CONDUIT

CONDUIT

Leif Garbisch

Alkion Press

ISBN: -10: 0-692-87721-5
ISBN-13: 978-0-692-87721-0

First Edition

Printed in the USA

Published in 2017
by Alkion Press
14 Old Wagon Road, Ghent, NY

Title: CONDUIT
Author: Leif Garbisch
Cover: Leif Garbisch

Fork Again

ONE

COMING DOWN THE MOUNTAIN, Games Shepard saw the world sincere. The roots, rocks, the dappled sunlit ground – everything was itself. Perfectly so. The bare deciduous trees stood free of deceit. And the evergreens, sleepy now in the January still, selfless as an open door, would never succumb to corruption. In these woods, essence was master, the only convention. *My friend,* said a patch of dazzling light to the left. *Don't slip,* said the loose and considerate stones on the path. From behind the limbs, between the laced branches, poked blue fragments of sky.

Say what you make of us, said the fragmented sky. I bet it's something up, like a mountain of a molehill. Which reminds me of a riddle.

The fragments played on Games's mind in spirited blue fun:

A robin and a golden retriever walk into a bar. Said the robin to the bartender, "I've made a spectacle of mornings, of evenings, too. I've made a break in the clouds to let the sun shine through. I've made a fuss, a face, and later amends. I've made little and much and light of all days. But when will I make my move?"

What began as a play on words, ended with a thud of earnestness. Games looked to the branches, unsure how to answer. He was distracted by the blue coming clean, coming through. It was hundreds of windows, shards of heaven, shifting perspectives as he walked.

Windows, said the sky. *Shards of heaven.* Is that what you actually see or simply how you lay meaning on things?

Games continued down the path, not wanting to debate it. Everything, including his footsteps, expressed the slope and goodness of the place – not a particularly steep slope, but an unmistakable goodness, at least to his way of thinking.

Naïve optimism, suggested the sky. Rose-colored glasses.

You'd think I'd share such a view. I, however, am no panacea, just one voice overseeing the earth.

And I'm all ears, thought Games. Trying to make sense. Behind me, the summit. Back there, Mr. M. Dead. His ashes probably still drifting down. And before me – what? I mean, what's his new place in the grand scheme of things? Or mine among these trees. Even hers, if I asked. She's. So beautiful in that black coat. But everyone's unsettled. To the left are problems I forgot I had. And to the right neglected solutions. Confusion. Perspectives. It all comes to break whatever unity I had. I was feeling it – one big self. Now it's back to pieces. Where's everything headed?

Home, said the sky. Not in a hurry or a haste. In a heartfelt way.

Games didn't hear this. Meaning he wasn't quite all ears. Yet somewhere lodged in his 27 years he held to the thought that life was created ultimately to increase order in the universe. The opposite of entropy. So even though he was a bit anxious as he approached the bottom of the mountain, because sometimes at the end of the day people go their own ways and all that has been established falls apart, Games trusted things would be well.

Good luck with that, said the blue bits of sky, now only whispers.

Did you say something? thought Games.

Just talking to myself about your brave new life.

Games listened through the trees. It was difficult, on the path, to hear with conviction. Difficult to know whether the tone he received was encouragement or mockery. He listened for a sense of the dead after attending this memorial. Some voice that might wish to enter him. He listened for reminders, for notes of understanding, actual words that would make a symphony of the day. He listened for the sound of others, both living and dead. A ghost, a squirrel, maybe the sigh of the girl a few feet ahead. Yet it was more the crunch of the earth he heard as he walked.

Games lowered his eyes to the path. There were jests of dry leaves and the soft snap of twigs underfoot, sounds entwined with the wintry air. His feet spoke to the path in wisecracks and rustles, the sound mixing with the January cool. Intriguing smell, that cool. Games inhaled the fresh, crisp air. It reminded him of birds, of bird names: Coot, for one. Jay, then junco. A gentlest dove. And that riddling robin. The robin perched on a branch in Games's mind in the low sunlight. Then off it flew, taking with it the warmth of the sun, leaving a chilly though still luminous late afternoon. Pure light. Light that enriched the world. That's what Games smelled, not an actual bird, but what all birds, all people, leave behind – the light of their being, which was their essential story. It was a fragrant seen. It was music to Games's ears. It was an invigorating sense that returned him to wonder, to the world around. It brought him to life, to…

Even more life. Games looked from the path to the woods nearby, as if now his eyes were ready to read. Blue blazes marked the path. He breathed the Appalachian air of the Taconic Range. Massachusetts, Connecticut. Which state exactly? Games could've asked, but he kept to himself. Nothing to say. Just continued down, as did the sun upon its consenting slope, both he and the sun careful not to slip, and Games, for one, going over the day.

He'd awoken early. Spilled tea on the floor. He'd met Abe at ten o'clock and had come to the mountain in a green car driven by a man whose name may've been Weed, a car with a tape measure in the cup holder and drill bits on the dash. He'd ascended to the dwarf pines atop Mt. Everest. Everett. Not Everest. Two *t*'s. No rest. Till finally there was a break. One far seeing, slow breathing, reflective moment up top. There, Games had listened to words set to the rhythm of the few high clouds, words that remembered Quincy M, that tried to capture the man's life in simple phrases. And Games had watched the release of those phrases, those words. He'd seen them float off – balloons, no, birds, no, the spirit of love, floating like Quincy's body of ashes set free. Drift of ash and words at the top of the mountain. There at the peak, Games had felt the day come to inexpressible significance. And now he was coming down. Through old-growth hardwoods. Past bare limbs, pines. Over the dry, uneven ground. Through crisp leaf smells and the many shades of bark, both light and dark. The dead of winter. The quiet dead.

No one much spoke coming down. It wasn't only Games, though his introspection may've been the boldest. It was a lot to think – about human life. Those gray remains of a man scattered far and, Games remembered, wide. He re-watched in his mind the ashes as they settled. Into the valley. Over the land. Bald Mountain, it's also called. Massachusetts – that's the state.

For the first time perhaps, Games saw the world as living. He heard words, a voice among the trees, coming from the dead man himself. A soulful urge for connection: "Find what you find on earth with opening eyes and hands and heart." That was the gist of it. Not to dwell on what's gone, but to see more life in the world around. The particulars. The beautiful each.

There was, for example, that young fresh skin, a baby's skin, a quarter mile back, held by her mother. This baby was a contrast to death. She was Hope. Hope wasn't her name, just – the baby represented a new beginning. And closer, much closer to Games, a girl, no, a woman, young skin, perfect shape, unshakable light, her name like a river, inches away, beneath layers of fabric. She walked one step ahead. She moved like water. A flow to her form. A beautiful view. Sexy curves and lips. Her lines. Step by step, she made her way among the leafless trees. And there were other people, mournful people like that mother with her baby, people deep in thought, farther up the mountain, following Games. They were all warm, living bodies on the path, coming quietly down.

Games walked in this world. He couldn't stop the landscape from speaking through him, which was an unfurling story, plotted not according to the crunch and carefulness of his strides but rather aligned with his shifting attention. The highs and lows. Ins and outs. The living and the dead. It was a blast of sun followed by weightless shade. Crisp winter air in the late afternoon. And fantastic shapes of light that moved him, as had always been of interest since he was a boy.

At ease in such unremitting privacy, Games found a familiar home. He could've remained there forever, in that friendship in his head, had he not acted against it, had he not looked for more substantial, more real, intimacy. And with an increasing urgency that filled his heart and quickened his blood, Games turned his body, his intentions to

The Girl Who Walked Slightly Ahead

She, this young woman, did not occupy Games's whole mind, but when he looked her way and there she was, the back of her at least, indisputably beautiful in the afternoon, she stole his attention. Such thievery had happened earlier when the girl first stepped from her car at the base of the trail and later when she offered Games water on the way up. As happened also talking with her at the top of the mountain among the pitch pines and scrub oaks.

Games thought back to her profile in the breezy two o'clock light up there, with views to the west all the way to the Catskills, and views to the east to the Atlantic almost. And now as he raced down the trail with this girl just ahead, Games tried to see around to the full of her face, to her eyes what they saw, and to her lips in their large pink playfulness. He wondered whether some day he might kiss her cheek and neck and those lips and feel the thrill of familiarity throughout his body. And wondered too if there might come a time when, driven by a need to unite, he would seriously listen as she'd lounge and disclose herself further, telling of the time with the goats in Tunis Mills, of the seven-day adventure in the Andes with her father, and more of that encounter with the Dalai Lama in a field full of white dandelions and black cows in Eastern New York.

Did you really meet him?

Yep, she said, biting into a sandwich at the top of the mountain.

What was he like?

He put his hand on my arm, she said. It was sunny.

His hand?

The day.

What did you do? asked Games.

Let it stay there. I thought of telling him that I wasn't that kind of a girl, but maybe I was.

Must've been nice, said Games.

It was. Sort of a weightless feeling, almost part of me. Then he took it off.

What did he take off?

His hand, said the young woman. What did you think?

Wasn't thinking, said Games. Just listening to your words.

Weren't they clear?

Cloudless, said Games. It's just me.

You're the cloudy one?

I guess so.

Anyway, said the young woman, he took his hand off my arm. He never stopped smiling. My whole body went warm.

Numb?

Warm.

Oh.

Games thought as he walked of the bare of her arm, and the brave light that would dare to touch it and make it tingle-o. Warm bare arm. Brave weightless touching. It must've been good. And he thought of what tantalizing words she might use if she talked on her own, just to be clear, speaking only to him, for his benefit. Then – what he would say back to tease her.

Coming down the mountain, Games Shepard hustled to keep up. It was possible that the girl kept her separation to save herself from talking. Or perhaps she simply was fast. Games's heart beat loudly in his chest, so loud it beat that she and everyone must've

must've

must've heard.

I know they hear it, he assumed, thinking of the thirteen other hikers nearby. No one wants to ask about the strange sound because it would undo the somber mood. It'd be wrong in this situation. Of course, not everyone is tied to etiquette. I know of one person, at least one person who –

What's that sound?

The call came from above. Games imagined the voice as that of his friend Abe.

What sound? Games asked.

Ba bum ba bum ba bum, Abe yelled from behind, up the mountain path. Sounds like a heartbeat.

It's not, Games yelled back. Ca cloof ca cloof ca cloof. It's horses. Hoofs.

Who's Orvis Oops?

Horse hooves.

What horses?

Appaloosa, Games suggested, because he liked the name and their leopard-like spots.

And though there weren't any horses, Games imagined them anyway, galloping cryptically through the brambles and dry leaves. He also knew that he was being too flippant, a bit disrespectful to suggest horses, which were such an upbeat and confident creature. Even kept to himself, the picture seemed overly sanguine for this melancholic time. So Games got off the horses, disposed of the picture, and thought more appropriately as he walked. He thought of the dead. He thought specifically of the man who had recently died, the thought of him somewhere. There was no stopping the thought and no stopping the dead and no stopping the life that surrounded the dead.

~

Mr. M. Mr. Am. Games remembered his short friendship with the man. Mr. M was the reason the small group of family and friends was here, having hiked up Mount Everett and now coming down. And where was the dead man at this hour? His ash, his body, his resounding soul. Games tried to see if Mr. M ducked in and out among the bramble or if he journeyed on in some more spiritual place.

Ah, Mr. Am. Old Mr. M. He'd come to the end of his life on earth. He'd climbed this way a hundred, at least a hundred times, or so his daughter had earlier recalled as she looked across the valley holding the box of her father's ashes. "A hundred million steps and more. Up and down the stairs, in and out through doors," she'd said. "For others. For others were those steps, mostly. The steps and trips he took in his life were all about others. In the very beginning he fell for the world, which I think was an easy fall to take because he loved the world every inch and everyone, no matter the difficulties, no matter the disputes."

Games had heard the daughter choke on her words, as if

perhaps she was remembering a long-ago dispute with her father. Some difficulty to rack her heart. That filled her with tears at the top of the mountain. And then a sudden wind. Wind out of nowhere, which brought with it an unshakable feeling of forgiveness. No dispute is as powerful as love. And Games knew coming down that Mr. M was the wind. And he wondered if the old man had chosen his time to leave the earth, if he'd chosen this perfect time to become that gust of wind.

Games slowed his pace. Thinking of Mr. M added considerable weight to his steps. Welcome weight. Awesome weight. And he figured he wasn't alone in considering the man. So, Games sped forward again and said to his new friend just ahead to his right, black coat like a crow, blond hair singing out,

What do you think of it all?

It?

Death, I guess. This whole experience.

Is it a hole?

The whole of life and death, I mean, said Games.

Doesn't feel like anything to do with death to me, said the young woman.

You think this is a trick to bring people together, suggested Games.

The young woman now slowed. Games came alongside, wanting what she had to offer if she chose to give it.

More like a celebration, she said at last. Her words mixed with splashes of sunlight and cool – the birdless air.

Games nodded. They picked up the pace, side by side. If all went well, she would take his nod as agreement, which it was, and not as swift dismissal of her feelings, which it definitely was not. And to keep on her good side, to keep things going, Games added,

There's a difference in the world, I think.

What's different?

I don't know.

Of course you do.

He's happy, said Games. And I didn't even know him that well. There's a bigger picture he sees. Now that he's gotten rid of his body.

That's a funny thing to say.

What's funny?

Gotten rid of his body, repeated the girl. Like it was garbage.

Maybe it wasn't quite what Games meant. He didn't mean that Mr. M had been trapped in his body or that it had been a burden on him. He simply meant that he no longer had the thing. The more curious issue, however, was why the girl hadn't questioned his word, *bigger*. She also was unconcerned with how Mr. M, being dead, could even see at all, how he could get any picture, big or small. Games wasn't sure where his new friend stood on the subject of afterlife. Not that he had it figured, though he was convinced that death puts no end to a person. Mr. M, Games trusted, was still aware of the earth. Its people and needs. Its purpose, even. And the man, dead as is true, carried on with life as well. Whatever that means – *carried on*. And *life* – what is there to say about that? Games didn't have much light to shed on the subject. Still, he would've welcomed talking about it further, listening to ideas, walking with them. He wanted to exercise what was weak inside him, what was imperfect for sure yet loaded with curiosity. If only this girl were willing. Or if only he could find the words to keep her going.

I stopped you, said the young woman.

No, said Games. Just thinking.

Keeping it private?

No.

Yes.

The word reverberated, yes yes, emphasizing the truth of it. The word sung yes for his ears and would not yes stop. There was no denying his inwardness, though it wasn't the whole story. Games chose not to fight the girl's implication, much as he wanted to.

I remember the first day, the strange evening, the… Him, Games began.

What hymn?

Calling me a coot. Some kind of bird. Inviting me into his room and talking. All his talking. No reason, it seemed, other than to say things, to get them out. Don't know why to me. I was there, I guess.

You're talking about Quincy.

Yeah. It was five weeks ago. Before that, I hardly knew he existed.

What'd he tell you?

It was. I don't mean to be vague. His words were wind coming through. I felt it. Wind. Who he was, I guess. That's what I heard. At the time I didn't quite get it, but now I feel fortunate. Full of fortune. Do you know?

Do I know a wind like that? said the young woman. I wish.

Really I'm wondering if I'm making any sense?

Yes.

It was a ride worth taking, said Games. I leaned in. Caught him with a sail I suppose I was holding, and we went together across the lake. Or it was a sea.

Bet you're glad you didn't have a net, said the young woman.

Annette wouldn't't've been much help.

So, you catching anything now?

He's gotten quiet, said Games. Which I take to be good.

Maybe it's just you, she said.

Me?

Quiet and happy in your interior world. Thinking it all to yourself.

Games didn't want everything to be for himself alone. And how wrong it somehow seemed to be happy at a death and burial, even if it was a celebration. Any happiness here would be appropriate only if it were an appreciative feeling about Mr. M and his life. Some greater recognition. So, Games looked again for the dead man, to try to know him better. He wondered as he searched how Mr. M must now feel, seeing the remains of his body dispersed among the pitch pines and maples, those dusty ashes having mostly settled by this time upon the cold January ground, 2,700 feet above the sea.

And Games saw, every so often, walking with the girl, what may've been hints in these woods. It was the entwining of certain trees. It was the way the light unleashed his mind. The old man, Mr. Am, balanced well with a continuing world. He minded his approach and seemed to be learning of things from the inside out, deciding what to do with his newfound timelessness. Games took freewheeling steps down the mountain to keep pace with his friend. Everyone has decisions to make, he thought, not speaking up about what he saw of spiritual things, even though the young woman would've been receptive.

She picked a stick from the path and carried it, like a cane at first, then like a torch. The stick was a tool, it was enlightening. To the left, what appeared to be white droppings of birds. To the right a draft of cool air that felt like confirmation. No worries just now. Continuing release. And the light through the trees though fading came free.

~

Now it was the last steep section of the trail. Soon the leveling out. Games stepped carefully. There were roots and rocks and slippery places. If he fell, would the girl rush to help him regain his footing? As rivers rush. As it was the rush hour time. Would she kneel beside him like the river she was so he could get in her way? Not in her way her way, her room her way. Not her bedroom, her body. And not her body either, not only that. It was her entire flow he was after. Games saw her knees and feet and other fleeting things. She of many lush forms, wrapped in cotton and wool. The young woman did not unwrap for him, never quite naked, not in his mind. She became, however, subtly suddenly more real than words the closer they came to the end of the hike.

Games saw all the possibilities ahead. Nothing to stop the adventures. Not for him, not for Mr. M, either. Not even death was a wall in the way. Death is no final resting place. No Mount Ever-rest. There comes a door at the end of the day for sure. Death, this day, both were new beginnings. Each a brave new life.

The anticipation sent Games reeling, his mind spinning, and he didn't stop rolling, not even at the bottom of the mountain. He didn't go still till he got back to his town, to Troy, the city of King David. No, not King David, King Prius. Not King Prius, either. King Someone. It was the city of the Hudson and the Mohawk both, one of which was a wide river he knew and the other a bird, a lone mo hawk, sitting on a fence post, on the lookout for a meal. And the city itself was plenty of places to eat, plenty more places to be quiet alone. And it was night there when Games finally arrived, and much colder, too. It was nearly eleven by the feel of things. Eleven o'clock, not degrees – an approachable time, a spiritual awakening if Games was ready for it. He was ready and watching, like the mo hawk, that silent bird, with a river of feelings inside him, and some weightless touch like that of guidance upon his skin. Games wished it were hands, but it wasn't. The streets were empty, fearless, soft. The untiring world was there for conversing. And looking up, he could see the stars.

~

Sometime on his way home following dinner with the others, after being dropped off by Reed so he could walk, Games had made the curious decision to go on Fillmore – Fillmore being a U.S. president he'd never considered. Traffic didn't consider the road much either. Milton Fillmore. Or Millpond, or Millard, or. A full sounding name, a round name. Thirteenth president. Thirteen colonies. So much for the history he'd learned. Eleven o two o'clock. He walked the street in fugitive silence.

Games crossed one street, then another. Three doors down there was an abandoned building, and beside that a lot with a chain-link fence. Something about the lot depressed him. The disuse, the rubble, the hopeless feeling of the place. He looked away.

Shift from the swift move of things. Still in the gentle night, the occasional streetlight lit, those few yet encouraging stars above. This was close to Games's apartment. He stood in the January cool, a few blocks away, looking up. It was the sixth day of the month. Epiphany.

Games Shepard, twenty-seven, had had a good life. He was willing and ready to be someone, a member of the earth, free to move about and make himself known, not chained as was that lot, not hidden as was Fillmore Street, which was tucked unnoticeably between Washington and Lincoln. There was nothing for Games to be down about, either. Though considering the recent burial of Mr. M, he was somber. If he could've spoken to Mr. M, he'd've apologized for his mood.

No worries, my friend. It troubles me, though, if I've brought you down.

I'm not down.

No?

Just thinking.

You can't do it alone, my friend.

Most thinking is done alone, thought Games.

Thinking itself is a relationship of yourself with another – a person, a thing. It's a spiritual connection. But you're missing my point.

I'm sorry.

Nor worries, my friend. Get out a bit more. Of yourself a bit more. Be who you are meant to be. A bit more. It takes practice. Include the stars in your landscape. Include people and cars.

Watching the road, Games nodded. A car went by, the driver glancing his way. Their eyes locked and released. Was the driver heading home or was he leaving the city or the earth for good? Thinking about it, picturing that driver, there resonated in Games a deep unknowing.

He re-watched the car. Over and over. Going, re-going. It meant real slow. Went real slow. Perhaps Games was just looking for things in the world that echoed something similar hidden inside him. He didn't know why he stood motionless on the street, not making his way home. Must've been the mood this night, which was something to pay attention to, like the thoughts exposed when looking at the stars.

~

Once when he was seventeen, Games met an old woman who lived by herself on the outside of town. The town was North Adams, where Games lived much of his adolescent life with his aunt and uncle. He couldn't remember the old woman's name or the department she'd once chaired at the nearby university. It was over ten years ago, and he was bad with names. The woman, on that night, made a point of one name she insisted Games remember.

Susan B. Anthony, you must know who she is. She was born nearby. February 15, 1820. A Quaker.
What's a Quaker?
Susan B. Anthony. The one and only. Write it.

The woman had him write the name on the table with his finger, which was the closest thing to a pencil. Then she showed him a profile in some book as they both drank coffee. Games hadn't known she was about to die, not Susan who was already dead, but the old woman – whatever her name. *It's a great mystery,* the old woman said, sitting at her table, *what I'm going to eat for breakfast tomorrow.* She was alive in her kitchen when Games left her late at night, and in the morning she was gone, just like that. Shortly thereafter, Games saw the photo of her in the newspaper on the kitchen table with his uncle's books. He never read the paper, not ever, but he read about her. The fullness, the final failing of her heart. Release of her heart. Definitely her heart, he read.

People rarely told Games the crucial information. For one out of six, however, it was always the heart. Not that the woman should've told Games she was going to die. And not that death was important, except as a window to life. It was that window Games thought of now. It was where he was trying to get to: a better view of life and why people live it, relations with others and how those relationships play out. He had to figure these things for himself. He had to pause and think.

So Games stopped, not yet home. He took in the stars and reflected upon both dead Mr. M and the young woman he'd just met this day – the old man's life and ashes, the girl's friendly, unforgettable face. He was a clue, like the driver of that car. She was a one and only, like Susan B. Anthony.

What's it mean to be a person on earth? Games wondered. A name to begin with, but it's more than a name that each person is after. There's an untold story in each star. And upon the earth there is a light each person stands for. It's a slow-saying light of existence that dissolves the shadows to reveal a picture of individual beauty. For each, it's a landscape that mirrors a deeper being. It's a mountaintop maybe, or a city skyline, the open ocean or a field of wildflowers, a place by the river. But do we see how our landscape fits in the world? It's a puzzle piece, really. The river meshes with its banks, the banks with trees, the trees with sky, and the sky with sun and clouds. Then, yes, stars at night. The landscape we each are, the way we see ourselves, involves other landscapes all around. The many landscapes, the many people, that make a world. The more landscapes we include in the picture of our self, the more human we will be. I have a picture of myself, Games thought. A bird's-eye perspective of earth and sky. Stars and storms they fill that sky. Sometimes there's a passing car on the road, one amazing river through the trees. It's all the relationships I come to. There is a landscape that's beautiful and difficult and unavoidably mine. It's how I orient myself to the world, and there's a terrific cost in minimizing the others I meet, an even greater cost of disregarding.

Games looked back to the street, black of the pavement, red taillights way down the road. To Mr. M. Nice Mr. Am who was dead. And to the girl – what a spring-like person. She was a seedling Games saw leafing out, not leaving. A flower with a bee right there in its cup. Be flower, be flow, be full of nectar. What a promising current she was. Curves and crazy good looks. A river to sea, a sea inside, a see you around, stuff to discover, an ocean of... Definitely, she would come later. She wasn't someone to say goodbye to. She would take better root, for sure. She was alive – that's the point. She was here, still. Somewhere on earth. Flesh and fresh and probably standing in her bathroom right now, taking off her shirt, her bra, and her aura of perfection – nobody's perfect, impossible to be perfect – washing her face with cold water, her breasts exposed to the mirror.

She and Games might try one another on some day. Clothes they'd be for each other, if it worked out that way. Ripped shirts, shirts with buttons, shirts with pleasing seams and colors. But the man, Mr. M, was no longer flesh. No shirts for him, no more seasons, no hikes into the hills and winter bird studies, no living narration. It was easy to remember that the man was dead, ageless now. Old Mr. M –

cast into the valley. He was doing whatever the dead do: They drift about for a while on wind. They drift about for a while as ghosts. They roll past people in their cars and look. They fill the sky as do stars with wonder. The spark of their names. The hint of their wholeness. A heap of questions. They start things moving. They motivate, unseen. And the man, Mr. M, is the one who started all this when he was alive. He's the one whose words were startling at first. Starlings, even. He loved his birds.

The time with Mr. M was strange to begin with. It was like walking on Fillmore for the very first time, and the very first time with Mr. M was only five weeks ago. Games had been in the evening apartment and the old man, for whatever reason, started talking to him as if he were his grandson or an old high school buddy, a longtime companion or colleague, some expected guest. Maybe Games was a guest, but it was all unexpected. He had never even met Mr. M before, but there he stood outside the old man's bedroom, and it was as if his presence was reason enough for everything that followed.

~

Hey Coot. Starling. Rook, said the old man, spotting the young man lurking at the entrance. It was all birds. Name calling. Games looked into the room. He hadn't even known someone was there.

If you were a bird, what bird would you be? asked the man from his bed

Excuse me?

Excuse you? You just got here.

Games stared blankly at this statement, unable to form a response.

Don't act so befuddled, said the old man. You can't be excused, not yet. Just imagine one.

One what?

Papa, leave him alone. The man's daughter came through the doorway, pausing to look Games in the face.

Are there more? thought Games, leaning in.

Just us two, she said.

What two?

People in the room, said the daughter, having, it seemed, heard his thought. You're easy to read. The daughter continued to study his face.

I... Games wanted to say more, but how to proceed?

He's a tease, said the woman, walking off. Just ignore him.

Like you're not the same as me, said the old man from his bed. Though it was unclear if he was speaking to his daughter or to Games. What're you doing out there? the man continued. You're like a marsh hawk or a mo hawk, I can't remember which.

I'm waiting for Abe.

Abel?

Yeah.

Danni's son?

I don't know.

My spontaneous grandson?

Maybe.

Your certainty is contingent.

Games heard *contagious.* He stood in the yellow light of the hallway knowing the word was wrong, but it made him smile.

What's funny?

Contagious certainty.

I didn't say that.

I know, said Games.

We were talking about birds, said the man. Then you brought him into it.

Him?

Abel, the man elaborated. I'm certain you remember.

Yes, sir, said the younger.

I call him Bamboo, said grand Poppy, leaning against the headboard, supported by pillows. After the fast-growing plant. You know Bamboo? The old man's hand wavered a bit as he lifted it to show how tall.

I do, said Games.

He's twenty-six feet by now.

Years, you mean.

Hear what you like.

Yes, sir.

I've got three of them so-called children, four grandchildren, and a great granddaughter, little Veery, said the old man. And don't be surly with me. I don't deserve it.

Games was caught. Netted. Tugged. He allowed himself to be reeled, an inch at a time, into the room.

I had a wife, and even though she died long ago, I'm still a bit sad.

I'm sorry, said Games.

I wish she would visit.

Games nodded.

I wish I knew what's become of her.

Games remained quiet.

I don't remember ever being angry with her.

Not even once?

Maybe you're right, said the old man. I had my bad days.

I didn't mean –

I wasn't a perfect husband. I'll be the first to admit it. Makes me sad to think though, because why would I've gotten angry at her? Ever.

I didn't mean... Games had not wanted to cause troubles. He remained in place, just inside the room, shifting his weight and watching the old man, whose thin gray hair held tightly to the evening light of the room. You were probably just stressed or tired, Games finished.

I hadn't retired, not when she died, said the man.

Tired, I said.

Not really.

I mean –

You mean, you don't mean. You go back and forth, said the old man. It's like watching tennis. Or one of the road workers leaning on his shovel. First one foot, then the other. Nothing ever gets done.

I'm...just –

I know how just you are. Just how you are, too. I get your gist.

Where could Games go with these statements?

Don't be confused, said the old man. I'm having fun with you. Like you, I'm full of thought. Nothing to restrain it. Some of it's junk. Everyday clutter. Not all.

Games nodded.

Keeps me awake.

Games nodded some more.

Keeps me going. Examining my life.

Games finished his nod.

I miss her, though, said the old man. Even now. How about you?

I'm okay.

But do you miss her? pressed the man.

Miss…

If you reflect. If you think deeply into your life.

I don't know who you mean, said Games.

Weren't you listening?

I was.

You haven't come all this way just to perch in my doorway. Maybe it's not a hawk that you are, but a fish. Reminds me of myself back in the day. Fishin to take away some vital information, not knowin how. Lookin to robin the world of its riches. You lookin to robin me?

To rob you?

Rob in, rob out, said the old man. You could steel yourself against the world. Or you could make a move to know it better. Have you come all this way just to be a wall?

It really wasn't far.

So, you are a wall?

No, said Games.

Yet you stand there, blocking the door like a load of bricks.

Sorry, said Games.

When I see someone at my door, I say vitamin. Vitamin.

The old man gestured for him to enter fully.

I live nearby, said Games, moving into the small square room at the speed of honey. Twelve by twelve feet by the look of it. I'm waiting for Bamboo, he continued. We play hockey together. Sunday afternoon pickup.

Vinegar's what you need for that, said the man.

For the pickups? said Games.

I had a truck one time, a blue one. But I'm talking about

hiccups. When I was a boy, they bothered me.

I used to get them, said Games. My mother gave a spoonful of vinegar.

Didn't I just say that?

You said they bothered you, remembered Games.

Been a while since I played hooky as well, said the old man. Do you like it?

Hooky or hockey?

No, vinegar?

It's okay.

I never was any good at it, said the old man.

Swallowing the vinegar?

Playing hooky. I was better at school. Did my work. Tried not to listen to all that blabla teacher noise. Annoyingly noisome, if you know what I mean.

Not really, said Games.

Kids called her a urinal, said the old man. Miss Field. You remember that smell?

Not really, Games repeated. I did have a Ms. Field though. Everyone teased her right to her face.

Remember her shaking her finger? said the old man. "Take your seats. Take your seats," she'd say. Day after day. "I won't put up with any shenanigans." Now that was a word to make us laugh.

I remember it, said Games. Sixth grade.

That's right. Threw spitballs at her, too, they did. Not me. Paper airplanes even.

Yeah. Mr. Chester came in with his outrage. So red in the face.

Mister Chester, repeated the man, liking the sound. I felt bad for her.

For Mr. Chester?

No, for her – Miss Field. Not him.

Oh, said Games. Middle school's the worst.

Did you like your teachers as much as me? asked the man.

I didn't mind them.

As much as me?

I don't know you.

Why would you say such a thing? Give yourself more credit. We're connecting. We're sharing experiences.

I'm sorry, said Games. It's just –

Do you know what diffusion is? The old man interrupted. His gnarled hand moved smoothly toward his face, stopping in front, trembling a bit.

I've heard the word, said Games, noting for the first time the wrinkles of the man, his bright and playful eyes.

It's the intermingling of substances, the man defined. The spreading of light evenly, so the whole world gets some. I was actually a willing student, back in the day.

I'm sure you were.

Do you think I still am? asked the old man.

Well, I doubt you're a student, said Games.

You're so sure of everything.

It's just a guess.

You're more than a guest. You're a starling.

I thought you called me a hawk. Or a fish.

That's because you keep reminding me of things. Be who you are meant to be.

Games had no clue, so the old man supplied one.

If starling is not a good start, begin with bobwhite.

Is that a bird? asked Games.

Pull up a chair, Bob. Don't be a stranger.

Games spotted the only chair in the room. He really was a guest, however, and a stranger to the place. He just happened to be there while the old man's grandson borrowed money from his mother who was making tea in the kitchen for them all to drink. Oolong? Darjeeling? Keemun? What was her name? And the grandfather, the old Poppy, took advantage of Games as he stood outside the room. Must've been some invisible birdfeeder in the hall that had attracted him. That's what Games remembered most — walking into the apartment and standing in the hall, right under what must've been the bird food. Then the old man called him to his bed, bobWHITE bobWHITE, had him pull up a chair.

Hesitantly, Games went for the chair, stole it, no, borrowed it from the desk and sat by the man's right shoulder, wobbly.

That chair's a piece of junk, said the old man.

It's okay, said Games.

He adjusted his body and looked at his mood for misgivings. There was an alarm clock on the bedside and a print by Chagall on the wall. Games flicked a piece of lint from his knee, then settled.

Was that so difficult? asked the man.

Games said nothing, and his reluctance faded.

I'm not a great talker, either, said the old man. Despite what you hear.

His face held the light, not light from the window, which was dark, but from the hall behind Game's chair, which carried a warm yellow glow. It was six o'clock, almost time for hockey.

Do you always...

What? asked Games, after a long pause.

Take your time with things? said the old man.

Maybe.

Maybe? That's such a guarded answer. What do you think?

I'm not thinking much of anything now, said Games.

Nothing?

Well...

A feeling of joy came into Games as his weight filled the chair. Though joy was too large a word. Better to call it a sense of ease and comfort. His hands rested in his lap, and he waited for what would come next. Not hockey. Forget the hockey. First to arrive was a memory of stillness, a bright frozen lake from when he was a child, sitting at the edge with his mother in some Midwest state in the middle of December. Then came a picture of Christmas, which wasn't about toys or a tree with decorations. It was the picture of his young self sitting again to the right of his mother as she drove into the Christmas morning solitude, away from the sun. Next, as Games sat in the room, appeared a memory of himself picking blackberries, also with his mother, and pausing to eat them by the side of the road, he on her right again, just as it was here with the old man. Seffi, his mother, with muddy boots and disheveled black hair. Games could see her so clearly, picturing that time: an occasional car passing at their backs, and the in-and-out sun stinging their eyes. It was summer then, clearing and cool after a thunderful, muddying rain. Games remembered the brambles, the wetness of the ground, and the sparkly light on random bits of earth. And he remembered his mother on a similar afternoon telling a story from a book she was reading about a lady of some lake, the dark water of that story that sloshed in the moonlight, and a sword and a king, Excalibur, Arthur. Then a sheep fly landed on Games's arm. He brushed it off. Don't be so afraid of things, his mother said. Or maybe it was the moonlight of her story telling him this. Don't be afraid of things, the moonlight said. Go bravely through life. His mother was at his side, having finished talking, ready to leave. And Games could've probably remembered other things, too. But now was not the time. The time in this room wasn't about Games himself, was it?

You like that spot? asked the old man.

It's not bad, said Games.

You comfortable now?

I'm good.

~

That's how it started. The old man introduced himself as Quinnem, M for short, which sounded like Am for sure, got Games Shepard to sit and used his young ear as a notebook for his scribblings. Mr. M rattled off his life, pieced it together as the night grew late. Trays of dinner came into the room. Something with kale, black tea, lentils. The story continued. And though Games questioned his reason for being there, he felt increasingly connected to the man, welcoming Mr. M's telling words, interlaced with his own, until at length the old man yawned and fell asleep.

Three days later, Mr. Am for sure took a turn for the worse and died, just like that. Pneumonia, heart failure, the end of the road. It's got to be something that kills a person, that takes him from the earth, thought Games. If it were nothing, how meaningless death would be, which is to say life, also, would be meaningless. Games preferred thinking there was a sense to things. You just had to find it.

Quincy, that was his given name. Quincy Mesch. Father, grandfather, a great grandfather Poppy to a very young Vireo. He died surrounded by a few friends and family. He died at his daughter's home in the country, which used to be his home in the country in Upstate New York. He died in his own handmade bed with a carved mountain on the headboard and a carved sea at his feet. He died as Bach played softly and a good gold dog ground away on a bone nearby. Seashells lay on the window ledge. Winter wrens poked among the brambles. Up starling up. Good Quincy Mesch. He was slow to anger and quick to forgive, always ready to offer a hand or a word to anyone in need. At his least generous, he'd've given you just a fraction less than his entire self. And at his most generous, he'd've tossed in that extra for free. He'd hug you for the hello of it and offer whatever he had in his home or heart. Never a day went by that he didn't feel for the world. Never a day went by he didn't open some door and go for a walk, even if only in his mind. Never a day went by he didn't think of his wife, the one and only. That's what the obit said. That's what was written in the Tuesday *Register Star*.

Games stood almost home, city of Troy, his hands stuffed in his pockets, deep under the sky. Wrapping around him, the thoughts of dead Mr. M. And fleeting pictures of the girl in her black winter coat. She was the beginning of something. Springtime, summer. She was sweet like wildflowers, the names of which were lost to him.

Light of the world. Of the world alive. Particles, waves, glinting reminders. Games fished for things as he stood halfway on Fillmore Street, the sky like a landing to rest upon, a place to gather his thoughts. There were some names that came his way, people he knew – Seffi, Aunt Julia, Quincy M. Places he'd visited – the Hudson River, Maiden's Lake, hills and dales what were they all. Blue and purple flowers in August, bearberries in September, dandelions in the sun. Winter jays and juncos and millions of blackbirds. The names of products like *Pepsi Neat* and *Hope Valley Yogurt*, the names of produce he'd taken home from the reject bin at work, and the names of produce he'd unpacked and layered so perfectly in its display at the Jake – red kiss us apples, am juicy pears, green roaming lettuce, and a corn squash, too. And how about the titles of those books Seffi his mother carried like candy in her large pockets. She in that oversized coat. She, reading in the sun. *Sweet,* she'd say. *Listen to this.* As if Games was always nearby, just waiting for her to speak. Titles re titles: The Morte d'Arthur. The Once and Frugal King. Some mockingbird tale. Oblique House. A Wild Christmas in Wales, where a robin died whose fire kept burning on its breast. A poem by Dickinson, inebriate of air. Poem by Poe, in a kingdom by the sea. And a legend, or so it was described, of a young woman at the base of the Blue Pine Mountains, so entranced by the wind as it whispered through the leaves that she died, actually died, listening.

What a waste to live and listen and not make good, a mind full of wonder but nothing to show. Such was the picture of Games's mother with her books. She'd read in the car, with blackberry stains on her fingers. She'd read in the woods with the dappled light. She'd read curled tight into a ball by the dirty window, losing herself to the words, wishing to enter those plots. The stories lured her in and satisfied her longing, the way the lives of the living couldn't do.

Games felt a nudge from the night, close to midnight. Get a move on. A move on. But why so fast? He had plenty of time left. Years and years to work with. Not so for some people. Not so Mr. M. Quincy Mesch. No more time on the earth for the dead man now, unless it came as light, as inspiration, unless it came to Games by way of his attentiveness as he stood on Fillmore Street, recalling.

~

Games had driven to Mount Everett in the morning to pay his respects. Almost a two-hour drive with sun blasting through his window from the east. He drove with Bamboo Abe in Abe's brother Reed's car along with Blue, Reed's wife, and Veery, their infant daughter. The baby had a blanket for protection and a knitted hat for her head. Vireo was her real name, with and without the winter knits.

Games sat in back, left side of Veery with Blue on the right. He watched as the infant slept, and he played with her when she woke just before they arrived for the hike. One two three four five, he counted on his fingers for Veery. One two three four six, he teased. There were also Quincy's daughter and son, Danielle and Jesse, Jesse's two children, and a spritely old friend of Quincy with an Arabic name. Finally, there were three students from years back, and the daughter of one of those students who, at twenty-five, was a nurse in a nursing home and still studying part time. Botanical books. Sweet potato blossoms. Honey bees. The evergreens in winter said she was the one. The real thing. Games stopped with her halfway up the mountain for a drink of water.

Want some? she asked, turning to Games, offering the thermos. It was the first words she'd spoken to him since their earlier introductions.

No thanks, he said, immediately annoyed with his decision. A person might die on the outside of doors, afraid to enter.

So, what's your name again? Games asked as the girl walked on, not that he'd forgotten, but to keep things going. He wanted to hear her speak. Dollops of sunlight flowered her hair. A patch of light on the side of her cheek. That skin, her cheek, its light – irresistible. Games would've saved if he could've the economy of her words and skin, to bring it out later in privacy as riches, though better to have it in the original. Always. If only she'd've offered more of herself, Games would've been content to listen and look. Instead, she asked Games about his connection with Mr. M. How had he come to know the man?

It's weird, Games said. He shrugged. I'm not...

You're not?

Good at talking about myself, Games was about to say, before a sound deep in the woods distracted him. It was careless the way Games lost words and couldn't re-find them. They weren't in himself, it seemed, and not on the ground either, where sunlight and shadow played separately like oil and water. A small wind shook the pines. No birds. No animals. Only trees and spaces between the trees.

Near the top of the mountain, the girl put her hand on Games's arm. A gesture, it seemed to him, to accommodate his feelings about Mr. M. The still pines became stiller, and the quietness of the air turned time into opportunity. Games offered this:

I only knew him for hours, but it felt like a lifetime.

Must be something special about you, said the young woman.

Games couldn't think what that would be. He didn't like alcohol, which was the same as Mr. M, who'd stopped drinking, just like that, at twenty-three. But that wasn't special, just strange. Fresh pressed apple cider, however, was delicious. There was this tree he knew where its limbs lowered themselves to literally hand you apples.

Is that the tree of literal life? she asked.

Figuratively speaking, said Games.

The young woman nodded. Anything else about you I should know?

I like a good cirrus cloud. They whisper, which not every cloud can do.

And you have to listen close, said the girl.

Same with birds, said Games. Birds tell you things about yourself. Mr. M liked owls and vireos, robins in the rain.

Me, I like ravens. Crows. Crows most. Red-winged blackbirds.

I saw some crows back down the mountain, said Games.

Anything else? asked the girl, as they neared the clearing at the top.

Used to be, Games then told, he rode his bicycle everywhere, until it was stolen. But that was all he could think to say, and the two continued silently on the path. If only Games could've said it all differently. Come across as more interesting. More all together.   Altogether what? He should've shown his sensitivity for this time. And the chance was nearly over. Filled with his silence. He needed to show he understood why they were here. It wasn't to talk about himself. It was to remember the dead.

I saw this movie once, said the young woman. *The Bicycle Thief*. With my sister. A grainy black and white thing.

Your sister is grainy?

She's older than me, said the young woman. It's sad, because a bike might be everything to a person.

A *life*?

A *bike*.

Games nodded. He liked the connection she made with the bike and the thief and her life and his.

I feel bad talking about these things, he said.

Don't. It only makes things worse for him.

For Quincy Mesch?

Yes, said the girl. Keep going. Climb on. Forget what's only reflection and remember what's alive.

Isn't this a memorial? asked Games.

It isn't a death march, she said.

Games loved that the girl said those words, that she carried such depth of perception, such height of it, too. So, who are you, really? he wanted to say. There's something about you. It was you, wasn't it, who stole my bike? He wanted to say this as well.

Games then realized what it was about this young woman. He knew her name, knew he liked her. Rianna. He'd known it from the beginning with the crows. Rio, Rio. Her name was a river. At least it sounded like one. Over the river and through the woods. Ri the river. Be the river. Games wanted to flow with the girl a while, to wind back and forth together, the two of them from bank to bank, drinking apple cider as they passed under some bridge. High whispery cirrus in the late afternoon. He wanted to listen in, to think about her a moment before saying more. Before asking:

Rianna?

Yes.

Did you steal my bike?

I did.

It was a name that now he'd said it he would say it again, to play with and tease in his riotous ways.

The thing is, they all had names, all the people on the hike, but it was mostly Bamboo Abe, itsy bitsy Veery, Quincy Mesch, of course, and the fine Rio Grande who Games could remember. Three cars for everyone to ride in. One was green. The other two... Games wasn't good with colors, either. The group had driven and parked and hiked to the peak, a two-and-a-half-hour trek through the cold bright day, no snow on the ground, luckily. A path to follow, no signs of spring, a few birds though – one vireo, three crows at the beginning, and a floating hawk way in the distance – no snakes this time of year. And Games had never much considered the habits of snakes or the names of birds. He'd never much considered how the months arranged themselves over the year, each month a mood, each day a possibility – something new going on, an invitation to think. Had given only slight thought to either life or death. And never, never had felt in himself such a struggle for the right thing to say. Never'd had a need for these feeling or thoughts till now.

Standing, warm in his jacket in the chill winter air, Games played with the coins in his pocket as he followed the stars. Change, change. Become who you are. He knew he held something of value given to him, maybe earned by him, now his to care for. Not money, of course, nothing material. A brightness in his being that had been with him always yet he couldn't say how. And not his alone. The brightness really was very little to do with his personal life.

Each of Games's thoughts led him to others. The connections took root as never before, making trails like vines, like veins, filling every crevice with a network of life. Games stood in this network as if for the first time. More likely he stood in the mysterious presence of his origins. And say that this inner experience was a new beginning for Games, that from now and from here, increasingly forever, life were to flow through him like channeled water, as irrigation. Say he were to experience that flow more and more each day, as the fullness of life and a need to release it. What would he do, what could he do, to express what he felt, to convey such drink to a much thirsting world?

Twelfth day of Christmas. Thirty-three degrees. Just above freezing. Games had no true love, though maybe he was working on it. He looked up from his introspection, and saw he was almost home. Those few and circling stars were faint night birds, dim ideas out and about. Truth, he'd read, was a revelation emerging at a point where the inner world of man meets external reality. Not much help in that description unless it were actually to happen. He looked from the sky, back to the ground.

It was nothing different, nothing remarkable, nothing yet. Games felt the earth beneath his feet. Was tired after so much thought and made his way, finally, the last block home. The remains of the day settled around him – ashes, ashes upon a long leafless view. A memory of ashes. The particulars of life filtering to the earth. It was a sense once more that filled Games with reflection as he climbed the steps to his apartment house door.

~

Everything's nice up here, Rio said after she and Games watched Mr. M's ashes settle over the land. They stood for as long as it took, and then a bit more to stare at a bird floating high upon the sky.

Nice, Games echoed, keeping the agreement inside.

Games had witnessed the burial and now saw Quincy Mesch everywhere in the windshaped oaks and pines. He saw the old man in the bird, too, the one floating on the sky. He saw the old man in each person, even in tiny Vireo as she chewed the leg of her stuffed lamb. He saw him in the light of the sun caught and exposed by the earth. Quincy Mesch was inextinguishable. He would not go away.

Rianna turned to Games, who kept his focus upon the distance.

At first I wasn't going to come, she said. But Dad wanted it. People I don't even know up here. Trees, the sky, that bird out there. Thing is, feels I've always been a part of it. There's this, and all the things I'm not seeing, too.

Games nodded, struck by her words about waking up to what you see and maybe also to what you don't. Her words reminded him of weeks ago in the old man's room. Quincy Mesch alive on earth. Oolong or was it Darjeeling tea? Forget the hockey, remember. That sport went right out the window. Time spread like a welcome mat, that day. The evening turned to night. And Mr. M fell asleep. Then his daughter who had brought the tea, whatever her name, and had brought the pasta and kale on green-apple trays and had kept her distance curiously close, said to Games as he was leaving,

I don't mean to be…

What? asked Games after a long pause.

I'm not sure how else to say this.

Games waited.

It's like you're someone.

Games wanted to be someone.

Someone I should know, the woman continued. Do you believe in reincarnation?

Believe?

That's the word you choose to repeat, said the daughter.

Well, whether reincarnation is true or not doesn't depend upon my belief.

You see?

See what.

That's just what she would've said.

Who?

You're not my mother, are you?

What was her name again?

Calico, said the old man's daughter. Her name was Calico.

No, said Games.

Yes, it was. It was Calli Cormorant, like the bird. Papa called her Calico.

I mean, said Games, that I'm not her.

I know, said the daughter. Don't listen to me. You're too old, I think.

But Games was listening. And he wasn't too old.

It's like you've always been a part of this, said the woman. Don't ask me how.

I like the chair, said Games.

Quincy's daughter looked him up and down.

But I'm sure, said Games. I haven't been here before. Ever.

All things resonated for Games as he stood at the front door of his apartment house, looking over the night. Every encounter, every relationship, all silences and words, worked him as if he were clay. He sensed this making, this creating or re-creating of himself, the same way he sensed the light through his eyes, or knew the door handle through his hand. Games felt a place in his body open, first around his heart, then in his throat, and finally at the very tip of his tongue where thoughts and feelings came to be said. It was one great place to carry the world in a communicative way. It was a place to take in life, to know it and say it and not hold back.   And now the assembly of stars above the roofs of the city seemed the perfect echo of what he bore inside.

Life was greater than its matter alone. It was, in fact, a prerequisite for matter. The material world simply provided a room for life, a space for it to take place. Games knew this to be so.   Standing as he was, just outside his door, Games corresponded, through the avenues of his body and routes of his being, with some universal quality of life.   In a few minutes he'd be leaving this correspondence behind. He'd enter his apartment and return to himself. But for the moment he remained connected. It was as if life held tight to Games for help, as if he might do something to assist its cause. And though this cause, an unrecognized truth of life, had always been part of Games, though it had always been nearby, nudging him urging him never coercing him forward, though it had befriended him at birth and before even that, Games had not till this time honored or honed or even acknowledged the friendship in all his twenty-seven years.

~

Games was the first and some say only child of Seffi, his mother. He never met his father, not at his birth the way others had met their fathers in large, attentive hands, and not in the many days that followed, either. It wasn't until he'd turned four that Games first became aware that others had fathers and he did not.

In the Country of Gillikins, which is at the North of the Land of Oz... His mother sat in a wooden chair by the window. She'd just opened her book and the words floated off the page, filling the room with story. Games wanted to look at the cover.

Can't you see I'm reading?

He could see, but the cover really interested him. His mother closed the book.

Look. Quickly.

The cover had a picture of a blue-suited boy walking in stride with a gangly pumpkin-headed figure. The two walked on a curving road with a great sun behind them. Games studied the picture.

Who's the pumpkin?

What?

Is that his father?

I'm reading, Games, said Seffi. Don't ask stupid questions.

Still, he wanted to know. If a pumpkin could be a... Could he... Did he have a... His mother turned her back to avoid further interruptions. She hardened in her chair, part of her becoming wood, another part dissolving into the book. And Games, not knowing now who to say anything to – a hard person or a gone person – went quietly to a corner where he had a few metal cars and ramps made of cardboard, and his own books, picture books – Bill Peet books, *Moominsummer Madness*, *D'Aulaires Book of Greek Myths*, *Frog and Toad Are Friends* – all borrowed from the library for his birthday. Potatoes boiled in a pot on the electric hot plate. The water hissed when it hit the heating surface. What water missed the hot plate splattered on the floor.

~

Late one afternoon, years later, yellow sun through the trees, it was a different perspective. Seffi's reluctance had faded. Her voice sounded softer, subdued. She suggested, when Games brought up his father, that the best thing he could do was to say his father was simply no longer.

No longer what?

Does it matter?

Games didn't know how to answer.

No longer part of the story, said Seffi over the phone. It was a February afternoon. And when his mother, from wherever she was calling, said those words to Games, he wanted to say...or have her say...or. Didn't really know what he wanted. Standing near the western window in his aunt's house, Games played with the sun. He hid the radiant disc behind the trunk of a tree by moving his head to the left a bit. It was his birthday, and he'd just turned ten. Neither sad nor angry that his father was no longer. Simply curious.

Why? he asked.

Why what?

Why's he no longer part of the story?

Games moved his head slightly right. The sun edged from behind the trunk. He continued to move his head. The sun reappeared full blast.

Oh, Games. You, said his mother. You've just got to accept what is.

Games did accept things. He did not dispute the world as it came. Still, he wanted to know details. He wanted the story of his father and how his father then had been cut out of the narrative. The boy stood alone in his aunt's house, listening back and forth, first to the sun through the window, then to his wordless mother on the phone. The sun, his quiet mother. Sun. Mother. Sun. He kept his emotions in check, traveling stoically on his own. At least, it seemed he was on his own, even though Aunt Julia was in the next room chopping onions, and his two cousins played somewhere in the neighborhood, even though right there in front of him blared the sun that so obsessed his eyes. And of course, as always, Uncle Orro would come home later, put his books on the kitchen table before stepping outside to drink his wine.

Things were easy to know. There was a certain rhythm and rightfulness to the structure of days. No problem accepting how things took shape and moved through the hours. Still, not everything was as it was meant to be. Not as it should be, perhaps.

Games took a deep breath.

Are you part of the story? he asked.

Games heard nothing over the phone. Every day it grew more obvious to him that this place with Aunt Julia, Uncle Orro, Peter, and Michaela – this was where he'd be forever. Not that he was unhappy. Truth is, he could be happy anywhere. Didn't need much, not even answers to his questions. Silence was okay with Games. And yet there were times when he...he drifted off. When he...

Sometimes Games imagined a mother who was touchable, touching, too, her hand on his arm or back, not pushing or pulling, and a father who would come sit beside his bed at night before Games fell asleep, and he, that father, would bring Games out of any funk with well-placed words. The three of them, Games, his mother, father, would be their own mutual admiration society. *You're so great. No, you're the great one. No, you're the best of all.* And he sometimes imagined a brother and sister, as well. A sayable brother, a seeable sister, ones more of a piece with his ideal family than Peter and Michaela, no matter how okay, truly okay they –

Okay then, said his mother over the phone, as the day grew heavy.

Okay what? said Games.

I'm going to put a...I'm going to go now, but...

Where're you going?

I put a present in the mail, Games. Keep your eyes and ears open. Listen for...

He thought she was going to say *the delivery*, but instead she said *clues*. And when the sun stung the boy's eyes as his mother said clues, he slid a tree in front of the brightness.

Anything's possible, said Seffi. Thus ending the call.

~

Who's Ernie?

It's no one's earning anything. Not you or me. Does the sky earn its keep? Do the trees? Why would they? But I've got to find a way to make it work.

Games didn't know what she was talking about. Most days, he wore his favorite blue shirt with a picture of a small airplane on the front. *Take off*, it read on his chest. *Keep on*, it read on his back. He was the same good kid from morning through night, barely old enough to have memories, even. He had no idea where money or food or each situation came from, really. A few silver coins now and then on the floor, dollar bills plucked from some man's wallet when only Games was looking, strange sounds coming from that same man who slept on his back on the bed, a large man, a loud man, who muttered and snored and sputtered and snorted, sometimes scratching his nose and rolling. And there was fruit for the taking from the *River Street Store*. There was easy bread from the farmer's market on Saturdays in the spring and a whole bunch of books from the library shelves that were free if you tossed them out the bathroom window and collected them from the rhododendron. It was all the possibilities of life that were available to Seffi. She read about them in books and saw what they could be. She invented them in the world and said they were so.

Games's mother loved to read. She took in stories the way others took in air. She took other things, too – advantage and risks, took refuge and pleasure, took men behind the curtain she'd set up in the one-room spread, took hold of Games's hand when she was in a hurry, took leaves from trees, took blackberries and honeysuckle, took little or no care of her skin or her hair, never took a hint or anybody's shit, not a backseat to anyone, never took much aim either till she took the whole damn place apart, even a few floorboards, looking for something, and left one day, dragging young Games by the arm.

Off the two of them went. *Finally.* Not to her sister Julia. Yes. Yes to Julia. No. Yes. Fuck it, said Seffi, stomping on the sidewalk. It was rivers of cracks that Games saw. The loose and busted concrete. He stood there, waiting. Maybe Seffi could take a hint from the wind what it was telling her right to her face: *Don't mess with your boy's future, keeping him here.* A hint from the nonjudgmental trash by the side of the road, from the stop and go cars making for home, and from the long-gone birds having already migrated. *What're you waiting for?*

They boarded the bus, sat in the back. She's going to hate me, thought Seffi. But then she already does. She and her pretty it's so perfect home in that Godawful cold old cotton or is it paper, paper-mill town with professor physics her better-half Orvis Horton or who gives a shit, just try, just try, just... Hold your own, be polite.   Seffi was trying, but it didn't come easy.   And two kids like out of some fairy tale, which makes it the most farfetched. The most perfect picture. Her picture-perfect life. And leisure. Magazine feature. Happy endings. A million clichés. Not for her, though. No cliché for her. It's...it's...

The bus was a loud long bumpy ride. Seffi pulled a book from her bag, turned to it. The sun poured from the south, then at length from the west. It arced behind them as the bus drove on. Games pressed his face against the window, watching the fields and the traffic blur. He liked the glass, the cool on his cheek. And another thing he noticed – that the closer they got to where they were going, the more snow that lay on the ground.

When they arrived at the station, Julia was waiting. It was a chilly night and the sisters were cold together the long car ride home. Not Games, though. Heat blasted at his feet. Julia handed him a cookie with a smiling face made from raisins. Fresh baked today. Lots more in the kitchen.

You can go to sleep, if you want, said Julia.

He slept on the bus, said Seffi.

Well, it's a half hour home.

He'll sleep if he's tired. If he's not tired, he won't.

Of course, said Julia.

Look, it's going to be, began Seffi, and stopped.

Yep, said Julia, curtly. It's going to be. Always always. Going to be. Just up ahead there's a difference. Never now. And the rest of the drive was quiet.

At Aunt Julia's, the professor and Games and the older boy, Peter, drank steaming chocolate at the kitchen table, Orro doing most of the talking, of doubles tennis and binary stars.

You know Carl Sagan? Peter jumped in.

Carl's a gun, that's what Games heard. He pictured Carl as a rifle, hopping on the butt of his handle, tiny mouth on the barrel, small sad eyes.

You mean like a hunter?

What? He's this scientist who. Dad, what'd he do?

He –

And there are billions and trillions of stars, said Peter. You know how many is a trillion? It's –

Too many to count, said Uncle O. Let Games drink his chocolate.

But Peter didn't care much about chocolate. Instead, he asked if Games knew about entropy.

I don't like peas.

Michaela cried from her crib. Peas, peas, laughed Peter. There are no peas. Orro put up his hand. It caught the light. Someone must've gone to turn Michaela off because everything went quiet. Peter began again.

First you have to know the first law of thermodynamics. So do you?

Games nodded his head in agreement, though it may've been in sleepiness. It had been a long day. Julia led the way to a real soft bed with green sheets and a blanket with trains and planes and boats and busses. There was another bed in the room for his mother, flowers on the table, even though it was winter. As Games lay in his bed, he listened to voices murmur and blend and then came sleep.

Seffi and Games stayed a while in the basement, Seffi pretending to look for jobs and a school, but instead the two of them drove to the mountains and streams, they walked the trails nearby. They'd return at night with stories of hidden graveyards and frozen ponds they'd seen. Once there was a book left on a picnic table. Another time a hockey stick and a puck there for the taking.

You can't just take stuff you find, said Julia, when Seffi showed her the stick.

Sure you can, said Seffi. What, you think the world wants everything for itself? You'd rather pass through the world and not take any interest.

Taking an interest is one thing, said Julia. Taking stuff's another.

And they ate together, as a family. Peter built fires in the woodstove because he knew how. Sometimes Julia with Kayla in a front pack baked cookies and bread with Games on a stool to help. He rolled the cookie dough flat and cut animal shapes with cutters. He watched the yeast bubble and foam in warm water. He waited for the bread to rise. Then spring came and daffodils, dandelions, mud. Seffi got a look in her eye and told Games they were going. She noticed Julia's keys near the address book and took her sister's car without asking, helped herself to some money from the kitchen drawer, a credit card for gas, and books from the shelf. She put five-year-old Games in the front seat. She put their clothes and some food in the back, and off they went to visit the one and only, the original world, where amazing stories told themselves, if you just listened right, and where things made sense without human help.

There's nothing for us back there, you know.

Games didn't quite know.

You've got to think for yourself, his mother told him. If you're stuck, take off. Remember that shirt you used to wear? Got to do, got to invent your time on earth. Can't wait for it to be handed to you, like some scientist pinning his hopes on data.

God, it was good to get away, to get on course. Not to tell anyone, just to go. They lived in the backseat and at rest stops heading west and in rooms now and then, and Seffi knew people somewhere and one of them asked Games to wait outside, and his mother rubbed his back, which felt different to him, saying there was a ditch behind the dumpster where there might be dragonflies or honeybees. No one notices dragonflies anymore, she said. Damselflies, too, purple flowers, honeybees. The world's abuzz. You've got to believe it, she told him. Don't take anyone else's word. Don't let others fill your eyes with crud or load your ears with crap. Not me, not anyone. So, Games went to see and hear on his own, and when he came back to the camper everything hummed inside him as a lush world of bees and blooms. The same man asked: Syy, wmmmm yrr nmmmm, bmm?

Hmm?

Said, what's your name, bud? He seemed to be interested. Lit cigarette. Little red light.

Games, said Games, watching the smoke.

Come again.

Games said it again. He always said his name as clearly as he could when anyone asked, because he wasn't ashamed, and he didn't mind talking, just didn't do it much. And summer was coming on so everything was warm and becoming loud becoming colors becoming berries becoming very, very becoming, which was his mother's favorite word of all – becoming.

And off they drove. Somewhere else. Games looked in the sideview mirror at the becoming world receding. He didn't mind missing out on things, didn't really mind which way he was going. He looked out his window at the river on his right. Games was the water he saw through the trees, the sparkly water. It moved along. He moved along. He was going somewhere, like the water itself. He didn't ask where he was going and his mother never told him. Then the river called out to Games. *Turn around*, it said. *Come back. Come.* It was something in the river – a body, a broken, a loose floating voice, lost. Games saw a black mass bobbing near the bank. It pleaded so loudly that Games startled his mother with his sympathy.

He needs us. He needs us.

Seffi stomped on the brakes.

What! What!

Go back, said Games. There's someone in the water.

His mother turned the car around and pulled off the road. She and Games got out and walked toward the water's edge where the thing floated. A half-submerged car, a calf, a bloated deer, a brother beast, sister log. Lumber. Human. What? There was a leg and an arm, a decomposing face.

Oh God, don't look, said Seffi, as she and Games got close, entering the smell that hovered in the still air.

She turned Games, pushed him back to the car, but he wanted to see.

Don't look, repeated his mother. An old dead person. Nothing we can do. Her hand was at her mouth as she walked, holding back words, looking all around as if someone, as if something sinister might be there. She stood at the car, not talking, not looking not once toward the river. No cars going by on a Sunday morning in the middle of nowhere. *Doesn't matter*, she stood. *Makes no difference now. Someone drowned. Long gone.* Games discovered her mood as if it played inside him. She was afraid of something, but he wasn't afraid. He wanted to go back and see more closely. If up to him, he'd go back. He'd stay with the person till the day ended or till someone gently guided both of them away.

And yet none of that happened. Games stood by the car with his mother, because he didn't want to leave her, either. Then, while she peed in the bushes, Games ran to visit with the dead, not really knowing why, just hoping to see better what it was that had frightened his mother off, or if there was something maybe he could do – bright wind blowing, one bird real high, water lapping through the grasses – to help.

~

Because Games was truly a helpful boy. He was no trouble at all. Easy to travel with. No problem, either.

Mother and son pulled into the grocery store lot late afternoon, practicing math. The day was like all others, synonymous and separate. Six times nine? No problem, fifty-four. Nine times six? No problem, fifty-four, said five-and-a-half-year-old Games right out of his head like The Calculator Kid.

Okay smarty. His mother reached into the back for a book. What's this word? She pointed to a word in the middle of the page.

Grr, gra, Games read. Gratitude.

What's it mean?

It's when you're way up in the sky.

That's altitude.

Oh.

It means Thanks, said his mother.

Altitude?

Gratitude. Remember it. And who wrote this book I'm holding?

What is it? asked Games.

It's *Great Expectations*.

Chickens, said Games.

That's Dickens. Charles Dickens.

What's Dickens? asked Games.

His name. Not Chickens. Dickens. I told you about the orphan Pip.

You said it was Tip.

Tip's someone else. He's from Oz. Pip's from the marshland of Kent. That's England.

Games had a faint memory of marshes and a Pip who was born there. And someone Jaggers. Maybe a mansion. That Singland, too.

It was his thirteenth novel. Thirteen colonies. You were born on the thirteenth, right before Valentines.

What's Falan Time?

Not Time. Tine, said his mother. He's a saint.

What's a saint?

Your questions are boring. Then, after a moment to let this sink in, she said, It's someone who's in heaven after they die. But more than that, a real saint's got God in them even when they're here on earth.

Games tried to picture a person, a saint, walking on earth with Zeus or Poseidon living inside them.

And what did Jesus do? asked his mother.

Who?

From the Bible.

Told stories, said Games.

They're called parables, said his mother. And how about Mohammad?

Why's he so mad?

Mohammad. He's not mad, said his mother. He listened to God. Why don't you listen?

I do.

If you listen, you learn.

I do.

What do you listen to? You've got to ask yourself that. Do you listen to the world that talks to you? Don't listen to others telling you how things are. Take the world as only you can. Take it and like it and. There's no need to do any of the shit convention tells you to do. Not school, not business, none of the man-made laws. Figure stuff out on your own. Make your path. Don't let anyone tell you who you are. Don't be shaped by convention or by the aggressions of others. Shape your own life. Do you know what I mean?

Games stared blankly at his mother. She stared back.

What?

He didn't have anything to say. Just, he wanted to eat.

I know. You're hungry. But what about Helen of Troy? What'd I tell you about her?

Games knew that one.

She made problems for everyone. And Paris is a city in Frank.

Forget about Paris. Who cares about Paris or Frank? The thing is, Games, maybe Helen didn't actually make the problems. Maybe it's just that others were stupid. How can one person make problems for another? We all only make problems for ourselves. And we solve them for ourselves, too.

Games was tired of questions and words. What he really wanted was a Snickers Bar. Or a fish fillet with tartar sauce.

How? his mother repeated. How could she've done it?

Who?

Helen.

She was, began Games. Was she...was too...

Wishy-washy. What're you saying? Too what? Too beautiful? Too outspoken? Too –

Beautiful, said Games.

You're just being a parrot. What's it mean? What's it mean to be beautiful?

Games didn't know what it meant. He was hungry. He wanted to get out. Go somewhere. Be different than this. Why did others just get to go, play baseball, soccer, ride bikes, skip stones for hours, watch shows on TV? His mother hated TV.

Seffi sighed.

Don't say something if you don't know what it means. Beautiful's a big word. It's what they all saw in Helen. It was unmistakable. Of course, they just thought she was a beautiful body with a mixed-up mind, a cause of wars and unhappiness, not a spiritual being with beauty in her soul. But that's what I see. I'm not saying she was perfect, I'm saying she was good where it matters most. And that's what you've got to see about people. Not the bad, not the problems, not the false things people make up about others, but the beautiful good they really are. Can you do that?

Games stared out the window.

Do you know what I mean? asked his mother, more softly.

The parking lot was alive with people, cars. The low sun stocked their car with light. Rocked it. Rocketed it. Sent it shining. The sign above the store was glowing red letters. MAKE IT WORLD. MARKET WORLD.

Okay, said Seffi. Let's get some food.

~

Early in winter, when almost six years old, Games swallowed a fly at breakfast. The diner was warm, packed with people. Their table rested unevenly on the floor. There was a smell of bacon and the music of plates and forks. Games's mother, whose restlessness made her difficult for most to understand, had a beautiful voice. She sang to herself when she thought no one was listening. She sang to her son when the two were driving. The song that came to mind after his unfortunate appetizer was one about swallowing a fly. Games did not wish to die, but perhaps he would.

What's wrong? asked his mother, noticing the boy's worried expression across the table. The table wobbled just thinking about it.

I don't know, said Games. I think I might die.

Of course you'll die some day, but not for a very long time, said his mother, spooning her oatmeal, holding the table still with her left foot pressed upon one of its legs.

What happens to dead people?

Do I look like a medium to you?

Games didn't know what her size had to do with it.

I'm not a fortune-teller, said his mother.

But what happens?

Why're you so worried about it?

I just swallowed a fly, said Games. It was buzzing and my mouth was open and it flew right in.

A fly. Who cares about a fly?

But it's a fly, like the song.

Seffi sat still, staring out the window, her oatmeal cooling, the spoon in her hand. She liked to stare and think. She took her son's concerns seriously when she wasn't occupied by her own. Though largely an unavailable mother at best, Seffi could now and then be counted on for ideas, especially if it was her son's birthday, which it was not, or if she'd been reading a book, which lucky for Games was the case. It was one of the books in her permanently borrowed collection. *Myths That Remind Us How to Live*. No problem sharing what she'd recently learned. This day had begun with bacon smells, with coffee, too. Light lay upon the morning, ready to roll. Seffi didn't hesitate.

Do you want me to tell you a story about someone else who swallowed a fly?

Who?

It's a good one.

Okay, said Games.

Okay, said Seffi, and she told her son about Zeus, Olympian god, top dog of the Twelve, thunderbolt kingpin, big wig, big cheese, lord of the universe. He swallowed his first wife, Metis, goddess of good advice.

What do you mean, swallowed her?

Just listen, said Seffi, who leaned on the table and it tilted her way, toppling the salt. His first wife, Metis, turned herself into a fly as part of a game the two were playing. Zeus, who loved and needed his wife, also was afraid of her because someone had told him that Metis would give him a son and that that son would kill Zeus.

Why? asked Games.

I don't know why. Just listen. So, Zeus suggested a game of changing shapes, and Metis, who thought it would be fun, changed into different animals. You ready for the animals?

Uh huh.

First it was a horse. Then a pig. Then she became a cute puppy. And then a songbird, a chickadee I think. Finally, Metis turned herself into a fly and Zeus saw his chance. He swallowed his wife. He didn't want to hurt her. It was to keep himself safe. So, he put her inside him where it would be very difficult for her to have a child. You can see how it's not easy to have a child if you're in someone's head.

Stomach, you mean, said Games.

I mean, it was smart what he did. Metis changed to a fly and Zeus swallowed her and he wouldn't die and she wouldn't die, either. In fact, she found a nice place to live in his head, and from there everything went pretty smoothly for the both of them.

You can live in someone's head? asked Games.

I don't see why not, said his mother. Metis could offer her good advice, which is what she did best. She could speak to Zeus and help him decide what was most sensible to do. She was the goddess of prudence. Prudence is sort of an old-timey word, but when you have it inside you it tells you what you should and shouldn't do. Don't do that, Prudence will say. It'll lead to something awful. Or: If you do this, you'll be okay. It wasn't commandments, not orders, just good suggestions that Metis handed out. Not bad, right?

I guess.

So, think of the fly you've swallowed like that. It's someone who's there to help. You're a lucky kid. You've got a great thing inside you. You've got someone who's there to help you always. I promise you won't die for a real long time. Okay?

Okay, said Games. But what about school? I don't want to drive around forever. I want to go to school. I want friends. I don't like being nowhere.

What's the matter with driving?

Games didn't know what the matter was.

Every nowhere is a somewhere that's just misunderstood, said his mother.

Games said nothing.

There's so much no one cares about, all waiting to be seen. We can do whatever we want.

Games didn't. He just. Whatever we want. He didn't know. He…

Eat your breakfast, said his mother. Okay?

Okay, said Games.

You need any salt? She held forth the shaker.

No, said Games. He knew he didn't want salt. He knew he didn't want to drive anymore. So, what did he want? Games was a boy who liked bacon and sunlight, eggs were okay. He liked rain when it rained on the windshield and then the wipers came to sweep off the drops and for a moment the glass was free and clear. Pretty nice. He liked listening to songs, listening to bees, listening to rhythms, to everybody. And now he could breathe easy about the fly, though he did try hard to listen to what was going on inside him, too. Sometimes he thought he heard a buzz, or maybe it was a voice, but usually it was nothing he could make out as words. He was almost six, without formed ideas, without troubling thoughts. The world was people and food and tables that wobbled. Sun came shining through the diner window. The sun, more sun, made light with its power and warmth with its light. The sun rose upon the sky. Its warm yellow light filled each day, and the days spun by, bringing with them such things as were often strange and new. And Games accepted his life, as he also accepted his name, without putting up much of a fight.

~

It's an odd name, though – Games. People questioned it, beginning with Dr. Papermaster at the clinic, then endlessly with others who thought they'd misheard. It didn't much bother the boy, the mishearings. He was patient with the questions, too, even if he didn't know quite what to say.

Tell them it rhymes with James, said his mother.

They think it is James, said Games.

Jesse James was an outlaw, said his mother. Robbed banks and trains. Had a nice smile like you. He's not you.

Games shrugged.

Tell them you've got good aim right in the middle of you. Keep that truth for yourself, though. Don't let anyone get the better of you.

What's the better of me?

When you find it, you'll know, said his mother.

~

Games's life on earth was the result of a bad act and a good. He learned of both when, on his thirteenth birthday, his mother told him the story of his birth over the phone. Typical of her not to be present. Games stood outside the kitchen in Aunt Julia and Uncle Orro's house. The television in the background had a show about spelunking that Peter turned up when the phone rang.

Who's that I hear? asked Games's mother.

It's no one.

Games, said his mother. It was a tone he hadn't heard before. I've got something to tell you.

Seffi then told the events of his birth, his father, the whole nine yards. When she ended, the television was showing a commercial for toothpaste.

Okay, said Games, after she'd finished.

That's it? said his mother. That's how it makes you feel?

I thought you said he was no longer part of the story. Now you bring him back like he's, he's like this –

I never said shit, said Seffi, mishearing.

What? said Games. No one said *shit*. I said *this*. This totally evil person or something.

No one's equal, said Seffi. Life's unfair, but you can help make it right.

Evil, I said, said Games.

No one's evil. They just...don't... Is it a party at your house?

Peter keeps turning up the TV, said Games.

Truth is, we're all part of one another, said his mother. I'm part of your father. He's part of me. We're both part of you, and you, thankfully, are part of us. It makes for balance. Course you've got to find it for yourself.

Find what?

The balance.

I don't get you, said Games. You're always running away.

And you're always in place, said his mother. Which is a better way to be.

There was a long silence.

But really we're both here, she continued. The reception was difficult, so she said it again, full of sadness.

You're here and I'm here with you. There's nowhere else to go. We're trying to find balance we don't know is there.

You keep saying ballast, like we're in a boat.

Balance, I said. Balance. But ballast, too, if that's what you hear.

Games knew that his mother wasn't here. She was somewhere else. When she hung up, he thought about where people were. He tried to see what they saw where they were. What they didn't see. He thought about balance and ballast, of walking a tightrope without toppling and of seeing the light in everything as ballast to the dark.

Games held himself up. Nothing made him fall. He was like one of those birds who could stand on one leg forever. And not always forever in one place. He thought of other places he could go to break up the monotony: There were the train tracks at the foot of the town or behind the school where that tree with its long low limbs looked like his aunt offering food. He liked that tree. And his aunt. And the train tracks. And trains. He then came back to his mere-words mother and his meaningless father and why they acted as they did, or why they didn't act at all. His thoughts were stuck in his head or his heart or cells or soul or. It was a tangle of unknowing that he tried to sort out. He tried to sort out what his mother had said.

But ballast, too, if that's what you hear.

It's supposed to be my birthday and you're telling me my father raped you.

Raped. Who said raped? No one said raped. Abducted.

What's that supposed to mean?

Do you know the story of Persephone?

It's always stories with you.

Games waited and waited. His mother said nothing.

She was raped by Hades, he said, breaking the silence. And Paris raped Helen.

Who told you that?

I read it in a book.

I'm not talking about rape, said his mother.

Are you talking about books?

No.

That's a shock. What are you talking about?

Human freedom.

Games thought he knew something about freedom. His mother had told him about Frederick Douglass who was born near where she grew up, and he'd just learned in school of Sojourner Truth.

No one can take you, said his mother. You can take no one.

But if he raped you...

Stop saying that word.

Then he's not my father.

Take you, I said. No one can take you. No one it's impossible can take from you the person you are. You can't let that happen. That's what I'm saying.

And she went on saying it. Seffi wanted Games to know that a person who would belittle the spirit of life was not a good person. And someone, anyone, who would coerce another's freedom was anathema to her. It was the consciousness of the person who would consider the act, not the act itself, that was the issue here. Change the consciousness and you change the act. If coercion and cruelty was how humans thought, it was wrong. Wrong was the control over girls and women around the world. Wrong was the manipulation of others. Wrong were human beings who were refused their autonomy. It was the most illicit thing you could do to another to impose your own determinations upon that soul.

What do you mean, soul?

Person, then, said his mother.

So, was he a terrible person?

Your father was all about himself. Imagine what it must be like inside a person when there's complete isolation. His body and his soul were too closely connected, so when something hurt his body, it hurt his soul. Or when he lost his tenuous control of the situation, everything was lost. His words were knives cutting up the day. He tossed things just to smash them. He was like: *What's out there? Who cares? I only feel what's in me.* That's what isolation says.

Why didn't you just leave, like you always do?

I don't always leave, Games. I go somewhere different to help myself. It's just with your father I didn't know who was the most important person to help. And then suddenly I did. I knew I had to get away.

Why?

This brought out the second act, the better of the two, which was his mother's decision to follow through with her pregnancy, even though the man responsible was an oppression artist, living in his dark abyss, who headbutted her once in the parking lot and made her drink only his take on things and eat his barbed words and took her money for booze and threw plates at the wall and one day when he saw his name on a list of people who had died that year, it made him see that even life itself did not belong to him. It never had. Made him think that the one true thing growing inside a body was death. So, he put all his trust in death and hated living for the wrongness of it. The fucking façade, he called it. And he laughed at Seffi's body when she told him she was pregnant because didn't she know how she was being played? Didn't she know how futile it was? Didn't she get the inside joke? He must have been the only one who could see things clearly. Birth leads to the understanding that it's all a mistake – all the fucking light and hopefulness, all the days spent working, trying to get somewhere, all the hours of eating and drinking and waking and, every minute spent thinking about everything and…and, everyfuckingthing itself. Birth only succeeds at enhancing death. Doesn't anyone know? And he, Games's father, threw all his clothes on the floor because he was angered by their wrinkles, their fit, and how they always made him look, or maybe just because he'd become a prisoner to his feeling of inadequacy.

Did you say he headbutted you in the parking lot?

I meant to say that I only had myself to blame.

Whatever it was, Seffi wasn't going to take the drama anymore, now that she had a child inside her. She stood her ground with a book in her right hand, *Plays of Euripides*, as if it were a weapon. She stepped over his shirts, brushed past him and his irretrievable self, right out the door.

The sky was particularly blue that day, the trees freshly green in the park nearby. How nice, said his mother, to be out in the world with the sun and birds. To be free and be responsible for yourself alone. Just you in the world and the world in you. Looking for affinities.

Why infinity? asked Games.

I said *affinities*.

What are they?

Just what works for you, and who cares about anything else.

But –

I know what you're thinking, said Seffi. It wasn't only about me, was it?

I wasn't –

Weren't you listening?

Most all what Games did was listening. People with their words. The sky with its light. Wind through the leaves. Cars going by on the street out front.

I said *the world in me*, continued his mother. Because then there came the protagonist, Parzival. Learning to be.

Who?

Do I have to spell it out for you? You are the affinity, Games. Infinity, too. This story's not about anyone else. Just you.

Games didn't know what to say. Into the phone. Into the air. He didn't even know what a protagonist was. Or affinities, really. Parzival whoever. He was only thirteen. He liked Frederick Douglass, who, watching sailboats moving about unchained on the Chesapeake, knew how close he stood to freedom, and how freedom was the necessary prerequisite to a purposeful human life. He liked Sojourner Truth, who didn't run off but walked with both dignity and her daughter to self-determination. He liked all stories that fed on the light at the end of the tunnel. Because everyone wanted to be – because everyone needed to be – free.

So, as soon as Seffi had burst out the door, she had to stop and think. All her books on the floor in that tiny apartment. Most of her money in the drawer with her clothes. A jackhammer broke up the street to her right. Nothing came easy. She'd work it out later. Right now she had to ask for better help. She went to live in a shelter for the summer and the fall months, too, and then took a bus to Baltimore because it was north but not so far north as where her sister lived, and this nice man, a priest or rabbi, had a place in the basement of some building, but how would she find work again and raise a kid? She couldn't just drag him along. She couldn't just leave him behind. She couldn't just let other people tell her what to do. She couldn't just do nothing. Then came Ettie Pease, carrying a platter of her very best biscuits. She came through the door, and the rest was gravy, which wasn't even a cliché. It was real, for a while. Winter birth, warm healthy food, people being nice.

Because the truth is, people are generally good, the ones who care, Seffi thought. And, yes, she said it to Games on the phone. Though Games already knew this about his mother, that she had an idealistic approach to the world, even if she didn't wish to join its society. People for the most part are trying to make good. They care about others. They care about themselves. They take care. They give care. But they're also difficult to be around for any amount of time longer than five minutes. They all have their own opinions and ideas and they want to push you into things. Things you don't want to do. Things that aren't about you as a person. Seffi said this to Games, his ear to the phone, as he watched the television change from one picture to another. But it's your life, isn't it? she continued. It's how you choose to meet the world if left to do it on your own. No mess. No violence. No judgments,

then. You can do most everything alone, Games. Alone.
That's when you're most free to be yourself.

Seffi's decision to keep her child was an act of difficult
selflessness. She didn't say this to Games over the phone. It
was a thought she kept hidden. Or, more than a thought, it
was an unquestionably correct choice and in no way
something she debated.

So, came the boy, born to the earth. Which was, hands
down, a good beginning for Games. Seffi knew that things
would always work out. She had strong intuitions. She had
positive feelings, which flowed as her blood and kept her
warm. Things were in fact good if you saw them that way. If
you kept your eyes open, didn't fight with life, read things
right, if you listened deeply. Everything for a reason, or so the
story goes.

She even quoted the Bible where it made perfect sense: *Let
all that is done among you be done in love:* First Corinthians. Or,
as Tobit said earlier, though this wasn't always so easy: *Cheer
all those within you who are captives, and love all those within you
who are distressed.* And finally, because she saw it this way: *To
each is given the manifestation of the Spirit, and who knows why
except that it's good and don't let others get in your way and don't
get in theirs, and the wind is good and the ripples on the puddles are
good and the calm on the lakes is good and the road is good and
somewhere in your heart that sings is good and you've just got to
know it and do what you are and not what you aren't or the good
won't come forth and multiply like stars as evening turns to night.*
Though most of that was not a direct quote. Still, something
good was always coming, becoming. Something beautiful
was there all the time, behind the world, in the works, and
growing in each person's soul, longing to be out.

~

I don't get it, said Games, sitting across the kitchen table from his mother. They both drank apple cider from blue glasses.

What don't you get? said his mother.

Why you did it?

Did what? asked his mother. She played with her now empty glass, making large and smaller circles over the knotty pine surface of the table.

Named me my name? Did you make it up?

Where's this coming from all of a sudden?

Is yours made up like me?

Games and his mother were living with Julia again. This was after the fly, but before Seffi bolted on her own for good. Games was in Ms. Flood's second grade at Thunder Love Elementary. Serena sat behind him and teased him about his name. She teased on the playground. She teased him at lunch.

That's sort of rude, said his mother.

What's rude?

I don't make stuff up. Everything's real. Plus, I like my name. It makes me think of Persephone.

What's purr – whatever you said? asked Games

His mother briefly told him the story, as she knew many myths of the Greeks and the Norse, and the stories of coyote and his friends, of the raven the wolf and the spider and even Ida B. Wells's difficult life. The story of Pip was an all-time favorite, the Good Samaritan, the King Arthur legend, and the Grand Inquisitor. There was Frederick Douglass on the banks of the Chesapeake looking out at the white sails that assailed his heart. And *Master and Man* with freezing Nikita: to free oneself before one dies – another favorite of Seffi's. And Gallant Greki who built a house in the middle of nowhere for all mankind, not to mention the story of Anna, the woman who found love in the grim and shameful gulags of the Soviet Union, and Lilianna, who crossed the Rio Bravo on her own and only nine to find hope up north.

None of it's made up. All of it's true, said Seffi.

She also knew of Gilgamesh. Seffi pushed her empty blue glass aside, so as not to be distracted. Then she said the name.

Who's Gilgamess? Games asked.

Sh.

Why can't I talk? said Games.

It's mesh not mess, said his mother. Talk all you want. It's one of the very first stories. Gilgamesh was an ancient hero.

What'd he do?

Well, he was two-thirds god one-third man.

Did he have super powers? asked Games, leaning toward his mother from across the table.

He could build things.

Like what?

He built a wall around his city, and this made some of the people angry because it kept getting higher and higher. So, they asked the gods to create a man out of dirt. This guy's name was Enkidu and he was supposed to stop Gilgamesh from building. Gilgamesh and Enkidu fought, but no one could win because they were so much the same, so the two of them became brothers instead, which is always better than fighting. Together they hunted and fished and thought about girls and yelled at the gods.

Why'd they yell?

They didn't want the gods telling them what to do. Then they killed the monster Humbaba and the Bull of Heaven and they laughed about this and shouted some more at the sky. Because of this, the gods were pissed and said that Enkidu had to die. And he did die. And Gilgamesh grew real quiet, and then angry. He paced and shouted and he threw things at the sky. What right did the gods have to take his friend? Gilgamesh figured a person should be able to live if he wanted. It bothered the king a lot that his friend was gone from the earth just like that.

You never said he was a king, said Games.

Well, he was, said his mother. And he had to find how to get Enkidu back. Gilgamesh had to learn the secret to immortality. So off he went to learn what keeps people alive. It was a difficult journey, and the closer he got to the secret, the more it slipped away. That's a terrible feeling to run and run and get farther and farther from what you want. Gilgamesh always got what he wanted, but not this time. Finally, he had to accept the fact that on earth everyone dies. Nothing you can do about it. He was sad for his friend. He was sad that beasts die in the fields and people die in their beds at night, but maybe it was for the best, he thought.

So, he didn't even save his friend, said Games.

He learned about life, said his mother.

What's so great about that?

No one could stop him from learning, said his mother.

This didn't impress Games.

You've got some of his name in you.

Games didn't see.

His mother took a pencil from her pocket and wrote Gilgamesh right there on the table. She underlined a portion of the word. She circled the name "games."

Games nodded at the upside-down word.

I thought about going backwards, with Magli. Or maybe Me or Gil. I remember a Gil when I was young. He tortured cats. Julia and I hated him for it.

Poor kitties, said Games.

So, it's okay? asked his mother.

What?

Your name.

Yeah. It's a good name. I'm okay with it. I'm okay with everything.

Everything?

Well... Games thought. Not torturing cats.

~

In Troy, the city of kings, of rivers, of soft urging stars, Games Shepard stood at his apartment, looking back across the night. He liked his name and storied background. He was well rooted in the world and had built himself from the ground up. He'd met himself from the sky down, too, with thoughts now and then of being the hero Gilgamesh, Captain Easy, or The Fly. *Everything for a reason*, some voice kept telling him. Games wondered if it was his mother from her inconsistency, or his father from his discontinuance, whose voice he heard. More likely, it was a less familiar part of himself trying to get through.

Games could never figure the voice. So, he stuck at first with things he did know. When younger, this was information he learned in school and what the world presented as truths: his kind Aunt Julia who baked cookies and bread, and smart Uncle Orro who put *light speed, entropy,* and *multiverse* together in one long sentence. It was his cousins Peter and Michaela, and all the capitals of South America from Caracas to Buenos Aries. There was also this fact he once read in a book – that if you were floating in the freezing cold water, three hours was all it would take for the heat to leave your body and you'd have to kiss your life goodbye. Games remembered this fact of life and death, which spoke to the fragility of the human body and to the support and the warmth it needed.

Games stood outside his apartment. Time slowed in the January air. Each passing second was composed of thoughts that became music in his body. Listen to yourself, said the thoughts. Musical, bluesical, rock solid, pop – how your life was built from antithesis. Games knew he was the result of good and bad thinking, of living dying cells, shadowed days and light. His father was an unfortunate gesture that at first seemed unforgivable and later may present itself for greater empathy. And his mother clung to separation as if it were the air she needed to breathe on earth. But the important thing, thought Games, is to keep an open mind about it all. Point yourself forward. Save yourself from closing by putting wide doors in front – fields, horizons, skies, these stars.

Games knew he would never give up on anyone. Not ever. Not when a person's alive, he thought. And not after he's dead, either. Days like today I see only connections. Brothers, sisters, family in the night, light in every window. Untiring windows, the inside life. That's where we're moving, eternally together, and I don't know why it's together unless it's to converge upon something better, the opposite of entropy. Days like today I'm responsible for the world. I'm saving the relationships, no matter how lost they might seem. And no one tells me to do it. And I don't ask why.

~

Games Shepard entered his apartment, threw his coat on a chair. In the chair sat a person. Games looked again. It was no one. His familiar wooden chair, now with a coat. A print by Chagall hung on the wall above the chair. He was happy to be home.

Other things made him happy, too. It was very pleasing to jimmy a knife under the lid to open a jar. Games loved the sip of air and the release of pressure. He loved it, too, that there is doubt, and that after doubt there is darkness with a possibility of understanding and after understanding there is work to do and after work you can play hockey or go for a drive or out on a date at Turn Up Café or Banjo Mountain or the Cineplex to see a movie.

What date again? The sixth of January. Epiphany, still. Games had no girlfriend. He had no distinguishing talent, no college degree, and no great love.   He'd had a serious girlfriend, once. Claire, about two years back. She often sat in that same chair, the one now with his coat – maybe it was she he'd just seen – legs crossed, hair pulled back. *Give me an honest answer.* It was what she always said to begin a question.

Games thought of Claire now. She was a nice girl, black hair like much of the night sky, very pretty, one who maybe he could have loved.

Give me an honest answer, do you think I can be one?

One? The one?

What did you say?

I don't know, said Games. What are you asking?

Can you see me as a psychologist? Like maybe a socialist or something.

A social worker, you mean.

Whatever.

Of course, he said.

It's what she wanted, though she also wanted to paint. Not walls so much as abstracts in oil. Games gave her paints, once. A canvas, too. She analyzed his gift, wondering if he was trying to tell her something about her chances with school. He gave her one of his apartment keys also, and they made out on the sofa. They made love when she wanted all of him, made stews together because Games worked then at the market where he still worked now and could get organic food, which was the food of choice for Claire. He helped her with money so she could take the classes at the community college, and he gave her his bike so she could get to and from school seven miles away. Which meant, because he didn't have a car back then, he had to walk to Jakes, but that was okay.

One day, Claire came into the apartment, carrying a book about consciousness written by her professor.

What's for dinner? she asked. Something nice, I hope. Which was a different way to get his attention, no need for an honest answer.

She and Games talked Jungianly, reaching into symbols and the primitive unconscious. It all made Games a bit uneasy. Claire could analyze any dream, telling what butterflies meant, and oceans, airplanes, dragons, you name it. She was a wiz with archetypes, too, all thanks to her professor. But when she drank too much she lost interest in everything. Her voice softened to a whisper and then to less than that. Sometimes she hid in the closet with the mop and dustpan. Games had to knock and coax her out. Had to lay her in bed, lie beside her grammatically, even if it was still light outside. In the morning, she was better or wasn't. If lucky, ready to go. Or not.

Her professor, Clayton or Odim or something, had said Claire was the brightest in the class and if she took his advice and applied herself, she'd get somewhere fast. It must've been advice she'd taken, because one day when Games came home, the bike was leaning against the wall and there was 307 dollars in an envelope on the table. On the envelope was a drawing of an airplane and the word *Thankyou* without a space, but Claire wasn't there. She was gone. Clayton Odim must've had real power over her. Games wondered if he'd see Claire some day in the future, walking with the professor, holding his acclaimed books under her arm. Would she feel awkward, he wondered, upon seeing him again? Guilty because of leaving? Or did the 307 dollars more than make up for any impropriety? And he wondered, too, how long it would be before he'd have sex again.

What is it exactly that a person's supposed to do with his life? Sex is one thing that was on Games's mind. But sex did not sustain him. Maybe, he thought, he could move up to produce manager at Jakes Market Fresh. He could assert himself and become floor manager, store manager, even. Or maybe he should do something different, work with people and not so much with fruits and vegetables.

The nursing home where I work is looking for aides, said Rio, when they were coming down the mountain, near the end of the hike. They train you and everything. You know, she reasoned, as a road to something.

To what? asked Games.

Or you could always finish school. You could get work as a respiratory technician. Everyone has to breathe. There're all sorts of jobs in hospitals.

Games kept quiet, as if giving this some thought.

Maybe you could teach.

Teach what?

Whatever you're good at, said Rio.

I'm good at inwardness.

Don't teach that. Teach children.

Children, you think?

I don't see why not, said Rio.

But teaching children was no option at the moment. And an aide in the nursing home was no kind of money. Besides, Games had a strange rapport with death, which made him think twice about such a job.

When he was sixteen, Games had a near-death experience. And though it wasn't his own death he came in contact with, it was a remarkable encounter.

Walking home one night after leaving a party, Games entered a house he thought was his. The night was moonless, dark, and Games slightly drunk. The door had two panels just like his, with steps leading up. Games, however, didn't notice the blue of the panels, the white dove knocker, or the number, 307, all of which were clues that this was not his house. Nor did he brush with the potted flowers that should've been on the top step, where Aunt Julia had put them. Instead, he pushed the door and it opened much like his own, squeak and all. It was good to be home. And sitting in the dark at the kitchen table, the chair was a perfect fit. Games looked for the clock on the oven. But the clock wasn't there. Not the oven either, not where it should've been. In fact lots of things, the more Games's eyes adjusted, weren't in keeping with his house. Some windows were missing from the walls, for example. Others had moved to the left or right, thus taunting his sense of order. Where the floor should've been tile, it was wood. Where the phone should've been was a basket of pinecones. The house was a mess, total chaos, piles of books and papers, collections of junk, animal bones, small mammal skulls and... entropy. Entropy. This isn't my house, Games said aloud, sobering on the spot.

What's all this nonsense about entropy? Order is everywhere, if you can see it.

Games jumped at the voice. Noelle Bestmartin, daughter of the late Joseph Bestmartin, eighty-seven years old.

Didn't mean to startle you. But imagine my own surprise.

Games stood. He scanned the room for the speaker.

Oh, do sit down, said the old woman, turning on the light. No need for theatrics.

I must've, began Games, seeing the woman standing in the doorway. Sorry, I'm.

Why're you sorry?

I'm. It's, said Games. What are you. You doing here?

What am I. I doing? said Noelle. This is my. My house. You should be. Be happy I'm not calling the police. Drunken kid. Breaking and entering. Deputy Sirani'd have a field day with this.

Games played hockey with Sirani's son, Josh.

Okay, he said.

Okay?

I mean, thanks for not calling the please. The police.

You're welcome. I mean, please sit down. You are welcome.

So, Games re-sat and the old woman made coffee by boiling water in a pot and spooning in the grounds.

What–

It's almost three, said Noelle, answering. But before you go on, let me have my say. It is my house.

Games didn't argue. And she told him about the good work of honeybees, the underground network of mushrooms, and the curative properties of the letter *c*. That, or the endless sea. She rifled through a book. Showed Games a picture, an old black and white.

Who's that?

Susan B. Anthony, said Noelle, making Games write the name with his finger on the table. She was born near here, 1820. Not all that pretty, is she. Sort of like me, don't you think?

I...

Of course you know I'm right. I was never much to look at.

After a quiet moment, Noelle told of the time she walked in on Robert Oppenheimer as he chalked and figured on the board, a certain opportunistic principle, o, or was it d, that he put near the end of his equation to make everything work.

The atom bomb guy?

Now, I am become Death, the shatterer of worlds.

Games gave no response to this line.

It's from the Bhagavad Gita.

What's that?

Something to talk about another day, said Noelle.

She went on about her time at the university, and Games's mind blurred and buzzed with the words of her medical research into cellular metaphysics and cancer.

Cancer cells are only trying to express the soul, said Noelle. All illness is imposed upon the body by the soul. Why are we so angry at illness when the real problem is ourselves and our lack of consciousness?

You've got to cure it though, said Games.

The greatest cure comes upon discovering the spirit behind existence. We must not talk about what's right or wrong with our bodies or the world. That keeps our attention on gauges and graphs and whatnots. It's as if we could measure wellness with a ruler. Instead we must realize how the well-being of ourselves and the world can transform with our consciousness.

The words were lost on Games.

Everything on earth is soul evolution, said Noelle. Soul

building, not body building. From the materialization of spirit to the spiritualization of matter. Do you know what I mean?

Not really.

Do you even know what the soul is?

It's...well...I...you, stuttered Games.

That's nothing but gibberish.

People say it goes to heaven, asserted Games.

What people?

My aunt. Lots of people.

Heaven's a way of avoiding thinking much about the soul, said Noelle. Sure thing, it comes and goes. But it's here to stay because here is where it's needed. Not in heaven. Why in heaven's name is there an earth anyway?

I don't know, said Games.

How can you not know?

I never thought about it.

The earth is for taking time with your soul, said Noelle. For building it.

Like a factory?

Like a womb.

What sort of room?

One you are free to move in, said Noelle. You build your soul and it's a bridge from the center of yourself. You build it in both directions.

Left and right, said Games.

Out to the physical world and inward to the spiritual.

Out. And in words. Games repeated what he heard.

Those are the directions you need to go, said Noelle. When you see a bird or butterfly, look to the spiritual. When you see a police siren in your rearview mirror, come back to earth real quick.

How do I bill I mean how do you... How? attempted Games.

You don't build your soul with alcohol, said Noelle. That's for sure. And she gave him a book by someone named Steiner. Games stared at the book and focused on the font. He nodded and his arm fell, book firmly in hand.

I guess, he began.

You're a nice young man, I must say. Well, I don't have to say it. I say it in freedom.

I guess I think I should go.

Veni, vidi, vici, said Noelle.

So, Games said he was sorry about coming into her house, that it was a mistake. And Noelle said it wasn't a mistake and that she wasn't sorry at all, but she would be when he was gone because the earth is amazing, and she had a cupboard full of coffee and very little time left to brew it.

I've asked myself often if I should save time in the day to drink coffee, or rather should I drink coffee in the day to save time? Marilyn Monroe said something similar about poetry. What do you say?

I mean, I'm sorry for barging into your house.

There once was a barge from Barcelona. At least you didn't barf in it.

Barf in the barge?

My house. I hate that word, *barf*, don't you?

Games considered *barf*. He considered other words, too – their rhythms and rhymes and, at times, their ill repute. Re-puke. Whatever. No nausea, luckily. The coffee had done the trick.

Thanks for not calling the cops, he said.

Why on earth would I do that? Bring in the police, and everything becomes a matter of worldly laws. Our lives must not be reduced to physical constraints. Don't you ever think about the meaning of things? Don't you wonder why things happen the way they do, or why things happen when they do? Do you even know what synchronicity is? I'm fascinated by it.

Games nodded, hearing electricity.

It's pretty cool, he said. The stuff that atoms do. But I guess I should probably go.

They held each other's gaze a moment.

There's the door, said Noelle at last. You know, it's not atoms in the end that matter. Not gluons or photons. It's your life and mine. You might choose not to consider me. I might choose not to consider you. I don't want to argue about it. I'd rather be amazed that we've had this moment to catch up.

Catch up? It was a funny thing to say, because Games had never met this woman before.

Don't be so reticent, either.

What's *reticent*?

Uncommunicative, said Noelle. Aim your will at the world. Connect.

Games looked around the room. He nodded and stood. His chair scraped the floor, and he left Noelle Bestmartin in her kitchen with the light and the coffee mugs, with her books and well-ordered mess.

The next day he saw an ambulance at her house. Noelle Bestmartin had died sometime that night. Games considered exactly when she may've died. If Noelle had died before he arrived, then she'd've been a ghost. If she died after he left, then he felt partly to blame.

Later, Games read about the old woman in the paper. Noelle graduated with distinction and taught at the university for forty-nine years. She was predeceased by her husband, Michael, and son, Leon, who died of Duchenne muscular dystrophy. She was founder and climber of *99 Peaks* and an avid butterfly watcher. In accordance with Noelle's wishes, in lieu of flowers, those who wished could take a hike with the disabled. They could visit the elderly unexpected or spark an interest in somebody young. Noelle's black and white face came at the beginning of the obituary. It was a profile and, to Games's eye, she looked a lot like that picture of... He wrote the name with his finger. Susan B. Anthony, born 1820. See you in the morning, were the final words of the piece.

~

Death entered the picture when Games wasn't looking. He'd walk outside and something very much alive would come to him. It was a chance encounter – a drop of water, a ladybug, a streak of light. The next thing he knew, it would be gone – the star extinguished, the water drop dry, the ladybug dead.

Games remembered trudging through the snow one winter afternoon, a teenager out alone. The snow was piled high and blackened along the side of the streets, no signs of life. And then, beside him, out of nowhere, appeared a crane fly. It stood on a patch of snow, having lost two of its legs already. Games stopped to watch the insect in all its remaining grace. How did it get here from California or Egypt? Games lowered his palm as a stepping-stone, but the crane fly just stood there, a frozen, ungrateful thing. Games pulled back his hand. Maybe he was the ungrateful one.

Which reminded him of something else. Games pictured his insect collection for biology, tenth grade, all those pinned and frozen lives, the beetles and ants and wasps, the potato bugs that had walked onto his books and died for him when he wasn't watching. He didn't thank them. Nor did he think it was odd, their sacrifices all gathered in one box. He disliked pinning them, though, and especially hated the one time the cricket he'd stuck to the mat was alive and singing when he returned after dinner to label it. How could he be so cruel? he thought. I'm as bad as people who torture cats. He'd pinned it alive, and there it was suffering, which was all for the sake of a good grade. He was a shatterer of worlds. Death for an A. And it was his fault, his responsibility alone. The Cricket Lord would certainly frown upon him.

Then there was Mosey, his aunt's cat, who came into Games's room shortly after she'd eaten an unforgiving mouse. This was years ago. The poor cat died that night beneath Games's bed as he slept. And later something else: The flapping and batting at his window. It was a curious moth. Games let it in. The moth landed on his open book, page 139 of *The Origin of Species*, which added coincidence to his homework. Hello moth, Games said. He watched the creature read, hopping from word to word. Or maybe it was trying to speak, as on a Ouija board, moving to make clear its innermost thoughts. There were many words on page 139. The moth said: *If...physical...it is incredible... if...connection...I fully admit.* Then off it flew, as unexpectedly as it had arrived, right out the open window. The next day when Games came home from school, he found a dead moth outside his front door. Same brownish color, with stripes on its wings like lines from a book. So weird.

But the very first death, Games remembered, was of a bird, olive green and white. Games was five at the time. A solitary bird, loosened from the sky. It stood tame at his feet for at least a minute or an hour, maybe all morning. Time for a five-year-old had none of the laws of a clock. Games and his bird stared at each other. The bird cocked its head and shook its wings. Cheery. Cheerio, peeped the musical thing. Games was happy watching.

Then the bird hopped off, but not very far, and Games looked away. When he looked back the bird was on its side. He didn't often see a bird on its side. It was a warm spring morning, the June sun out. Games ran to his mother asleep in the car.

Wake up. Wake up.

What's the matter with you?

Wake up, he cried. His mother just wanted to sleep.

So, the boy returned to his bird, but it was gone. Some dog was running off with a mouthful of feathers. A white dog with black splotches. Games had nothing against the dog. The dog hadn't killed the bird, simply had found it. Maybe the bird had run out of time. Games wasn't a bird to understand birds better, and birds weren't people. Games didn't even live in this place, did he? No, he didn't. And he didn't live elsewhere, either. Used to be, only months before, he was with his aunt and his cousins. Now he was driving, and he wasn't even driving now, he was standing. Games stood in the morning and wasn't a bird and he didn't know where he lived. He wanted to live where others did also, like Aunt Julia and Kayla and Peter and... He wanted a home but didn't know why. He didn't know how to say it, either. Games followed his mother. That's what he did. Even though now she slept in the car. It was spring and he stood on the grass, he was five. He was five, and a dog way off in the distance – that's who he followed. With his eyes, Games followed the dog till it was gone. The dog was gone and now he was alone. Alone on the grass, the sun in the sky. Low sun green grass. Green grass blue sky. Blue sky real high. That's all.

~

The first obituary Games ever wrote was for the cricket. The second was for his father. He was sixteen years old, living for good with his aunt and uncle and his two cousins. Julia handed him the phone. It was February 13. His birthday again.

Happy birthday, said his mother. I sent you something.

Thanks. Where are you?

It doesn't matter.

Sure it matters, said Games.

Don't let it matter, said his mother.

Okay, I won't. And he meant it, because what was the point of making problems?

How're you doing? asked Seffi.

I'm okay.

What're you reading?

Reading?

You still read, don't you?

Why do you care what I'm reading?

It's something to talk about, said his mother.

I just finished *As I Lay Dying* for school.

You like it?

It was okay. I liked the end, but sometimes it felt made up.

Made up?

What was the point of this conversation? It wasn't like Games's mother was part of his life. It didn't matter. Just go on:

Not really happening, he clarified.

What did you want it to be? asked his mother.

I don't know, said Games. What should a book be?

A bad story is content with itself, said Seffi. A great story is never content. It wants to be everything.

How can a story be everything?

It can't, said his mother. But it can try.

You just want to lose yourself in fiction, said Games.

Maybe. What I really want is a direct revelation.

What's that supposed to mean?

Something straight from God, said his mother.

What's God got to do with it?

Seffi laughed. You sound like a song.

I don't know what you're talking about.

I'm talking about something that inspires awe. That's when I like a story best. Say a story were the Grand Canyon. Say a story were the ocean.

I like a story when it doesn't confuse me, said Games. What I like about the world is it never confuses me. Only sometimes.

What I like about fiction, said his mother, is that I can include myself with the characters. I feel we're all part of something and whatever it is, well, we're trying to work it out.

Work what out?

Whatever the problem is, said Seffi. We're masters of our future.

Why's there have to be a problem?

There doesn't, but things can always be better. Good writing shows the possible truth about people, even when they are far from it.

Far from what?

The truth, Games. Are you even listening to me?

Maybe.

His mother felt bad.

I'm sorry.

About what?

Sometimes there's nothing else, said Seffi. Everything's a story and we're in it.

You said there's something bigger than the story, reminded Games.

I don't know anything bigger right now. Story is all. There's no escape.

Who wrote it, then? If we're all in your stupid story, who wrote it?

God.

Isn't God bigger? asked Games.

It doesn't matter, said Seffi. We're trapped in God's book. That's all I'm saying.

I don't want to be trapped.

No one does. The point is to imagine it.

Imagine being trapped?

Not being trapped. Being not trapped. Imagine the book.

So, God's writing a book and we're characters, Games summarized. And who's reading?

That's like asking an ant who's studying it with a magnifying glass, said his mother. The ant can't see the whole picture.

We're not ants.

I'm just saying. We'll never know anything outside the

book because we're in it and that's the only language we've got to know things with. It's the only place we can know. We can't know who wrote it, because that knowledge is somewhere else. And we can't know who's reading, because that's in another place, too. It's interesting, if you think about it.

It's depressing, said Games. It's just your thought. It's not the way things are. They don't have to be the way you say they are.

Silence. Quiet. Walls and windows. Floor and ceiling. Waiting for something to arrive. Games listened for his mother. Maybe he'd said something insulting, he thought. But he wasn't her master. She had slipped away herself. It was all her doing. At last she returned. In her voice, the sound of reconciliation.

Some things are, well they are, really interesting to think about.

I guess, agreed Games. I don't want to feel trapped, though.

Of course…

I don't want to be in a story. I want to be here and unlimited.

I know, said his mother. It's all I can do to send you some books to cheer you up.

I'm not sad.

You just said you were depressed.

No.

Yes.

No.

The pendulum of exclamations swept left right left. Could've swung forever.

Mama, you're all about books when you talk, but that's not how it is. I don't think in books. It's not how I am.

Silence now of a green cushioned chair. Games watched the chair, expecting nothing. He thought of his mother listening to the time becoming emptier as it went by – a flowing river but there was no water and no river bed just Seffi staring at the wall, wherever the wall, wherever she was. Games didn't know. He knew so little. The green of a chair. What else to say? Seffi was the adult. Games didn't think this. Still, she should be the one to come up with words. Something resolute to give her son.

Never, for the sake of peace and quiet, deny your own experience or convictions.

What? said Games.

Just something I'm reading. This man, Hammarskjold. I don't know what else to tell you.

It's someone else's words, said Games. Like a greeting card. Always someone else's. Say something that's from you.

Why do you think so poorly of me?

I don't think poorly.

Of me, I said. You don't think well of me. Thing is, everything's so fu –   So full of pathos. Pathos and uncertainty. It's a restless life.

Endless?

Endless, restless mess, said Seffi. I didn't ask for this.

They became quiet again.

So, what are you doing, Mama? What's happening?

I'm sitting here, talking to you. Can't you hear me? It's your birthday, Games. Are you happy?

No. I mean, yes. I mean, what are you really doing? The truth. If God is writing you, or if I am – what's the truth?

Soul in desperation on the earth, never settled, never tranquil, except in moving. The rest is love. *Love never ends.* First Corinthians.

What's that mean? asked Games.

It doesn't matter. Read them if you want.

Read what?

The books I've sent. Didn't you get them yet?

Mama?

What?

Why are you there? Why aren't you here?

Don't ask me that.

Why not? It's my birthday. I want something present.

You still like it with Julia, don't you?

Sure, said Games. She's real protective.

His mother laughed.

What's funny?

I thought you said provocative.

Protective, repeated Games. And Orro explains all the

science so I get good grades. He thinks I could be a doctor.

A doctor? You want to be a doctor?

Maybe, said Games. I like to help people.

It's better, said Seffi.

What's better?

You being there.

Games didn't know what was better. But thinking of Orro reminded him of fathers. The subject was always ripe for revisiting. I was... he began. Just thinking.

And?

You know. My birthday. Birth. Whatever. About my –

No, Games.

Father.

Games heard a sigh, as if the conversation suddenly deflated.

Not now. Not again.

Games made his way, no matter.

Who he is, and was he really, you know... I mean, where is he and...

I told you, said Seffi. He's not part of the story anymore. I told you other stuff, too. Just forget it. Forget everything. It was wrong.

I can't forget something I don't even remember.

The story goes on without him. Try not to think about it.

I do anyway, said Games. Sometimes.

Why? You said you were happy.

It's nothing to do with happiness.

Then what if I told you that he died. Would that end it?

Happiness?

Not happiness. Your need to dredge up the past.

So, when did he die? asked Games.

Sometime in between then and now, said Seffi.

You're just making it up.

I don't make things up. They are what they –

Is he dead?

Yes.

My father's dead, said Games. Why didn't you tell me before?

You never asked.

So, just like that, I ask and he's dead?

Not just like that. But, yes.

How do I know you're not just saying it because?

Because?

I don't know why because.

What do you want me to tell you? said his mother.

The truth.

He's dead, said Seffi. He's been dead a while. Now he's dead all over. Dead is dead is dead.

I don't believe you, said Games. What was his name?

He never had a name.

I don't believe you.

It's true, and I'm going to tell you what else.

What's that?

Love never ends.

That doesn't mean anything, said Games. It's just a quote. I have one, too: Never for the sake of something deny my confidence.

It's convictions, not confidence, corrected Seffi.

Well, it's something I want to know, said Games.

Then you need to do something about it yourself. You need to create a life. The better life. The real one of your father. And it's got to be good. You be God.

I don't want to be God.

A good angel, then, said his mother. It should be easy for you. A muse, yourself.

What do you mean? Make fun?

No. Write his obituary. Find something good to say. Something from your heart.

Why would he be there? asked Games.

Because everyone is, said his mother. Your heart is the most powerful place in the universe.

What's the point? Games thought. I just want a clear answer.

What's the point? he said.

To love this life, said his mother. That's it. The best answer I've got. If you say things with your heart, it's a great story to tell.

I'm not trying to tell a story, said Games. I just want to know about my father.

Know him, then. Write down his life as if it could talk.

When you've written it and it's over, burn it.

Burn it?

I don't see why not. Fire turns all things to light.

Mama?

What?

Julia's right next to me. She's moving her arms like she wants something. She wants to talk to you.

She's trying to be fire, said Seffi. But I don't want to talk to her. She loves you. And I love you more, even if it doesn't make sense.

I don't need to feel love, said Games.

That's a terrible thing to say.

I mean I don't *need* to feel it, said Games. Everything's okay.

You still like it there, right?

I guess. I mean, yes.

I'm going to hang up now, Games. Do what I said or do what you want. It's up to you. You're too good for your parents.

I don't feel too good, said Games.

He's dead, Games. He'll never call. He'll never knock. I'm sorry how things happened. I can't make it different.

The phone was silent. Games waited. A thoughtful silence. What would his mother do now?

The past enslaves you, but the present releases you. You are master of the future.

You said that already.

There's nothing bad in you. Bring out his life and then put him to rest. What do you think? Will you do that?

Sure.

You promise?

Okay.

Okay, said his mother. Happy birthday.

Happy birthday, said Games.

I love you. You know I do.

I know. I love you, too.

And the phone went silent and the silence went blank, which was even quieter than silence, an enormous debt of silence. It made a vacuum of the moment. Games held the phone, being drawn in. He felt the emptiness sucking at his ear, pulling him deeper and deeper even as he stood in place. He heard the hum of his blood like the sea in a shell. He heard the hmm of his mind. It was infinite questions all without form or words. Then he hung up and turned to his aunt.

She didn't want to talk.

Julia nodded, pursing her lips tight so to keep any judgmental words from slipping out. She hugged her nephew, squeezing him a little extra. Games felt the weight of Aunt Julia's body, the soft of her breasts. He felt the gentle sigh that released through her half-open lips. The sigh lingered a moment. It was sizzle in a frying pan. Garlic in oil. Onions in butter. Melting down. Soft down. Rich fragrant ubiquitous down. Put in some sugar if you want. Caramelize. Caramel eyes. Julia turned her head and her arms let go. Her body pulled away and she, too, was leaving, walking in measured steps out of the room.

And before Games had time to think, she came back, just like that. But it wasn't Julia, it was Michaela from the kitchen.

Hey, Games. We made you a cake.

No cake before dinner. It was her mother's voice.

Not to eat, said Michaela. To see. Come on. It's going to be good.

~

Back in Quincy Mesch's apartment. Near ten o'clock. Games studied the old man's face. He looked at the light that came from the hall and felt its warmth seep into the room. The old man, propped against his headboard, shifted to get comfortable.

It's getting late, said Quincy. I never got my ice cream.

Your story was good, said Games.

Not as good as rocky road.

My mother told stories, said Games.

How'd your mother get into the room?

Wandering about, I guess, said Games.

Got entangled, did she?

Something like that.

Games looked at his cell phone. Over three hours he'd been listening.

What you said...I was...sometimes I even...it made me...

That's nice of you to say, said Quincy.

I mean, the story of your life makes me think of my own.

The story's not the thing, said Mr. M.

You mean it's not everything. Not the truth.

I mean it's a substitute. Like a substitute teacher. A representative of the real thing.

Games nodded.

You were nice to listen. My old mind. The images. People, places. Sorrows, joys. In my room here, there's always that knot on the floor next to your chair. It's there whenever I look. It doesn't move. But in my mind, life flows on, and I don't know where and I don't know why.

I told you, it made me think, said Games, glancing to the knot on the pine floor at his feet.

That's what we're here for, said the man from his bed. To think it through.

Think what through?

This time on earth, said the man. I'm not the starts and stops I make along the way. Not the people and places I remember, the jobs I've had. More truthfully, I'm what gets me from one moment to the next. Do you know what that is?

No.

Was hoping you did, because I don't either, said Quincy. We're all built of moments: one followed by another then another. During each moment, I decide how to be. If I could go back to some beginning, to the first moment, I'd still be me, but without all the dressings of time.

Games thought briefly of this ultimate beginning of a person.

Naked life, said Quincy Mesch. But it's my naked life to dress as I will, to make into something.

Games sat in his chair beside the knot beside the bed. He'd been sitting this way for – what was it again? Nine-thirty. Ten. *I am built of moments.* The sentence passed through his mind.

Maybe it's all a person is on earth, said the old man.

What's that?

I'm the costumes, the exteriors I put on each moment along the way. The clothes are my actions and inactions: What I move out of the way. What I succumb to because I'm overwhelmed. What I gather from the wings. What I lose to the wind. The hurts I inflict. And the reparations.

I don't know, said Games.

That's all right, said Quincy. I wonder if you're ready to take the next step.

You want me to go?

I can't keep you. But that's not what I mean. The world needs our attention now more than ever. I see it in you. I wonder what you see.

Games's mind was a blur.

When Dante was in Paradise, began the old man, he spoke with his great-great grandfather. Canto something or other. Not Canto, of course. His name was Guida or Cassio. Maybe you know it. Long time ago, my mother gave me the book, *Paradiso*. Do you remember?

The name of the guy?

The book, said Quincy.

I know there's an *Inferno*, said Games.

Well, there's also purgatory. There's *Paradiso,* too. In the poem, the great old grandfather gave Dante some advice. He told him to write his *Divine Comedy* about known and famous people, you know, people in the limelight, in the news, otherwise no one would pay attention to what he wrote. No one would believe what he had to say. They'd only be interested if the stories were about big time events and if the people were known names, big cheeses.

Cheeses?

Big cheeses. Important people. What do you think about that?

I don't know Dante, said Games.

You can still have a thought about what I said.

I suppose I think that everyone is worthy of attention, said Games.

Quincy nodded.

I mean, there's as much truth in you as in anyone.

It's nice of you to say, considering I'm such a little Gouda.

There's more to everyone than meets the eye, said Games.

I agree, said Quincy Mesch. A shame it remains hidden.

The two sat quiet, almost indistinguishable in the ten

o'clock shadows. Mr. M yawned. His eyes were heavy and the heaviness grew. Light from the hall struck the bedside photographs with a reflective ping.

Are these pictures of your family? asked Games, noticing various people in small silver frames. He wanted to pick them up, to bring them close. One, from a distance, it had to be of young Quincy, looked surprisingly like Games himself. The old man, however, wasn't interested in the photos. He had details to work out.

I'm trying to think of another way to put it.

Your photos?

Not those pictures. Have you ever written an obituary before?

Is that what you want? Is that what this –

Don't get me wrong, said Mr. M. I'm not recruiting you. But have you?

I wrote one for a cricket, once, said Games. I opened with, *There's no death, only life, as I see it.*

Sounds arrogant.

I don't mean life as *I* see it. I mean, as I see it, there is only life.

A Sense of Life, said Quincy. I remember liking that book. Saint-Exupery. Did you write any others?

Did he?

You.

Write books?

Obits.

One for my father, said Games.

I'm sorry to hear that, said Quincy Mesch. He must've been a special man.

Not really. It was a long time ago. Then three years back I wrote a few for the paper, that and doing the *Mumble Jumble* word game. It was the only job available before I started doing fruits and vegetables at the Jake.

You write obituaries for produce now.

For apples pushing daisies. For moldy old peppers.

Veggies are people, too, said Quincy.

Sweet Potato Joe was a member of Plumber and Steamfitters Union, Local 77, said Games. I wrote that a few days ago. He was a good tuber to all who knew him.

You've got what it takes. Ever do an interview with the dead person?

You mean before he died?

Or after, said Quincy.

Once, recalled Games. Some big cheddar in town. It was supposed to be a profile, but it turned into an obit.

Because he died?

Games nodded. His life and times as major mayor. I whittled it down to almost nothing.

Funny how easy it is to reduce a life.

That's the worst part for me about obits, said Games. Putting life into words, and so few of them, really. Then, who reads it? Some grim reapers, the ones who obsess about death, or the few who might recognize the name and be curious.

Could be a person, began Quincy, maybe a melancholic sort, who simply wishes to see what final words are chosen to express a life.

And the occasional person flipping through who's got nothing better to do.

Did you ever talk to the families? asked Quincy. Did you interview as many as you could before you wrote?

You've got me wrong. This wasn't the *Times*, just a summer job. I got information from the funeral homes mostly. It was questionnaire stuff. All pretty standard. You know: Lori Gibson died after a long illness. Lori had recently been employed as a technician at Bennet Corp. She loved to crochet and was proud of her prize roses and pink lady's slipper. That sort of thing. Every day, as long as the sun came up, Lori's first words were *Thank you.* She welcomed the world and it welcomed her back. Survivors in addition to her husband include three children and seven grandchildren, her special angels. Calling hours will be from two p.m. to five p.m. The funeral will be held as usual and will be followed by a private burial. Contributions may be made to blankety blank in lieu of flowers. Stuff like that.

She welcomed the world and it welcomed her back, repeated Quincy. That's a bit unorthodox.

I doubt I actually wrote that.

I'm not saying I don't like it, said Quincy. And did you

ever write what the illness was?

I don't know. Maybe with cancer. People understand cancer.

Cancer is a small constellation, and its stars are weak, said Quincy. Still, I have great respect for it.

Why respect?

As a way to understanding. I told you about my Calico, didn't I?

I'm sorry, said Games. I forgot.

You can't remember everything.

But I want to remember. There's lots I want, and I'm this close to it. Games held his finger and thumb a quarter inch apart.

You're waking up, said Mr. M, yawning again.

There are many things that need fighting for in the world, said Games. That need fixing.

You see, said the old man. We agree. The world needs our attention now more than ever. But I don't think there's anything essentially wrong with the world. I do know we have to transform all the contentiousness on earth. Each of us has to move the argument into himself. We have to defeat that which makes us want to fight with others and look for the shared road that leads to the future. You change the world from the inside out.

This reminded Games of –

Gandhi said it better, said Quincy Mesch. Still, you've got to first accept that the world is good before you can see what the problem is. It's the same with people. Start with the good, return to its fundamental sense. And by good I mean as the word is spiritually discovered, not the shallow word that's used today.

Spiritually discovered?

Games didn't follow, and the old man didn't take it up.

So, why'd you stop writing them?

Writing what?

Obituaries. Isn't that what we're talking about?

I don't know what we're talking about, said Games. Then he explained how he needed more money.

More money is a plus, agreed Quincy Mesch. I never had more, just enough.

The old man opened the drawer beside his bed. He pulled out a wad of bills.

Take it.

I can't take your money, said Games.

Why not?

They'd think I was robbing you.

Who'd think that?

Your daughter. Abe.

Why do you care what people think?

Because I do, said Games.

They want what I want, said Quincy. My money is your money.

How is your money my money?

How is it not?

I didn't earn it, said Games.

That's because your definition of *I* is so narrow. I am you, only at a different place on the body of mankind. Let's say I'm in the hand and you're in the heart. Point being, what I have earned belongs to all others.

One big humanity, thought Games, picturing a giant walking between stars dishing out dollars.

It's getting late, said Quincy Mesch, yawning. You've completely missed your hockey.

That's okay. I'm not very good.

Think about it, said the old man. He pressed the money into Games's hand then slid down in his bed beneath his quilt.

Think about what?

And close the door on your way out.

Okay, said Games. But he wasn't leaving.

I'm not much of anyone really, said the old man to the dark of the room. I've lived a charmed life, though. Like a bird to begin with. Alighted in this body, I suppose. Well, not this stiff, wrinkled one, a fresher one it was. I was supple as a kid. Oily in the morning. Came down to live on earth in time. Human faces, oak trees, walking in the light. I ate a ton of burgers, till I became a vegetarian. I can't remember exactly when. Do you know when that was?

I...

Games shook his head. Though Quincy, lying in bed with his eyes shut, did not notice this. And Games himself wasn't even looking at the man, at least not in the room. He was, in his mind, seeing Mr. M – first as a birdlike spirit above the trees and the cirrus clouds. Then in childhood with hundreds of burgers covering the table and the floor. Later it was Calico with her ash blond hair. And three happy children in the morning sun, tomatoes on the windowsill, scattered leaves in the autumn winds. Some dark seasons, too. Deaths and depressions balanced by births and new highs. Birds again. Robins, vireos, goldfinches, doves. And now this. The old man sensing life, reaching for it with all his being.

It's the same with you, said Quincy.

Maybe, agreed Games. I'd like to be someone.

The charmed part is the same, said Quincy Mesch, eyes shut, speaking to the room. You'll do okay. I myself was blessed with a body and time, but I became tired of myself alone. Then one day the love of my life rode into town. I saw her on the path and knew things were going to be different. I wasn't sleepy anymore. I was waking up.

Not now, said Games.

It's late, Quincy said for the third time. Now, it's your turn.

For what?

To wake, don't you think? I tell this to Abe, but he doesn't listen. Wake up! Full of interest. Your attention touching all that is here and all that is not but should be. Why is that so difficult? I can answer only for myself. Still, it's in each person all the same.

Waking?

That too. But, love. Love's really what we're talking about, isn't it.

Games said nothing. The floor board with its knot, the walls, that print by Chagall. Mr. M was drifting off. Beyond, the night wove stars upon its loom.

I mean the possibility of love, continued the old man, returning for a moment. Almost forgot how much work is needed.

I don't know, said Games. What's work got to do with love?

There's a room like this in the next house over, said Quincy. Someone's walled in over there, longing out the window. Who's going to help him?

Help with what?

Games looked around the room. All he had were questions. He held what money had been pressed into his palm. He would return it to the dresser when the old man was asleep.

Don't put things back that are given you, said Quincy.

How did he know?

I won't.

Not behind my back, when my eyes are closed.

Which they already were.

Okay, said Games.

He sat for a while beside the bed. A while more. He could almost hear the old man's thoughts. Into the room and through and out. The quilt that covered Mr. M moved ever so slightly. Into the room and through and out. The two night windows watched from the wall.

When he was a boy, Games loved to listen: the wishful dark through the darker branches on a moonless night, rain on the rooftop, rain on the leaves, the oak at Aunt Julia's with its family of squirrels. Then driving away, being driven somewhere, deep and quiet, late at night. There were tires on the road, but Games was not tired. It was a large and telling world, and he was softly awake, hearing, just beginning to know. Darkness of dreams and wonder, stars coming through. And lights of houses off in the distance. It all covered his mind. Uncovered it. Set it free. As if Games might recover, no, discover something else. In his own good time, something more.

A few more seconds beside the old man. Games kept watch. Warm yellow light came in from the hall. Sliding the dresser drawer open was easy, so quiet.

And not when I'm asleep, came a voice. Not when I'm gone. Don't ever put things back that are given to you.

I won't, whispered Games, closing the dresser drawer. Inching away. Empty-handed, it seemed.

JANUARY

Quincy Mesch

Late afternoon. The light recedes. Shadows reach across the valley, which is a wide valley and it is also my mind. I'm preoccupied with an imagination that goes something like this:

Below me is the great expanse. It's a field, or rather, a metaphor, that contains everything of the earth: waters woods all light and air. There are boundaries to each object I see – the edge of some leaf, the bark of those trees, the exterior walls of that red barn. There are borders also to every face, and shapes that hold each body within a particular, inescapable form. A fence, too, keeps the field from escaping. I see this fence as a sinuous ribbon determining the field and restricting its reach.

The fence is what intrigues me most, as it seems to enjoy its control of the world. I look at its perimeter rising and falling in waves across the land, stretching the globe, circling back. No beginning or end, only the insurmountable keep of the fence. I listen to what it has to say. *My friends. My contents*, says the fence, imposing its mastery. Substitute the word *subjects* for *friends* and *prisoners* for *contents* and you get the gist. The fence goes on: *There's no getting around me. The earth, some say, is a vale of tears and despair. What can I tell you? They're probably right. Yield to your unrealizable hopes and manipulate things to make you happy. That's my advice. Don't trouble yourself to understand what is outside your ken. "Ken" is not the best choice of words, but I use it to close.*

The people in the field below don't care about ken. They don't seem to hear the fence, either. Though maybe its words enter subconsciously. I look from my hillside invisible home with a silent sense of responsibility. I'm given this scene in order to... Well, I don't really know why. What is it about me that I'm permitted this hearing and this perspective? I'm sure that others, that everyone in fact, could be in on this secret. But it's just me at the moment, as the sun sinks behind the hill. And down there in the field, the crowd wanders clueless in the shadowed, now darkening world.

The people accept the fence, even though they don't know it's there. What's not to accept? The fence doesn't get in the way of visiting friends after work or a fun day at the beach. Yet the people don't hear the undermining tone of the fence. If only the masses knew its controlling nature, maybe they'd become angry with the barrier, wishing to decide things for themselves, or at least to lift some ladder from the ground and peek over, even though I don't know what's to be gained from the other side. As I said, I'm barely more knowledgeable, even with this bird's-eye view. It's one thing to say: *Look. There's something holding us back. Knock down the wall. Be free.* It's another thing to know what tools to use to get the job done, let alone what difference it would make. Besides, what if the fence, like atomic forces or gravity, is what keeps things together on earth, and without it all structure would fall apart and all living things dissolve?

The dark grows deeper upon the earth. It's late now. I haven't made a move for the longest time. Looking from my secrecy, I notice a light in the field that allows me to see long after the sun has set. I consider this light with a philosophical eye. It is each person that creates light down there, as if, unknown to them all, they are a force to be reckoned with. There also is a hidden magnet that attracts many of the people as they stand at the perimeter wall and gaze, their spirits drawn to something that encourages them from the other side. I see nothing to elicit such inspired looks, though these people appear to be enjoying the effects and longing for whatever galvanizing forces have caused them.

I, too, am encouraged. I'd like to know what's beyond the fence that the fence would rather I not find. This added height where I stand offers no clue, only the teacherly suggestion of a gate that is each person's to open on earth. And even though I'm the one who thinks this suggestion, I have no insight as to how to arrive at its goal. I just push forward, combing the world for my personal gate. But it's a stupid way to look for something that I need, as though it's going to show up just to satisfy my efforts. And sure enough, because I am a bit headstrong, the fence laughs at me. *Stop troubling yourself. Here's that gate thingy you need.* And I try it, excitedly. But the gate's a dud. It goes nowhere new, just turns me back to the field in some paradoxical twist, as though the whole thing's an infinite joke. And I know it's not an infinite joke. It's just that my way of thinking is trapped. So, the key is to think differently, I figure. And the fence laughs at my efforts. But its laughter doesn't stop me from what I'm going to do. I'm going to break through all barriers and discontent. I will somehow make room for a revelation by enlarging my self. I will live an inspired life so to see inspiration better. I will increase my capacity to understand and to love.

Love, says the fence. *You're killing me.* I wait for its laughter to subside.

Laugh all you want. The joke's on you. The night spins deep and the stars circle high. My heart is the how to all great discoveries. Now, I'm going to stop this staring this standing these words and

–Quincy Mesch, age 33. From Blue Notebook #2.

Years ago, I first opened my eyes. A shower of light came from the world, and I was washed. Strange and wondrous things accompanied the light: forms and feelings, shadows, too. The thing that now I most picture about my birth – happy, welcoming faces. Better for me those faces than grumps or grouses, not that I don't like those birds. I'm just saying. I knew, at the start, that someone was happy to see me, even if I couldn't say who. It started things well to see a friendly face first, and it put me on the lookout for all good things to come.

When I was a boy, for example, there was this beautiful woman, a neighbor who entered my days by walking past. I don't know where she was going. Her face was clear but her form changed at will. One moment she came as the blue morning sky, the next as the shade on the evening sidewalk.

She visited me at night, too. Not as a real, physical body. I was only eight, nine. She was in my dreams, that's all. Sleep was good to me and this woman came as some angel I saw during that time away. During the day, I was happy being a boy on earth, making stuff and breaking stuff, playing down the street with Blink, Toofer, and Javier. Then, at night, like everyone else, I slept. I went places and did things that in the day were impossible. I went flying about without a plane, and no wings, either, just my body upon the sky. Then I landed in my sideways kitchen, bacon sizzling in the pan, the pan floating on a lake, a million-eyed elephant tree on the shore, and something frightening behind the cupboard door.

And just as that door was about to open, the beautiful neighbor woman passed through. She carried a carnival on her back, with a caravan of trucks and all the fun rides, especially the Gravitron and Ferris wheel. The world was a round-about whirligig. Sometimes I'd try to talk with the woman. Not much luck with that. Instead of the words coming out of me there was an eagle at the horizon with the sun in its talons, lifting the sphere into the sky. How great was that. The sun wore a crown and tossed it to the earth. I tried to find the crown among all the broken glass and cigarette butts in the ditch. What I found first was an old lighter. Then a flick. Followed by the light. The world became everything to do with light. I said light so loudly that I became what I said. Light on the window sill, light of my mind. Then, I awoke.

I got out of bed, like I always did, looked out the window, and welcomed the day. The eagle was gone, and the sun simply the sun. I could see no crown. If I was lucky, however, I spotted the woman walking to work. What was her job? I had no interest in her job. There was something else about her I liked. The way she walked in the world, or that she was always so happy. It filled me with curiosity. I couldn't resist her joy. When at my window, I'd press my nose. And when out on the sidewalk, I'd stare like a cat watching its prey. If she saw me, she'd wave. Hey, kittykittykitty. And I'd wave back.

No school today? she'd ask.

It's Saturday.

Oh, right. You must think I'm an idiot.

No. I didn't think she was an idiot. An ideal, maybe. Someone real, for sure, with words and a smile for me, for everything. And that's one of the first inspiring things I remember.

What I'm trying to say, though, is something much larger than my memory of this friendly woman, larger than her smile in sunlight or her shadow on the sidewalk and larger than my plot and my plodding through time as well. What I wish to express took root in me at the very beginning. It started with simple looks through my bedroom window, down the street, away from my second story room. It continued when I, a bit older, went down to the river where the homeless people lived, or when I went driving with my aunt in winter to watch the sun rise out of the ocean.

This something I'm trying to say soon filled me with feelings and rounded my days with a passion to touch and to taste and to know in my very own incremental way the makings of the world. It was a world that mattered to the person I was becoming. The light through the trees, and the tone of voice from my parents and teachers – it all mattered. This outward sensing grew inside me like a force to take me over. And I don't mean as something to rule me or destroy me or steal me away. I mean the opposite. I was waking to the fact that the things I collected from the world were affirmation of myself in life. And more importantly, given time, I would, if I could, convey that positive self back, in return for every look I borrowed, for all I received.

~

As a teenaged young man, working one summer at Mr. Jones's farm on the Maryland shore, I saw an adolescent swan on the creek. Pretty bird. Cygnets, they call them when young. The swan had a damaged wing and could not fly. I swear, I thought I couldn't fly either because of her. I should've remembered my childhood dreams. I should've had more confidence, but I identified with the bird. I wanted to be close, to be related, if not by blood or even by our burdens, then at least by proximity. She glided, day in day out, just beyond the reeds, mute, as was I in my quiet watch. Cyg and I passed the end of summer days floating on the surface and diving to the murky depths to feed and drink and to wash our minds of distractions.

Later, a girl came my way, Connie from California. She was almost the one, though nothing lasting became of us. I caught her approach in the corner of my eye. Sometimes we worked together in the greenhouse. Her face was radiant and her legs, tan and taut, teased me with their well-formed lines of light. I loved those thighs. I wanted that light. I hid behind the bench with the potted plants so she wouldn't see what I was doing with my eyes. And I wanted to be seen, everyone does, but I wouldn't allow it. I'm sure I wanted to talk to her. I'm sure I wanted to touch her legs and be touched by her.

Growing up, I was easily seduced by the physical world. There were smells of the warm leafy countryside and melodious tones just to tempt me. I looked for periods of unmeasured time, and time turned into pictures. I couldn't stop receiving the sun that came through the trees and the glass. The brightness alone was everywhere. There were birds and plants and girls stepping from the shadows. There were beautiful words too, such as *Cygnet* and *Solo* and *Etude*. *Umbrella* was always a favorite of mine. *Shoreline* I liked, when I was down at the farm. *Shorebird* and *Luminous*. The luminous moon roomed with me effortlessly. Star, street, lamp, and search – whatever the light that came, it was something I wanted to drink the way I drank water, and I wanted to eat the way I ate bread. Only more.

But nothing compared with the person who came next. She rode into town when I was older. I saw her, straight on. At first I didn't know her name. At first I didn't know her age. There didn't seem to be much time at first. Which was a false first impression. If there's one thing to remember about us – that's you and me and each person of the earth – it's that there's no shortage of time. Time is our staple, more prevalent than hydrogen or flowers. It's what you use to make confections. Connections, I mean. You need time and a bowl, interest and a spoon. Set the oven for warm. Things turn out for the best if you use time well. Just don't forget what's cooking, don't over-bake it.

As for myself with this girl, I became a better cook with time. We continued to see each other. There was no end to the seeing. Wherever. We were. It was a good place. To start.

And we'd go for a drive. Would get out of the car and hike the land, 3,000 feet above sea level, reading rock formations and rays of light. We'd look at things the exact same way or we'd say whatever differences we were thinking. Maybe try on opinions like new clothes for the season. Or argue a bit to challenge each other's notions about what's beautiful and what's true. We'd roll our eyes, dig into the ground, and stand, steadfast in our own stubborn places. The view was steep, the weather unfragrant. Each in our own certainty, we had turned away from the other, but would always turn back, suck air and sigh. Then, unfailingly, we'd make our way back to the car, offer apologies, and keep going. Because. What a waste of time to not apologize and not forgive. Because. There are a million new wheres awaiting us. Because. You could be glued like a grump to yourself, stuck like a stump in the earth, no chance of growing, of creating love. Or you could be loose and limber, able to bend to the heartland and turn among the stars. Which story is better, I wonder? Relationships take work, that's all I'm saying. Flexibility, presence. It's a sad separateness for sure when we miss each other in simple notes of affection, yet what's worse by far is if we miss each other by the nots of our effort.

Let me be clear: I'm speaking of Calli. Calli Cormorant. Calico, I called her. Callinectes sapidus, a beautiful blue crab. California, I sometimes teased. Calibration, celebration, revelation. Hemerocallis fulva, too – the daylily seen growing by the side of the road. At least that's what Calli told me one day, she with all her botanical wisdom.

Calli was good with plants. She stood tall and straight – a stately oak, a whispering pine. Her mind was a bud then a bloom then a butterfly. I watched her, trying not to interfere, though sometimes I annoyed her like a nosey camera. She carried her own water and a network of roots to share with others. She was a natural with the world around. It was just this social resolve about her that I was lacking, and though I never meant to hold her back, I couldn't let her go. So, I married her in June, right after her school let out. Her teaching, I mean. I was twenty-nine. What a long year it took for me to propose. She was worth the wait, however – those pockets of air in my underwater hideout, and all the doubt-filled, starless nights I lingered in.

Does anyone else remember her profile or the color of her hair in the sun? Can anyone besides me speak of her hair's length and its unperfumed smell? It was soft, too. I can feel the whim and the tease of it, as if we are yearning again, we're young again. The strands through my hands – it's spring again. Bloom again. Cumulous in the summer blue again. Bright clouds low in the autumn sky. Happy cries of children sledding on the hill behind the school in winter. The taste of every season. And the long showerslickness down her back – that hair again. I was never shy with her. Never at a loss for words. We were not cautious together either, often game. We came right out and said things regardless:

Ever told you, I once said, standing with Calli in a field, how much I love it when there's a cricket singing in the night, and he's bothering you but you can't find him so you have to stop looking and start listening?

A Cricket in Times Square? she asked.

No, in the country.

Ah, the country.

Ever told you how strong I love coffee? I said.

Yes. She sighed. You have.

Not the watery kind they sell at old Jakes. I love it strong. Ox strong. Cindi Strong from eleventh grade.

Love love love, she responded as if the word might go on forever. I love teasel and thistle. Who else cares about them, so I do. I want to care about things others would rather forget.

What things?

The scraggly blue hydrangea in the shade of that barn. Children who are poor and malnourished and an inconvenience to a nice vacation. Or some stick no one else sees drifting by on a stream.

That's some stick.

It is, said Calli. It's got a mood to it, too. Something suggestive. Like Cindi, right?

Cindi's got nothing on your stick. You think there's a stream here? I asked, wanting to see that stick and hear its story.

Streams are everywhere, she said. Sometimes you see them, sometimes you don't.

I'm sure you're right, I said.

We were standing on someone's land where there was a bull in the distance and a crumbling barn.

It looks unsafe, I told her, about the barn. Or maybe it was the bull. The charging, changing possibilities.

Come on. Let's do it. Let's go in.

Go where? I asked.

The barn. What'd you think I meant?

And she tugged, so I followed, and we did, we slid past the bull with the greatest of ease, we went in.

We made way for each other, too. It wasn't all easy. Was something we both needed, though – room for ourselves. Before we got married, there was plenty of individuality – our rocky, blossoming selves – that kept plugging away. There was work to do – doors to hang, tile to set, and metal to bang into art. There were trips to take alone to the shore, turtles in the road to brake for, and classes in the evening, moonlight on puddles, wind gusting by. And...

Intimacy, ah, which was getting to know each other, side-by-side, more for our physical places at the table than for any essential purpose. Take, for instance, a knife and a spoon bumping – silver against silver, smooth lines and curves – and see how each piece of cutlery remains independent while still touching. And so, we were separate and together, working our places, closer and clinking day-by-day for pleasure, which was nourishment, and for interaction, which was joy.

There, I've given a strange picture of us as silverware. Though also we were unfurling cloud fish upon the sea blue sky. That's another picture. We were fish who swam free, and sometimes one of us would vanish without telling the other. Still, there was plenty of time for returning. There was loads of time for coming together and for talk, late at night, down where the streetlight cast our godlike shadows. Or in the morning in bed, yes. Or standing beside the car, before work. That, too. The many times, the many places. But in the beginning it was the one. That barn and environs just past the bull – that was the spot. Our private venue for small revelations. It was there I told Calico things I'd never told anyone else.

~

No way, she said. You were never a rock.

Rock star, I repeated. And I was a boy once, too.

Prove it. What kind of a boy?

The kind nobody notices.

Calli nodded, but quickly added, because it was the right thing to say, I would've noticed.

I was an elephant tree, as well, I said. A buzzard, a tiger, a wren, an all-around difficult moth.

When were you difficult?

I meant math. It was math I had trouble with. There were so many problems.

This intrigued Calli. Her face lit up, or maybe it was just the sun that slipped out from behind a cloud and found her exactly where I was looking.

Go on, she said. Problems don't bother me.

Not even ones where there's no solution? Ones with traveling trains going in opposite directions at fifty-seven miles per hour, and a girl on a bike whose name was Theresa?

The bike was Theresa?

The girl, I said. Maybe it was Lisa. She was running away.

Biking, you mean.

Yes. Things felt hopeless. And once, I remember, I was this long beat on a drum I found in the basement of my aunt's house.

Were you ever any good?

Good for nothing's what my fourth-grade teacher said. Ms. Something. She teased me because I came in late so often. I was never in a hurry. Some say that's good.

Good if you're molasses, said Calli.

We never had molasses when I was a boy. My mother was against it.

Against molasses?

Honey, too. My mother liked to say I got my start in a high-rise in Lowell. Though she may've said it was a hellhole in Paradise. The Paradise Motel, that is. We stayed there almost a year, sometime after I was born. She said it was a heckuva rut.

That's depressing.

Not for me, I said. Course I was real young. What did I know?

What *did* you know?

It was never a bad thing, I said. Kept pretty positive.

I could tell that Calli was following my words, trying to envision things and come up with a clever response. I jumped in before she had the chance,

We rode in the car. My mother and I. I listened to sketches of the world she said in passing.

She spoke in sketches?

Her drawings of the world were her only haven, I explained.

And you're her only sun?

I think so.

The real sun or just some shining representation? asked Calli.

Well... A real son, I guess. In the beginning, it was spontaneous life. I never thought anything else.

You never thought *anything* else? said Calli. You'd wake in the morning and everything'd be bright as usual, and you'd say: Same old same old. Just me and my spontaneous life.

Wow. It's like you were there, observing. Sounds tedious, the way you say it, though.

Who said tedious? How're things tedious if they're spontaneous and bright?

Life's not a bed of roses, I said. No Shangri-La. Things don't really want to be perfect.

Who said anything about perfect, either? asked Calli. You're so manipulative.

I didn't answer. Neither of us spoke. And I saw her then, in light of her words, in the lead of her self, undeterrable. And I began thinking in quotes: *Here's looking at you. The true perfection of man –*

Tell me something of the earth that's not, said Calli, interrupting my stream of admiration.

Not what?

Perfect.

Easy, I said. Any painting, sculpture, musical score.

Even Bach?

I like Bach, but he's not perfect.

What else?

All books, buildings, and every schoolroom clock. They're all a little off.

Those things are man-made, said Calli. Of course, they can't be perfect.

A green pepper, then. A thorn bush.

What's the matter with a green pepper?

I don't like them, I said. They get spotty. I don't like the taste.

You ever been to the Spotty Pepper?

A couple times, I said. I don't drink much anymore.

What else? she asked.

What else what?

What else isn't perfect?

Me, I said.

What's wrong with you?

I'm bad at math.

Which means you're better at other things. What else?

Maybe if I hung out at the Spot and drank more, I said.

What's so good about drinking? asked Calli. Alcohol changes things for you so you don't change them yourself.

Should I change them, I asked.

You and me both. We have to do the work.

What work's that?

To see the world as it is, she said. To be with it no matter the problems. To do the moth. Math, I mean. As best we can.

I thought about math and moths, about drinking and how bodies need liquid, but I also had experienced how too much alcohol makes for slurry words and a sad morning. And I thought more about I and imperfections. Faulty grammar, color blindness, and my inability to remember people's names. There were lots of bad things to choose from. I decided to keep it simple. So I said:

I'm bad at merging in traffic, and I can't drive a hard bargain.

What's wrong with that? said Calli. Compromise is the key to happiness.

So, happiness is important to you, I said.

It's in the Declaration of Independence.

I tried to remember such happiness, but all I could think was: We the People of the United States, in order to form a more perfect –

That's it? said Calli, interrupting my introspection once again, wanting more of me.

I couldn't think. I tried to think. At last I said,

Sometimes I mix things up.

Who doesn't?

And lots of times I act one way when I should act another.

You can't always know what's best, said Calli.

I want to know, I said. I want everyone to be happy.

It's not up to you. It's up to each person to pursue it on her own.

Sometimes my imagination goes crazy, I said. I get mixed up in other people's lives.

Do they kick you out?

It's my imagination.

But it's someone else's life, said Calli. What gives you the right to get involved? Did you ever ask?

Maybe she had a point. Still, it wasn't as though I was doing it out of arrogance.

Okay, so maybe it's not arrogance, said Calli, as if in response to my thought. But if you involve yourself with others and it's only out of self-interest, that's no better.

I said nothing. Turned my head to the side and looked off to the trees. Light burned through the branches, stung my mind. She was right to question me, but it hurt what she'd said, as though I was wrong to care or that my caring was wrong.

You've got to be clear with yourself, said Calli. Know what you're getting into, then do it with confidence. Don't be a wimp.

Her words brought me back from the trees. Not a wimp, not a wren, not a squirrel, not a nut, but a person. How could I know for sure, I wondered inside, if my interest in others was only self-interest?

Sometimes I see myself at war, I said. And I'm no good at fighting.

We all have our own battles, said Calli.

I don't know what to do, I continued. So much trouble in the world. People unhappy, people at odds, people at loose ends. I see myself watching comrades dying, and I do nothing to stop it.

Comrades?

Keeping with the war theme, I reminded.

That's pretty bad, said Calli. But it's all in your mind, isn't it? You can change your mind. If you see a bigger picture, you increasingly become what you see.

Easier said than done.

So, what do you do when you see them dying?

I look for a while, then I turn away. I try to picture a better life. And when I look back, it's over.

What's over?

People are dead. Either dead or suffering. I hate to see suffering.

It's not your fault, said Calli. You can't save everyone.

But why didn't I try to help?

I heard a sigh, a shuffle of feet, sunlight landing in the thick of it.

War is an artificial situation, said Calli. It's man-made, like a clock. Living is more real. You're not guilty of living, are you? Not guilty of being human?

Well, I. That depends.

Ever think you could kill someone yourself? asked Calli.

The thought has entered my mind, I conceded. But not for long. I'm not much for killing.

Me neither, said Calli.

My father killed life, I explained. He focused his attention on alcohol and gloominess so he didn't have to care. And my mother killed time by running off and hiding.

My father, said Calico, could never kill anything, not even a fly or mosquito. He'd rescue bugs from the windowsill and put them gently outside.

Nodding, I said: Sometimes there's conflict. It won't go away so easy as wishing it. Maybe it's meant to be there. Conflict can be a bridge to change.

Calli thought about this, or so she gave the impression, though maybe she was taking a moment to rearrange the conversation. After that moment, she said:

Tell me something good that happened to you to make a difference.

I listened over and over to that request. There were many good things, but what difference, really? I sped through my life, looking for differences. Problem is, I was always myself. Too much myself. If I could invent some fabulous story, I thought, if I could think like someone else, if I could change my point of view – that would be the start of something new.

Okay, I said.

Okay what?

Once I was wounded by something falling from the sky, I said.

Is that why you have that fake limp?

That's just something in my shoe.

Was it a bomb?

In my shoe?

No. What fell from the sky? Could've been shrapnel, said Calli. From your soldier days. Or a branch, a meteorite, a cosmic worm.

Cosmic worm?

From a wormhole in the space-time continuum. Aren't you interested in what's out there?

Sure, I said, adding: It was amazing that something could fall out of nowhere. It made me think. Made me stop being so interior and really look around.

I always look around, said Calli. I love to look up.

At last! At last! Enough about me. I found my way out of self-analysis, and into her.

What else do you love? I asked. What else do you love doing?

I don't cook, if that's what you mean. Hate cleaning, too.

I don't care about that. I mean, if you open a door, what's there for you?

Well… Singing when I'm by myself, she told me. Saying hello to strangers. I'd also like to fly.

Fly how?

Not in my dreams, she said. I'd like to fly an airplane someday. Beryl Markham. Amelia Earhart. All on my own, up there. Banking left and right. Tilting my wings. I'd be waving to the earth from high in the blue. Rising's the thing.

Didn't Earhart die early?

I like to climb, said Calli. A bird's-eye view. It gives me perspective. What do you think?

Sounds fun.

Fun. Is that all you think about?

No, I said. Other things, too. Someday, I'd like to teach.

Teach what? asked Calli.

Charitable living. Or how to make a box with dovetail joints.

I'd like to see your work, said Calli.

Which was nice of her to say, though there wasn't much work, just a widening wake of days. A few scraps washed up on the shore. Three test boxes.

Sorry, I said.

About what? You don't have to show me anything.

I should've that very moment given her something hopeful of me to see – how maybe I could make a difference by teaching, by being a good influence on kids, by increasing the world through inner conviction. But I couldn't even picture it for myself, not yet. Calli then asked if I was becoming.

Becoming what?

Oh, just becoming, she said. You like *umbrella*, I like *becoming*.

I like *becoming*, too, I said to her. And I couldn't help it. It slipped right out of my mouth: You're becoming. I mean, you're very becoming.

She blushed when I said it, so verily archaic the expression. Blushing was her only weakness. I guess that made her imperfect. Unless it made her more perfect to me. I liked that she blushed and that I could make it happen at will with well-timed compliments.

Those reds, the reds of her cheeks, were good reds when we stood by the barn, when we walked inside its rickety form then out into the light again, and later when we sat near the stream that coursed through the woods, looking for that storied stick. We sat almost touching as the water moved by. Almost. Then inching closer. Then a bit closer still. Then yes. My leg her leg, no separation.

So, do you want to go climbing someday? she asked, out of

the blue.

Criming someday. That's what I heard. *Criming,* as if she was from China or as if we were going to be a team, like Bonnie and Clyde, like Jesse and Zee.

I thought you said criming?

Climbing, she repeated, as she watched the water run. Do you want to?

And I did. Yes. It would be something new.

~

There's a first time for everything. The birth of me, the death of me, too. Feels now that I'm ten months old, learning to walk again. Feels like I'm sixteen months, learning to say what's been trapped inside. The newness of this experience compels my attention. It widens my eyes and catches my breath. Everything's of interest. I'm a child again.

And yet, on the earth today, if someone were to think of me, he'd picture my advanced age not my newness. For those who remember, I'm still that splotchy man in his final days – stiff neck, sore back, slack and slouching form, a drip in my left arm, almost done with life, nearly touching death, close to... *Oh, how sad. Dear Quincy. Sorry to hear it. Could've sworn I saw him sitting in that booth just now, talking to Tina. He was a favorite in here. A big fan of our ginger cookies. Gave ten-dollar tips on five-dollar checks. Gave Nikki a hundred-dollar bill once when she was going off to college.*

Thing about me – I liked giving more than getting. I handed out money because it made people happy. Bills and change and wake and see. It was something new every day. And now that I'm a goner, death is my difference. My body, well burned, is onto something else. Its ashes scattered from the top of Mount Everett have drifted who knows how many millions of wheres, and have settled for the time being into the body of earth, into other forms of life.

I, howsoever I am, am an ageless form again, younger than an infant, more open than a clear blue sky. I hear the boldness of dawn quietly rising. I hear the roll of the ocean quickening inside. My outlook is fresh as soft first grass. I'm telling it true, I'm telling it to all who'll hear – I am. Not hard, not weighted down, and in no way dead. Just am. Very much alive. Recalling Nikki and Tina and delicious ginger cookies. Thinking for the time being till the time being moves on.

There was a poet once. He said, *Make it new.* And there was another poet my mother liked who said, *Nevermore.* I remember my mother showing me a picture of some raven and a picture of a dovelike plant she called *Concubine* and a picture of a suffragist named Susan or Sparrow and a picture of Death to round things out. She insisted I remember all names, because names have meaning on earth. But all I remember now is that mixed-up Columbine, and how my mother stole books from the library. I was thirteen, and not interested in stealing. She walked out the building without checking the books, and away we drove real fast.

Book. Not books, she said as she drove. Don't enhance the crime. It's just one book, and I took it for you because –

One book. Okay. What is it?

Airman's Odyssey.

The Odyssey?

Saint-Exupery. And it isn't stealing, she explained. Because nothing really belongs to anyone anyway. Your father's the one who. He –

What about my father?

Never mind, said my mother. I don't want to talk about him. Besides, how could a story belong to someone?

If someone tells it, it's theirs.

If someone tells it, she gives it to the world, said my mother. If she doesn't tell it, she's holding on, like it's a possession. And that's the real problem here. That's what keeps the world from growing.

What keeps –

Possessions and fears, my mother insisted. It's what isolates people and holds them back. Nevermore. Nevermore. That's what I say. No more possessions. No fear.

So, I looked at the books piled in the back as we drove wherever it was we were going so fast, and I saw those books as bridges.

We were always going somewhere new when I was a boy. I remember. We were masters of the road and what future we'd find upon it. I tried to listen to what was being said all around by voices of those far wiser than me. I heard people on the radio, songs and talk. I heard wind whistling across the edge of the half-open window. And outside – the tires rolled upon the road. And beyond – the grasses were drunk on wind. Thanks to the grace of each day, I heard the slur of words turn sure in me. Move with life, said the words. That's how you'll be able to find what's new. For if you move only on your own with no understanding of an evolving world, you are no more than an echo of old times, not a voice of the future, which in itself is very becoming.

~

But back to the climbing. The criming, the criming.

Yes, we did go.

2,700 feet one day. 4,800 another. Up Alander. Up Whiteface Mountain. Greylock, Big Charm, and the Kat. We saw a family of snakes. Vireos, warblers, ruby-crowned kinglets. That's the first time I found real joy in hiking. Later, I learned to make lean-to shelters and solar ovens out in the wild. I learned to make fire with sticks and to recognize the edible mushrooms, leaves, and berries. Eventually, I'd go with my seventh-grade class on trips to various peaks.

So, I suppose I did become a teacher after all. I took my class hiking in the spring every year. We'd camp out. Meatless chili. Indian flatbread. *Mr. M. Mr. M.* They'd call my name. I remember all theirs. There were Ben, Marco, Snow B, Yvonne, Suji, and J L, who wrote his name as an imprisoning Jail. *Hey Mr. M? Mr. M? Yes, J L. S'okay if I throw this apple core? No. Give it to me.*

We'd notice birds and name stars, watch meteor showers. One of my students was Ryan O, like the constellation Orion as seen by stargazers who make beginnings of the end. Later, he worked as a science writer for the *Times.* He made a number of well-received documentary films, including *Girls! Girls! Girls!* whose title reflected the seedy world of pornography and prostitution and likely attracted some unsavory sorts until they saw these girls were courageous, mindful, and completely clothed. What a shame. And not long ago, Ryan O came from the city to see his daughter, Rianna. They surprised me with a visit.

Mr. M. Mr. M, said someone from behind.

I turned and saw a twenty-something girl standing in the room with her father. A real beauty, fresh and bright. Not the man so much, but, yes, both of them, really. A light came on inside me.

Danielle let us in, said the man.

No way, I exclaimed.

Well, she did. She let us in.

But, is it you? I asked.

It was. Ryan was one of my most memorable students, incorrigible and unmanageable. I liked the way he resisted my approach in favor of his own. I could make nothing of him. Instead, I was the man who stood in his way. What kind of teacher was I to stand in anyone's way? I needed to get out of my students' ways and let them succeed as best they could.

I learned my lesson quick with Ryan O, and was happy to see him in my room, grown and telling me of his efforts to bring science to girls in Ethiopia, Uganda, and Pakistan. There he stood with his daughter, twenty-five-year-old Rianna. We sat and ate lunch together in the August air. Biodynamic cheese from Ryan. Bread, apple cider. I was carefree at first, and grew increasingly reflective.

When I was twenty-five. This I remember saying. When I was twenty-five, I lived alone across from the railway station. Once I saw a young girl hit by a car. A woman with a scarf got out of the car, frantic to help and desperately wanting to take it back.

Take what back? asked Ryan.

The accident. I went over, but. A policewoman was there. An ambulance fast. The mother, the scarf-woman. Lots of others, all gathered. I'd only get in the way, I thought. The girl, she tried so desperately I could tell, injured and all, to smile through this, through. Her pain and. I could see it so clearly. I felt it from the injured girl. She wanted to make sure everyone. That everyone else was okay.

A brave girl, said Ryan.

Exactly what I thought at the time. Made me question, What did I have to bring to the world? Courage like that? The opposite of suffering?

Or an antidote to suffering, said Ryan.

Yes, I agreed.

All young adults go through that, said Ryan. Questioning themselves.

When I was twenty-five, I went on, probably boring my visitors. Trains would come and go, shaking my bed and unraveling my sleep like a...a... I'm trying to remember a simile Calli once used.

Like a ball of yarn, suggested Ryan.

I don't think it was yarn. But maybe, I agreed. I continued my story: I used to wonder where the trains were headed. I heard voices calling, *All aboard. Get on with your life.* Of course, I was getting on. But who could tell?

You were being too hard on yourself, said Ryan. It's that melancholic side. Rio, on the other hand is sanguine. Ryan smiled at his daughter. She has it all figured.

Completely, said Rianna. You should've followed my lead back then, Mr. Mesch.

I should've, I agreed. Are you a time traveler?

I am, said Rianna. But it's supposed to be a secret.

We each took a moment to reestablish the secret, to shift our positions, give a glance to the window.

When I was twenty-five, I continued, I had my diploma and was ushered to the world to conquer reality. I saw myself as a person who'd take steps. It's just, where would they lead me? I never thought they'd lead me here.

Here's a good place, said Ryan, looking around.

Four years later I proposed to Calli and we married in the late spring.

Calli's not. She's. Not still living, is she? said Ryan.

No, I said.

I thought... Well, I heard... It was...

Twenty-five years ago, I said, to complete his thought. That's when she died. Which makes *here* not quite as good. Certainly different. I don't know what's gotten into me. Lately, I've been way too introspective. Heavy hearted.

Be how you have to be, said Rianna. No sense in being some how you're not. Which I thought was a wise, amazing thing to say.

It's all about twenty-fives today, I explained. Twenty-fifth of August. Rianna, you're twenty-five. Ryan, you must be –

I'm past 52, though that would've been nice.

Still, if I had to guess, it'd be twenty-five children in the park right now, twenty-five birds in the bushes, and twenty-five cents in a quarter. Twenty-five is the atomic number of manganese, and it's the final chapter of the book I'm reading. When I was twenty-five, Calli was very much alive and I didn't even know it. And when Danielle was twenty-five, that's when I lost Calico to cancer.

I'm sorry, said Ryan. We didn't mean to open this door.

Oh, the door's always open, I said. It's no problem at all.

Been such a long time since I've seen you, said Ryan. He looked at the far wall, then at his hands, then me. I thought, since Ri and I –

No problem at all, I repeated. In fact, I'm... Well, sometimes my mind does create problems. Not today. Today everything makes sense. But I do get disheartened when I lose things. Then I find her again. And everything's good.

Find her?

Calli, Papa. Weren't you listening? He's talking about Calli.

Calli, Papa.
Weren't you listening?

The words echo, that I may return to them with better purpose. Such meetings, as with Ryan and Rio, reminded me that time is not a one-way, dead-end trip on earth. And people are gone only when you're not aware of them. I should've thanked Rio for hearing so well. I should've given her my take on things. I didn't then, so I'll do it now:

Don't wear time around your neck like jewelry. It's not for

wearing, not for weighing you down. Time is what you've given yourself so you can be present. It's like one of those Post-It notes stuck to every door in your soul. Time says: Pay attention as you go through. Pay attention to this. Pay attention to everything, to the flowers in the ditch, the twig in the stream, and each person in the room. This is not sentimentality. It is searching for the truth of human life on earth. And when the stickiness wears off and those notes fall from the doors to the ground of your soul, when you think, That's it, my time is done, when you say to yourself, There's nothing else to look at here, no further work for me to do – you're wrong. You're not going to live forever on earth, but neither are you going to get rid of time so easily by dying. The treasure trove remains full. There's more time in the revolution. There are further notes on the pad waiting to be peeled and pressed to new doors in your evolving soul.

~

When I was a boy, I always thought that I was different. I didn't want to be the same as others. I wasn't better. It wasn't that. I was simply okay at being myself, like Ryan O. I winged stones sidearm at the stillness and watched them skip till they were out of sight. That was fun. I stayed around long enough to hear the gist of what people were saying, while in the corner of my eye I'd catch glimpses of things that excited me, and then off I'd run through the door or out the gate or down to the river. I'd look behind trees or I'd brush the weeds aside in hopes of an amazing find. And maybe it happened. Maybe I found an empty can with a spider inside or the bones of a small mammal. But such things, though nice discoveries, didn't satisfy the search inside me. There remained a mysteriousness I couldn't quite reach.

I think too much about such things, I know. Sometimes, even now, after my good life, I go on and on as if I'm still alive, still home upon the earth, hoping to understand the mad portion of my time with others.

Perhaps I remain tied to that place. But luckily, too, I grow tired of trying to figure everything, and stop. I drop all self-thoughts and pick up on things separate from me, like those glimpses and subtleties I noticed when I was most together with the world. Things like the blue of the sky, the curious shapes on the water, the quiver of birch leaves, or a three-year-old girl bursting into smile. Life then multiplies within, increasing until all walls, all fences are overcome. It's a freeing feeling. Time streams without constraints. I'm timeless and dark. I'm all time and light. The passing stream empties me, and, paradoxically, I am more myself than ever, carrying the whole of life in my emptiness. I am, in truth, a conduit, if only for the moment, conveying the genius and verve of existence.

From there I start to grow again with the world inside me. I am an open book, with blank pages as the soil and with all possibilities of the earth as seeds. The blades of grass are seeds, the stones are seeds, trees and birds and clouds are seeds. Birth and death and joy and suffering – all seeds. Each human life is a seed on my pages, a seed that germinates, taking shape and sound. And then all at once there's a word I wish to say, a sentence, a true story of life in the making. And as the life grows, the book grows with it. What's even truer – the life does not stop. There are always more pages, more letters and words. It's a curious mix of plot and purpose. Something happens to begin with. An almost indistinguishable glow. Then something else. A shift a change.

I wake and see.

~

The slow resurrection of the sun, its light streaming through the window. The fullish moon is setting in the west. Stars recede. Darkness retreats. The earth returns – here. This is no ordinary day. It is one I've been waiting for.

Danielle comes early. She plucks me from my apartment in this river city as if I'm fruit on a winter giving tree. It's her usual smile again, and her eyes are two blue open arms. I think she's happy to see me. She talks about moving me and all my stuff, about bringing me home to live with her. She worries about my health, my ability to care for myself.

Doesn't necessarily say I'm old, but she thinks it. Mostly wants to help. She wants to do what's right. I lead her out the door and she takes me for a ride.

One by one, I watch the buildings pass. There are overhead wires, church spires, and the dirty, broken sidewalks. There's a vet at the corner who is out of work, approaching cars for money. He comes to us, and Danielle gives him a twenty. There are signs and billboards everywhere: advertising slogans, sales in blue ink, office space for lease, and morning sunlight on facades. There is noise, information, business, inarticulation. We leave it all behind.

Danielle is a good driver, and it's not long till we come to what's more of the land, to the lyricism of rural life, which is sweet and animato in my eyes, like music. Into the opening world moves a score of trees with baritone brown trunks and tenor black branches against the soprano blue sky. My mind moves harmoniously at the moment. It is alert. I'm full of song and play, as if there's a child in my mind, which there is, I assure you. There's the thought of a sweet little girl, not to mention my ageless spirit. My body is not the issue anymore. It's the indispensability of everyone that matters.

All I want to do now is get to my old home and see that great grandchild who's a sweet little bird to me. Danielle drives fast. The fields are somewhat covered in snow. There is bright winter light rebounding off the road. I look at my daughter at the wheel and see in her face thousands of words I've never seen before. Danni, I think. Is that you? I should ask her, but I don't because it would be rude and confusing. So, I think, Yes, it is my first and only daughter. It must be. And it fills me with memory – dumplings in gravy and painted horses on the walls when she was five. There's a Christmas carol echoing inside me from almost eighty years ago, me on the piano bench and Danielle to my left, just as now. She glances at me, smiles, then back to the road.

I am her old Papa, and I stare for a moment back in time. I hope I was not a bad father, but I don't want to go there. I want to stay here in the positive light. It's her face I see, and her story moves over the earth as unfurling clouds, disappearing, reappearing. It's a story in the making that perhaps I could tell if I didn't have something else on my mind, something very exciting I'm looking forward to. I've mentioned this something already. I can hardly wait.

Now we drive into gaping space, and I open my eyes further just to keep up. Danielle's taking me to the house I built long ago. I built it with my hands and with tools I borrowed from Caleb and Jan, and Calli helped me build it, too. It was ours, even if it belonged to the Lark County Bank at first. 133 December Hill Road – that's the place. Now my daughter lives there, but without Glen anymore, which is sad to say. It troubled my heart when they split. But she's with her son Reed who I call Purple Martin, and his wife Blue who I call Sky, and their newborn little Veer who recalls me to life. And all of that is very o very o good.

Vireo is the most cheerful bird. She's why I'm so excited. She is my alphabet and my over-easy egg, cooked just right. I smile thinking of her, like a runny yolk, delicious and perfect. I love her beginning cheeks. I love her round face, her squishy belly, and her soft shoeless feet with toes curled tight. And I especially love that she's got a good house to live in, one that I built myself. O my darling Vireo, my little bird, my rhyme. So much to look forward to. But we've got to get there first.

Wallace Cummings's farm, the one with the barn and the bull and the stream through the woods. I must be dreaming. The hills and the valleys. The paths I am made of. It's as if I'm thirty-two again. There are paths that the cows cut through the land. There's a freight train calling from the distance. Freight train mate train afternoon late train.

A call comes to me. It's Calli. She's eyeing the bull in the field and the falling down barn. I go to stand beside her. We say things back and forth:

This is a nice place, I begin.

Not bad, she adds.

Native Americans called this place Heart of the Sky.

Iroquois?

I don't know what tribe.

Hyacinth?

Hyacinth Indians? I'm confused, I say.

Don't be, says Calli, adding, Sky's heart must be plenty green, though.

I look around. Calli at my side, and acres of green green green green green.

We could start here, I say.

We could.

Who knows where we'll end up, I tell her

Got to start somewhere, says Calli.

Once there was a man who started on a roof, I say. Then he fell. Ended up dead on the ground.

He should've considered better where he was going, she says.

She's right, as always. Wind blows her hair onto her face. She looks down to get out of the wind, and I look with her. And call it fate or chance or synchronicity, because when we both look up, Wallace Cummings is heading our way.

Welcome home, he says.

And just like that, I'm no longer dreaming.

Long and the short of it, Wallace broke off a small piece of his farm and sold it to us so he could build a new barn for milking, all the modern equipment and a house for the chickens, too.

Times are changing, he said to me. In my new barn, I'm going to play classical music for my cows to harmonize the milk. What do you say?

I say, okay, I said.

And I'll tear down that old barn for you.

No, said Calli. I like it.

It's an accident waiting to happen, said Farmer Wallace.

It won't happen anytime soon, Calli said. Keep it.

It's no problem. I've got boys.

We'll keep it, I said.

And we built our house just inside the woods, looking southeast. Lilac morning sun filtered in the windows. Ladybugs lived in the cracks at the jambs. I built a bed for Calli and me, a queen bed with a mountain carved on the headboard and a sea rolling at our feet. We had three children, one at a time. And I walked with my children to school, back then. Sometimes we stopped to hang on a branch. The older they got, the less they wanted to walk or hang, but when they were young, being together was the norm. We made our way out of the woods, past the old barn. Stopped for a moment, wondered about its disrepair: red wood unpainted year after year, its rafters exposed more and more each spring, and its beams beaming white oak right back at the sun. Would the barn give up its stubborn stand and topple?

The school where Calli taught first and I a bit later was straight through that field and down the road into town. I'd walk with Danielle, with Jesse, with Forest all in their time. We wore a path from the house to the town. We'd pause and listen to the talk of the water. We'd stoop and pat Jango, the farmer's wife's dog. We'd walk easy in the sunshine and quickly through the rain. We'd struggle midwinter mornings when the freshly fallen snow lay deep.

There are three children whenever I stop to count, not always together but always in me. And if we were early one morning, we'd invent stories of the barn, explaining how it had come to such ruins. Danni said we had to help it. Fix it. Paint it. We had to put it right. She could hear the barn crying like a baby lamb when we came anywhere near. But for Jesse, it didn't matter if the barn stood or fell. What mattered was getting to school on time to play ball with his friends. And Forest, when I walked with him later, he loved that the barn was falling down. He wanted to help it – not help it back up, but help it down. He wanted to pull the poles and knock in the walls. It's what happens to things when they're done, he said. Like that deer. Remember?

The buck by the woods? I asked.

The dead one, yeah.

Forest and I had stared at that rotting carcass at the edge of the woods, and Forest had thrown dirt on it and leaves to help it along.

But me, I still liked the barn the way it stood. I'd taken it in as a foster child some time back and always held it up as an interesting story. One day with Danielle and Jesse, I explained how the barn had long ago been a boy who loved to play tricks on his neighbors, painting their pets red, for example, stealing all the water from their garden hoses, screwing their mailboxes shut, and eating their melons from the inside out. So, a magician named Acres or Miles or Yardley or –

Which was it? asked Jesse.

All of them, I said. His name kept changing, and he turned the boy into a barn to be rid of the pest, but it didn't do much good as the barn was still a nuisance and an eyesore, to boot. There were wild parties on the weekends and there was gambling in the loft. Trolls and sprites and pucks and pixies came from Spain and China to dance in the hay. They'd jump from the rafters, and pound on the walls for no reason at all.

There had to be a reason, said Jesse.

But there wasn't, I insisted. They did it for fun.

Fun's a reason, said Jesse.

I guess you're right. Fun's one of the best reasons of all.

Then once, much later, and no longer part of the story, I was coming home alone a late spring day, which was an anniversary of Forest's death. It bothered me to see the barn still standing when other things had fallen down well before their time. And I was just so goddamned angry at the barn that I stoned it with rocks and clumps of earth, and I kept on stoning and throwing and cursing and doing everything I could to make the damn thing fall. But it wouldn't fall. You can't make something fall if it's still got time. You can't change the past, either. I was out of ammo and out of voice and out of sorts, and definitely. Angry not angry. But not any bit consoled, either. Such a beautiful day, too. I remember. I stood crushing young grasses with the awful weight of my body. It gave me no relief, having thrown those rocks, only wore me out. It provided no lift from the earth, no resurrection. It produced no answers about why Forest had died, none. But maybe, somehow, a bridge or a door. Because I wanted something to open. Longed for it, deeply. To be more connected even through death.

I felt ashamed after throwing and cursing and said so to the ground. I'm sorry – to the ground, to the nonjudgmental earth, I said. My feet, my grief, my light, my son. The woods, the trees, the forest near. And to the barn, looking up – I'm sorry, I said. And I loved it again, as never before. I needed it, too, more than ever.

Nothing remains one way forever. Sorrow dilutes in time until there's no more substance only the spirit of sorrow, which is easier to take and has the potential to transform your thinking. Is it really sorrow that I know? Because I do not feel bad any longer, no matter what I've lost. What I've lost is nothing compared with what remains in the folds and fissures of my being. It's not that I don't want to talk about death. It's more that what I want to say is life. I'm with life now, and there is no distinction, only meaning. Birth means more to me now. Earth means more. Time and space and winter sleeping trees mean more. Paths through the field. Knitted hats mean more. Light and love and people, birds and… I am not afraid. I am grateful.

~

Here we are, close at hand. Some things are familiar, others have changed. Danielle's on my left. She's still driving. That's good. But the barn's fallen, completely gone now. The cows were slaughtered years ago, and even the bull has disappeared. Wallace Cummings sold the rest of his land in the spring of the buttercup rains. A developer bought it and a few houses have been built so far. Good school in town, everyone says. People from the city want to come. You can still hear trains certain times of the day, if you listen.

We drive up the drive, Danielle and I. December Hill on a January morning. Man with modern daughter, in search of a soul. A young soul. A child. I'm just playing with words. And who's waiting for us in the window? It's Veery in the window, held by her father. "Great Grandpoppy," Reed mouths. I see him pointing. "It's Poppy the Great," he tells his six-month-old daughter.

We enter the house, cedar wood, number 133. Such young and smiling faces. I hug my grandson, Reed. I hug his wife, Blue. I look all over the room for the tiniest of girls. She's everywhere I look but nowhere to be seen: the toys and the blankets, the sheepskin on the floor, the mess and the mayhem from so little sleep and so much to learn. But where is my sweet, my endlessly describable Veery? O, Vireo. Vireo.

Where is she? Where? I feign unseeing, unknowing. How sad to be alive in the world and yet not to notice its life, so friendly and faithful in every corner and in everyone. Oh, woe is me. Woe.

Don't be silly, says my granddaughter-in-law, Blue. She's right in your arms.

It's true, she is. I find my little bird at once where I hold her.

Ah, there you are. You little peep, you imp. Trying to get away from me, are you? It's a wide winter day, sunny, mid-thirties. The perfect weather for a walk together. I'm like my young self again. I've got the body of a schoolboy and the mind of a king. A thin king, perhaps. A cran king. A chin king. It doesn't matter much what kind of kin king I am, I'm ready to go straight. Out the door. You up for it? I ask.

Veery says nothing. I take that as a yes.

So, I put her in the frontpack. Some might think an old man such as myself can't handle the weight and responsibility, but they'd be wrong. Reed puts a hand on my shoulder. It's a strong hand, I feel. He's an excellent father.

You're looking good, he says.

I feel good, I tell him. I'm chomping at the bit. Like some kid ready to –

You set, then? he asks, cutting me off.

I'm ready set go.

It's a beautiful morning, says Reed.

Don't worry about a thing, I tell him. All will be well.

But Reed's got work to do. He's got a faulty furnace on his mind. Things to take care of. Problems to fix.

I'm not a wart, he says. Why worry?

I pat my grandson on the shoulder.

I like the way you think. We've got our songs and our mittens. There's a big world to see.

How long will you be out? asks Blue.

We'll be back in an arm's length, I assure her. Don't wait up.

Wait, says Reed.

I just said not to.

No, he says. She dropped a mitt. He puts the mitten on his daughter's hand.

Thanks.

It's a good day to be out, says Reed. There's air to breathe. There's –

Exactly, I say.

I just fed her, says Blue. I've given you a bottle. And that hat, you can pull it down to keep the sun from her eyes.

Perfect, I say. But we won't be staring much at the sun.

And here's a blanket, if the wind picks up, says Danielle.

A blanket and socks. A hat, two mitts, one bottle, no worries. We're off, I say. We're off. But we stand inside for a minute, unmoving. How much longer, I wonder to myself, will I be in this world, this entryway, saying goodbye? The Time Being moves slow today. Then Veery and I go out the door into a blast of light.

A blast of light of air of earth. Up somewhere in the sky there's a distant hum. I look for it. You've got to look up, I tell Vireo. Always look up. And she does, kicking her feet. We see what the sound is. It's a plane overhead. A plane overhead, sharing the day. Sharing the day and waving its wings. Waving its wings hello hello, wishing us good fortune. The plane flies on, and we walk to the field where I once walked with my children. Same field only different.

Hello, morning blue. Hello, winter trees. Hello, quiet planet.

I see this world with Veery for the first time. I see what has been building inside me forever. My inside is outside. It's as if the etching in my soul is exhibited and now hangs on the walls of the earth around us. I am here with Vireo, warm in the sunlight, taking in the surrounding air. And I know that in this child the world is becoming. Very becoming, I hear myself say. The sky blushes red as ripe holly berries.

You are my sunshine, my only sunshine. I sing to Vireo.

No, she says, kicking her feet. Up there. Up there. If she could only point. But I know what she means.

You're right, I agree. There's a sun up there, too. Summertime, and the living is easy. Fish are jumping and the cotton is high.

What's caught in his eye? asks Veery. What's summertime? she asks.

You're right. It is confusing. You're still a tiny girl, aren't you?

What's summertime? she chirps again.

It's when you were born, about six months ago.

I'm six?

Months, yes. Coming on seven.

And what are fish?

Fish are animals that swim in the sea and in streams. And streams are bodies made mostly of water. Look where we are. If angels were water they'd look like this happy and rippling stream.

Vireo and I pause to watch the stream.

Hello, stream, I say. Hello, rushing water. What are you late for? Are you trying to get to the ocean? Are you in some kind of hurry, or just in some kind of hurray?

We've got business, sure, says the stream, but we always feel good about what we do. So, yes: Hurray. Hurray. Off to the ocean we go, we flow. Off to the ocean we go, we flow. Hurray. Hurray.

Well, I say. Come visit us again as rain.

Vireo and I take in what moves. We listen to the sun and the water-talk.

If you listen, I explain to Veery. You can hear the secrets of the world.

We stand, still and quiet. As if. To hear. Something revealed. I look down at my great-granddaughter. She's bothered.

I usually like the light, she says, her face loaded with sun. But now –

I'm sorry. And with my body I shade her from the glare. Too much of a good thing is too much, I say.

We turn back, but slowly, trying to establish the perfect amount of bright.

This land is your land. This land is my land. From Cali... fornia...

What's the matter, Great Poppy? Why'd you stop?

Oh, don't pay attention to me. I'm just thinking.

What's thinking?

Remembering things, I explain to my littlest bird. Making connections. This earth has made me very happy. Very happy indeed. I'm so full of...

Sad things? she asks, sensing something melancholic in me.

Sadness, happiness – it's all part of my fullness, I tell her. But what I'm beginning to think now is completely new. No memories attached. Pure amazement at this world and this life and I, I'm very happy you're with me this moment.

I'm happy, too, Poppy the Great.

Vireo kicks her feet and she moves her arms. She lets the light shine into her eyes, not minding it much.

I will always work for you, I tell her. I'll return like rain to water your roots. I'll return like some kid to pluck fruit from your branches.

What fruit? G-Pop.

Plums apples grapes peaches pears. You name it.

Beaches? Bears? she asks.

If that's how you grow, I say.

Whimsically we wait in the winter warmth. Each of us has something different to grow. Each of us has something unifying to say. The ground is brown, with patches of snow.

I have to go soon, I say.

Okay, says Vireo.

I might not be back for a while, but I'll take you home first, don't worry.

Why worry? she says, echoing her father. I'm no wart.

Exactly, I nod. You've got near perfect skin.

But when you do come back, begins Vireo. When you do, and if we come here again, I want to walk. I don't like being carried. I want to do things myself.

Sure, I say. You can walk.

And talk for myself, she insists. I don't want to rely on your words. I have my own.

It's a deal. I promise. You've got to be yourself.

But for the moment we stand united. I hold Vireo to my chest, feeling her heat and her heartbeat resonate to my core. She's the feast in my mind and mood. She's the focus of my appreciation. The sun rises behind us and our time is now. Bare tree branches in the January sky. Blues whites browns and blacks and and.   The plane my plane our plane has returned. Never a day goes by. It dips its wings. I haven't forgotten. Goodbye, it dips. And sweeps and sows. It heads into the west to dust the earth with light. So, let there be light, I say to whoever is listening. Let there be a sense of life. Let there be good thoughts to live by. Let all you do uphold the world. And the world in return will serve you well, will share its seasons, its weather, its birds.   And the reason for everything. For everything is love.

TWO

Just before three, a single engine plane hummed westward overhead. The February air, slow near the ground, lay cold. Games Shepard paused outside the brick building. He breathed deeply. Took in the sound of the plane as if it was part of his breathing. Looked up. Where was the plane? It was inside him now. He was about to enter the building with a plane inside him.

The nursing home had two large glass doors with black words affixed. Games pulled on the right door, not bothering to read. Didn't matter which door he chose. Today he began his new job – a nurse's aide. He'd chosen the three p.m. shift. With that shift, he could still get up early to stock produce at the Jake.

The sky was crystal blue, a cloudless jewel as Games opened the door. When he looked back, still holding the door, the plane was nowhere in sight, though the sound for sure still murmured in his chest. Then the door closed and the single engine hum closed with it. Games was in another world, a contained place, no longer out. He smelled the antiseptic cleanliness, and saw the shiny, waxed floor. His shoes squeaked on the gleam as he walked where he needed to be.

~

Games shadowed Andrea for the first week of training. Having worked at the home for over twenty years, Andrea knew the place as someone would who saw everything through the lens of responsibility, commitment, and kindness.

You have no idea, she said.

Games waited to be given one.

Sometimes these people have no one else, said Andrea.

It was a modest idea. Games held its weight. As the day grew dark, the two continued down the hall, room by room. Never much time for praise from Andrea, never much need of it for Games.

So, James, said Flory, during a break that first week. What do you think?

It's Games, said Andrea.

Andrea was direct and outspoken, daughter of Arp and Natty Parkins. Both parents were Unitarians, unlike their daughter, who put all her faith specifically in Jesus. Andrea was mid-fifties, broad shouldered with short-cropped hair. She had no family other than her still-living parents who she took care of at home. A mother hen to pretty much everyone, Andrea insisted on smiles.

Got to have it, she'd said to Games his very first day. Carry a smile like the sun, even when there's rain, no matter the worst storm ever. You tell me the thickness of your clouds, I'll still tell you you've got to find that sun. You don't need to see the sun to be the sun.

Andrea's hands were confident, pale, and strong enough to move the surliest patients. The bulkiest as well. She liked to see men taking part in caregiving.

Games, Andrea repeated. Not James.

And I'm asking what the man thinks, snapped Flory.

Look at his face, said Andrea. That's serious smooth. He's no more than a boy.

How old are you? asked Flory.

Almost twenty-eight, said Games.

You're not twenty-eight, said Andrea. Twenty-four, I'd say.

Maybe she was right. It was difficult to argue.

Don't go telling him what he is, said Flory.

It's my job, said Andrea.

Since when's your job telling people who they are?

My job's to instruct, said Andrea.

Flory looked around.

You call this a school?

I call it the world. Women do all the intimate work in this world. We get right in the middle of things. We get involved. Men need to learn what it's like. They need to step up to the plate.

You tell that to my Pete, said Flory.

Your Pete is beyond my jurisdiction, said Andrea.

Don't bring my Pete into this, said Flory. James isn't interested in my life.

It's Games, said Andrea.

That's right. And ask him if he cares about what you're saying. Nobody cares what you're talking about.

With all that's wrong with our society, began Andrea, leaving the phrase dangling. Unsettledness. Selfishness. Your Pete. Everyone's Pete.

Don't go bad-mouthing my Pete.

Okay then.

Okay then what?

I'm talking how children are unraised by their own parents, and the elderly ignored, disposed of like chicken bones.

I'm a ribs person myself, said Flory.

If women ruled the world, there'd be none of this carelessness. What mother's going to let people spill chemicals on her children's dinner or contaminate her family's water? What mother's going to say it's okay to bomb away your disagreements? It's men who've made this mess. Everything would make better sense if women were leaders.

Don't let her preach to you, said Flory to Games. Not like she knows everything.

What don't I know?

About being a mother.

It's being a woman's what I'm talking about.

I'm telling you James, she'll turn you to one of them.

A woman? asked Games.

A bleeding heart's what I'm thinking, said Flory. Always trying to change things.

I love my work, said Andrea to Games. Just that no one should ever be in one of these homes. I'd never put my parents in here. Worst thing, you'll see it – no one comes to visit. And when they do, they just walk out again. They leave their family behind like plates on a table when you go out to eat, something for others to take care of. How's a person become trouble just by growing old and losing some of the gloss?

I wouldn't mind it here so much, said Flory. Clean beds. Crackers. All your meds. Good staff.

Oh… You're no help, said Andrea.

What about Mr. Rickaby? asked Games, referring to the patient on C wing who couldn't do anything for himself, who was strong and belligerent, who once broke a nurse's wrist by pulling her onto his bed.

Pervert, said Flory. I'm never going in there by myself.

Mr. Bob needs what we give him here, said Andrea. Still, could be at home. That's my say. I'd have him at home, if he were my father.

Bruises and all.

No bruises. Just the business of taking care.

You're special, said Flory.

I'm not special. Stand in the hall when you've got a free minute. Think about your car, your home, your kids, your friends, whatever it is you've got outside these walls. No one's going to tell you that you can't leave. Everyone's special. Everyone's got a life that's about more than television all day long and waiting for clean sheets and flavorless food, and if you're lucky a chance to sit on a real toilet.

It's fudging good food, you ask me, said Flory. They like it. God, just let them have what they like. You want to take everything away?

I don't want to take anything.

Right, I forgot. You just want to give.

Maybe this was mean. Flory didn't intend it to sound that way. She enjoyed pushing Andrea to her limits, but didn't want to hurt.

Andrea shook her head no problem, said nothing. Then she spoke:

So, do you want to live here, Games? I don't think so. I mean, do you? I'm just asking.

Games didn't answer, but his expression, the way his eyes went around the room and out the window then back to his thinking – it all said *No*. He didn't want to live in the nursing home, but he didn't mind the work.

~

The late afternoon sun blasted through the western windows. Andrea took Games down the hall, room by room, to close the curtains, to turn and clean the occupants, to shower and shave them and to chat.

The nurses aren't much to look at here, said Andrea. All nice, but, I'm thinking, for someone like you… You're really just twenty-three?

Almost eight, said Games.

Married.

No.

Girlfriend.

I…

I?

Games said nothing.

Don't be so tight-lipped. Remember that smile you carry.

I'm not doing this for dates, said Games.

Of course, there's Rianna, reminded Andrea. She comes a bit later, but she won't stay long.

Games said nothing.

You know her?

Not much, said Games.

She's got the smile, easy. Full of light.

I mean a bit, Games clarified.

You're bitten?

Just a bit, I said. I know her just a –

Sweet girl, said Andrea. Pretty. She won't be working here long.

You said that.

Just want you to hear it.

Games took up the prompt.

Why won't she be here long?

Neither will you, said Andrea. It's not right for either of you. I can tell.

Games had given her nothing to read him by. Very tight-lipped.

Are you a fortune-teller?

I see what things are coming to, said Andrea. Yes. These halls are soul-sucking halls. It's an artificial place. People come here to shut down. More prison than home, really. But you're like a stream of water, carrying the world on your back. And Rianna, she's a breath of fresh air. I like her lots.

Games said nothing as they went from room to room, visiting, cleaning, emptying, lifting, tucking, brushing through, and being with. They entered Mr. B's room, 101N. Ms. Lott's room, 103N. Joy Rimes and Lorenza Pitman roomed together. Malachi Boyce and Grey Larimore. Molly Swirr and Miss Charlotte. On down the hall. Some took a lot of work to get them to roll or help them out of bed. Others were cooperative. At the end of North Hall was Angeline in 115N – room of her own.

Hello my angel, said Andrea. Sitting with the sun in your eyes. I'll just close these curtains.

No you won't, said Angeline.

I've brought someone new for you to see, said Andrea.

Angeline sat up in her chair. The sunlight slid from her face, down her cheek to her neck. She turned from the window to see who had come.

Hey, Coot, said Angeline.

Games had heard that name before.

Hello, he said.

You're back.

It was difficult to know what she meant.

You finished with your running away? she asked.

I guess I have, said Games.

Does Mama know you're home?

I don't, Games began.

Angel, said Andrea. This here is Games. You may've seen him poking around before. He'll be helping you in the afternoons.

I don't need any help, and don't need introductions. Coot, you tell her for me as because no one lets me speak for myself, anyway. Tell her I'm okay.

Games was about to say it, but Angeline cut him off.

Mama's been talking about you. Every day, like a broken record. I'm not scolding, just telling you. I mean, you hurt her by leaving without saying.

Games didn't know what to say. He'd never left anyone.

Every day, she repeated.

Well, I...

You know where the fishing poles are at? asked Angeline.

No, said Games.

That's okay. I'll find them. We don't even have to fish. You know, some people don't like fishing on account of the killing.

Where are you going? asked Games.

Out. You coming, now that you're home?

I don't know, said Games.

Mama and me are going camping, said Angeline. Up in the mountains. There's a big lake and bears.

Angeline, this is not your brother, said Andrea. His name is Games. He works here.

My brother is Coot, said Angeline. Like the duck. That's a game bird, I suppose. You can tell her it's so, Coot. Are you still a pilot? Mama said you were. Delivering mail to the desert.

Not anymore, said Games.

I'm not going to school this week. You want to know why?

Why? asked Games.

I'm not talking to you. I'm talking to miss-know-it-all.

Why aren't you going to school? asked Andrea.

Mama and me and Coot are going camping. Did you find the fishing poles?

Not yet, said Games.

That's okay. Angeline looked out the window. Speak of the devil, she said, watching an airplane.

We'll have none of him, said Andrea. Not in my house.

You said you'd take me flying, remember? I want to fly up the coastline. I had a dream about it the other night. Chesapeake Bay up to Jonesy Island. When are we going?

I don't know, said Games.

It must be beautiful. All alone up there. Talking to the clouds. What's a cloud got to say?

Gray white words, sometimes rain, said Games.

Clouds are like movie cameras, said Angeline. They see it

all.

Games nodded, thinking maybe that was so.

It's too bad you can't come camping with us. Mama always asks about you. Why'd you run away when you did?

Sometimes you just have to go, suggested Games. I was chomping at the bit, I guess.

That's a good reason. You really hop a train to Oregon?

I don't remember the details, said Games.

That's the worst thing, isn't it?

What's that?

Trying to remember, but you can't. The truth is out there. You know it is. Or, it's inside you. But where?

It's hard, agreed Games.

You've got to trust what's in your head to show up when you need it, said Angeline. She hates her sister, though.

Who does? asked Games.

Mama. Did you live with her in that funny town?

Who? asked Games.

Mama's sister, said Angeline. Over in Massachusetts.

I used to live with my aunt, said Games.

Same difference.

I guess so, said Games.

You coming camping with us, then?

It's February, said Games.

It's not February. I'm not stupid. You must think I'm an idiot.

Games felt bad for what he'd said. He had to do something to fix it.

I'm sorry, he offered. Sometimes I get confused.

That's okay, said Angeline. You didn't mean it. Want an ice cream?

And where're you getting that? asked Andrea.

Orange Creamsicle. Root beer float. Buster Bar. You name it.

Maybe some other time, said Games.

Is she your girlfriend? Angeline was pointing at Andrea.

No. I just work...I mean...

You know me, said Andrea. We've been friends for two years.

Well, it's not like you ever come over, said Angeline.

Usually we go for a walk together down the hall, said Andrea.

Angeline nodded.

Maybe you're right. I don't always take notice. It's. Everyone's a fool here and then look what happens right out of the blue. My brother has come. It's a special day. He's real good looking, isn't he?

Like a movie star, said Andrea.

Have you really been in a movie? asked Angeline.

The only movie that came to mind for Games was *The Bicycle Thief.*

I like *To Kill a Mockingbird*, said Angeline. Not the movie so much as the book. And mostly because of Scout. She's real outspoken and honest. Then there's Natalie Wood in *Rebel Without a Cause*. Do you like her?

I don't know that book, said Games, fiddling with something in his hand.

Oh, she's real pretty. You'd fall in love. Are you in love?

Not yet, said Games.

It's no sin, you know, said Angeline.

This conversation! said Andrea. Who'd ever think that love's a sin? But I'll tell you a secret if you want.

Angeline turned toward the telling of the secret.

Games, I mean, cutie here, is staying for a while.

You can stay in my room I mean on the floor with a blanket till Mama finds you a bed.

In his own room, said Andrea. He'll be coming by to talk with you every now and then. When he's not busy.

I'm never busy, said Angeline. Not bored either, not with everything to do. It's just I don't work a job like some girls my age.

You used to work, said Andrea. What did you do?

Of course, there's school, but I hate it, said Angeline. Mama's never around much to help with my math, and when she is around she just sits and reads. She treats me with courteous detachment. I always liked that expression. Scout said it. Courteous – I like to sit and read, too, sometimes I do, but not when outside's knocking at the window. Hot days like now they open the windows at school, just to make it more tempting, but if you get up and go over, they yell at you: Sit down, young lady. Back in your seat. Eyes on the board. You're testing my patience. They scold like that. It's a teacher's job to scold. It's not my job. I don't like school, and I hate to be scolded. You know, maybe I just won't go back. Mama and I are going out, anyway. Soon as she gets back. If the both of you, if you're his girlfriend, you can come.

I'm too old to be anyone's girlfriend, said Andrea. Maybe Rio would step in.

I know Re-Annie, said Angeline. She's Annie all over again.

Andrea laughed.

How'd you come up with that?

She's my friend, said Angeline. Do you like her, Coot? She's real pretty, like Natalie Wood, only with lighter hair. And not a delinquent, either, if that's the right word. Hey you, I say when she comes to my house all smiles. Hey you, she says back. It's just how we are.

I don't know her as well as – Games dropped the piece of string he'd been rolling between his finger and thumb. You, he said, picking it up.

Andrea looked at her watch and made a slight move to speak.

Ri-Annie she comes over and we decide to go fishing or hunting for snakes, said Angeline. She doesn't like to fish, but she'll do it with me just to be nice. She's real good to sit with, too. Once when I had bad poison ivy, she sat with me all afternoon and played cards. Who else will do a thing like that? She had this ointment made from jewelweed, but I couldn't stop –

Angeline stopped talking.

What're you looking at? she asked.

The sun coming through the window, said Games. It's almost down.

Angeline looked out. She saw another plane or the same one flying low.

Reconnaissance. That's what Mama says they're doing. I used to know what that means.

It's spying, said Games.

But how do they fly when it gets dark?

They use their instruments, said Games.

That's stupid, said Angeline.

Why?

You mean like a flute or trumpet?

No, altimeters and gyroscopes, said Games. Those kinds of instruments.

I guess you would know all the fancy words, said Angeline. You're going to take me flying someday, aren't you?

It's real expensive, said Games.

Tomorrow, I'm free, said Angeline. But soon, I'm going to the mountains.

I'll come by tomorrow and we'll talk about it, said Games.

All right then, said Andrea, who was ready to go.

Is she your girlfriend? asked Angeline.

No, said Games.

Do you have a girlfriend?

Not yet.

So, you can come camping if you want. It'll be like it was. God, Coot. Mama will be so happy you're home.

Okay, said Andrea. We're going to go now. You want to walk with me out to the hall till dinner?

Why do I want to go in the damn hall? I'm sorry.

You like it, said Andrea. You can watch all the people.

I don't want to watch all the people. I don't like all the people, only some.

Of course you like people, said Andrea.

Some people, repeated Angeline. You're okay. And Re-Annie. And Coot.

And your mother, said Games.

Where's Mama? asked Angeline. I hate being stuck inside on a nice summer day. I like it outside, not in some goddamn hall.

Okay, said Andrea. But when Games comes back, he can take you if you want.

I can take myself, said Angeline.

She held out her hand to Games.

Mama's been so sad, but she'll be happy now. When you left, she cried for a month. Nothing would assuage her. That's a word I like.

Games took the old woman's hand in his. Bony, cold,

spotted flesh. He noticed the word *Mockingbird* in bold font.
It was a book on the floor, partially covered by a framed
photograph of a girl and a boy.

We can go to a movie sometime, if you've got a dollar for
me.

Games nodded.

I probably have a dollar, he said.

They held each other's hands until Games felt awkward
and pulled away. Angeline turned from Andrea and Games
as they walked out the room. The sun, just about to leave the
world for now, poured light through the window in a final
burst of empathy: We're going to the mountains. One-dollar
movies. Natalie Wood, and Scout and Jem. The soothing
trees against the sky. Flutes that make it easy for flying. See
the world that others see. The low pink clouds like far off
roses.

~

She's getting worse, said Andrea. Used to be she knew who I
was. I'd put her in the hall and she'd talk to Philippa, but
Philippa just wanted to sit quiet. She got angry with Angeline
for talking so much and pushed her away. Angeline pushed
Philippa back and Philippa fell and broke her hip. That was a
couple of weeks ago. We've got to be more careful now.

Who's Coot?

Her brother, sounds like, said Andrea. She has a framed
picture.

Does he come here? asked Games.

No one comes.

They walked back down the hall, toward the nurse's desk.
Rio's shift had started at five, and there she sat, head buried in
her work.

She's been here two years, said Andrea.

Who? asked Games, looking at Rio.

Miss Angeline. Only once did I see some woman stop by
for about seven minutes. I was counting.

What do you mean?

When I went in later, she was naked on her bed.

The woman? asked Games.

Not the woman. She wasn't there. It was Angeline. Said she was going for a swim.

In her head she probably was, said Games.

Andrea looked at him.

Where's the sense in the world, she said. What...can... The words sputtered and caught in her throat. It's anyone's guess what she wanted to say. Games's eyes stayed down. It was a mad crazy world on the shiny white floor. The reflection of footsteps. A final, relinquishing sigh.

FEBRUARY

Angeline Finch

When I was thirteen. No, not anymore. When once I was. When I was real early getting out of bed, like a daffodil in February. Sitting duck. Not very smart. Winter's gonna get you, Mama said. No, I said. It's not winter. Not anymore.

Whatever it is, it's mixing kind of nebulous at the moment. About the only thing that's making any light is Coot, who comes and talks with me. He comes by and it's easy to be myself. He reminds me maybe how things used to be but mostly how they could be. I like that about him, how he's a reminder and a promise, too.

The world's a crazy place sometimes. It's a hindrance and a burden. I mean, I like some things about the world – heat for one and how ice melts in your mouth, but other things not so much, such as how people mostly are mean. They're cold in their hearts like it's winter inside them. And when Coot comes to talk I've got plenty to say about it, but when he's gone, I'm quiet. I hold it in. Then this bitterness and frustration comes bursting through the dam when I see him again. Why, when I'm not around, do you hold back? he says to me. What are you waiting for? he asks. It's just him, I guess. But I don't say this so he hears.

Like I reminded him earlier, he's the one ran away. Of course he says it wasn't him, but it really was and it was wrong. I was alone with Mama mostly. Papa died by his own hand when it was before I even knew him, so I never felt what it was to have a father living at home. And I'm sure that sounds a lot like other people's lives, too, but it's true for me, and I'm the one saying it. Thing is, though, none of that setup is what makes me me. Sure, it's important but. It's not who I'm with or who I'm not with that matters, it's what I do with what I've got. At least that's what people keep telling me.

People will always tell you things. But do they listen to themselves? They tell you how important it is that sometime in your life you see things different than you think they are, and try to put it all in some bigger perspective. You've got to make sense of life, that's what they're trying to say. It's something special when it happens, but you likely don't see it at first, not when you're young, not when you're older even, not if all you've ever been doing's been getting by and frustrated with it. Then, you're still an outsider. You see things real and true, I'm told, only when you're able, only after looking out for a while, after taking everything in and thinking whatever you want to think like you've got your private God-given license, then looking back and thinking different about it, trying, like I said, to see it from another point of view. Maybe that other point of view is a person you respect, like Coot. Or maybe it's just a bigger way of seeing. And then, if you're lucky, something lights up inside you. There it is for the first time, like you wouldn't believe. I'm not saying it's come to me yet, but lately I've been watching for signs.

Coot's the one got me thinking, and I thank him for it. I hate sitting fidgety all day, like I'm in school again, looking at the clock up there on the wall and the teacher standing up front by her desk with her hair all up in knots and her face twisted like a red licorice rope, telling me things how I's better than we except at the sea, and making me print when I can write cursive better than anyone, and keeping me between the lines when there's so much room outside, plus teaching me literally nothing about the moon. I like the moon because it's a new moon each day. But I don't want to wander all over the place with what I'm saying. The moon doesn't do that, so neither will I.

~

I already said it, that when I mostly lived with my mother, Coot wasn't there. My mother told stories. Like once Mama said she was driving with her drinking friends and they were heading out where the black people live near the train tracks, and her friends wanted to throw empty bottles and yell nigger nigger watermelon nigger, but Mama didn't want to do any of that, so she said, *Let me out,* and they said, *Why?* and she said, *Just stop the damn car,* and they said, *Here, where the niggers live?* and she said, *No, just here.* So, they let her out, and it was dark, and they went on and yelled whatever they wanted to without her. But Mama wandered in the woods the other side of the tracks and came upon a man sitting beside a tree with a campfire going. He was peeling a peach with a knife and humming. Why're you doing that? she asked. What part confuses you? he asked. Peeling your peach, said Mama. So I can eat it without the fuzz, said the man. And the way he said *fuzz* it made Mama wonder if he meant police. But mostly it made her like the man right then and there and never again want to even think of doing anything hurtful to others. Funny how one word can do so much good, isn't it? And it doesn't have to be a fancy word, either. Like *serendipity* or *assuage.* Then he gave her a big chunk of his peach and the juice was delicious and dripped down her neck, and he told her that if she wanted to get home, he could show her the best way, but she said she just wanted to walk it herself and get wherever her feet took her, and he said he understood perfectly and thought it was a smart thing to do and that he wished he could do the same, but he couldn't on account of one of his feet was missing. Mama hadn't noticed that, but then she did. And that's the first time she knew where she wanted to be, which was out in the world in the heat of discovering, not trapped inside, like meanness in a car or hatred in the heart. But free, so she could see for herself what was true and good.

Do you remember any of that?
    No, I don't, said Coot.
    Mama didn't tell you that story before?
    No.
    Well, it happened.
    I don't doubt you, said Coot.
    But you don't care, either, I said. Do you?
    Yes, he said back. I do care.

And I believed that he did. So I went on:

Once it was a day real hot like today, I explained. I was hiking with Mama. We were planning to go camping but we couldn't find the fishing poles and we couldn't find the tents, either. So, we just had to make do. Mama was the type of person who could make do with whatever. She found berries to eat and could make fire from sticks if she had to. She painted the walls with boiled milk and grass clippings, which made a faint green paint. When it was cold, she heated the house with sunlight and candles. She and I stuffed straw in the walls then patched up the holes, and she borrowed money from the priest who lived by the Orthodox Church. She always said she'd pay him back and she always somehow did, because I went with her to do it and had cookies and ice tea right there on his front porch while I listened to that solemn voice drone on and on about the Christian thing to do, about having a man in the house and education and a few good books, especially the Bible.

The thing of it is, Mama already had lots of books and a bible, too. And maybe I wanted to go to church, maybe not, but what I did want more than anything was to go swimming. It was always so hot growing up, and the kids in town would go down to this swimming hole whenever they wanted. I always wanted, but never went. Till one time I was by myself at home and things were that August-can-hardly-breathe kind of hot, and we didn't even have a fan, so I decided to go. When I got there, there were six seven other kids and they looked up like their heads were all tied to the same puppet string. I went to go in the water, but they all told me that it wasn't safe to swim like that.

Like what? I asked.

You've got too many clothes on, said a girl I knew from school, Minnie Higgins.

And even though I only had on shorts and a tee shirt, she explained it that everyone at first had to swim naked. With your clothes on she said the snakes and turtles and po-dings would grab hold of your shirt and shorts and drag you under and you'd drown.

What's a po-ding? I asked.

Remember that girl Eileen used to go to our school, said

Minnie.

No.

Well she doesn't go anymore cause last summer she died. They took hold of her blouse and. There was a whole thing in the paper. And this guy with the TV news came out and did this story. You got to swim naked first so they trust you. It's like code or something. Then they leave you alone.

What snakes? I asked, looking into the water.

They leave you alone, but it's got to be done right.

They trust all of you, I said, looking around.

Sure do, another girl, Tracy, told me. We've been swimming forever. But 'cause it's your first time. My father says one day all the animals are going to take over the world.

So, I took off my shorts and shirt, right down to my unders. Then I took them off, too. What did I care. It just was so hot and everyone encouraging me on account of the snakes. And that, it seems is when Mama just happened to be walking by, which I don't think she was spying, though maybe she was, and she saw me without my clothes on and all the kids laughing and splashing me and I don't think she saw the snakes or even knew about them. So, she came out of the trees and the others all backed off and got real quiet, and she told me to get out of the water and get my clothes on and not to go swimming with a bunch of miscreants and reprobates, which I didn't know at that time what she meant, but I was hot and wanted to swim and really didn't mind. So, she told me she knew a better place, up in the hills where no one had a license to be cruel.

Freak, someone yelled. It was Minnie Higgins again.

Mama very calmly went up to Min and extended her hand. When Minnie didn't take it, Mama took my hand as maybe a better offering anyway and we walked on.

We ate our dinner that night and hardly talked. Next day, I think, I had something to say. It was dinner again, and I still hadn't gone swimming. Overcooked carrots and mashed potatoes with butter.

I saw Coot today, I told her.

I know, said Mama.

You know.

Yes.

Well, why didn't you, I almost screamed. Why didn't you tell me?

Nothing to tell. Now eat.

So I ate. We had canned peaches and graham crackers for dessert.

Then Mama said, Tomorrow morning, real early, you and I are going hiking.

Swimming? I said.

Swimming, camping, everything. You find the fishing poles yet? she wondered.

No.

That's okay, said Mama.

Is Coot coming? I asked.

No, said Mama.

Why not?

Because he's not. He's got to stay and work.

What's he do that's so important? I asked.

He takes care of fruits and vegetables at the store, said Mama. He also looks in on old people now and then.

I thought you said he was a pilot.

I never said anything about him being a pilot. But a person can do lots of things with his life.

What am I going to do? I asked.

I'm not your author, said Mama.

But what do you think I'll do? I asked.

You, my little angel, are going to do what you want, and you're not going to let anyone tell you you can't. It doesn't matter the particulars, it matters the spirit. You're going to live long and hard and one day at a time, like the cliché says.

Who's Queen Shay? I asked.

Never mind, said Mama. It'll all go as planned. You'll find your mark. You'll have your say. Then the colors'll be fading and you'll grow sort of tired. And one day, a certain afternoon will drop by, late, and you'll decide on your own it's time to pick up and leave. Might be real hot like today or it might not. You'll've had your dinner just like we did. You'll stuff your pockets with graham crackers, and you'll look out the window at the night sky with stars.

Will there be a moon, too? I asked.

I don't see why not. Sure, there'll be a moon. You'll see it rising from your room. All through the night you'll keep an eye on it until it rises out of reach. When the dawn breaks rosy on the morning sky, you'll sneak out the door. You'll go for a walk, just like we're going to do tomorrow. There'll be cows and sheep everywhere. There'll be the sound of a train in the distance and the sun slowly rising. And there'll be the moon as well, over on the western side, saying goodbye with the last of its night light. Sometimes things say hello. Sometimes things say goodbye. It's all good, if you don't judge but just let it be. No anguish in your soul. No loss of your identity. If you see things as good, they'll be good to you.

What about for Coot?

He'll be okay. He's got a future to meet that he's had a hand in preparing. A girlfriend and a happy life right up ahead.

Is my life...I began. Mama looked off. I don't know what she was listening to. Going to be happy, I finished.

That, said Mama, as if that was enough. She then swung back to me, completing, depends on how you go with it. Like I said. It's all good, if you see it as good.

Something changed for me then. I'm not saying I had everything figured, but a curtain blew open and I went from total blindness to all-out seeing. This lasted as long as the curtain was lifted. What a waste of time it is, I remember thinking, not to go with the good. And that's how it's going to be from now on. No matter where I am, no matter what it's about. I'm going to see things as good.

~

Now, Coot's left me alone and gone to work. That's okay. It's late at night and I don't want to sleep. I'm too excited. Bits and pieces are falling like snow, but it can't be snow in August. It must be moonlight, or dust from cleaning, or sparkly nuggets of sky. I look through the window and, yes, it's flakes of moonlight I'm sure.

I'm alone again, waiting for Mama. Don't know where she is. I'll have to go looking for her when the sun comes up. We're going swimming and fishing in the mountains. I might

as well go
to sleep if
I can.

And just as Mama said it would, it's getting bright out there already. So, I put on my most summery shirt and shorts and hiking boots and carry with me a spare pair of socks. I bring a book to write in and one to read and some graham crackers that are stale like always but it's the best I can do. I don't have the fishing poles. I don't have our tent. Maybe Mama found them. She's waiting outside for me, somewhere ahead on the trail. I just have to – Oh, that's right, I almost forgot. My swimsuit, which I don't even have one, do I? It doesn't matter, though. It's all good. I'll swim as I am, like the fish and the frogs and the black water snakes.

Mama sometimes locks the door, but not this morning because she knows I'm following her out. Coot's asleep in his room upstairs and there's this lady outside with a cigarette who doesn't see me because I hide in the shadows as I go. I'm glad she doesn't see me. I don't like the look of her, or her smoke, which makes it difficult to breathe. Besides, away from here is where I want to be, not explaining stuff to people I don't care about.

I thought it'd be warmer than this, but it isn't. It's just because the sun's not all the way up yet. And the moonlight's still falling like snow. I see it. And I hear the cows lowing, ready to be milked. Milk is something inside the world that you need to get out. Food is trapped in plants and honey in bees. Voices are in everything. And I feel sheep wherever I step, soft and cool to the touch, like walking on wool.

I'm debating which way to go. For a while I debate, but I go toward the lightest part of the sky, which is sunrise. I look everywhere for the moon, but can't find it except in pieces. I feel real thirsty, and lucky for me there's this stream, at least some of it that's not dried up. I stop to take a drink, which is real cold water and amazing colors like a rainbow.

It's a personal thing for me to take a sip. In fact, I feel the water was put here for me just this morning and if I hadn't've stopped for a sip I'd've been hurting its feelings. Lately, I've been thinking the world cares what I do. The whole world's alive and part of me. It's in my blood. It's here for me, to help me and for me to get to know. Mama always said that the world had a beginning and I had a beginning and that that beginning has nothing to do with the solid stuff I see and feel, but with something invisible, what she called spiritual truths, which makes more sense to me now.

We all began together from a wish of God, Mama once said. Out of a wish grows a world.

Why would God wish for a world? I asked. Why would God wish for me? Why is there God at all? Why me?

Mama didn't answer. Nobody did. And I just stood there, unknowing and confused, wanting to ask more questions, not knowing how.

It's quiet this morning, too. It's okay not to get a straight-away answer. I might be here when word comes. I might not. Thing is, I'm going on.

What I like best about this place is it lets you wonder. It lets you ask questions. Nothing's stupid. The world outside doesn't judge the things you feel but lets you be you, which is first things first what I think any child needs. And I'm happy as I drink. I do wonder some about the trash in the stream, though. It makes me sad, all the pollution, and what people do to hurt the earth. So, I take the bottles and stuff from the water and gather them from the banks. There's so much, it's disgusting. Sometimes people are such slobs. A pig is neater. A goat or a duck. A rat, even.

Still, I can't wait to get to the lake. I can't wait to be so hot and ready. I can't wait to get there and strip down, swim, and soak in the blue, and the sun'll be shining and sparkly on the water and I'll be me all over, under the water, unable to tell the difference between inside and out. That'll be real beautiful, I know. I'll be alone with the world. Together.

I see the path that Mama took. It's up ahead. And behind me is Coot who's somewhere in my house right now. If he's asleep, he's dreaming what this is like for me. If he's awake, he's thinking about me just as I am, and if it makes him understand himself more, I guess I've been worth something to this world.

Yeah, my life is good. And it's not because it pleases me, it's because it actually is good. I've taken my life and observed it some and liked it well enough. I like this moment especially. And if I could thank someone I would, but I can't think of anyone. I'd rather be out where I am, not inside and thinking or inside and talking.

The world is everything that I love. It's more questions and answers and always new life. It's about the attitude you bring, and that's the only thing I want to say. I could walk and walk here for hours and days. I wouldn't get tired. The soles of my feet would sing and be happy. Sing me the moonlight. Sing me the nearby sun. My arms would swing and be free. Sing me the hope of a new tomorrow.

The thing about my body is, it's not so important anymore. It's a piece of the world. It's the one-time ship of me docked at shore. And now I'm going wherever it is I'm going without it I guess. And where is all the stuff I've collected? And what time's it anyway? The sun when you want it most – it's coming. The warmth when you need it most – it's here. Heat round me like arms, a blanket. I'm held. On fire on fire on. I've got to let go. And where in the whole wide world am I going? Where in the whole wide world am I now? Under the sky with flakes of light, lying upon the earth, looking up.

THREE

Snow again, settling on the ground. Likely, wouldn't amount to much, not this gentle reminder.

Games opened the door to the nursing home, midafternoon. He was here to work. Coming on three. The snow brought with it thoughts of Angeline Finch who'd wandered off one morning and died beside a drainage ditch. It had snowed then, too. The boy who found Angeline had cut across the lot because a straight line was usually faster than going around. His name was Kayvon or Kelvin, definitely something beginning with a K. He was a good student, a considerate boy. He went to tell someone at the convenience store that a woman was sleeping outside. But maybe she was dead. Games had heard the whole story on the local news in the back of Jakes while sorting through a shipment of bruised bananas.

~

Games walked into Curtis Bridge's room. Just after three. He was tired. Two jobs. Abe had left on a road trip without telling anyone. Well, Games he'd told, but it was their secret:

Sold all my hockey gear for 250 bucks, he'd said a week ago. That should get me where I'm going.

Abe never gave a location. Still, he was a good friend and Games wished him luck. Not many close friends for Games. No sex for him, either, since what seemed forever. It pierced and stung him like a knife in the stomach. His lack of serious relationships caused much anguish. It was the weight of emptiness. Ample time and space with little, he felt, to show. There was distance between Games and others, though it was nothing he could confirm with an odometer, and his heart, had he been able to measure the separation with that organ, would've told him he was much closer to people than he perceived. Consider, for example, how many of the elderly men and women enjoyed seeing Games in the hall or in their rooms. They filled his hands with their hands and oiled his ears with stories.

James, my man, said Mr. Bridge. Get over here.

Mr. Bridge knew better, but he liked calling Games James, which went back to the first day they met, over a month ago:

I was telling our new man here about Rio.

It was Andrea who'd begun the conversation that day, as she and Games stood waiting for Mr. Bridge to turn his wheelchair from the TV and engage them.

Redoing what? said the man, watching the soundless anchorman move his mouth without disturbing the air.

Rio, said Andrea.

I know her, said Mr. Bridge, spinning to his visitors. A table with a chessboard, brown and white pieces, stood beside him. I don't know you. You are?

Games, sir.

Jameser.

Games, repeated Games.

Like Jesse James.

But with a G.

Lethargy? Are you making fun?

No.

You must think I'm an old fart?

No one's saying you're old, said Andrea. Just telling you his name.

I already know it, said Mr. Bridge. Said it's Jesse James, like the train robber.

He didn't say anything like that and you know it. Don't let him play with you, said Andrea to Games. We came in to ask you a question.

What question's that? said Mr. B.

About Rio, said Andrea.

That's not a question.

The question is, She's a nice girl.

When I was up to bat, said Mr. B. They called that a statement.

Just tell Games what you think.

Mr. Bridge settled in for the discussion.

What I think. You're giving me the floor?

Andrea turned off the television.

You're impossible, you know.

That's your opinion. As for mine, I think blue's a good choice of color for the sky, but I also think there's someone isn't going to like the choice.

What you think about Rio, said Andrea.

Ah, back to your thesis. Painted Lady. Red Admiral. Monarch.

Are you –

There's a butterfly that's maybe as pretty, clarified Mr. B, but it's debatable.

So, it's safe to assume you like Rio, said Andrea.

Am I not speaking? He looked at himself, he looked around the room. Am I not here?

We hear you. You're being obtuse.

You honor me with such compliments.

The choice is yours, said Andrea. How to be. Pleasant. Unpleasant.

So fucking annoying, thought Mr. B. But he would do what he could.

Tell me, then. What's going on? he asked. Hasn't been fired, has she?

No one's been fired.

She up for promotion? If you want me to give a reference, I will.

No one's up for anything.

Then, why the inquisition?

Just want to hear your thoughts, said Andrea.

No one's ever been so interested. I sit unable to move while everything changes around me. People come, people go. The troops are deployed, sent into action: We move out at dawn. Very good, major. But what about the civilians stuck in their rooms? Fuck the civilians. This is our call, not theirs.

What are you jabbering about? asked Andrea. You and your language.

Without you and Miss Ri, said Mr. B. I'd turn against life.

You never turn, Curtis. Not even if I asked nicely.

Mr. Bridge nodded. He knew he was difficult, maybe even obtuse. He also knew he could put on a show.

A few things I'm against, he said. This chair, my bed, these walls. Generally, I'm pro.

Pro what? asked Games.

Pro vita, said Mr. B, making a concentrated effort to be precise. Just today this girl comes up to me, whiskers above her lip, smelled like cigarette smoke. You know the one. She spilled milk on my bed and froze.

I hope you didn't snap, said Andrea.

Where's your faith in me? said Mr. Bridge. I'm a new man.

Andrea's expression showed she didn't trust the transformation.

Jameser?

Yes.

I'm guessing you know something about fighting.

I...

You have a minute?

One, said Andrea, who'd already heard many of the stories she was sure would follow. Guatemala, Central America, South Korea. It was difficult to locate the conflict. You're a man of battles, she continued. My friend, Colonel Garber, would love to talk.

I'm not interested in your Gabber. I'm talking to Jameser.

Well don't fill him with nonsense.

She was pinned under a beam following the explosion, began Mr. Bridge.

Who?

It was very rugged country, and when we got down there, they'd just blown up the bridge. Or we had. Someone blew the damn thing with everyone on it. Everyone. Worlds unraveling, fallen. Her legs were destroyed. She couldn't... Well. I'll need an arnica compress, I thought. It was something my mother used to put on me when I had bruised my leg. How ridiculous it was for me to think of such a cure. All I wanted was to help. Something to put it right. To have her tell me her name, not to lose her. So I stayed. No way I was going to move that beam or stop the blood. I looked her in the eyes, trying to see what she was seeing.

She was seeing you, said Andrea.

No. It wasn't me. I held her hand. I was only a kid, like you Mr. James. I was fighting a war.

What war were you in? asked Games.

It's all about the relationships, my friend, said Mr. Bridge. Problem is, you barely know the people around you. You don't ask their names or where they come from. You know so little, really. And then she died the next minute.

I'm sure you were very helpful, said Andrea. We do what we can.

And it's never enough, said Mr. B. But it might be a chance for a fresh start in life. A new direction. The worst thing ever, I killed a man.

I'm sure you did, said Andrea. She'd heard this story, too, many times. All the same, we're running –

Never once growing up did I wonder what it would be like to kill, to take a life. Oh, there were bugs, mosquitoes, but out there in that rugged countryside, I saw him go right up to heaven. I watched him walking toward the spot, carrying his broken body.

Now how's someone going to walk and carry his body at the same time? asked Andrea.

Do you know how we ascend to heaven? said Mr. Bridge.

No, said Games.

An angel comes and takes our soul. Plucks us right off the earth like a piece of fruit. I don't know about if you're rotten, though. You probably hadn't figured on that, Mr. James? You and all your badmen buddies. All the people you've killed. You really think an angel's going to come and take you off? You should rethink what you've been doing with your life.

I know, said Games.

Now you stop, said Andrea. You're making him think what you say is true.

Isn't it?

Andrea sighed.

I'm just playing with you, said Mr. B. I know you've never killed anyone. Am I right?

Yes, said Games.

Enough nonsense, said Andrea. This place gets loonier every day. Games here's going to be the one taking this wing in the afternoons. You be nice to him.

Mr. Bridge looked him over.

How old are you?

Twenty-eight soon.

When's soon?

February.

What crime brought you here?

No crime.

By the time I was twenty-eight, I'd killed a man.

I've heard, said Games.

There's a mystery to it.

What mystery? asked Games.

Did I say mystery? I should've said misery. You see, I didn't see it coming. I didn't see how bad it'd make me feel. There's no worse feeling than doing something you know is wrong but you do it anyway. Then the rest of your life you're alone with yourself and the wrong you've done.

You're not alone, said Andrea. Jesus is always with you.

I don't believe I know the man, said Mr. B.

Because He isn't a man, least not the way you're thinking it. But He's with you, nevertheless.

What good is it, if he keeps his presence to himself?

Jesus cares about you, said Andrea.

I'm glad to hear it, said Mr. B. Still, I think it's better that I do the caring.

You can care all you want, said Andrea. What's the earth for if not for helping one another? Just some of us need more help than what a mere person can give.

A meerkat, you say?

You heard me the first time.

Mr. Bridge shook it off. He turned to Games.

Tell me, could you ever kill someone?

I don't see how.

By accident. In self-defense. In anger.

I don't ever get very angry, sir, said Games.

All in good time, said Mr. Bridge. And stop calling me sir.

Sorry.

Don't be sorry, either. God dammit, the way you talk,

you'd think I was someone important, not just a *mere* person.

You know I don't like swearing, said Andrea.

Our outlaw here set me off.

You be nice to him, Curtis. He'll help shave you.

How's he going to save me?

Shave, I said. Might even play chess, if you ask him. Or bring you a book.

Curtis Bridge took a moment. Reflecting on books. The books he'd read, the ones Games might bring. He wiped his face, he felt its bristly stubble. This room was his home. His chair his bed his fortress.

You like to read?

Sometimes.

History?

No.

Newspapers?

No.

Comic books?

Not much.

What the hell you read, then? asked Curtis Bridge.

Just books, said Games. My mother had a library in her car.

Alexandrian?

No.

New York public?

No.

Library of Congress?

Not quite.

You ever read philosophy? asked Mr. B.

I read something by Nietzsche once. I read some Plato and Jung.

Modern Man in Search of a Soul?

I don't know, said Games.

Synchronicity?

Games thought about the word.

That rings a bell.

It tolls for thee.

What?

You ever read the *Iliad*?

The *Odyssey*, in school.

You probably think I'm your father, said Mr. Bridge.

Not really.

I'm just playing with you, Games. You see. I do know your name.

Okay, okay, said Andrea. We've got better things to do than spend our time listening to you.

Go do your work, said Mr. B. I ought to think more about others, less about myself.

You ought to take up a hobby, said Andrea.

I think you're right, said Mr. B. Like painting or horticulture. Or falling in love.

He looked to his wall for a piece of art, just one. The walls were empty, not even a smudge. He looked for the cutting of a twig in water or a potted plant on the sill. Nothing on television. Nothing to see. So, he thought how long it had been since he'd been in love. If there was someone he'd loved, she was dead to him. He'd forgotten her face. And if there was someone he'd killed, he was afraid to name him, too. Names he missed saying by mere inches. Meerkats of the Kalahari. Meer people. Only relationships mattered, and they existed in the air and the air was thin and difficult to breathe. And yet Curtis Bridge did not consider himself an unlucky man. Maybe unfortunate to've gone through life so much on his own, but for the most part he was content. His walls displayed his contentment. No content at all, not even a smidge. No cost to his life. Just alone with himself, nothing to show, nothing to share.

Maybe you could paint a picture of flowers in love, suggested Games.

Daisy and Rose, you think?

Perfect, said Games. Or two tulips touching.

Enough, said Andrea. You make fun of love. You make it into a hobby, into hotel art. But the real thing is, it's endless work.

Yes, said Mr. B, sounding sincere. I am remiss. And I envy you both.

No sense in envy, said Andrea. It kills each person it touches.

So arrives my executioner, said Mr. B, smiling. And don't be deceived by the smile on my face. It is the smile of last things. Inevitability. Trust, even. A smile of trust. In what? In life, you idiot. Life.

I'm going to bring in the Colonel, if he's willing. I can't remember what –

No Colonels, said Mr. B. I've stopped talking now. You both may leave. Dismissed.

He turned from them and switched on the television, the sound on mute. *Jeopardy*, whose answer: What is Armistice Day, was written by all. Games and Andrea left the room and continued down the hall to visit with others. Mr. Bridge didn't see them go. He hated the news. He hated the shows, the sports. The flickering light reminded him of something. He shifted in his chair and looked out the window as a plane went by. Then he waited to see. What would come next? The sun set soon and stars came out. Mr. Bridge had his dinner. Played chess against himself. He read a magazine and later was lifted into bed. He shifted his weight and looked out the window. He saw shooting stars, there and there. Then he fell asleep in his flickering room. Later, Games turned off the TV and drove home. Tracer stars, visible lines in the sky. The clock struck twelve, which sounded like notes of remorse, and by the end of its striking, the first day was done.

~

Now it was another day. March already and Games was twenty-eight. Snowy afternoon, just after three. Mr. Bridge saw Games crossing the doorway and called him into the room.

James, my man, said Mr. Bridge. I need a shave.

Games changed directions and entered the room. He took the electric razor and shaved Mr. B's face. Mr. B was not satisfied at first, so Games shaved him closer. Finally, the old man, rubbing his face, nodded.

Good enough.

Games put away the razor and was getting ready to leave when Mr. B called him back.

You have a minute?

Not for chess, said Games.

Hand me that newspaper.

Games did.

Obituaries. Obituaries. Always obituaries. I probably know some of these people, said Mr. B, looking.

Do you? asked Games.

Do I what?

Know any?

Here's one, said Mr. B. Frank Meier. I knew Frank. He was a good man. A history teacher, no wife no children, an ardent birdwatcher, it says. Didn't know that about him. Do you watch birds?

If one flies by, said Games.

Mr. B put the paper down.

You seen the new hottie in 115?

She a bird?

An old biddy, more like it, said Mr. B.

No, said Games. But it sounds like you have.

I see everything in this place. I observe objectively, impartially, the way Goethe recommended.

Who?

Goethe.

Oh. I thought you –

I know what's going on, interrupted Mr. B. I see you looking at Rianna.

We both work here, said Games.

You do anything besides work?

Sometimes I watch birds, teased Games.

You take her out yet? asked Mr. B.

She doesn't have time.

No time, said Mr. Bridge. What the hell? You live in the same world as me? He was looking around the room, trying to figure if the world had somehow changed before his eyes. This world is made of time. I never once heard of not having it.

I mean…

Games didn't want to talk about what he meant. He didn't want to talk about his social life with this man.

You're creative aren't you? You're young. Energetic. Make time. What're you waiting for?

Games didn't know what to say.

Some things don't matter so much, said Mr. B. Other

things do. When I was a boy, I killed a mouse, he said.

I thought you killed a man.

It was a mouse first, later a man. You ever read that book?

I think so, said Games, assuming he meant *Of Mice and Men*.

Not that one, the other.

I...

When I was a boy, began Mr. B, we lived in two rooms. Small place, I remember it. There was a mouse in my room. I didn't mind, but it would crawl over me at night and wake me. Maybe it was just lonely. Maybe it wanted to talk. I never asked. I would've asked my mother what to do about the mouse, but she was never there when I thought of it, so I figured on my own a way I could catch the mouse so's not to hurt it and then I could take it outside into the weeds and let it go. I was seven. Were you ever seven?

Yes.

I made this clever trap where the mouse would step on a lever to get a peanut and then the box would fall and I'd have it. The problem was, I set up the trap in the afternoon.

And – mice can't be trapped in the afternoon? wondered Games

I put in a couple peanuts and waited. But it wasn't even near time to go to sleep, and then my mother came home before dinner, looked me in the eye and said: Say goodbye to this shit. There's a 100 percent chance we're leaving now.

Leaving? said Games.

That minute. No delay. Never going to sleep in that hellhole again.

You just went?

Packed our stuff, which wasn't much, and what we didn't pack, we left behind. I had a bag and my mother had two and she made me hold her arm and we just, as you say, went. That was that. It was the last time we were ever in those rooms.

And you forgot about the trap, said Games.

All I remember is it worked when I tested it, and I had left it set, ready to trip. Do you know how many nights I stayed up thinking about the mouse caught in that trap, eating his last peanut supper, then dying in the dark, unable to get out?

You don't know, said Games. He might not've gone in.

It's possible, said Mr. B.

He could've gnawed through the box, said Games.

You might be right. But those were never the pictures in my head. The picture in my head was of that trapped mouse. It suffered and died. It's the picture that keeps playing in your head that you've got to deal with.

And you're telling me this because?

I'm starting fresh, said Mr. B.

Pro vita, remembered Games.

I'm taking a different route, said the old man. Developing better pictures.

I'm sure the mouse forgives you.

It's not about the mouse anymore, Games.

And hearing the old man say his name put things in a quieter mood. Games stepped closer to the bed, leaned like a flower toward the dark, severe sun.

I've been thinking about it some, said Curtis Bridge. Now, I've never been a very religious man. For a while I was an outright atheist. These last few days, however, I've become very spiritual.

What's that mean? asked Games.

It means I've been thinking, said Mr. B. How the world is made of difference.

I thought it was made of time, said Games.

Tick, tock – there's your difference. Time without difference is timelessness. So, to repeat – the world is made of difference.

Games tried to sort these words in his mind, but they came to nothing.

Between everything on earth there's a space, said Mr. B. Doesn't matter if that space is a space of time or inches. Those spaces between things make all differences in the world. It's a law.

The space is the law? asked Games.

The law is that there must be differences on earth. And there's no possible movement, no advancement in life, without first there's a difference.

Never heard that law.

Maybe not, said Mr. B. But you couldn't move from right

to left without it. You couldn't take one step, forward or back. And not just your body, your thoughts and emotions, too, would rest in stillness. Some call that paradise, but I say it would be hell on earth.

Games tried to imagine his mind and body not moving, not needing to move.

By difference do you mean opposites? he asked.

It can be opposites, I suppose. Good and evil, the holy and the profane, or just what makes you happy one day and sad the next, but usually people don't move so much between extremes. Usually on earth, we move between things that lie closer together, like between this room and the next, or between that doorway and my bed. The old farts in here are very close to death. It's one simple step for us from life to death. I might take that step tomorrow. It all seems so perfectly laid out.

To die. To move between things, thought Games. From one moment to the next. He knew all about this, but right now, this moment, he had lots to do, people to tend to, beds to make.

I've got to –

When I was young, interrupted Mr. Bridge, I went from despair to fear and from fear to hate in a matter of seconds. I was someone way back in time. I'm someone else now. When will I stop moving and quietly know?

Is *this* about the mouse? asked Games.

It's about everything, said Mr. B. Mouse included. Don't you see what I'm saying?

No.

Two people stand close, but are miles apart. I'm talking about bridging the gap. I'm talking about human relationships and if you can ever really know someone else.

Okay, said Games.

The Law of Differences reads, Life on earth is a matter of differences. Here, it is all pieces of a puzzle and where those pieces fit in the whole.

Unless everything's random, said Games. And there is no fit.

A typical thought in today's world. I'm not buying it. That's why I told you, these last few days my thinking's been spiritual. There appears to be meaning.

But differences on earth, said Games. That just states the obvious.

Which is why there's a second law.

Games looked at the clock on the bedside table. Tick tock, tick tock.

The Law of Convergence, said Mr. B. It's a silent agreement. It moves everything together.

And these laws are yours? asked Games.

Not anymore. I'm a mere person with nowhere to go. They are your laws. I give them to you. You and Rianna. It's how I see things.

I don't know what you're seeing, said Games. Or giving, either. There's nothing to say about me and Rianna.

That's up to you, said Mr. Bridge. But I've got eyes. Been looking for a fresh start for a while now. What else can a person do in a place like this?

Games passed by Mr. Bridge and his clean-shaven face on his way to the window. The old man seemed almost young again.

Go ahead, then, said Mr. B. Look at things your own stubborn way.

Games stood at the window. The world outside – fresh with snow. No tracks, no trace of the ground or road. The tree limbs, the rooftops, appeared clean and new.

Take what's given, when it's given with affection, said Mr. B. At least, Games thought the old man had said this. It may've been the softhearted snow he was listening to. Soon a plow would come to push away the snow. People would trample the newness, and blowers blow it off. Soon the clean white ground would be dingy and drab. There'd be gray, dirty, everywhere piles of snow. People would grow weary of the mess. They'd empty a wealth of expletives into the drifts and banks. Enough is enough, they'd say, cursing the unending winter. They'd try to put an end to the cold with deadly stares, while longing for spring in their green growing hearts.

But for now, Games heard: Take what's given, when it's given with affection. Watch the snow fall and collect on the earth. It's a good picture of the world, if you let it be so:

Snow covers the old, making room for what's to come. There's peace for the mind. And infinite possibilities. You could start here, start now. Could make your move. You, me, everyone can create a work of life like a work of art, which is a work of discovered relationships.

A person doesn't always get a new beginning, heard Games. Doesn't happen every day he gets the opportunity, standing near a window, watching the snow. But here it is, a fresh, clean world. What possible problem could there be with that? Well, only one I can think of. A world at ease and at peace, an infinite world without differences, doesn't move forward. A world at one, a person alone, has no chance at love.

Games watched the snow out the window. He listened to whatever voice sounded nearby. He turned to the clock on the bedside table. He knew he had work to do. There was a wing of others to tend to, someone else to talk with down the hall, someone to take to the shower to bathe.

All encounters are threads in the weave, he heard. Relationships, relationships. That's the picture. A revolving earth that relates to the stars. We'll talk about that some other day, if you have a spare moment. Life-affirming harmony, life-changing dissonance. We spin through the minutes, the hours, the days. Are you even listening? On and on in my head not knowing. I'm tired of all this aloneness I feel.

MARCH

Curtis Bridge

So much for that room. The television, the clock. Seems now I'm on a mission to find the wisdom in this new arrangement called death. I have nothing to report as of yet.

Back in time, Rianna Olivet put her hand on my body, lying as I left it upon the bed in the early morning hours of that home, which was no home. Heart attack, they said. Not the heroic death I would've wanted, but it makes its point: With things of the heart, I'm a failure.

Here, so far, what I most understand is stillness and aloneness. I see myself as a vacant sky, reflecting upon a quiet, unhorizoned ocean. There is neither splash nor ripple to break the sameness. This goes on for...   If time here were comprised of chapters, I'd've already passed through a million million by now. Yet the story has not changed one tick. And how is this any different from my living days? Likely this changelessness will continue forever. Lucky for me, however, because of someone's pity, I'm allowed a reprieve.

Consider yourself fortunate, I'm told.

And I consider it, I really do. I let the possibility roll through me, echoing its way down the corridors. I definitely feel I'm a small bit of wind, traveling alone in darkness. Yet the moment the light leaves the sky for good, the sky breaks open, revealing stars. Never thought much of the stars before, but now I am that sky with each and every star, which is something I've never felt before.

And then comes a second consideration: In death as in life,

I'm built of associations – with stars as with people. And after that, a third consideration: It's a corrupt business that does not include others and does not make others its work. I gather this information to put in my report. I'm not sure who will read it.

~

On the day I was born, a car killed our cat. I didn't even cry, or so I was told. As I grew and had friends, they were not friends I put in my days but friends I left standing outside the front door while I played quietly in my room. They'd knock on the front door and maybe my mother would answer. Maybe not. I never knew what it would be like from one minute to the next with her.

Then, one day, I woke. It took me all morning to recognize that my eyes had been open all along. I'd say now that I was becoming accustomed to the earth. I smiled at things for the first time. Light was okay, voices tolerable. There were occasional people, neighbors, who seemed reliable enough, but I didn't much need them. I figured things out with my own two hands. I had a mother who taught me with her stubbornness and a father who stayed away as best he could. Both of them were good at what they did.

A short story: I saw my parents kiss once. It was early afternoon. A pack of Winston cigarettes and two dead squirrels lay on the table beside them where they stood in the kitchen, joined for three seconds in that kiss. The end. That was the only time I remember them showing affection. And some historical fiction: I had a brother, I think, who wrote books I never read, and a sister who swam so far away that she disappeared almost for good from my memory.

More for my report: Once, I trapped a mouse and allowed it to die. I didn't mean for it to die, but I did nothing to stop the death and did everything to make it happen. Other things I did: I threw rocks at the pilings under the Slaughter Creek Bridge, and caught minnows, putting them in a jar, for no better reason than that they were alive and fun to watch. I dug a spade in the earth, bringing worms to light on my way to other treasures. A gray gem, a grub, and a suffering toad. That was the last of my digging, slicing that toad. Later, I killed a man before we'd even had the chance to exchange names. And sometime in the midst of it all, I lost use of my legs. I don't want to talk about any of that, though. Because none of it is who I am.

~

Just the other day when alive in the home, I was sitting by the window in my wheelchair. Games came by as usual.

Mr. B, he said, standing just inside the door.

My man, I said, turning.

The room was my private sanctuary at the beginning of the hall near the nurse's station. Lucky for Games, he could stand where he stood and talk to me while at the same time keeping an eye on the nurses. It wasn't even his day to work. He came to visit out of kindness, bringing some book I never mentioned to him though I did give the author's name to Rianna because she, too, wanted to fly. Of course, anyone with a brain knows how Games got wind of my words. Young people talk. They exchange information. They cross paths with each other, as if by chance. They drive each other places and hike for fun. They play trivial pursuits because one of them loves it. They sleep together when it's not even night. It's all in my report, though I myself remember very few such adventures. Anyway, it was good of him to bring that book.

What's that you've got? I asked.

Games stepped further into my room. I had a chess game set up on the table, just in case. He showed me the book, eyeing the kingdom.

Ah, Antoine, I said.

It was a book by my late older brother. He wrote others, I think. One about a little prince. Didn't ever get the chance to read my brother's work when I was living: meditations on relationships and meaning, and the fucking future of life and war. I am sorry, Andrea, for cursing. It wasn't my fault. Just being reminiscent of myself on earth. Overcome with emotion, I suppose. Problem is, I won't get the chance to read the book now, either. *Flight to Arras.* Did I say brother? I mean the spirit of. So be it.

The Games kid reminded me of myself when younger,

without the dark nights or the vinegar I put into days. It was something about him, something buried inches under the surface that needed to get out and breathe. That's the part that's the same as me. Every time he entered my room, he stood there, hopeful.

I remember that first day. I was sitting in my chair, looking out the window, when he walked in with Queen Andrea. They thought it was the television I was watching. Never was the television. It was the time slipping by – December, January, February – and I was measuring my choices, my slowness at learning things.

Then just that other day, waiting for a change. Games came, as I said, carrying a book. He showed it to me.

Ah, Antoine.

So, Mr. B, he said. You want a shave while I'm here?

No shade, please. Give me the sun.

A shave, he repeated, as if I hadn't heard him right the first time. I played on:

Shad's a good fish, too, I said. You ever eaten blue?

What's blue?

A fish where I grew up, I explained. You want directions?

To cook it?

To get there.

Get where?

Wherever it was when I was a kid, like you, I said.

Sure, he told me, coming close, putting his book down on the table with the chessboard. How about a shave first, though? I'll get you real close today.

Promises, promises, I said back, fingering the bishop, so Games might instead see I wanted to play. I'd been practicing that line for a month. I needed things to keep me awake in that colorless place.

It's why I'd taken up the mission to get Games and Rianna together before the two of them went their separate ways, away from the home. All people leave the Hit P home, which of course stands for *House in the Pines*. Home, I suppose, is redundant. Who in their right mind would ever stay?

The only one who won't leave'll be Andrea. I recall giving her hell about Jesus. I liked to give people a bit of hell. Not that I have a boatload of hell in me, a forkful if I'm lucky, but it's enough to keep people guessing. And I've got nothing against Jesus, either. I don't really know the man. Talking shit was my way to connect. Like playing chess. I was good at saying foolish things. Good at winning chess, as well.

You're leaving your queen unprotected, I told Games, midway through our match.

I don't know what I'm doing, he said.

You've got to think seven moves ahead. See yourself winning.

I don't care about winning.

It's that moment that sticks with me. I saw my opening. How could he not care? I thought. Winning is a matter of will, your will. It's a matter of wanting, really wanting something. It's about seeing a bigger, better person just up ahead, seven moves in the future, or maybe seven thousand, and saying to yourself, I'm going to get there. I'm not going to let anyone keep me from that person. Not going to succumb to something less. He's mine, if I can do it. Leading the charge, connecting with what's up ahead – that's winning. Or maybe it's more accurate to say "reconnecting," instead of "connecting." Because, as I'm discovering in this afterlife, I've been the entire universe from the beginning of time. Been and still am. It all.

Here's how I put it in my report: After death, I'm more than I ever imagined. Surprisingly close to everything. At least, that's the picture I'm getting here. It's strange here, and at the same time familiar. As time fades from consciousness, they say you grow accustomed to the universality. Of course, when you open your eyes again on the earth, that universal feeling fades. I suppose that's so you can get used to the world in time, your own time. On earth, you've got an allotment of time. It takes a while to get used to the colors and bird songs, to all the streets and cars. It takes a while to get used to being someone in the world, and to not be clueless. I was the most clueless of all.

Curtis. Pay attention Curtis. Give me an example.

A next apple?

Yes. That's what I said. A next apple. An Ex Ample. Example of the second law.

The...uh...uh...the...

Second law of thermodynamics, yes. An example, before we all die of boredom.

Which is the reason, I told Games, as I moved my bishop to put him in check. That I ran away and joined the army.

I'm confused, said Games.

You're about to lose. No wonder.

Maybe, but where'd it all come from?

I'd've rather he inquired about my legs. Entered the narrative and asked, "So, is that where it happened? Were you hurt in a bombing or some kind of military incident?" Not that I was going to tell him the truth, which was that I was always really only half a man, but still I wanted him to question my reality. He never had shown much interest in my legs, however.

I mean, why'd you want to run to the army?

Different weapons to help me win, I suppose. I fought in places no one's heard of. I held a woman's hand who died. I killed a man rather than know him. To kill a man. Or know him. Which sounds better to you?

Games nodded, as if the answer was obvious. Just then that book he'd brought me fell from the table to the floor. Must've been it was sitting on the edge. Fell and landed, table to floor. The book. Antoine. The brotherhood of humanity. We stared at it for a while. Then, Games picked it up. Put it back, securely on my table, next to the board, near the king. Check and mate.

That's the last thing I remember about Games. Chess pieces scattered about. A book on the table. He was a good person, like a son to me. I never had a child of my own. No wife. No lasting parents. Only one true friend in my slipping memory. That sister I spoke of, never did swim back. And my brother was dead, like a closed book on the table next to the pawns and the rook.

But everyone dies. Everyone dies, don't they, even if they do write books that fall to the floor. And now. Now nobody is left. Not Games. Not Rianna. Not Queen Andrea. Not even much me. I wonder, if I was anyone, really.

~

One thing offers some proof of me. It was sometime, maybe…
Well, I don't exactly know when. But here's the gist:

It happened very near to where I am, I'm sure of that. Was
the night I visited my friend, the friend who I hadn't seen for
years. Only a few people have names I remember. Jesse
Games has a name. And Rianna Olivet, she has a name. And
Andrea, the queen — a name and title. Antoine, a first name,
at least. But pawns like me don't have a name to use on
themselves. My friend, though more like a king, has no name,
either. Not at this moment of my telling.

When I arrived at his house, I stood briefly at the door
before knocking. I heard protests inside, not inside the house
but inside me. I knocked anyway and soon the door opened.
My friend looked me in the eye and said he'd been expecting
my visit. Was happy to see I was walking again. I hadn't
noticed. He invited me in for a drink. I was never much for
beer or wine. Tea is what he offered.

Darjeeling? Oolong? Keemun?

Whatever you're having, I said.

He poured the hot water over the leaves, and we watched
it steep.

Milk?

Thank you, I said, and he handed me the cup.

What brings you here on this cold March night? asked my
friend.

I thought you were expecting me?

It's true. Still, I wonder if you know why you're here.

Not really, I said. Does there have to be a reason?

Usually there is, said my friend.

Well, I was floating around, I told him.

Floating?

Walking in the cold. Was getting a bit numb. Then I saw
your lights. It's nice to be somewhere real and warm.

I'm glad you came, said my friend.

The stars, too, I went on. They're circling around. Maybe
they are the reason.

Why are stars a reason?

They urge and harass me.

That must be hard on you, said my friend.

I looked across the room to think. Sometimes it was hard, I

thought. The night is seldom easy. Especially when –

There's no moon, I said.

Not yet, agreed my friend.

Thing is, I began, with some hesitation, I've been feeling a bit disappointed in myself.

Sure, sure.

What do you mean, sure, sure?

I mean, How so? asked my friend.

How could I explain my disappointment? I didn't want to relive it by telling. I just wanted to forget. When it comes to making progress in your life, you've got to start off new, you can't rehash forever. Then my friend put a hand on my shoulder, which I took to mean affection.

You've always been far too sensitive, he said.

It surprised me to hear what I took to be praise. I, myself, would've said *insensitive*.

Remember when you killed Egrett?

Who? I asked.

The man you killed, Egrett.

His name was Egret? I asked.

Not Egret, Egrett, said my friend. With two t's.

Why would his name have been Egrett?

Everyone's got a name. His was Egrett. He was like a bird only different. He had a wife and three children.

Well, all I remember's the small flat nose on his face, I said. That, and the short black hair, and the loud glint in both his eyes. We stood alone near the sandbags, debris scattered on the ground, broken glass, black and white night – I remember that, too. Plus, being fucking afraid but not knowing it.

You remember a lot, said my friend. The stories you can tell…

It was dark that night, I continued. Like now. Stars were out, like now. Planes overhead.

Not like now, said my friend.

No, but like halos, I said. They flew behind me, wings on my back as if I were an angel. How about that imagery?

There's a romance to war, but there's no bit of love, said my friend.

I never even wanted to be there, down on the ground, I told him. I wanted to be up, to fly like my brother. Not to kill anyone, but to fly.

You've never told me about your brother.

I never knew he existed till now, I said. Someone brought me one of his books.

Ah, a writer.

I guess so, I said.

So, what made you shoot the man with the short black hair? asked my friend.

I wasn't looking at him when I shot, I said.

So, it was easy.

I'd never say easy. I was trying to win.

Did you win?

I didn't want to be afraid. I wanted to live.

Living is essential to life, said my friend. Are you afraid now?

Not now. No. There's no conflict now, no chaos.

It's a moment of truth, then. Things are coming together for you now.

Truth, I said, feeling skeptical. I don't... It's not...

There was silence in the room. I don't... It's not... Far as the ear could hear. I don't... It's not... No way I could finish those sentences. So, I sipped my tea and felt the shock of my friend's presence. Such things as I should have known, yet I was still so unaware. There was a wintry mix of darkness and stars at his window. There were only two swallows of tea remaining in my cup, two birds.

And as I sat in his chair, I saw others, not an audience but a stream of curiously engaged people, come through his door and walk right past me. They were dressed in simple clothes, women carrying children, children carrying dolls, men in coats and hats, some among them with gloves and scarves. They were not there for me. They were there for my friend, it seemed. They were his community, his affirmation of life, not mine, and they all disappeared into his kitchen where the smell of something cooking made my mouth water, my stomach burn, and my heart ache even more.

What food is that? I asked.

It's dinner. You are staying, aren't you?

I don't know, I said. It smells like lamb.

I can't imagine we're having lamb. Though it does smell

like lamb, doesn't it?

It does, I said. Why can't you imagine it?

My wife's a vegetarian, said my friend. I am, too. We have a baby lamb in the field out back. Well, three of them. I can't stand the thought of killing. Can you?

Killing, dying, death: It all lives on this earth, doesn't it?

Ironic choice of words, said my friend. But I agree with you, killing does live. Mostly we kill and we don't know it. I wonder, were we more free to decide, would we oppose all killing?

But your wife, I began. She wouldn't've killed the lamb for my benefit, just because I...

No, no. I'm sure not, he assured me. It must be the spices. She's become very fond of the new spices since we moved here. Would you like to go in with the others?

Not yet, I said. I'd like to tell you something first.

Of course.

I had this dream the other night. About him.

About Egrett?

How did you know? I asked.

Well, we were just talking about him, weren't we?

Maybe so.

Are you sure it was the other night? asked my friend.

Not really. It could've been earlier this night. Could be I'm dreaming it now.

Could be, said my friend. Every day brings surprises. Why, it was a rainy day in fact that brought my family here, where we've got our small farm out back. It's everything we've ever dreamed of. And the stars of tonight have brought you and me together. This, too, is amazing.

Now you're confusing me, I said.

I should be quiet then, so you can be clear.

My friend and I sat face-to-face in his room. There were windows at my back and at his, a door at my back and a door at his. We were close in age, a similar height. Much ran parallel, but nothing quite the same. The warmth of some unseen fire comforted us. How many times had I been in his house and not known it? How many times had I tried to explain things to him? I felt ashamed I'd never listened much to him before. I felt ashamed I'd never invited him to my own room, not once.

So – your dream, as you call it, said my friend.

Yes, I began. It was of the war. The pictures don't leave me. It's pictures of hands tightening around the necks of birds and strangers. It's pictures of me plunging into an abyss. It's pictures of statues and monuments and flags and falling. It's images of grandeur in man: purple hearts, valiant efforts, giving one's life, taking others. There is blood, there are bombs, sometimes children without legs. I see the faces of the children mostly, hungry mostly, suffering young people and no one to care about their needs and interests.

Don't their parents care?

It does little good, their care. It's severe economic and physical hardships brought on by the governing elite. Sometimes skies are blind with rage, and fields are dead, with nowhere to go. There is only selfishness leading the way.

Selfishness? said my friend, obviously wanting me to say more. I couldn't explain the feeling to him.

I was following orders, I said. It was a reconnaissance mission into the night to find out what the enemy was doing. It was an absurd, likely suicidal mission, but who was I to object? As I walked, I had to think something. So, I thought about winning. There were so many times I played chess back home in my room, and cards on my bed. I always came out ahead in the end. I thought about my shit-ass home and coming out ahead. And I thought how justified this war, that there was nothing wrong with this war. I thought that I had the truest point of view, the one that was infallible. God – as much of the deity as I could conjure – was certainly on my side, and if only I could convince the enemy of the rightness of my way, there would be no need to call them enemy. If they simply would agree with me, we could, in fact, get along. We could succeed together.

Sounds a bit naïve, said my friend. And somewhat inconceivable to be sneaking around on your own at night. Are you sure you weren't looking for a way out?

I ignored this and went on:

Egrett, I suppose, was given the same orders as I. And as he approached, he too must have thought the same as I: how right he was in his point of view and how wrongheaded were all of us, his enemies. I, of course, did not see him on his way toward me, did not imagine it, either. I moved trying not to think about what might go wrong. And then, there he was, right in front of me, out of the blackness, like a beast.

A beast?

We met halfway on the empty street, near the pile of sandbags. The wild, black-haired bird and I. A starling, I thought. A raven or a crow. Thirty feet apart. Starlings were always a favorite bird of mine, you know. Crows are common, but I like them, too.

Crows will eat meat, said my friend. They also like fruit.

I didn't know, I said.

Egrets, of course, eat minnows and tiny shrimp of the salt marsh. Not your Egrett, but the egrets with one *t*. Where I live now, there are occasional egrets.

How did we get onto the diets of birds? I asked.

I'm sorry, said my friend. You were saying.

A sudden wind came upon me. Not much, but enough that I was blown off balance and my mind teetered on the edge. Dogs howled in the distance, and a full moon flooded the sky with light.

Where did the moon come from? asked my friend.

I don't really know. But it was there.

Hmm, hummed my friend. And I continued:

Egrett, if that was his name, looked at me. His eyes were ripe with hatred. That's what I saw. Ripeness. Ripness. They were ready to rip into me. We were enemies and I stepped back, creating more distance. My opponent held his place. Does that mean I was less of a man? The truth is, we were much alike. I mean, we were both loyal soldiers. We risked our lives and sacrificed comfort. We each had two hands, a heart, and parents. What a pity we spoke different languages. What a pity this war had been declared that filled the air with so much demand for recognition, because that demand alone was enough to asphyxiate us all. How impossible it is to breathe in war. What a misguided way to change the world, by fighting.

Fighting, said my friend, is often an unhealthy breath to take, or to let out.

Yes, I agreed. It's just that each person in battle has his

own point of view, which he equates with his very being. And he wishes to defend this. There's no time to think or soften. It's all rock-solid stress. No calm moment comes when you can offer something of yourself or accept it from the other. There's no negotiation. That's where I stood.

Could I get out of my contract to kill, and walk on? Or must I act decisively? I had a cause to defend. It was not fraternity. It was not reconciliation. The cause was a grand one of honor and country and right versus wrong. The reason I fought was for a better world. Truly, I loved the world so much. I'm sure I did. I would've done anything for it. No one else could have loved the world any more than I. The clouds and birds, all moving things, were particulars of my love, even if I never much said it. The busy streets, the changing colors, and people every so often who didn't disturb my equilibrium. Sometimes things were actually good for me. Did I not try and smile at strangers I saw? Did I not like music and stories, sweet potatoes and beef?

I'm not saying I'm perfect, I told my friend. I'm not saying I'm the only one who loved the world. I'm just saying I am able to love. I have it in me, that's what I'm saying. I enjoyed joking around and watching movies at night. I was fond of a good thunderstorm and ball games on the weekends out by the old school where the trees cheered in the wind like a crowd going wild. And how amazing it was to watch a woman, whispery blond hair, stooped in the dirt, a stick in her right hand, as she drew on the ground, meaningful marks, speaking to someone, anyone, it didn't really matter – but if that someone were me, just once, just me in her voice for once – oh, how full of hope the world would be.

Same thing now as it was then. Plies of time layered my mind: imaginations, pictures, and peaceable days. How greatly I've always wanted friendship and peace. That on that night, when I came back to my senses, I was distressed to see where I stood. Because I stood in such chaotic dark, with my enemy in front, saying something, muttering it really. I didn't understand him. What are you doing? You are not...me you're not...I'm. It frightened and confused me. Who the fuck are you? What fucking language are you speaking?

The moon was trapped behind a cloud. So be it. And he

stepped with me as I tried to back away. He stepped at me, his words charging, changing, ringing, lies. Planes flew overhead like haloes, cries. Wings at my back, I couldn't even fly. The distant howl of dogs – their barks. Go back, go back.

He drew closer, kept moving toward me, gesturing, trying to reach out, reach what? Go back, you fucking insane person. You crazy vulture. Don't come near me, I wanted to say. But this was his land. This was his home. This was his street. This was his move, his shining life. What could it ever be that would unite us? I saw him reaching. Out. Reaching. I've been... I've... Where was his gun? What could be a more gentle voice than an open hand with no weapon, no fear? My own gun was raised against it all.

Been expecting you, he said.

And so I shot.

The sound of one rifle and a volley of gunshots returning from the distance. I felt my body for life. I felt the thought of my own life leaving, me bleeding to death halfway on the street and the last look of my eyes, my last smile somewhere behind me, fading. I didn't want to leave the earth. And if I didn't want to leave, what did I want? Why was I there to begin with? I wondered.

Wasn't it to see the shared image of all humankind? said my friend.

What?

I said, Wasn't it –

The moon came out, I interrupted. But I couldn't see straight. I was alive, for sure. Not so, the other. What right had I to kill someone? I felt a great numbness throughout my body. My legs couldn't hold me up any longer. I fell at his side. It was a terrible nightmare just beginning.

You tried to mend the wound, said my friend. You wrapped his chest.

I did. How sad it was. How pathetic. His blood poured all over the ground as if he were a fountain. I knew then that I could do evil.

You were only twenty-eight at the time.

Twenty-three, I said.

Twenty-three, said my friend. Don't judge yourself so harshly. His face frightened you. You were outside your element.

It was a mistake, I said. But I was weak.

Don't be so hard, said my friend. It's just as true that you knew at that moment that you could *not* be evil, that you in fact were a human being for the first time, remembering the sacredness of life.

I was a hypocrite.

You took a step forward. You went toward the man.

I don't see it like that. I went backward. I began to crumble. I didn't think or care about any life but my own.

That's war, my friend. You felt the imbalance of the situation.

If by imbalance you mean that I was alive and he was dead – that I knew.

Try to look for the peace in your actions, not the war any longer.

I killed a man, I reminded him, as if he didn't already know. I don't find much comfort in that. I find only weakness.

My friend nodded, as if there was nothing more to say. Then there was:

What if I told you that Egrett was moved by the possibility he saw in you? What if I told you that you never in fact killed the man? That he lived on and lives on still.

I'd say you were making it up to ease me, I said.

And does it?

I don't know. I'd like to think I'm different now. I'd like to think I would act now more out of peace, as you said. I'd like to think…

I stopped in the middle of my thought. I'd said enough. I was quiet and looked around. Light prodded my mind. Something through the window, bright and flickery – maybe stars, but they were so far away. And beside me, on the table, were empty homes from the sea, bits of oysters and fully formed whelks and snails. I hadn't noticed them till now.

Have these always been here? I asked.

What do you mean, always?

And from the kitchen I could smell the onions and the lamb. It must be lamb, I thought. I could smell the thyme and the oregano. The smells pleased me, even if it wasn't meat. I didn't need meat. I could do without meat. I could make better choices. I could win with my heart. And people kept coming in the front door, passing through, carrying things, and heading to some unseen table in the other room.

Who are all these people? I asked.

I don't know yet, said my friend. I'm becoming interested, though. Aren't you?

It's a bit overwhelming, I said. I'm usually very private.

My wife loves to cook for others. She's always opening the doors, trying to help. She's got these projects, you see. Wants to make the world a closer place.

You're married? I said.

I'm sure I told you, said my friend. With three children.

Three, I nodded, familiar with the number. How old are you anyway? You don't look very old. And how old am I, I wonder?

That depends, said my friend.

I nodded once more, in agreement.

It's time for dinner now, if you'd like.

I would like it, I said. I'm hungry.

And my friend whistled like a robin. And a coo came back, like a dove. Around the corner peeked his daughter. Her face was young. Her body small and spiraling out, blossoming more each minute. Maybe twelve, I imagined. Thirteen.

Papa, she called. She ran to him, kissing his cheek. Where've you been?

Not far, said her father. Where are your brothers?

They're at the table. Being supper annoying.

Don't you mean *super*?

Do you want to know what happened in school? asked the girl.

Yes, said her father.

We're learning all about the moon. I'm going to carve one out of wood.

Hardwood?

Soft, she said. It's easier. There are seas on the moon, but they don't have any water. There are lots of shells, though, and I found them all because the moon is a magnet to the oceans on earth.

The moon is a magnet. You said that in an interesting way. I'll have to think more on it.

Thanks, said the girl. There're so many things I like. I can't wait to learn. Are you coming, too? This, the girl said to me, smiling.

Yes, I said.

Do you want one? she asked me.

What do you mean?

You can have any one you want.

I'm confused.

Take a shell, if you want, said her father to me.

Thank you, Daisy, I will.

That's a funny name, she said. I like it.

Well, we all have names. You look like a Daisy.

Daisy left the room and my friend got up. He gestured for me to follow. I did, but slow.

Are you and I, by any chance, dead? I asked, as I moved his way.

We might be, he said.

And all the people who've come through the door?

They keep coming, said my friend. I can't close it. It would be cruel if I did. I don't want to be cruel anymore. Once I was cruel, at least not very understanding of differences. My eyes may have shot a bit of hatred. I'm sure I didn't mean it. When I was young, I was my own thoughts, only. I was not a particularly good person. I drank a lot. I hit people with words. I hit a young man with my car. I'm ashamed of who I once was. You don't know how terrible I feel about it. I call that time regretful. It wasn't who I am.

No, I agreed.

Only that which gives meaning to life also gives meaning to death, said my friend. I read that somewhere.

What gives meaning? I asked.

Why, love, of course, said my friend.

It's always love, isn't it? I said. Couldn't there be something else?

What else is there?

Something more practical. Something useful.

I suppose meaning could be a good pair of shoes, said my friend.

Shoes wear out, I said. Especially when you're able to walk.

That's true. I'm not sure what else to tell you.

It feels there's nothing left of me on earth, I said, afraid.

Does that bother you?

Yes. I always knew I'd die someday. It's just I never wanted to leave without a trace.

The moon is out again, said my friend.

I'd rather see the sun, I told him, as I picked a shell from the beach-like table. A moon snail, a periwinkle, a whelk, whatever. It was a good feeling in my hand as I walked from one room, into the next.

And there was the table laden with food. It was surrounded by people unfamiliar to me, but who I would certainly get to know. Some of them were listening, others quietly watching, and all of them were waiting for us, it seemed. Let's get in there. Let's get going. Let's move on, I wanted to say. It was the start of something new. It was a beginning for me of who on earth I truly am.

FOUR

One by one, Rianna Olivet picked shells from the window ledge and fiddled with them. Scallop, moon snail, razor clam, mussel. She rubbed the smooth pieces and traced the spirals with her fingertips. She took a pure white shell – half a clam – moving her hand along its surface, pausing her touch, resting the piece in her palm, and finally leaning in as if listening. It seemed she wanted to penetrate the hardness, to descend into a secret language embedded in the architecture of the shell. There were ridges to run with, edges to follow. There were chinks and chipped places from having been tossed about. There was a convex shape to cup in her palm. Light weight. Sweet form. A concave offering, too.

And say there was someone who looked from halfway across the room. He would've seen what Rianna was doing. Provided he was a good witness, he could also've described in details down to the sweet hairs on her arm what he saw. But what clue did Games, the witness, have of the thoughts going on inside the young woman? As much as he followed her obvious movements, so he hoped to find those elusive thoughts even more. There was undoubtedly some interior experience to Rianna as she caressed these former homes.

Imagination was an easy inroad. It was a tool Games was happy to use, and the imagination, as Games watched Ri, went like this: A sense, a scene. No, not a sense or a scene. Not a show, or an explosion of landscape, not a blast of light, but a path. A simple path to begin with.

Follow the path to a vibrant blue ocean, so vibrant it's jumping with fish and dolphins. And there, beside the blue, looking onto the beach, stands a house. There are many rooms in the house, which has only one story. The story inside is a girl named Rianna who walks through the house as if it's a museum. There are field flowers in the corners all wanting to be seen, a still life of sea birds, and many sculptures of people, heroes and heroines, old and worn, some with wounded hearts, others missing limbs. Rianna attends to them all, one by one. Farther along, decorating the walls, there are drawings and watercolors by children. This art brings a smile to Ri. It's exuberant, full of salt spray and joy. She breathes the art as if it's air. The colors sure are breathable here. The world has many surprises.

There are windows and doors, for example. One door flies open at the gentlest touch, which is how Rianna touches things so they open for her. Out she goes. It's a beautiful day. Ri stands on the shore, with gulls on the sand, with reams of seaweed, not to mention an inexhaustible supply of waves. Again and again, the waves run to her feet, crashing the party, offering foam and cold water. Yes, a shell now and then that rolls into view. Is that a nautilus, a gleaming nautilus? Who knew this beach had nautili? And it's only a hint of what Games saw in Rianna, as she held the shell in her palm. He wondered if it was an accurate picture. *A penny for your thoughts. A nickel for your feelings, if you look my way.*

Rianna gently returned the clamshell, not quite a mother-of-pearl nautilus, to the ledge, aligning it with the other shells and adjusting them, one by one, so they each had a view out the window, as if a good line of sight to the earth was what the shells most wanted. Then she looked up to face the morning.

It was an act of light and a large cast of buildings. There were scattered spring trees and that full western moon near the horizon. Rianna studied the moon as it fell from the sky, taking in its roundness and its handful of seas. Sea of Tranquility, of Showers, Serenity. She could almost hold those seas, or the whole of the moon like a shell in her hand.

Rianna contemplated the setting moon, sweet round form, and its last, hopeful overview of the city. The moon watched over the earth with a depth of feeling that made everything it looked upon an emotional experience. So long, you streets. So long, you rivers. You amazing spring blooms. You...you... The moon's face shone searchingly, as if looking for someone. Where was its someone in this entire world? Then the moon dipped regretful behind gables and trees to join the crusty earth again. How difficult it is to leave sometimes. A quarter, halfway down, two thirds, almost completely gone now. Rianna watched the descent, listening to the quiet finale of the moon.

And then, in the interest of a different story, the moon turned back, as though for an encore. Pushed from below, pulled from above, or powered by a will of its own, the moon rose again in the western sky. The crowd went wild. No, not that. The crown of the moon came first followed by the eyes. Eventually, the whole yellowish face was back in place, having opposed the natural course of things. Incremental in its return. Incredible, too. Certainly newsworthy. Or was it simply a ruse?

If only a trick, thought Rianna, it was far from simple, well beyond the scope of acceptable physics. And though Rianna herself was imagining this re-rise, it would be fair to say she didn't know she had it in her. She had plenty in her, including concern for others, including love for the moon, but she wasn't one for willy-nilly making things up. She preferred to see the returning moon as a remarkable and provable event, though likely she'd keep the re-rise to herself, saying nothing about it.

Not even to him? said the moon.

Is he looking at me? asked Ri, softly.

Sure is. Like you were topless or a brand new bike.

Me a bike. I wish. Should I turn?

Not yet. Stay with me a bit longer.

Well, said Ri to the moon. As for saying nothing about this, Games doesn't count.

Why doesn't he count?

He'll believe anything I say. I'm so comfortable with him.

I can see, said the moon, who once again, took to setting in the west.

The round face peered from low in the sky. Its light fell softly across Rianna's small city, grazing on the streets, glancing off the asphalt and rooftops, gleaming through the window, into her eyes.

I like the moon, Rianna said aloud.

Games looked at her from the bed in the middle of the small room. Ri sat fully clothed by the window. He liked what he saw.

Who wouldn't? said Ri.

Games couldn't think of many who would not like the moon, if that's what she meant.

Starwatchers, he suggested. Sunfish, sunflowers, moonhaters. And day lilies. Day lilies don't care for the moon, but daisies love it.

Why daisies? said Ri, finally turning his way.

I know a Daisy who likes the moon.

Daisy's got a good head on her shoulders, Ri told him. Moodhaters are lunatics.

Games considered this mishearing, missaying of moon. Moods could be difficult, he agreed. And, yes, to hate them was loony and pointless, as Ri suggested. Hating your mood was as helpful as hating the rain when you're hiking or the calm when you want to sail. Every mood, as each weather, has its purpose in the grand scheme of things.

Moonhaters, I mean, corrected Ri.

For Games, however, nothing needed correcting. His mood was good, and the moon proceeded to disappear from view, as was in its nature. Mostly, there was this beautiful person at the window before him, backed by early light. He'd been enjoying the show: Shoreline Rianna with shells. Morning Rianna with moon. Rianna Seanna Diana.

I'm going to call you Diana, said Games

Sorry, wrong number.

What do you mean: Sorry, wrong number?

What do *you* mean, calling me Diana?

~

The sun rose in the east. The moon set in the west. Sometimes there's a purposeful composition to life. What purpose exactly, Games didn't know. He did know, however, that everything was working well. The sky was a balance. The room was balanced, too. He sat happy in the east. Rianna looked good in the west. Sometimes things are close to perfect, like a line of shells on the windowsill or the lay of the world in morning light.

I remember an image my father once read, said Rianna.

He could read images?

It was a picture from Dante he liked.

You mean, Dore? asked Games, thinking of the pen and ink illustrations he'd once seen.

Dore, the little witch?

He wasn't a witch, said Games. He was an illustrator.

Well, I'm talking about Dante, said Ri. An image from the *Divine Comedy*. It was of the moon setting one side of the earth and the sun rising the other. Things were equal and ordered.

All I know of Dante is that story of the guy and the girl who got caught having sex and were killed by the girl's husband. They were in love with each other, and both went to hell.

Seems unfair, said Rio.

There can be no true love in this world, said Games.

Do you really believe that?

No. Do you?

It's sort of depressing, said Ri.

Love is a many wearying thing, said Games.

I don't know about that.

Me neither.

Then why'd you say it? asked Ri.

Had to see if you would deny it. And you did.

You set me up. Everything for you is one big manipulation.

Rianna looked out the window, and whatever it was she saw no longer held her in place but seemed now to make her restless. She looked back to Games.

I should probably go.

Games swung from the bed and moved her way from across the room.

What does probably mean?

He stood next to Rianna. Shells on the windowsill. Nothing to do. Nothing to move. Light seeping in. Lift a hand and steer your future. But Games didn't reach out.

There's no problem, if that's what you think, said Ri.

I'm sorry about setting you up. Didn't mean to scare you off.

So now you apologize, when things aren't going your way.

It's my manipulative nature, teased Games.

I like it, said Rio. It's just. I told you. I've got so much stuff to do.

By stuff I thought you meant spending the day with me.

You said you had to work today, said Rianna.

Work. Right. Yeah. I…

Games had two jobs – Jakes and the nursing home. He had a pile of dirty clothes in the closet and a half-finished book on the floor by the bed. There was plenty of time in each day, and plenty more at night. Sometimes it was difficult keeping everything balanced, but not now. Now things were easy.

There's this lady, began Ri. Gertrude. She lives on the ground floor of my apartment house. Her son asked me to check on her.

Why?

He's not very… Well, he's… He lives far… I. I try to go almost every day. Been doing it a month. He lives in the city and was so relieved. He gave me a thousand dollars up front. He doesn't seem interested.

Interested in…

His mother.

Maybe there's a reason, said Games.

I'm not interested in his reasons.

You sound like Andrea.

Rianna didn't like being told that she sounded like someone else, and Games was angry with himself for having said it.

Sorry.

Why are you sorry? Once she tried to kiss my mouth. She doesn't eat. I leave food for her. Soup. Whatever. The bowl's always cold and full when I return.

I didn't know, said Games.

Why should you, said Ri. So, it's okay?

Of course, said Games. I'm just…

Rianna looked at just him and considered changing her mind. Go slow, don't justify. There was plenty of time, as was suggested before. Two, three hours. How long until…

When do you leave Hit-P? Games's question interrupted the thought.

What's hit pee? asked Rio.

House in the Pines.

Oh, she said. The end of the month.

I was kicking it around, said Games.

Kicking what?

You think I should finish school? he asked.

Elementary?

I was thinking more like college.

Yes, said Rio, decidedly.

I think I'll leave, too, said Games.

I'm going now. You want to walk with me?

Well, sure. But I meant: I think I'll leave Hit-P.

It must've come as no surprise to Rianna that Games would leave the nursing home, because she didn't ask why.

I'll miss the people, she said, as she put on her coat. Her skin deep within, completely unprovocative now. The wrap. Unsexing his thoughts. Breasts sapped of light, stored for the day. And her core even further away. To cover the body and go. To see no soul was a shame, Games thought. He didn't want to be shallow, insensitive, thoughtless – fill in the blank. He put on pants and a wrinkled shirt and then another shirt, ironed and blue like a cloudless sky, and the two of them walked to the door. Knob. Open. Closed.

Teaching is good, said Games. I wonder what people would rather do – teach or take care of other's ills.

What people do you mean? asked Rio. I'd rather teach. Caring's good also.

They headed down the inside stairs. Outside, the April sun cut low across the eastern edge of the apartment house. It blossomed at the corner of the building, a first spring flower, bright and warm.

I like the sun, said Games. Who wouldn't?

I guess we're just so different, said Rio. Me and my moon. You and your sun.

She went her way and Games followed. She was a fast walker but he kept up. The morning welcomed early risers. The streets revved with songs of resolute cars and rippled with scores of light. The world was an orchestra. Games listened to the music.

Do you go in today? asked Rio.

No.

I'm just saying…

What? thought Games, as Rianna paused. What're you saying?

You could come by later and we could both go to Trudy.

Trudy?

I just told you about her.

The woman who kissed you.

Who tried, said Rianna.

Are you afraid of her?

What's to be afraid of?

I don't know, said Games. A weird old woman with a passion for kissing and groping.

A lonely old woman, said Ri. No groping. You're making fun.

You must be someone she likes if she wanted to kiss you like that.

She thought I was someone else.

But you're not. You're you.

You thought I was Andrea.

And I apologized for that.

Oh. That's why you apologized.

Is there something else I should know about? asked Games.

There's always something, said Ri.

Games waited for it.

I think she's going to die, Rianna told him.

This isn't what he expected to hear.

Because she's not eating? he asked.

Because her heart is broken.

I'm sorry, said Games. And he was. Suddenly he was sorry about other things, too. He felt bad not so much for things he'd said, but for people in the world whose lives were lost. Mothers in the world. Sons who weren't very… Women sitting all day alone. Children who had no reason to care, no one to care for them. People who had no food or warmth or… His mood was slipping, he didn't know why. Maybe he was being too sensitive.

You should check out her book, said Ri.

What book?

She had it on her kitchen table when I first showed up.

What is it?

She wanted to read it to me, recalled Rianna. But I was in a rush.

Then later she did? asked Games.

I don't know what she did. She never told me about her work or anything. She grew up poor, but she has thousands of shells. So, I guess she's rich in calcium. She always talks about freedom.

And she shell be released, said Games.

Her apartment. It's sad. It's empty except a few things from nature and this piece of a mirror that someone…that she…that… She treasures that mirror. This scrap of a thing.

And now I can say that I know everything there is to know about this book of hers, said Games, sarcastically.

Don't be mean. It's a couple hundred pages. I don't think she'll hold on much longer.

To the book?

It's weird, said Rio. Trudy reads it to me while I brush her hair.

What's weird about that?

She doesn't move all day, I don't think. Just sits at her kitchen table. It's the only place I ever see her. It's got a title, too.

Her table does?

The book, said Ri.

What's the title? asked Games.

From, on the first page.

Smart place for a title.

But the pages are just scribbles.

Doodles?

Not really pictures, said Rio. Looks like patterns on water. Skittering lines on the river.

Sounds a bit crazy, said Games.

Sometimes there's a word, like *beautiful* or *burn* that pops out on the page. Then a while later it's *beggar* or *bed, beach* or *boy*, and at the very end, the last word – *blooms*.

She only likes *b* words, said Games.

I like blooms, too, said Rio. All kinds of flowers.

Games knew this about Rianna. He was curious about the book.

Anyway, I thought you'd be interested. You're good with people, no matter what all the experts say.

What's that supposed to mean?

It means come over after work today. I want you to meet Trudy.

No problem, said Games.

It means I think you give people courage, said Ri.

People usually want something else, said Games.

I've heard you've given people books, said Rio.

They usually want something different.

What do they usually want?

Money mostly. I've got millions from my robbery days.

I used to have money, said Rio. Now I have debt.

Is that what you want, then? asked Games.

Debt?

No, money?

Money's okay, said Rianna. But what I really want—

She went blank after want, so Games filled in.

The moon?

The moon's okay, but I really want to be with younger people. It's so much age around me always.

The light fell increasingly from the sky. Was it curiosity about the earth that made the sunlight pause upon the planet? Or was the earth just a thing in the way, like a boulder in the road?

Am I too old? teased Games.

Yes. That's just what I was thinking.

What were you really thinking?

Ri took a moment. Held it inside. Brought it back slowly, with words.

You know, she said, hesitantly. I want to be with creativity and health. Not so much with old age and sickness. Does that sound terrible?

It sounds like you've made a choice for yourself.

Maybe I can do some good. As a teacher, said Ri.

What good is that? asked Games. He didn't like how his words came out, but the damage was done. The words had been recorded on air, defiling space and time.

Just then a truck blasted its horn at the two oblivious walkers as they headed blindly across the street.

Games and Rianna jumped back, startled. They stood on the edge and recovered from the scare.

Here's the perfect place and time. Games saw Ri's lips, imagined their sweet consent. I am unimpeded, short of breath. But instead of kissing her, he said:

When I was in seventh grade, I tried to look up my teacher's skirt. Mrs. Marsh.

You remember her name.

No. It wasn't Marsh. Something else. I liked her legs. They looked good to me.

And what good is that, said Ri. Portrait of a pervert as a young man.

Just normal boy stuff, don't you think?

The two started walking again.

You and your play boy days, said Rianna.

I kept it a secret.

You were ashamed.

I was private, said Games.

I think I want to teach high school, said Ri. Botany or biology or both.

All *b* words. You're just like Trudy.

Ri nodded, unoffended by the comparison.

I could see myself with younger kids, said Games. More than with produce.

You like children better than zucchini and apricots?

Apricots are okay, but I think children are better.

They reached Jakes, two hours before Games had to be at work. There were newspapers by the front door and a sign that said, *Closed for Easter Sunday.*

When's Easter? asked Rio.

Week from today.

I never understood why they call it Good Friday. Seems that Easter should be called good and the Friday before it, bad.

My mother liked Easter, said Games. She'd buy candy and we'd go for a drive. All I remember about her, sometimes, is a car.

You remember the candy.

Games could've remembered more. He preferred looking at Ri and prompting her to talk.

I'll walk with you farther, if you want. I've got plenty of time.

That's okay, said Rio. I want to run.

I can run, too, you know.

I know. But then I can't think.

I keep you from thinking.

You give me thoughts, said Ri. I just want to think on my own for a moment, if that makes sense.

April Sunday morning light. Light April morning Sunday. Games and Rianna stood near the entrance to the store, both not thinking much now. There was the good night behind them, and a full day in front. There was a table of spring flowers on the left for anyone to notice, and a cloudless blue sky on the right adorned by the sun. Nothing else for the moment to disturb the peace, not one car or bird to shatter the mood. And nowhere on earth was it more suitable for affection than here, where every possibility descended and there was nothing to lose.

I guess I'll go now, said Rianna, not quite sure what was the right thing to do, though she did have a lot of studying to get done, and, besides, the sun was very bright in her eyes.

So she left, just like that, without saying goodbye, which confused Games, but only for a moment, everyone being different. Rio then realized her mistake and stopped. She turned and smiled, waving.

Sorry, she called. I was just –

It's okay.

Don't be bothered by me. I'm… I… It's…

I'm not bothered at all, said Games, and he wasn't.

'Bye, she said.

See you.

Call me, said Rio. Then she said, No.

No?

I forgot.

What?

You're coming by this evening. We're going to see Trudy.

Six okay? asked Games.

Six. I'll be there.

And yes, she would. Why not? If it were up to Games, she would always be there, not always in place, but always somewhere on earth. If it were up to him, she would not be leaving now. If it were up to him, he would've said, "The hell with work," and they'd've gone to where there's a waterfall he knew about. And if not to the waterfall, at least to that bridge for pedestrians, the one with the gentle arc and the hand-carved face of a happy gnome. If it were up to Games, light would talk to him and tell him how to see into other people's hearts, to know what they wanted, to repair them when needed. If it were up to him, the earth would work out as a perfect home for everyone, or each person would work his own way here – a million and one heres, a million and one hows. But not everything was up to him – hardly anything, really. And that was okay. And not everything was perfect – hardly anything, really. That was okay, too, as long as Games kept his steady place in the world and his unwavering sense of confidence in life.

He stood to the side, by Jakes, with the Sunday papers and the flowers on the table, watching what Rianna did, where she was going, and how fast it all happened. He didn't need convincing. He demanded no answers. He liked the world and that she was in it, making her way like the moon away, like the moon coming back and who can say why, holding a moment, offering hope, like the sun rising up, like plenty of time: Everything in balance on the fulcrum earth.

APRIL

Trudy Lynn Burroughs

They entered my room as angels. There were blue white shells on the windowsill that I don't remember putting there. She was the angel who'd come to visit before – Gabriella, Michaella, Uriel. She'd always arrive gentle as a pear blossom falling to the ground, saying, Hey you, Ms. Trudy. It's me again. And then she'd say her name, which has slipped my mind, even though it made me so happy to hear at the time.

He, however, brought an entirely different mood. I'm not saying that he was somber. Rather that he tried to look closely into my heart to see what my heart was missing, which made me feel a bit invaded, though I know he only meant well what he did.

He didn't put them there, did he? The shells, that's what I'm asking. He was a strange looking angel, more grime than glow about him, as if he'd been working all day in the fields with the crops, though most likely it's because he was lower in rank, not up there with the big three – Gabriel, Michael, Oriole. Still, he did have very blue eyes, and that set him apart. The way the ocean is set apart from the highlands. The way bluebells pop at the edge of the woods.

The first angel, she was pretty as a spring flower. I liked her lots. She came because my boy asked her to come. I suppose he had a right, but I'd rather he'd just left well enough alone. She had her wings on straight, and I admired that about her, but she spent a lot of her time pushing soup and bread on me. I tried to kiss her once when I thought she was the day. It had been such an uplifting day, and I felt good inside, like I was at the ocean and the whole world was in front of me. I think my kiss alarmed her though. Not everyone wants to be kissed, even if their spirit is beautiful and free.

The girl angel, like I said, she gave me peace and comfort. I did wonder, however, if the newcomer, the man angel, had any sense of the ocean, or a sense of good days and bad, or a sense of humor even. At the very least, you've got to have a sense of humor in your bag. A sense of others is important, too. I've tried my best at that with limited success.

I wanted to test him, if I could. And because he seemed like a decent listener, I began with a story:

Once in the city there was a poor beggar woman. She held by the hand a scraggly child named... Well, it doesn't matter her name, does it? Every day the Prince would walk past with such a capital *P* to his name. It made him look out of sorts and definitely out of touch. He'd see the two unfortunates with their eyes open for offerings like outstretched palms. Day after day and month after month, it was always the woman, her clean pleading face, together with her same dirty, raggedy child. Then one morning in springtime, the Prince stopped to ask: Is that dirty, raggedy child yours? Well, sir, said the woman. You have your eyes half open. The dirt and rags are mine, but not the child. The dirt but not the child? Yes, sir. Are you mocking me? he asked. No, sir, said the woman with deference. Whose child is it then? asked the Prince. Well, you know how it is, said the woman. I know how what is? asked the Prince. At least, I assume you do, said the woman. Do what? asked the Prince. Know, said the woman. No, I don't, said the Prince. Hence, my asking. What do you mean, I know how it is? I mean, said the woman, that the earth is devoted to this child, no matter what she looks like. But a child cannot live on earth alone. Yes, yes, said the Prince, bored by these bleeding-heart words. I'm not inquiring about the earth, but about who is responsible for that girl. Well, said the woman, direct as could be, that would be us. Us, repeated the Prince, hissing the *s*, surprised by the word itself or perhaps surprised to be included with this woman inside the word. Yes, said the woman. I wouldn't want you to think that the responsibility falls entirely on you.

That was all there is to the story, which isn't as funny as I'd hoped. Maybe it is more in line with a parable. There are, I think, as many unrecognized parables in a day as there are fish in the sea. Of course, I'm sure my angelic listeners understood that the child was not the fruit of the Prince's loins. The point is, and I repeated this to my visitors. The point is, it's our duty to be concerned about others. Don't you agree? I asked. Yes, they both said, one from the left of me, the other from the right. And we all wondered in unison if the Prince had received the message.

~

I had a selfish purpose in telling that tale. I wanted to bring the newcomer out of his shell. Selfish, shell – I seem to be playing with words, but I'm not. I thought the story might arouse a sense of injustice in him, and he'd go about ranting against the wrongs of the world. And if not injustice, I thought it might at the very least amuse him, the way I'd told it. Yet he, to the best of my seeing, never even cracked a smile. I guess it was too serious a telling the way it came out. But still, what's the world without a good laugh now and then.

Of course, maybe I'd just told it wrong. Or maybe he didn't hear it right because of the shells on the windowsill that divided his attention. That young angel stood beside my chair at the table and his eyes kept wandering over to the shells on the sill, as though I'd put them there for him to obsess upon. And maybe I had, but it doesn't mean I wasn't also in the room, for crying out loud. Must've been hours, must've been days, he stood there looking. Shells, the window. The window, shells. The sun rose, the sun set. Again and again. Blooming spring was upon us. Bluebells popping somewhere. People starving. People dying. Day out the window. Night with stars.

Then all of a sudden, Easter morning. It was a few hours before sunrise. I never in my life spoke much about Christ, and I'm not going to start now, either. But I wanted to talk about something before the sun came up and everything was lost. I wanted him to look over at me. And by *him* I don't mean Christ, I mean the tall angel. I'm talking about my new friend. I wanted him to listen with that heart-searching self of his, as I felt at that moment how time and the earth were both slipping from me.

Yes, well… Those were his exact vague words to me.

What do you mean, Yes, well? I asked him.

He shrugged and said: Probably should've eaten the soup Rianna brought you. Which was rather rude, I thought. Then he said: Probably should've let your son take you back to the city. He said this as if he knew something about it, a glint to his eyes like the glint in the eyes of the very son he so flippantly mentioned.

I remained quiet. He let out a sigh to soften his ways.

I'm sorry, he said. That was wrong of me to say. Forgive me, please.

He was a real queer angel if ever there was one, and I accepted his apology.

Then, all at once, everything went still, almost effortless. And what I mean by that is, I remembered I was no longer alive on the earth, which is a strange thing to think. I remembered my death. I remembered how quietly it had happened. I remembered an assortment of living days, too. But mostly I knew that I didn't have to work to hold myself up any longer, or struggle through conversations, or wait for things that never would be. I was alone in my room, which was a room of feelings and whatever truth lay behind them. And my angel, he was alone with me. Me and him in my amorphous, muddled room. Likely the other nice angel, the girl, had gone for a drink. Or maybe she had other soon dead folks to attend to. I don't mean to sound irreverent, I'm only telling things as they are.

He, my blue-eyed, accompanying angel, then spoke inside my mind, or maybe it was to my soul, asking me things I don't know what. It sounded more like chirping from a bird, and it went on and on and it wasn't even morning yet. Clear cool Easter, before the sun had risen.

Calm down, singer, I said to the bird. Please God, give me peace and comfort, not a load of questions. I meant *God* merely in the exclamatory sense. At least give me strength to tell my truth my way.

And I waited, till finally there was an opening. My heart loosened and my thinking made room for such words even I was amazed I held inside:

I wish I could just vanish, I told him. Not take up any

more space.

Well, you can't, said my angel. Not yet. We've got to get somewhere first.

Where are we going?

I thought you'd tell me, he said.

And he was right. Angels usually are. He sat there, unable to fly off, trying to unshell me, treasure me, I don't mean *treasure* I mean *measure,* measure me more. And I don't know how long it was, but sometime later, when I looked again, neither of us was completely in the room any longer. He, in part, was a lingering ear, a listener, someone who wanted to be helpful. And I was bodiless on the bridge of Death, or, as I prefer saying, entering A Better Place.

Still, I want it known, I was fully aware. Something of me hung on in that room. For what? I don't know. Who wants to hang on to an empty home life? It was not a place I really wished to stay.

I used to think there was more to me. I used to think if someone'd just read my book, maybe they'd find something I'd missed along the way. It makes me sad to think I may've written my life in vain. Didn't Lincoln say something like that? Truth is, I suppose, that I'm not much of anything. I'm whoever I am, who I haven't quite mastered, but who, also, I don't mind. I keep to myself like a pain in the soul, like being holed up. I don't shout my name or look much in mirrors. I don't get out, either. Others invade me with their being.

I can't help thinking, though, that *out* is what I want of me. Not these acres of inwardness. There is something of the world in everyone, something more social even in me. Let me first go deep. Then I'll toss myself out of the sea, a gift. I'll sort myself out in air. I'll land on the shore, like in that book I read way back about shells, the one written by the aviator's wife, Anne, which wasn't really about shells but rather about who you've got to be and how, and not being trapped, a blue empty bivalve on the window ledge always, but seeing yourself as an important part of the world. Someone. With others. Somehow. Kissing and caressing the muscular day.

~

Way back – that's what I'm talking about now. There wasn't much community in me when I was younger, mostly private chaos and discontent, like that time I was twelve and our house went up in flames. Of course that wasn't just about me, but I'm trying to give a picture. I stood alone by the trees, watching. The fire leapt from room to room. It smoked like a carnival worker and laughed like a demon. It spat on the floor and destroyed all structure. I lived that summer in a flimsy tent. Mama and Papa were there, I'm guessing, and my little sister June. Hammers clapped, saws buzzed, and the tent flap flip-flapped. Flip flap. Flip flap. All through the windy nights. I woke each morning, opening my eyes to what was never made right. A teen magazine tucked in my sleeping bag, and *Lord of the Rings* or some such book pulling me elsewhere. I listened for quiet, looked to the sky, but there was no escape. Life brought me to tears, and it wasn't even suffering for me, nothing terrible like war, it wasn't poverty or sickness, nothing tragic, just feeling wrong where I was. I had a terrible longing for other places, other things, some different life. An obsession, really. Mostly, it was my own shortsightedness that was the problem. Which is ironic, because I had a strong imagination.

I always knew I had one. Teachers told me. Papa said. Growing up, I knew my imagination was powerful as a knot on the floor that turns into an ocean. And then the ocean into the night sky with singing stars. Skipping school with Jilly and Birk, I knew. Making up stories, love songs. Making up towns and countries with winged creatures like Bloons and Trobbles and The Lost Fricassees. Then, later in the day, going to the quarry with Ari, with Wags, I knew. Making out, I knew. Drinking rum and coke, touching swollen cocks. That's the rub. Lying naked with Nick. Taking busses, hopping trains just to have my own private room, I knew. A room in which to read something I carried in my pack. The daylight slipping fast. The bleating rhythm of the tracks.

Oh fucking stupid world sometimes. Amazing created world, too. I ran without stopping, and the earth spun on. I only halfway knew the place. There had to be another half, a different experience waiting just ahead. I could feel the possibility of it, like looking to the horizon, out over the ocean.

I could feel the waves of what's more. What is it? What? There at the edge. Always the edge. Teetering, tottering. Either I'd sink or swim – that was the feeling, my constant companion. What would you do in such a situation?

Me? my angel asks, startled out of his passive listening.

No. I'm talking to the air. Of course you, writer boy. Get with the program. Your words are to balance me. Do your job.

He holds out his hands, like a scale.

Who says I'm writing this down? he tells me.

Well, somewhere it's written. How else is anything known?

I never thought of it like that, he says. So, why don't you keep going and I'll stay alert.

Whatever. Where was I?

At the edge, says my angel. About to swim, to jump in.

Right. Well, nothing really changed. Always the edge, never what's different. Like later, serving eggs and bacon with a bit of extra leg for good tips. I was still off-kilter. Living on my own. Scraping by. Providence. New Bedford. Hartford. Troy. Every place had a name. Had a boss named Block once who pressed me hard, his cock in his hand, till I gave him my mouth. Sometimes, I'd lean in so men would see my boobs. Other times, I'd find a moment to look at the clouds through the dirty bathroom window. Mostly, I'd walk across the parking lot like I was someone else, early nights, the neons blinking blue blinking green blinking red, making rainbows on the asphalt.

Then I'd go left down Water Street, thinking far off, imagining better places, when all of a sudden I'd see some guy who'd change my mind about my inglorious situation. The look of his wavy hair or his unshaven face in the sun – that's all it would take to change my mind. Or, I'd be standing in Loki's Bar and whenever a guy, say, with long black hair, would pass within inches I'd feel the heat of his presence and would wonder if he, too, felt mine. So, maybe he'd sit. Then lean my way. He'd put his hand so close to my own. He'd lay it on the bar, aligned with my hand, not quite touching but so close that I wanted... I wanted to explode. I'd feel that hand, just hairs away, I'd feel it more than if it was on me. And his face near my face, I'd feel breathless and my cheeks would burn. Kiss me, kiss me. Someone inside me screamed for attention. The passion of being. You're alive for love, someone was saying. The body electric, lights of the city, the loose flames rising, it's what everyone wants. That was the kind of kiss I needed that I never did get. Instead, he'd loosen his tie, pleasing his eyes down my shirt. I'd ask if he'd ever read Whitman. What man is that? How about *Don Quixote*. Donkey oaties? Sure, he'd say, looking up. Why not? he's say. Great stuff, donkey oaties. But he was saying it only to have fun with me. I knew he didn't like to read.

What did it really matter, though? We'd leave and find my room together because his place was too far away or it was being painted or exterminated or Route 27 was closed for construction. Whatever the excuse. Detour takes me three times as long to get home, he'd tell me. I just need a place to crash. So, we'd go my way to my apartment, and we'd listen to music and make coffee in the sink, him hanging on me, unbuttoning my blouse. We'd make love in the kitchen, again on my bed. I was fucked for good, got nothing out of it. I'd look out the window at the thin of things, at the bony black night. My endurance was strong, but eventually, I knew, I'd be running on low. Go to sleep, my friend, I said to me. Go to sleep, sweetie. I'm by your side, protecting. It was the most comforting thing to hear those words.

And before I had time to slow and restore, I was flying, as happens in dreams. Out past the land, far over the ocean. Clouds in the moonlight. A suffering of clouds. Something was wrong. The flashing light shouted its warning. Mayday, mayday, the radio static. There'd have to be an emergency landing. Someone on the radio was singing this song: "There'll have to be an emergency / emergency, emergency / There'll have to be an emergency / landing in the sea. Bum-bum." The singer had a scratchy voice that sounded like dry leaves in autumn. Then I was down in the water, sinking into darkness, trying to swim back to the surface to breathe. Which is when I'd awake, caked in sweat, my back against that same mattress, no one beside me, a family of mice chewing in the walls, and my bathroom light flickering like always. I'd pull the sheet over my body, quiet. And that was. The end of that.

But it got me thinking. It didn't have to be like this. So one day, some nine years later, if I'm doing the math right, I was at this beach. Imagine it if you can, my angel.

A beach?

Yes.

Ok. I'm seeing it.

And on the beach there's a woman, who may be a mother, because there's a smiley kid about eight years old nearby, playing in the sand. He has dimples on his face and sand on his arms and legs. I'm not sure this is my greatest imagination, on account of I'm dead. But still, it's worth you taking a look.

So. A woman.
She's got her ups and downs, her
highs and lows, her
out like spring flowers and her inwardness, too. Sometimes she's a circus cloud in the sky, swinging on high, other times she's stuck to the surface like ground fog. And then there are times she feels washed up – a piece of driftwood or a crappy, plastic jug, and no one's near to save her from the dumps. At those dispirited times, she's as sad as can be, full of unwelcome things that don't hesitate to visit her. Why was she even born? she wonders. What good is she? And where's that smiley kid, when you need him most? But. Don't come, don't. Come – I don't. Want to see you now, she says, her connection breaking up, making her feel lost and small.

Then the tide turns on her, a gift of free counsel, and she's okay. In fact, now, this new moment, she's in a good mood, full of spunk and bright ideas. She wants to throw off her clothes and dance her way across the dunes, to run in swimming because she's burning so, or because why in this big beautiful world, why not bring yourself to it?

And that's exactly what she does. She dances in. She leaps past the breakers. She floats on swells. Then, after rising and falling for hours, it seems, she begins to swim. Water water at her feet, a crown of jeweled unclouded sky. She swims without burden. She swims as long as time allows, or longer. The ocean is lovely, far, and deep, she recites as she swims. The ocean. Is lovely. Far. And deep. Stroke after stroke. Is far. And deep.

Only, it is a precarious arrangement, because how can this good feeling go on? It can only go wrong. Always things change, grow tired, and drop. And to prove it, the tide turns once more. Waves and wind push for her return. The lifeguard's whistle orders her back. Why do things go this way? Just when she's getting somewhere, she's yanked back.

On the beach again, she stares across. Perhaps she never did go in the water, just stood here and pictured the act. **No Swimming Allowed** – there's a flashy metal sign in the cool morning light. Blond sand, blue eyes, naked hair, blush. She's dry before an untiring ocean. She's burnt upon an impossible world. I am mad for you, she says. Hot like a cinder, she says. My soul.

Yet, there's a kind light that wants to germinate inside her. Whether it takes root or not, who knows? That's the thing about kindness and life and madness – who knows? In the end, she thinks, There's no one to blame but myself. No one's to blame, but someone's too blue. Hue of the sky. Who is she?

Is this a riddle? asks my angel.

It's whatever it is, I say.

This imagination, this woman, is yourself. Am I right?

My God. Aren't you listening? I thought you said you'd be more alert.

I am, says my angel.

Of course, the woman is myself. Sometimes, I'm less than whole, unshining, no way perfect, and other days I'm filled-out, with something of a sweet glow like translucent candy. In that changeable way, I'm reminiscent of the moon, phasing in and out of days, never getting to something lasting, very little gravity of my own. Don't you agree?

Well, I...

I see myself as the moon. It's a perfect description. I'm mostly a thing to lay eyes on, always have been, maybe something to carve out of softwood and leave on a windowsill like half a clam shell that offers itself as a chalice.

A chance at what?

A chalice. Not chance. That's what I said. A cup of some kind for someone to put his paperclips in.

Paperclips? questions my angel. That's it?

That's not it at all. As the moon, I get out of lots of things, like having an atmosphere or amber waves of grain. I don't even have to bother with human interactions, don't have to support any life besides my own. As the moon, I don't have to lead the way, and I have little significance to offer other than reflected light. True, it's not a very cheerful view, but at least it's an honest assessment, as I sit here in the early morning sand, looking. At.

At what? says my angel

This kid beside me, for one. He's about eight, like I said. Sand sticking to his hands and feet. He's the kid from earlier, the smiley one with dimples. I don't know if he's her kid, the woman I imagine, or if he's mine.

Aren't you and the woman one and the same? says my angel.

My God. Can't people be different? Why do we have to all be the same?

No one's the same, says my angel.

Regardless, I go on. Somebody really ought to engage him, don't you think?

The boy? Yes. And I think it should be you.

Okay, my good angel. If that's what you think. I do want to spend time well and not have it cost. I know I should live for others a bit more. Really what I need's to stop this bullshit imagining. I need to find a way

OUT, I say. I say it loudly.

My kid looks at me strangely, wondering why I just said what I did. Probably thinks: I'm not in the water. Why'd you tell me to get **OUT**?

It's not you. It's me, I tell him. I want to make something for the world.

Make what? says my kid.

I don't know. How about a song. *You are my sunshine, my growing sunshine.*

That's not how it goes.

You're like the smartest kid ever, aren't you?

He doesn't object.

Okay, I say, because I have to say something to break the silence. Help me make something else then.

I'm hungry, my boy tells me.

We'll get to that later. First let's build something from all of this nonsense.

What nonsense? he asks.

From all of it, I repeat. From it all.

And I lie back in the sand, eyes closed, writing words of water in my cindery soul, sizzle of seawater in my changeable soul. My boy digs in beside me to listen. His stomach groans. It rumbles and groans in my empathetic soul, and he waits for my story, real patient.

~

FROM

Chapter Four

Once upon a time, there was a beach and a boy –

You can't say *Once upon a time* in chapter four, he says.

I can do anything I want. Just listen.

I am listening, he tells me.

I lie on my back, eyes closed to the sky. It's a warm spring day, the first real heat of the year. I feel the morning on my cheek. My son, the most amazing most remarkable boy, plays nearby. I hear him digging, and when I open my eyes, I see his hole. It's empty.

What's it for? I ask him.

What's what for?

The hole.

It's not for anything, he says. It's just for fun.

I get up and we both walk to the water and kick at the waves. We dig our bare feet in the sand and our toes turn cold blue. Seagulls, hearing of our arrival, come to hang out.

From the minute one lands, we're never without them.

I've got nothing for you, I tell the birds. But they don't seem to care.

Fact is, I'm poor. I don't remember being anything other than poor. Well, maybe once when I was given a five-hundred-dollar tip. And another time when I found a hundred-dollar bill between two pickets of a fence. But I have very little money saved. And I don't want to call on my sister or parents for support. How'll I make do for my son? The kid needs things. He sees others with riches, and I can almost hear the envy hiss out of him from so much pressure of wanting. Of course, we have to eat. We have to keep warm. I've got one rusty car with half a tank of gas. I have some saltines in my coat pocket back up the beach.

The sea rolls in, as we stand and watch. It tosses pebbles and shells, flotsam and jetsam. My boy searches through the stuff and comes to me with enough cockles and broken dreams to build a castle. There's this carcass of a crab to guard the front door.

It's not called a front door, says my son. It's a gate.

Okay, then. A carcass of a crab to guard the gate.

Is it dead? he asks.

Is what dead?

The crab.

Yes, I say. And he places the carcass as a guard, just the other side of the moat. The seagulls above sing songs of need. It's a fleeting pleading music that never stops circling.

Got nothing for you, I repeat, but they're very persistent. Out on the horizon, I see a boat.

Look, I almost say, but don't. It's the size of a small toy. I want to pluck the boat. My heart goes out. It returns, but brings back nothing – no toy, no boat. A wave crashes near, edging toward us. Water fills the moat. My son takes some sticks and shells and builds a bridge from outside to in. Another wave comes and washes away the guard crab. Then an even larger wave cuts into the castle. Things are going from bad to worse. So, I go back to the higher ground near the dunes, just to be dry. My boy, in contrast, isn't bothered by any of the destruction. He'll stay with his castle to the bitter end. He waits on the waves for whatever they'll deliver.

Waits and waits. I close my eyes. Next thing I know, he has sidled beside me.

Wake up, he says.

I am awake.

What are you doing? he asks.

I open my eyes, say to him:

Not doing anything, unless you call thinking of saltines doing something.

Not really, he says.

You hungry? I ask.

Yes.

I take out the package of saltines and give him half.

I'm still hungry, he says, after scarfing them down.

How about a story? I say. A different one.

Okay, he says.

Do you know where it's from? I ask.

From?

Yes, from.

You? he says.

Not quite. It's from out there, I say, pointing to the ocean. My heart went out there and brought it back instead of a boat. I didn't know I had it in me till now.

Oh, he says, probably disappointed about the boat.

Once upon a time, I begin.

I've heard this before.

Just listen, I say. Once upon a time there was a beautiful woman. She didn't own anything except her beauty, and when she tried to sell it, she got in trouble with the police.

Why? asks my son.

Because the law says that beauty is free. Ask any physicist.

What's a fizzy zit?

Someone who knows how the world works. So, with beauty, anyone can just have it. You can't charge money.

Oh, says my son.

Can you tell me something that's beautiful? I ask.

He looks all around, but sometimes it's difficult to *see* all around.

No, he says.

No what?

I don't know what's beautiful.

Well, you'll see it some day. I can look at a bone on the ground or a feather or shell and say, Wow. That's really beautiful to me. And the thing is, the bone doesn't charge me a thing, and not the feather, either.

How about the shell? asks my son.

Nope, I say. It's all free. When things are simple in your life, you get to have the beauty, no charge. But sometimes life makes you pay.

I'd like a bike, says my son, changing the subject. It could be any color but not pink or purple. And not orange. I think a bike'd be pretty cool.

A bike is cool, and that's why it costs, I tell him. Cool things cost, like air conditioning in the summer, and a cold soda cola.

Did the woman go to jail? asks my son.

She did. And she was there a long time. Even longer than the longest road, but luckily she escaped.

How?

Not by digging.

By how then?

By being quiet, I explain. No one could hear her. She was quiet as a mouse and no one knew she was there. Then it was just a matter of walking out the door. Thing is, if no one knows you're there, you can do anything.

What'd she do when she got out the door?

She was free to do whatever she wanted, I say.

But what'd she do? persists my son.

She looked at life differently, that's for sure. Maybe she got married and had a real family life. Maybe she took her kids to baseball practice when summer came around. Maybe she shopped at the Red Market for all her meats and veggies, and at the Blue Market for her ice cream and toothpaste.

Uh huh. My boy seems bored.

Not too exciting, is it? I say.

I thought she could go on an adventure, he says. All the way to the end of the world.

Would that be a better story?

Yep.

What would she do at the end of the world?

First she'd look for treasure, then she'd find it. The minute she finds it, she puts it in her pocket, but someone real mean wants to take it from her. He chases her and she gets away by jumping off a cliff. Lucky for her, she changes into a bird.

That is lucky.

Then she flies to the field where an evil man and a good man are fighting over who gets to eat the last piece of fruit.

What fruit? I ask.

An apple.

Any old apple?

An apple that if you bite it, it'll give you what you most want.

Like what?

Like a bike, says my son. Or something else. And when the bird comes down, the men stop fighting. Then the bird eats the fruit, because she's hungry. And turns into a pig.

A pig? Is that what the bird most wants to be?

No. But I like pigs. I guess the bird wants to be a person again, like she was. So, after a while, she changes from a pig, and then she's someone again.

Who? I ask.

A real nice woman like before, only different. And she's got this box with a sun and a moon painted on it and stars all around. And the woman says: Whoever can answer this question gets to open the box and have what's inside, plus a sandwich.

A sandwich sounds good. What's the question?

Where are we going?

Is that the woman's question or yours?

Yes.

Well, I say to my son. It's a good question, and it came all the way from the end of the world.

Do you know what the answer is? he asks.

No. What is it?

To find out soon.

We're going to find out soon, I say. That's the answer?

Yep.

Did someone say that? I ask.

Yep.

Who?

You sort of did, earlier. And I did, right now.

So, who gets the sandwich? I ask.

We both do. But not yet. It isn't made.

That is a problem, isn't it. So, what else was inside the box?

This.

And he hands me a shard of mirror, a triangular piece about two inches across. I look into it. My face just fits.

Where'd you find it? I ask.

In the box.

But before the box, where was it?

When I got up this morning. It was next to the car.

I like it, I tell my son. Are you ready to go, then?

I guess, he says.

We've got to get those sandwiches, I remind him.

And we pick ourselves up and I look once more at the ocean. The waves are coming. Nothing'll stop them. Surf and seaweed and broken shells. I'll go with my son. I'll try to find work. I'll try to find home. Things'll be different soon. I'll get a job selling shoes or serving lunch and dinner at Big Mike's. The green of the marsh behind me is blowing. The song of the seagulls makes me want to run off. But by the look of the sky, the day's got my back. It'll always be with me no matter where I go. Can't shake my life, can't shirk responsibilities. And by the end of April there'll be even more light. More life, too, if I can just bring myself to it. Which I'm trying so hard to do right now. And there where the sun burns a hole in my being, and there where the sun rises achingly bright, lies what I'm looking for, if I only could see it through – new life in the springtime, all possible blooms.

FIVE

Games and Rianna examined their reflections on the plate glass. There were pads, pens, and calculators. All colors available through the sliding glass doors. But mostly, where they stood before the doors parted, Games and Ri saw themselves.

I like my reflection in tinted window, Rio said.

Not me, said Games.

You don't like my reflection?

I like you better in person, said Games. On glass you're too thin and flat. I hardly know you.

Ri lifted her breasts.

I'm not so flat, she said.

That's what I'm telling you, said Games. In person, you're much better.

But in the window, Ri suggested, it covers up the flaws.

Games was looking at his girlfriend, her flesh and clothes, her hair pulled back, the translucent details of her face.

What flaws?

There's no point in talking to you about it, said Ri.

There's no point in talking to you about her, said Games.

He meant the reflection. Rianna looked at herself in the plate glass.

You can see right through me, she said.

Games played along.

It's your deceptions and lies that make you who you are.

I want to be someone else. I want to be her. Rianna nodded to the glass.

You could be anyone. Why her?

Could I be a mechanic? asked Ri.

You could work on it.

How about a comedian?

Very funny.

Or a thief?

A bicycle thief, said Games, knowing her history.

I didn't take your stupid bike.

A car thief, then.

Catharsis. That's what Ri heard, blending the words. She was absorbed in the reflection. A man went past. Shirt with a tear in it. He entered the store.

It's called a stationery store, said Games. But there's movement everywhere.

The world's a crazy place, said Rianna. Come on.

They went inside to buy printer ink she needed. Mad color choices. Magenta, black, cyan. Oh, what a goose cyan. Sayonara. Cyanide. An employee dressed in red, streaks of purple in her hair, did not nod, nor did she ask if they needed help. Green notebooks. Pink and fuchsia Post-Its. Pens with unwritten proposals. Rubber bands with nothing to bind. Labels and pushpins and rulers to live by. For example, *Invest in staples rather than glue.* And, *Since you can't support yourself on love alone, make money instead.*

As Games and Rianna headed to the ink, a girl squeezed by. She bumped into a display and a plastic container of paper clips fell on the floor. The colorful clips scattered, red to blue: a rainbow, and there wasn't any sun inside. Some of the clips landed in difficult to reach places. The box said 450. Only a few remained home in the clear container. Rianna and Games helped to pick up the strays.

Mind doing this yourself? the girl asked. She seemed annoyed. It was a nuisance, sure. Though, it was her fault.

We've got it, said Games.

The girl didn't say thanks. She didn't say anything. Just stood. Her father, the man with the shirt that had a tear in the shoulder, was looking for her. He carried paper, 500 sheets in his left hand, recycled.

Vanessa. Get.

She looked at him coming down the aisle.

Come over here, he called.

Shit, she said, under her breath.

Nessa. We, said her father.

The girl backed away.

You're not my father.

The man froze.

Of course I'm her father, he said, looking at Rianna and Games as he spoke.

He smiled at Ri. Nodded at Games.

Kids, he said.

Don't listen to him, she yelled. He's not my father. You're not. You're not. She backed out the aisle, knocking over merchandise, drawing the attention of others in the store. A woman in pens. Another with a young boy near the printers.

The man did nothing for a moment. He wanted the public on his side. Sympathy for his difficult job as a parent. He shook his head. Shaking's what he did. Rule number one: If you shake your head at the crazy world, others will agree that it's not you. You're not to blame. *My girl's, she's a bit crazy*, the man wanted to say. *Course, maybe crazy's too strong a word. Not the right word. Just she's got a problem, an emotional disorder. Aspergers, Autism, Socialitis. You've probably seen stories on the news. She's been like this since, well, ever since, ever, since she could...* This, of course, was the perfect time to choke up a bit. *No one's been able to help*, the man said with his eyes. The things he wanted to say. *We've tried every doctor, acupuncture, homeopathy. She was two when we lost her happy, carefree self. Began knocking over things for no reason. Lashing out. First time she ran away, she was only six. You should see my wife's bruises. And the wounds on the inside, they're even worse. You wouldn't believe what we've been through with...*

Vanessa, the girl, ran out the door like a wild child, a hooligan. Thief! Delinquent! someone should've yelled. Nobody yelled it.

She's probably stolen again, said the father-like man, unconcerned. Please, excuse me. He said these last words as if this meeting with Games and Rianna had been planned but now he had something unscheduled to attend to.

He walked fast toward the door, and then started to run, still carrying the recycled paper. Out the door he went, into the May afternoon. The alarm went off, a car drove by. There was an old man walking with a shopping cart past the entrance of the store. The shopping cart was filled with empty bottles and cans.

Come on, said Games, who thought there might be more to the drama.

He and Rianna stepped out of the store. They saw the girl running across the parking lot with someone her age. Maybe twelve, thirteen. Blue jeans and a light red jacket. Blue and red, like the clips. The man was nowhere to be seen. He hadn't seemed creepy, not like some pedophile. In short, he may have been her father. Who knows?

Should we go after her? said Rianna. Maybe she's...

The girl didn't look like she needed help, but it was difficult to tell. The sun shone in Rianna's eyes. In Games's eyes, too. Cars piled up at the red light, trying to get out. It was a poorly designed lot. And with the sun in their eyes, Games and Ri lost sight of the girl. It was over. She was gone. Leaving them to think. Because sometimes you wonder – should you've acted differently? Ri wondered it. If she should've followed her instincts to go after the girl. To at least make sure if –

Should we've done something? asked Rio.

Maybe we're being filmed, said Games. Some kind of study.

He didn't know exactly what kind of study. A social study. A study of how humans act in suspicious situations. Or of how responsible they feel when it comes to strangers. The data would be collected and analyzed, later published in *Psychology Today* or the *Journal of Social Disorder*. The report would consider all variables and take into account such things as the low angle of the sun and what type of shoes people were wearing. It would prove a point, a very important point, mapped out scientifically, not only showing how people respond to uncomfortable events, but also digging to the core of humanity and revealing the truth, the ultimate answer of why. Why are we the way we are? There'd be no further debate about what makes us human. The facts would be clear, and the author would've driven home his point. His conclusions would be irrefutable. Might even win the Nobel Prize. This study would change the world, making it a better place, or at least a more understood place, for sure.

If it had been a study, Games and Rianna wondered if they'd acted well. Where did they fit on the bell curve? Had they responded in only the most typical, conventional way? Were they partly to blame for the woes of the world? Or did they fall on the side of moral champions? Games looked for a camera, but it was too well hidden. Neither of them wanted to be part of this study. So, they went back inside for the ink. An employee asked about the girl, who she was, if they knew her, if the man was or was not her father. A slew of questions. It must've felt to the employee that Games and Ri were in on it.

Milton called the police, said the employee girl.

Who's Milton?

Store manager.

That's good, said Games.

They found the ink. Black's what Rianna needed. Games and Ri headed out with the cartridge, no bag, just a receipt. Milton called over.

Excuse me.

They turned. He asked for their names and phone numbers before they left, jotting down the information, just in case.

~

The two drove to Rio's apartment, near the college. A bird was standing on the sidewalk when they got out of the car. A robin, noted Games. The bird hopped to the side as they passed it. Springtime. May birds. Warming. Fashion. Trends in manufacturing never interested Games. Rio dressed nicely – few colors, but style.

Are you coming in? she asked.

Yep.

Games's mind went to Trudy Burroughs who had lived on the ground floor. She'd died on Easter morning, not long after he'd met her. He was about to say something about Trudy to Ri, but as they approached the door to the building, it opened. Out came Nat, Rio's roommate. She closed the door behind her, even though Games and Ri were about to enter.

Hey, did you hear? she said.

What? asked Ri.

They had like 200 cops and everything right out front. They were all over Prospect and everywhere.

For what?

For that guy who the guy. You know who. The guy I mean.

What guy?

Oh, shit, she said, reading off her cell phone, texting back. I've got to.

What is it?

He'll kill me. Fime late again. Really. Fucking kill me.

Billy?

What?

Who are you talking about?

Sorry, Nat called, as she ran past, to her car

Rio got out her key. Games remembered the robin. He remembered there was something else he was going to say, but he'd forgotten. They went in the building and climbed the stairs to Ri's apartment. Rio tossed her ink onto a chair and sat at the table.

You worried about tomorrow? she asked.

Not really, said Games. Who's Billy?

Someone. Maybe a boyfriend. Who knows?

Games was to begin a new job, working for Reed Martin, Quincy Mesch's grandson. Bamboo Abe's brother.

I like to build, he said. Well, I think I do. I might.

What've you ever built? asked Ri.

A bench, once. Out of a log.

I built an entire resume, said Ri. Games tried to top this:

A neighbor asked me to put new screens in his porch. I didn't know what I was doing, but got paid for learning.

They should pay you to go to school, said Ri, thinking about learning.

They should, agreed Games. You're not doing it for yourself, but to be a good citizen. The only reason someone goes to college is they want to make the world a better place. The government should pay.

That's right, said Rianna. So, where are you going tomorrow?

Outside Hollowville.

Where?

About an hour away. Out in the boons.

Are you sad about Jakes?

Not really.

How about Hit-P?

A bit, said Games. I wasn't there long. I don't think I'm a caregiver.

Games went to get a glass of water. When he returned, Rio was reading a book, studying for something. Her blond hair, pulled back, spilled loose from its hold. Strands of it came free and lay on her cheek and shoulders.

You never stop doing it, said Games.

She looked up.

What?

Her legs were crossed, intriguing lines like graceful branches, like sinuous cracks in the sidewalk, only the lines of her legs goaded him, excited him sexually. How would he respond? Typical, typical. And her shirt was unbuttoned just enough that Games could see where her breasts took shape. A bird flew past the window, which was a third-story window, very nice. Stupid word, nice. Very fine. Stupid word, fine. Very... The trees down there were leafing out. Flowers, flowers, very flowers. It was... There was this thing she did with her lips, her mouth, at the very corner. It was a book about propagation.

That really bothered me in the store, said Rio.

The man? asked Games.

Whatever the troubles are in the world, she said. I try to keep positive.

They were probably just working together, said Games. You know, con artists.

It's not the crime, it's the why, said Rio. The dreary landscape inside someone. I'm not saying I'm perfect. I'm no work of art.

Everyone's a work of art, said Games. But it's a matter of taste.

What's a matter of taste?

A person is, said Games.

How's a person a matter of taste?

His own tastes, said Games. A person is how he thinks about things. He likes something because it works for him or he doesn't like it because it doesn't work. That's how it's a matter of taste.

That's depressing, said Ri. It's too limiting.

So, you can make yourself less about taste. You can think bigger. See around the roadblock of your personal take on things to what's really there. But I don't know why I'm telling
you this. It's what you do.

Even so, said Ri.

Even so. Even so, Games repeated in his mind. He liked how she'd said those words. Even so. Eve-n-so. He liked how she crossed her legs, how her legs were crossed, how uncross she was. Even so. Her mouth – that thing. He liked her hair a bit messy. He liked the cluttered table and the small room. He liked the light through the window and the leafy world below. Games put his glass on the floor. Then sat beside it.

You can sit on a chair, said Rio.

I know. It's a matter of taste.

Well, you can always think bigger.

Maybe tomorrow, said Games. Even so.

That doesn't make sense, said Ri. Even so, she got up and left the room without explaining. Why had she gone? Had he said something wrong? Had he offended her with his even so-ness, with his chosen seat on the floor somehow? Then she was back, holding a drawing.

My father had this project years ago. He went into prisons, Virginia or Carolina or somewhere, and got these prisoners to make self-portraits. This drawing's one I liked, so he gave it to me.

Games took the paper and studied it. A green-eyed man. Jonesy or Jones Y. A scar ran from one cheek, the left one, down his chin and across the right side of his chest. His shirt half open, half torn, half tucked. Light from the right, above, cascading.

Why'd you like this one? he asked.

He's so old, but he's smiling. He's in there for life. His face is half in the light, half dark. You can't know everything, but you can know enough to see there's a good, a real beautiful human being in there.

Games followed the lines and the light of the drawing.

So many lives begin imprisoned the day they're born, he said.

You don't mean literally, do you? You mean some people are born with one foot in a trap.

Something like that. Not literally in prison.

Yeah, but don't be distracted by the problems, said Ri. Take away the mess of a person's life, and what d'you have?

Clarity? A bigger picture?

Obviously Rianna thought this was so. Games had no reason to question it. A better question:

What's the tattoo on his forearm say?

Utopia, isn't it?

That's sort of sad, said Games. What's the viney plant under it?

Sweet pea.

He's a gardener.

Rianna shrugged off the statement.

What I like is that the only way you can see him is to look and to ask, she said. You can ask him anything. He's all there.

What do you mean by… Games didn't finish his question.

Turn it over, said Ri.

Games did. On the other side were the sentences: *Look in the miror. Thou shal not kill.*

He wants us to be merciful, said Games.

Why do you say that?

I could say something else if you want.

Say what you think.

Games had nothing to add at the moment.

I think he's seeing himself for the first time, said Rio.

Was he on death row? Executed?

I don't know, said Rio. Is it important?

Probably to him, said Games.

So ask, said Ri.

Games wasn't sure what Rianna meant by this statement. Instead of questioning it, he asked instead:

Do you keep this drawing beside your bed?

No. I just remembered it because of what you…

What I…?

I've got this box, said Ri.

Your treasures.

What, you don't keep anything that's meaningful?

I… began Games. Maybe he had.

It's things I've collected, said Rio. When I look at them, I think about my life.

Game turned the phrase over: *about my life, about your life, my life, yours.* He liked that she looked at things. He liked that she stored them. He liked that she thought about meaning and that a drawing could make her thinking thoughtful. The portrait was well drawn. It was subtly shaded.

I like it, he said.

Everyone was a child once, said Ri. A fresh human being. The world holds itself up as a million possibilities. It's like magic what the earth does for life.

Birds fly through the sky, said Games. How's it happen?

Shadows play on the wall, said Ri.

Peas grow in pods, said Games. And I eat them.

Light holds still on leaves so I can see it, finished Ri. It's amazing, if you think about it. Wonder is second nature to a child.

Even so, said Games. We lose it.

I'm not talking about that, said Rianna. We come to the world with an open mind. Seeing miracles. The plants and animals and stones, the puddles of water to splash in.

We're sort of a miracle, too, said Games.

Exactly. And we feed on the world wherever we are. So, it needs to be healthy. We're each a seed held in many different hands of the world, and all those hands need to be rich, nourishing soil.

That's a nice picture, said Games. Now he understood why Ri wanted to teach, why it was important to her. You can't start at the end to make a difference. Start at the beginning, from the ground up. Or at least near the beginning. With children. Fertilize the ground with love and attention. Make it a good start, without walls or traps or restrictions. Even so.

Do you have other drawings?

Not of prisoners, said Rio. They're all in a book my father wrote.

He wrote a book?

He's written lots. This one was *Mirror Text – Portraits of Prisoners.* There were maybe fifty portraits. I've got lots of plants.

Lots of plans, thought Games. What was the connection Ri was trying to make?

Plants, I said. Not *plans*. I've got my own sketches of plants that I've done.

Oh, said Games. He wanted to see them.

Trees. Ferns. Dandelions. That sort of thing.

Petal, sepal, calyx. Games rattled off the botanical terms he knew. Stigma, style.

You've been studying.

I've got a dictionary, said Games. Also've got eyes.

You're a potato.

A peacock feather.

Argus, said Rio.

This is so boring, said Games, yawning. He closed his eyes and feigned sleep.

Rio nudged him.

Why? she asked.

Why what?

Why's it boring?

I was just being a myth, said Games.

Something's always amiss with you, agreed Rio. But it's not boring at all. Each plant comes out and takes shape in the world. I think it's amazing.

You think like a child.

Rianna took this as a compliment.

People, too, she went on. We're fascinating, really. What spark do we come from? What shape are we going to take?

Games thought about this, metamorphosis. Maybe people didn't used to die. Weren't even born. Just flowed from one thing to another, like a story without periods. On and on. Morphing throughout. Games used to write like that. When he learned that things needed to pause and even to stop, he added punctuation.

I was just teasing about how you think, he said.

I like how children do it, said Ri.

Can I borrow that drawing when I go?

Be careful with it. Ri put the portrait on the floor by the door, so they'd both remember. It's all you've got of him.

Did she mean *you*? Games wondered. *All you've got to*

know him by. Or did she mean *I*? *It's the only drawing that I have of him.*

~

Later, walking to his car, Games went over things in his head. He remembered the cow and Hermes and Argus, the monster with a hundred eyes. Those eyes, as the story went, came to adorn a peacock's tail, thanks to Hera. It was a myth he'd read years ago. After that, Games remembered the robin from three hours earlier. That bird wasn't a myth, and had only two eyes. Now the creature was gone. Nowhere to be seen. Hera hadn't done that. Nobody had. The bird used to be a physical, living thing. Now it was a picture in Games's head, brought to life by his thoughts.

The evening was warm. Games liked the spring when it felt like this. He didn't need a coat. He didn't need much. College students in the distance. The year would be over soon, not the year year but the term. What terms would he use? What temperature? Should he, too, get his degree? Go back, complete his college education, take on something more?

He started his car, pulled out. A bicycle swerved past, went on. It was lucky Games hadn't hit the rider, who was just a kid, maybe twelve or thirteen. No helmet. Games swore at himself for being so careless. He put his head in his hands. Took a deep breath. Took another, and then continued to leave the space.

And beneath his car was the robin, red breast in the evening, dead on the road – true story. But the sun, red sun, was alive in the sky – just as true. Games didn't see the death behind him, only the life in front, right in his eyes.

Even so, he shouldn't forget the stuff on the passenger seat. Games glanced at the drawing on the seat beside him. It was the face of a prisoner, light falling on it from the sky, upper right. Green eyes. Nice shading. Something's always trying to emerge in the world, to break out and be free. To have the chance to express itself. Or impress someone.

Games turned onto Mulligan Street. A person is a member of the whole interconnected team of things. By *things* he meant what? By *team* – did he mean *team*? But sometimes a person does something to leave the group. He skips out. He breaks with himself and others. There's a schism, a disconnect. He commits a crime just to express himself, maybe to make a different connection. Something new wants to bud. And somewhere in his soul he knows it's wrong, the crime. If soul's the right word. If wrong. If crime. Somewhere he's fighting. Or hating. Hurting. Unable to transform how he's got to transform. Locked in some cell. Maybe from the beginning. And what if he dies in there without the least bit of help, without the wholesome sun? Crushed light instead, a scar on his chest. Still, isn't he a member of life for good, even so?

Even so. What's that mean?

It means, maybe he's just forgotten his part in the whole.

Yeah, his part. Must be he's not seeing the bigger picture.

Or never thought much about it, said Games to himself.

There you go. If he'd only given it a thought. It would've solved all troubles, erased all woes.

Maybe he was never given the chance.

A chance is all anyone needs to put things right.

Games felt mocked by this interior conversation. That he, that someone was mocking him. No one else in the car, however. Just him. Even so.

What's that mean? Even so.

It means living is difficult enough without knocking yourself, thought Games. The most difficult of all things on earth is to… is to live – He stopped at *live*, as though there was a red light before him to put a halt to his words. And his car. Which was true. There was a light. And lucky, too, that Games had stopped because of the police car across the way.

Now the light turned green. Games drove on. And he finished his thought: The most difficult of things on earth is to live consciously, to understand the lives of others, not to be stuck in personal perceptions. Even so, how easy it is not to think bigger, sometimes. Comes naturally, in fact, to live as if you are part of only your take on things, your personal tastes, as if it's all about how you just you feel, how you alone see the world, as if there's no other way. Everyone does it. Yet why not do things differently?

Your words make it seem easy. They don't make it come true.

Games nodded. He drove toward his apartment, wanting to think better. So he went on, Why not be a sentence that is not a sentence of punishment but a meaningful idea expressed in a stream of words that flows left and flows right in melded time.

You call that a better thought. That wishy-washy nonsense.

I mean, thought Games, turning left onto Sungold, be someone who is the past and the present and the future at once. With pauses and periods and new beginnings.

New beginnings. Sounds good to me.

It is, thought Games. It's nothing to mock. Nothing to knock.

No. Nothing to knock. No more mocking.

As the red sun dipped into the hills, thus ending. And Games drove on, even so, even so.

MAY

Jones Y

Some evening, least it wasn't solitary. About six o'clock if I was to give it a time. Round me air all loosen limber, but my mind made taut like a guitar string quarter turn from snapping. There sprung this young fellow from a whole other world, sat with me might've been a table between us might not, air all round, way I just said, smelling of days out back like I was a boy again, clear spring day, hour after rain, mix of green willow limbs and the smooth cool of mud. He counted my blessings, corrected my misspellings. None of it bothered me much. Said he, too, wants to teach.

Who you gonter teach? I asked.

Kids, he said.

Which kids?

You got any? he asked.

Sure. I got kids. Got three. Too old for school.

Where are they?

Body language, I told him. One's down my arm, she's Utopia. I call her Pia. One's on my shoulder. He's my first boy. See?

I peeled my shirt. Showed him the design.

What's it say? he asked. I can't make it out.

RJ. Means Renny Jones. That's sweet pea wrapped round a heart. Must be well over fifty now.

You said there are three.

Third, he's always got my back. That's Perfect.

What's perfect?

His name's Perfect. Not one thing wrong with that boy. His mama's the one gave me trouble.

She gave you Perfect, too.

Say it how you see it. You got any more of your questions?

Did you ever read the book, *Mirror Text*? he asked me.

Read it?

You seen the book?

Looked it through once, I said. Made me right sad.

You were in it, he reminded me, like it was news.

Some of me was.

What did you think? he asked.

That was years back now. Man came in the prison. Ryan it was. Ryan O, hopping from here to East Crum to Saint Dorothea for women to Absalom down Point Lookout. There was a group of us what in our stupidities had decreased the world.

What's that mean?

You ready to hear what I'm really saying?

I am, he said.

Used to be light was at my back, which you might say is a good thing but I was always walking into my shadow stead of leading the way.

Hmm.

Hmm? That's all you've got to say? Cause it makes no sense to me anymore. I'm all about growing things. Anyway, he got us to drawing and painting for this project of his. I was okay with it.

Self-portraits, right?

Whatever self came out, I said. I recall some poem shaped like a tree, and the word freedom painted to look like one man's face. Myself, I wanted to draw. I never knew I was any good.

Were you?

Not bad, tell you the honest truth.

Was it better than the yard?

You're trying to be someone you're not by saying that, I told him.

I... I'm just.... Sorry, he stumbled.

You're young, I told him. Everything here's just rehearsals.

What's that mean, rehearsals?

We've got our shows: *Heart Times, Heart Case, Heart Labor, Heart Drive, Counting to No One,* and *The Business of Dying.*

They the only shows in town? he asked.

Depends how you look at things. Some people act like it doesn't bother them a bit. But you miss stuff: a real sharp knife, a windshield in the rain, stopping at a red light, moving with a green.

Like, slowly it eats you up, the young fellow said.

Gets old in here, I explained. Lockdowns for sure. Solitary sometimes. We do things the same. We've got our soap and paperbacks to make us happy. But there're so many terrible feelings. Regrets, missings, misgivings. You just have to let them ride or else. Boy like you, you won't ever know how it is.

I'm trying.

Trying. Shit. Things'll suck you, keep you hopeless, dry you up. You got to let them go, else you'll be emptied, not a broken bone not one gray hair or a single good thought left to you. Nothing even for the turkey buzzards to pluck. There's not much chance to grow like that.

Is there any garden here you can work in? he asked.

What put that in your head?

I don't know. You mentioned growing.

What kind of growth you have in mind?

A garden, you know. Seeds and plants and vegetables. He explained it to me in the simplest terms.

I know what a garden is, I said. I've been in the fields here. Shit, I worked on a chicken farm on the outside. I worked with corn and beans. Tomato plants leave the smell right on your hands. Once I had a little plot, man gave me back his house. Weren't no guard in that garden. Weren't nothing but air and dirt and clean sun. It was a good chance for me. It was way back.

Way behind his house? the young fellow asked.

Another time's what I'm thinking. You've got me recalling lots of things, some of it pointless, like the color of his front door.

What color? he asked

Blue. But it don't matter none.

What man? he asked.

I don't know his name. He was a white man, pretty decent. He came from the Midwest. St. Paul or somewhere. Had him a real white wife.

Real as in...

Some white people are okay, I told my interrogator. He didn't charge nothing.

Did his wife suffer from too much time? Did she sail the dingy Saturday mornings when her husband slept? Did she smell of rose water? Of vinegar? Did she lie naked on her side in bed by the window?

That I couldn't tell you.

But you went to her.

I went around. I did what I had to besides the garden. I needed money.

Did you take his wife?

Take her?

Have her?

How my gonter have her?

Look, I'm just making this up as I go. I don't know the precise language.

Ask what you're asking again.

Did you kill his wife?

As in burn the place?

As in kill, he repeated. To die, to sleep, no more. And thus end.

The boy leaned in, resting his elbows onto his legs. Or might've been on that table between us. Who my to –

No, I told him. I mean... Who my to say?

Let loose a big sigh had built up inside me. Young fellow just sat there, nodding his head, which shook me some to see it. Then stillness. Then this:

Did you ever have friends you could do without? he asked.

I couldn't get away from them, if that's what you're asking.

Didn't you try? Didn't you ever wonder what other things were like? If you could've been free –

Free! What gives you the right to use that word?

I just wonder if you ever walked through the field where the winter wheat grew?

Things were always right muddy.

And was your shirt ever ripped at the shoulder?

You been thinking about others, looking at pictures.

Maybe, he said. Then, after a pause: Were you ever in

love?

Come on, son. Why're you asking me that?

He had no answer.

Man I know had a tattoo, I said. *Love is Hell*. Another man had one: *Love/Sick*.

Is that who we're talking about? he asked me. Those men?

I don't know *who* we're talking about? I said to him. Sure not me. Like you said, you're making this up.

Not anymore, he told me. I'm working it out.

Fair enough.

So…

So, keep working it, I told him.

I still want to know about love, he said.

Not from me you don't.

Yes.

What for? I asked.

For love, I guess. Love alone.

Love alone is loneliness, I told him.

Is that how it is for you?

You ever seen a buzzard on top of the empty sky? That's how it is for me. Love – hell, everything's so far off, it's well past wishing. It's a truckload of wind let loose in emptiness. Nothing for it to brush against. That good enough for you?

So, what got you arrested?

Stupidity, like I told you. Course, alcohol had a role. Also, had taken the edge off.

What were you doing on the night in question?

Counting my chigger bites.

Anything else?

Out hoeing.

At night?

There was a full moon. Too many weeds.

Where were your kids?

Each with a mother.

All different?

Everyone's different, I told my young friend. Haven't you heard?

You ever tell stories, like to yourself or your kids or to me?

I'm not gonter lie to you.

Not lies, stories.

Once upon a time a person came down from the sky, I told him. He was thunder and he was lightning. He did as he pleased. He didn't think twice. He wanted some space and time so he could start fresh. I make up shit just like I'm made up.

I told you, young fellow said to me. We're working this out, the both of us.

I nodded. He nodded. We sat there, nodding.

Well, you make sure it comes out true, I told him.

Not up to me, he said. Then he asked: Who do you think it's up to?

A long pause.

Would you say God? he asked.

Why would I say that?

I don't know. Maybe you'd say it's up to you if things come out true.

If it was up to me...

A short pause.

So, did you wash your hands in the utility sink? young fellow asked.

There wasn't any blood, if that's what you're after?

Dirt? Mud? Crud under the nails? The smell of gasoline? Some.

Were there any pictures of the man and his wife?

Place was full of them.

Any of her in particular?

A black and white in the kitchen by the telephone. She was early in her thirties. Ivory skin like it never tasted sun. Light streamed from the upper right corner.

You remember it well.

I'm full of pictures now.

Back then, that night, you must've been hungry?

I hadn't eaten all day. But that wasn't my problem. My problem was – You taking notes?

I am.

My problem was that fool – myself. He didn't think, only did. Young fool he was, like a blade needing to cut. Hurry up. Slice through. Take meat, take flesh, take that jewelry from the drawer. Thought everything was his, didn't he? Take the cap off the bottle, take it up with the world, take it down. Was full up with empty. All he did was take. It's who he was. Couldn't hold him back from fucking things up, could I. Didn't have no sway over him.

I was talking about you wanting food.

I know what you're talking about. When's a man know, really know for sure? That's all I'm trying to get you to see.

Look, I don't mean to harp on it, the young fellow said, wanting to bring me back to some past where it was no good sense being. Just piecing together the facts so we can put right something of this.

Putting it right, are you.

Yeah, he said. You and me both.

You've got me wrong, just like the others, I told him. But young man sitting across from me, he didn't want to be like the others. He thought he was different. I told him to take that up with himself, if he had the time. Like I said before, I hadn't eaten all day.

So, what did you see in the kitchen besides the photograph?

There were a few crabs from the creek, but all I had was a biscuit.

Who made the biscuit?

I found them in a basket on the table.

Was it real quiet in that house? Were the windows full of evening light?

Now that you say it.

So, were you afraid? What were you thinking?

Thinking, then? Thought I told you I wasn't. Was messing around, gin down. I took a swig. I took the cash from the top drawer by the phone. I struck a match. I let my insides burn slow. The outside, quick.

Till everything was gone.

It's never gone.

Did you know she was in the house?

I didn't know a goddamned thing.

Is that what you told them?

Didn't matter what I said. Why would it?

And is that what you do now? this young fellow asked me.

What're you saying?

Strike out. Burn slow. Think back on things that make no difference.

You know me bettern that, I told him, saw him nodding.

Thought you said I was getting you wrong.

Well there's your wrong and then there's my wrong. I try to keep my spirits up, though. My head up, too. I've been thinking about my life, lately. That's something can change anyone.

Have you discovered anything new?

Me?

You saying you've discovered yourself?

No one said that. Been thinking about children, though.

What about them?

Nobody's bad to begin with, and that's the truth, I said to this fellow, sitting there. But not everything's always good around you. And even if things turn sour and a boy gets sucked in, he's the one's got to draw his self out – that's the truth, too.

An even shorter pause. Then he said:

Let me ask you this: Did you ever kill bugs when you were a boy?

There were ticks and flies and frogs. Want me to count them for you?

How about birds?

Why're you going there? I'm not about killing. I want to take care. Care. Care. Care. Care... I kept saying the word. I couldn't stop. I let it pour like water from a bottomless bucket. I let it drip like my faucet. I let it...

Are you okay? he asked.

There's always something else: When I was sitting in the jailhouse and they told me she had died, I knew it was over for me. Five forty-seven, I remember the clock. Just before six. My heart left my body, my mind went numb, I couldn't stand on my own two feet. You ever had that feeling? It's like you're out in a boat and there's a storm and you can't see the shore. The boat's going down and you can't swim. You know what's happening, and it's bad, real bad, but that bad's not the worst of it. What's worse is that you know the world's tired of holding you up. It's given up on you. And that feeling – that's hopelessness for you. Terror comes alive inside, takes over your breathing, your heartbeat, your whole fucking mind. Nothing's gonter save you. There's no saving for you. And it's all because you weren't yourself the way you were meant to be. You were stupid. Let yourself be used. The world isn't stupid, you are. The world's just what it's supposed to be, like a chicken or a pig. People think there's a good world and a bad one, but there's only one world and it needs you here all the time, needs all of you here all of the time. What's bad's not the world. It's that you let yourself be taken over. You slip away from the world, don't think for yourself. That's the only way the bad can exist. It exists when you give yourself away, then bad's got you by the throat, like you're its dog. It fills you with bark and growl. It speaks for you. You think bad, you think bad's something real in the world, but it's not. You think it's the truth, but it's a fucking lie. Bad's just a lie. And that's not me. Not now, I mean. Not any longer. Tell me if you see it when you look me in the eye. Honest truth.

I was asking about birds, he said.

And I'm telling you about all the ones I've hurt, and that I'm done with it. No more killing, ever. No more violence. No more prisoning thoughts. It's not what this world is for. Holding eggs in my nest hands like those eggs are my seeds, that's what I'm saying. Seeing things born, helping them grow, caring for everything in my soul.

Your soul? he asked.

You have a problem with that? I said.

Not one bit. Is that who you are now?

I need answers, not a brickload of questions from someone

like you. This ever gonter end? Ever be different? Ever?

Yes, the young fellow said. I suppose he was trying to be comforting. It is, he said. I'm sorry, he said. I'm making it worse, he said, reaching out with his hand, but not quite touching. There was a table between us, or maybe there wasn't. I don't much know about the furniture.

I was born into trial, already convicted, I told him, explaining myself best I could. Now's my time to be released.

Bear with me, he said. I know there's a way to get you out.

How much longer? I asked, though his answer wouldn't make any difference to me. I can't even tell you where I am anymore. But I can tell you where I'd like to be.

Soon, he said. Real soon.

~

Don't know where the young fellow went after that. I think he was still in the room, just didn't talk much. Kept to himself. He had a picture of me in his head, but I can't say it was true. I told him I'd give him a better picture if he'd listen, and he nodded he would and said he was real sorry if he'd assumed shit about me, and that he believed real firm in my life and goodness. And, again, that he was real sorry.

Belief, I sent the word back at him. Life's nothing about belief. It's about what is. It's what's in here, and I tapped my chest, right near the scar, tapped it just like they do in the movies, but this wasn't a movie, it wasn't a story, and it wasn't some feeling to knock. It was real as food when you're hungry. Things that are real, the good kind of real, you don't believe them, I said. You know they're true because they feed you. And you grow.

Show me, he said.

So I did:

> It's a garden, I said. And I drew it
> out of myself
> like with a pencil
> on air.

Everything's a garden of sorts. Just trying to make something good. You live your life and you beat on your walls, on your stomach, like the sun beating on the weeds in some useless field. Hell, you go around not caring, and you get beat on by your father who's not even your real daddy who used to be he was in jail and might now be he was dead, or might not, you don't even know. And you take shit, you take bags of chips, you take the man's gun from under his bed and shoot a hole through the floor by accident, and mice come in and roaches, too, for whatever food might could be. And the man who thinks he's your father tries to cram you through that hole, bruises your skin with his shove, breaks your arm with all his shove, and laughs at your every tear, saying, You aint no bettern a cocksucking roach. Might could be that's the best you are, he says, he says it with his chest all pumped to say it. Then one day your own mama makes to throw you into the wall for taking money out her purse, and you didn't even do it, says you'll end up in jail just like your fucking worthless, that's what she says, your worthless daddy hisself. She's washed her hands of you, she says, even while she's smoking and trying to burn the place down, striking matches, dropping them on papers without even knowing what she's doing, yelling her crazy shit. Leaves the house, ashes everywhere, slamming more slamming. Forget this, says the door. Forget fucking this, says the door to your ears. And you think it's not them but you, it's you who's had enough. So you put out the fire on the floor, go to Bonita's, to Roob's. You go to Li'l Griff's. How old you anyway? Twelve, thirteen. No one's keeping track. You go hungry sometimes, then someone says: Bring the boy something to eat, and they bring it. It's usually chicken. Or else, it's sugar, like pie or a soda or honeydew melon. Later, there's this girl who smells of alcohol. You fuck her because she wants it bad, and it's the first time you ever did such a thing, so now you're grown. And you don't give a shit about her. She's a crazy girl anyway with greasy skin. You live with your aunt who tries to get up inside your head like she's got something to say. You pretend to listen, all the while looking out for yourself, because you're grown and can pretty much do anything. Then there's this other girl, not bad, and you want her pussy and she doesn't smell like whiskey, she smells like fried pork, and along comes another and another after that, all the sweet meat. But then one day this girl shows up who smells something different from the rest, like sugar snap peas winding up the fence, blossoms on the vine. You look at her real and you look at her slow. You think because you're a man now that you're a true man, but you don't really know how to think like one, let alone like anyone resembling a real self. And you let her slip by. Then this guy you want to stab shows up, bothering your days and even your sleep and it's just because of how he believes he's alpha shit, like he's better than you, which who cares if it's true or not, it's his fucking attitude. He's like thistle, like gnats. Fucking Johnson grass. He's like some weed. Like thorn and burrs. So long, motherfucker. But you don't do it. You grant him life. You go into town and roll for money instead. You got to have money for your kid. What the fuck. Where'd he come from? And then two more, just like that. And where's that girl smelled fresh like sugar peas? What ever happened to her? She's long gone by now. Never even had a chance. So, you go out back where there's the old willow and mud. Something's got to sprout soon, you think. Where's the fucking sunshine? Where's the fucking green? Why things got to be like this?

So, what say you rule? Say you take over the world. Say you're the man. I mean, to rule over everyone else, the weather, too. Say you bring things on that have no business being brought, like maybe you mess with some man's wife, and the cows behind her house in the evening make soft noises, and the frogs in the spring pond peep all night. Say you shout down storms and drive yourself as loud as you can. You carry your tune like it's a choir. You do your dope. You drag your ass from bed. You eat fried pickles. You slaughter chickens. It all gets old, and whatever you do, nothing good happens, no matter that it should, no matter that you say it should. I mean, it's no good garden, is it? Not a whole lot that grows, not even peas or string beans, which are easy. It's rubble and confusion, and whoever it is inside you, he's right angry and silent, like he's disappointed in you, like there's this person inside you and he's angry with you constant. So, you get angry back. What else can you do? You hang out with others who also don't know. They don't know the taste of real, fresh fruit, let alone that a person can change. All those others they keep telling you what's wrong and you listen to that shit. But nothing grows. There's not a job that's right for you. There's not a whole lot you can do. Maybe there's something, but when's it gonter be yours, and your woman she calls you a goddamn lazy fool. And she doesn't like the peas in her salad you put there. Peas. Everyone likes fresh peas. But not her. She likes fucking scrapple and cornbread. And this is what it is: It's wasted. This is what it amounts to: It's all about the garden, but there's a concrete wall around the place, no gate out, and the ground's no good. It's no good soil, and weeds take over, aphids, Japanese beetles, too. It's a fucking garden where nothing new gets in, nothing gets out, and nothing healthy grows. So, what do you do about it? Do you kill everything bad? Do you burn it up, burn it down, wipe it clean, start over? Do you throw pesticides onto the ground and put up nets? Do you deal the wall with a sledgehammer? Do you load your gun with a scowl on your face, unchain the dog, attack?

~

Bright early morning. There was a shitload of trouble all around, and maybe I'd done it. Maybe I'd messed up. I wanted to put it right. I wanted to put on my shirt and not see my scars, but feel the sun on my face. I wanted to do things real for a change. And I was ready to plant. I turned away from all my mess. I turned toward. To start the day in a good way. This is it, I said. All right.

It was the first week of May, early on. Felt good, somehow. The moist ground was ready for turning and the sun showed up strong. Things were heating up more steady each day. And I had my boy, Perfect, with me. He was only six, but already he could tell the difference between a sweet pea and a sugar snap just by how they came calling out of the ground.

Run and get me my hoe, I told him.

He ran.

We worked together all through the morning hours. That

was the time to loosen the ground from its winter hold and let it take on the growing things. I had my plants I'd grown in my grow box. I love a good pea plant. I love a red tomato. Cherry ones, too. I love all onions. Love love love. Sweet carrots and cantaloupe ice. Problem with strawberries, the squirrels and the chipmunks eat them.

Then this young fellow from the paper comes along while we were sitting in the shade. Came walking across the field. At least, I thought he was from the paper. He wanted to take a picture of me and my boy, which he did with his big old camera sitting on a tripod. He came out of nowhere. Aint never seen him before, but he was a nice white fellow somewhere in his twenties who shook my hand and listened and showed Perfect how to frame a picture.

Later, he came back to give me what he'd shot, but never did see it in the paper. Course, I don't read the newspaper much. It was a good picture, though. All blown up and framed in a wood frame he carved himself. I've got it in mind now. It makes me happy to have it. Makes me feel alive again. And I'm okay for the time being. I feel alright about my children, if nothing else – all three of them like sweet honeysuckle climbing and vining around me. Their lives are something special, growing real good.

But there's a lot to think about when you're planting. I always like to talk to the plants when I put them in. Make them know that everything's gonter be okay, and even being eaten's only part of life. Some of the time you live, sometime you're gonter die, but it's not about killing. It's about living with respect for others, and if I didn't do that, if there was a time in my life I didn't do that – well, it wasn't me. Not saying it wasn't my fault, just it wasn't the real me. I was different back then, so listen to me now. Don't listen to me then. I mean, hell, you're not gonter take to heart a sprout if it's talking punk, if it goes on like a crazy green about its killer fruit to come. But you are gonter consider the plant after it's taken up with life, when you see that flower and the flower speaks to you with sun-shaped words. That's the time when the conversation grows serious. So, if I couldn't find the words in me at one time, long ago, maybe they were buried in darkness.

On the other hand, listen to this: It's a picture of me and my boy. Happiness, I mean. Mutual respect. Responsibility on my part. A sense of duty. It's digging, planting, starting to grow, and the sure thing of fruit on its way. There's always a good picture somewhere. You've just got to find it, because it proves you're vital and healthy for this world, and no way in prison and no way a poison.

I'm a lot more healthy now. That's why that picture I drew for that man, Ryan, I drew with the sun on my face. Things began to change for me then. I hate seeing all these young kids with dark scowls and anger written all over them. What good's that do the world? But you can't say it to anyone. Things are meaningless that you don't have growing inside you sure as fruit. If you don't know it, it might as well not be there. You can't be happy if you're going around looking for the meaning of the word. You can't be helpful if you're hurting inside. It's not about schooling, but about self-education and germination. And it's not about learning from others what they know nothing about. It's real hard to know who's wise. So, who do you listen to?

Best to take it from the world around. Take it from the earth, first. Take it from the sun and the rain and the smell of leaves living and dying. Take it from a storm, if you have to, but not from some person who's all messed up. Don't take it from me, either. Least, not yet. I'm still trying to make the soil good. I'm still sending out roots and shoots. I'm still trying to flower. Take it from a better plant – a tree, a sugar snap pea, even some strawberry with its tiny white flower. Just take it before the chipmunks do.

A child is born to the earth, and the earth's got nothing bad against him, just her good body. What most the earth's got is patience and love. I know love's the word I didn't want to say earlier, but I've got to say it now. I wasn't ready earlier. Now I am. The earth's got love. It's what I'm saying. And all winter the earth builds love inside, and it begins to show that love each spring. Then the land bursts forth its love throughout the summer days, and in the fall with apples and gourds and colorful leaves the love of the land lets go. The love that's grown falls to feed the earth again. And then comes winter. It's time to rest and restore and reflect on things, not to worry so much but to know that better days are coming, maybe not now, maybe not tomorrow, but soon. Even so, it's always up to you to find those days and make them true. It's up to you to take what you've got, what the earth provides, and make it your own. You're a plant, too. At least your growing part is. You're more than some weed. You're a growing person. And you're full of love, no matter. No matter what you know or don't know, it's true. And you don't have to take my word for it. In fact, don't take my word for it. My word's got nothing to do with you. What good's my word? Take your own word. Plant it. Let the rain fall rainfall. Let the sun shine sunshine. Let the earth work its magic so your word grows good. Let the world know you're there and you've got leaves and you've got flowers and you've got fruit and you've got seeds and nothing's gonter stop you from giving your life up to someone other than yourself alone.

Aint that right, Perfect?

My boy's in the garden. The world around is every bit an open gate. He looks up at me.

We done yet? he asks.

Not quite, I say.

And I take out some paper and pencils I just happen to have. We find a place to sit down by the sweet peas in the bright of the sun.

Now, you draw me a picture, I say.

And he's happy to do it. He's got a million good pictures to draw from inside. And he draws a lot of them. Some are plants. Some are birds. Some are cars. Some are people. He lays them out, one by one. We sit for a while, looking them over. Then we get up slow, gather, and go. And this, my friend, is a beautiful day. We are free, untroubled, and everything's coming true. Walking home under the big blue sky.

SIX

What's this?

Games handed Rianna the sketch.

It's supposed to be wild columbine.

It is columbine, said Ri. But why?

I saw it in the woods. What do you think?

The day was free and the June sky cloudless. Game's apartment smelled of coffee. And down there on the street below, he pointed out a woman carrying flowers.

It's a sign, he said.

Let's go, said Ri.

It was decided. They'd drive to where the columbine grows. Games had found the red-yellow, droopy flowers in the woods behind the site where he worked with Reed and Foster. Reed cut timber frames. He'd said he could use Games for the summer at least. Not, he insisted, as a favor to Abe.

I need the help. Fifteen dollars an hour. Cash okay?

Sure.

We'll see in the fall, said Reed. I might could put you on the payroll.

It made Reed smile the way he'd said this. Might could be it was an inside joke. Measure the laughter. Raisin the Rafters. Plum Bob. Saw Saul. Bill Don.

~

You like it? asked Rio.

What's that?

Your work.

Yes, said Games. They drove along the empty road, midmorning sun coming straight on. There were rolling hills, and sparrows passing among the trees, and to Games's surprise what he thought was a meadowlark perched on a fence post, overlooking a field.

You know, I've been thinking about college, he said.

And?

Yes.

Yes?

Finishing, said Games.

Finishing what?

The thought, first. Then maybe college.

Good for you, said Rio. Almost immediately, she regretted saying it this way. Sounded like her mother. *Good for you, Rio. Good for you, sweetie,* which made Ri mad at herself to sound like someone else, and sad at the same time to think of her mother, who she missed. Still missed. Wishing her back, no matter the things her mother'd sometimes said, those measured sentiments, her parental responses. The missing never transformed into something less melancholic. Nor had it subsided over the entire year.

I didn't mean to say it like that, said Ri.

Games shook it off.

Everyone needs a push, he said. I know I'm in a rut.

As if on cue, he drove the car off the road, onto the soft shoulder.

Hey, said Rio. What's going on?

Don't worry, said Games. No peril.

Ri thought he meant clothes – apparel, which is what she heard, and it made no sense to her. Driving off the road, saying, *Don't worry. Apparel.* Games eased the car back from the shoulder, into the lane.

No more ruts, no ruts, he chanted.

You're a comedian, said Rio. A barrel of laughs.

Laughs aren't perilous, said Games.

A barrel, I said.

~

Games and Rianna talked with ease, scattering playfulness like sunflower seeds throughout their conversations. Rio gathered the handful of seeds that she'd accidently spilled into her lap, chucking them out the window into the passing ditch. Those seeds had tasted rancid, anyway. She didn't turn back to see how things fell.

Sometimes there was a car that passed on the left. Sometimes a groundhog by the side of the road, or a hummingbird that hovered near pink honeysuckle. And once two bicyclists dressed in bright biker apparel, their torsos hunched like hooks, caught Rio's attention – logos on their shirts, blue helmets, sunglasses, and, in their single-mindedness, no worries of automobiles.

They didn't even make an attempt to move over, she said, after Games had arced around the pair.

Words were free to use however. To express annoyances. To state the obvious. To gently steer the conversation in new directions. Sometimes words worked their magic by painting pictures and punning thoughts. They reeled and riffed, and the road didn't mind. Not the lush fields, either. Nor the dashboard at all. Words filled the car like farm-fresh, late spring air.

What do you think of Perfect as a name? asked Games.

The name of a town? Ri wondered.

Someone's first name, said Games.

You mean like Perfect Wilson or Perfect Heather Moore?

If that's all you've got, said Games.

How about Francine the Perfect Shun? suggested Ri. Prefect Paul. Or Liana Perfect Lee.

Prefect Paul. He's a bit off.

Why do you have to notice everyone's faults? said Ri.

Games searched the road for something better. Asphalt. Only asphalt. Don't even bring that up.

I guess Paul. If I have to come up with something. He's a good dyslexic.

Ri wasn't impressed.

Remember that time, Games began. Spencer, the near perfect failure, met with success down by the river where you left our raft.

You always bring that up. But it wasn't a raft. It was a rift in our relationship. And it wasn't me who left it.

And you, said Games, always say it wasn't me. Whereas I say it wasn't you. If not me or you, then who?

Us, said Ri, throwing down the pronoun. And this. This. She gestured first to everything inside the car and then out, to the world around.

Us. Games repeated the word. This. It's all illusion.

Yet it brings everything into question, said Ri. What we're doing. Why we wake in the morning. How we drive each other insane.

You're right, said Games. And he changed gears, switching lanes to avoid a problem up ahead. So, have you ever notice? he asked.

What? said Ri.

It's just a yes or no question.

He straightened the wheel and sped to near sixty.

~

Conversations, the quiet between. Messing and fooling. Noticing and not. No politics, maybe talk of movies. *Manos – Hands of Fate.* And the film by Ed Wood. *Plan Nine from Outer Space.* Or the more contemporary masterpiece, *Battlefield Earth.* So many good movies to choose from. And listening to music. A piece by Bach. Some sweet invention – the grapear, the sugarsnaplum. Fugue, said Games, means flight or flee. Oh, where? Oh, where were they going again? Not to Insanity. To see the columbine, remember. And songs on the radio, songs from memory, as well. Singing and feeling a simile in the soul. As weightless as possible. As high as can be.

Ri loved to sing. Songs from way back, because she liked the words. She'd do *Somewhere Over the Rainbow* or an old Joni Mitchell that her father liked about a parking lot, something else about the cost of a dog with a waggly tail, one about what God only knows, another about the spring and the summer, too, and one by Nat King Cole, considering love, which her mother used to sing when she was alive. Rianna withdrew for a moment.

What's the matter? asked Games.

I keep reminding myself of things.

Bad things?

Ri thought about this. No, she said. Nothing bad.

~

So, have you ever noticed? asked Ri, farther on.

Noticed wha –

It's really just a yes or no question, she said.

They both could play that game. Eyes on the road, the straightness of the day. Quiet yellow flowers in the field to the east. Ri opened her window and stuck out her head. The smell was delicious. Fragrant greens. The perfumey lavenders. Bursts of blue. It was very familiar. Then something changed. The road curved west and started to sing. Unless, perhaps, it was the car.

Do you hear that? asked Games, listening to determine if it was the engine or the tires.

Had he said something? Ri heard only the colorful world. She pulled in her head, closed the window and looked out, her face now turned so the back of her neck, the left line of her jaw, and her earlobe showed. The skin was soft and good to see. Near perfect, but Games didn't want to go there. The lobe had an old piercing but no jewelry. He glanced down to her legs, which were not bare, but what if they'd been bare? Light honey colored, sweet June flesh.

Look at the road, Games told himself. What was he doing? Luckily, that skin, the tease of her bare legs, was not present just now to tempt his eyes and hands. Not there to burn him, for him to turn over and over in his mind till he could take it no more. No luscious, fleshy legs to draw him in, the way the sun sucks planets, the way a black hole does. The event horizon. No going back. How lucky that was. Though it wouldn't've been Games's fault, would it, if Ri's skin had siphoned his attention and the car had crashed? Gravity would've been to blame. The appeal, the pull of the situation would've been too great. It was laws of the world that caused most things to happen: winds to blow, wood to float, balls to roll downhill, eyes to wander, hands to fall upon breasts and legs, bare or not. Games, most everyone also, had no control over such physics.

His eyes were on the road again. There were cows on the right, way off in the distance. The pasture looked green and soft. Green skin of the earth. Even fresh thistle leaves are beautiful. Yes.

You hungry? Games asked.

Well, I. Not really. Are you?

Games didn't have to consider it. He definitely was hungry. His pack of sunflower seeds had tasted rancid. He hadn't eaten since seven last night. He knew, he said, this place.

The fish? asked Ri.

Not that plaice. This one, up ahead. They've got good food. Organic ice cream.

Perfect, said Rio.

What is it with you and perfection, said Games. Remember our fight?

He turned off the musical road onto another, drove down a hill that wound into a hamlet. Things sounded normal now, nothing to worry about. When he stopped the car and got out, Games checked the engine and tires just to be sure.

He then bought two ice creams, even though it was eleven. Or maybe they were gelatos. He didn't know the difference. What did it matter what time it was, anyway? Some people make such a big deal about time. Other people make a big deal about food. The best cheeses. The best chocolate. The only good coffee you can get is in Europe, they say. The finest fish, wild sockeye salmon, comes from waters off Alaska, and the ancient grains – amaranth, emmer, millet, and teff – not only have the best flavor, but also, grown organically, help prevent cancer. Games and Ri sat on a log, beside a stream, eating.

My father wrote a book about organic farming, said Ri. Biodynamics, actually.

What's that?

A book?

No, biodynamics?

It's... Well...

Rianna thought for a moment, and the moment went on, the thought along with it. After a while, Games wondered if all hope for an answer had been lost.

It's... Well... What? he asked, in an attempt to bring things home.

Ri ate more ice cream. She looked at the water, the stream flowing by. The surface glinted with sunlight.

You've got a farm, she began, which is like a canvas. And everything –

Did you say *canvas*?

Yes. Can I go on?

Sorry.

And everything becomes a harmonious painting.

What are you talking about?

Biodynamic farming.

So, why're you talking about painting?

Because, if you think about it, said Ri. The animals, the cows, the chickens, the soil, the crops. All the pieces work together like colors on a canvas.

Games needed time to digest the thought. Rianna continued before he was ready: The farm's a creation, a living painting on a canvas of fields.

And the farmer's the artist? said Games.

I don't see why not.

Usually not how you think of a farmer, said Games. And you don't often think that a farm's a painting, but a provider of food. You use the farmland to get crops and livestock. Use it so people can eat.

That's the thing, said Ri. It's not about using. There's more to a farm than food alone.

Games waited to hear what's more.

A biodynamic farm is… Well, it's not just about getting what you can out of the fields – the highest yields. It's more about what those fields give of themselves. More about how the soil and the plants and the animals contribute to the well-being of the place.

You mean, they have a say in it?

They should have a say, said Rianna. Everything has a voice in the world. The problem is – do you ignore the many voices, or do you listen? If you insist that the land does your bidding, it stresses out the land. You know, how you can stress a person with too many demands. Maybe she just wants to be quiet and go slow with her words, but you poke and prod and get her to explain stuff just because you want it, never asking what she wants. I don't call that a healthy relationship.

More like torture.

Sort of. And then she breaks down because you won't stop forcing it.

You as in me? said Games

Yes. This is all about you.

Is it?

No, said Rianna. I'm just saying. Think what damage you, not you you, but someone, might be doing to the land by coercing it to provide high yields of food. And if you coerce the food from the land, if you don't let it grow of its own free will, how can that food be good for the world? How can it be healthy to eat?

You're saying that a tomato has a will of its own? said Games.

I'm just saying a tomato knows more about itself than I do. So why not ask it? Listen to what it has to say.

Games had no problem with this. Rianna took time with the stream, with her ice cream again, before continuing the lesson:

I mean, if the farmer only looks at profits…yields…well… You've really got to look at the whole picture.

Which is? asked Games.

Relationships, mostly, said Ri. The farm is a place of relationships. But to begin with, there's no farm at all without some reason to have it and people to do the work.

Okay, agreed Games, thinking that was obvious.

And maybe it is, said Ri.

Is what?

Obvious. Still, the work's got to be done with consideration. You've got to think about what you're doing. What does a plant need from the soil, from the farmer, in order to grow? How can you provide the best environment?

Take a seed, said Games. Put it in the ground. Add some sun and rain and…

And what?

Whatever else it needs, said Games. Nitrogen, phosphorus, potassium. The answers are out there.

Half answers mostly, said Ri. About the physiology of plants. Think of yourself, you. Are you nothing more than the matter you're made of?

I thought this wasn't about me, reminded Games.

But it is about what you think of the world you live in. It is about how you treat everything around you. I'm saying you can't assume you know something just because you've broken it down and analyzed it to your liking. Pay attention to what the plant needs.

You keep saying that, and I like it, said Games. But a farmer can't pay attention all day. He's got to pay bills, too. He's got to plow ahead. Reap the harvest. Whatever the jargon.

It's a lot of work, agreed Ri. To provide a healthy home for the seed, and then consciously allow that seed to become itself. Like a child's got to be born into a healthy environment, doesn't she? She shouldn't be born into a smoke-filled room where there's shouting and arguing and where the TV's blasting its distractions so no thought is given to what's growing in that room.

That wasn't you, was it?

I'm talking about a seed, said Ri. A sprout. What allows that sprout to express itself best? Healthy soil allows it to grow. Inspired workers on the farm who actually are interested in the plants. Other animals like bees and spiders and pigs and cows. Each piece is a part of the picture. Plants and animals and people and soil – they exist together. A farm is a family. It's great art, like I said. It works thanks to everything being interconnected in some underlying agreement.

Games remembered. A painting, yes. A social work, he thought.

A system of relationships, really, said Ri. Good relationships upon the farm depend upon the life and well-being of each individual part, weeds included. The sun and moon and stars are part of the picture, too. And then something more.

Something even farther than the stars? said Games.

It's nothing far, said Ri, looking out, across the stream. Closer, maybe.

Games wanted to know what Ri was thinking, what she was seeing.

I'm just rambling, she said. Don't listen to me.

I like listening to you, said Games. I want to hear your

"something more."

Rianna looked at her hands as if she'd find it there. She had finished her ice cream. The container now empty. Tiny wooden spoon. A lingering sweet taste in her mouth. And up, out there. Sun through the trees. A nod from the light. Greetings and shimmers and shadows of leaves. The stream going by – it moved like a song.

It's big as life, she said. Even bigger. But you hold it in your heart and hands.

A riddle, thought Games, glad he didn't say the word out loud. Rianna continued.

You want the food to be as full as possible. If everything –

Full, like stuffed with nutrition? interrupted Games.

Maybe I should just stop talking about it.

Sorry.

Why are you sorry?

Because I interrupted. And your thoughts need to flow.

It's true, Rianna was passionate about this biodynamic stuff. Food full of everything possible. Vitamins, sunlight, starlight. Love, even, if that's what she was getting at. But to Games, food was just something to eat. If you liked it, it was good. If not, it was bad. Food wasn't empty, your stomach was.

No one's saying not to eat, said Ri. But it's got to be healthy. An artificial farm coerces its food. An artful one creates it.

You don't like coercion.

Do you? I mean, a farm's man-made, but you can do it as best as you can. You can think about children and what they need in the world. And you can think about seeds and not selfishly try to get the most out of them, which is imposing your own wishes and not caring about theirs.

A seed has wishes?

We've been through this already, said Rianna. You are responsible for what you think and do. You've got to act with life and love, and not bend things to suit yourself.

Is that what I'm doing to you?

I'm talking about plants.

You're including lots more than just plants in what you're saying, said Games. Besides, do the plants really care?

Wouldn't you?

You mean if I was a plant?

Sure, said Ri. If you were a plant, would you want your life to be taken over and controlled so you had no say?

If I were a plant, said Games. I'd want you to take care of me. You'd do a good job. I'd trust you.

I'd have to water you, if there wasn't any rain.

And I'd want only encouraging words, said Games.

Biodynamics is about thinking it through, said Ri. It's about doing right by the land and providing a setting for healthy, happy crops. It's about all the animals on the farm, the cows and chickens, the birds and bees, even the insects, not chasing them off. You can't push things around. You can't manipulate the land so much that you destroy its character, depleting it of its true being with herbicides and pesticides and artificial fertilizers. Then the land loses its natural abilities. Left to itself, the land does pretty well. So, on the farm you've got to work together, with the weeds and the worms and the tractors and the goats, even the night sky, like I said. It's all part of the picture.

It's not just corn alone, said Games.

It's not anything alone, said Rio. Certainly not only the material world. It's spiritual, too.

That's where love comes in, said Games.

I never said love.

I know, said Games. I did.

Rianna said nothing. Who really wants to talk about love? She didn't.

The end result, though, is still food to put on plates, said Games, just to be sure.

And why not do it right? reiterated Rianna. Don't coerce. Listen to one another.

~

They'd both finished their ice creams and now listened to the stream, each flowing note of water, each calm note, too. Each one, each other. Games didn't mean to be dismissive. What did he know about good food or bad? He ate when he was hungry. Maybe he needed to think more about it. Why go through life without thinking? That would be like swimming through the ocean and not getting wet. But the ocean is full of wetness. And life is full of thought. So, if you say you're here in life, maybe it's time to think about it some, to figure for yourself what's going on.

Ri threw a stick to the water and they both watched it float. A bird in the low bush. White clover in the nearby grass. Butterflies, daisies, bee-like hummingbirds. Games felt comfortable with Rianna. He felt good and whole. But how did she feel? Not just to him, not just the softness of her shaded skin. Ri shifted her body upon the log. Someone had put the log here for sitting. It hadn't fallen in place. Its bark had been hewn to form a seat. Sunlight found passage through thousands of leaves. Rianna leaned forward, into the light.

Nothing lasts forever, thought Games. Beauty, youth, freshness, light – it's all subject to change. A relationship is ever in a state of becoming. But it's what you do at this moment that is the seed for what will come next. Ah, that's thinking for you.

Games wanted to reach over and touch Ri. He wanted to kiss her. He'd done it before. There were no laws against kissing. There were laws expressing physical confines, such as electromagnetism and gravity. There were other laws to accept as well – social laws, traffic laws, laws governing how oil companies treat the planet. And then there was an individual law specific to Games. This law spoke of things that guided Games's life on earth. He was a measure of that law, which governed his specific melting point, for example, his giving up point, his point of view, and the exact point when he decides to take action. Games wanted to wrap Ri with his arms. He wanted to kiss her lips as the sun kisses the day. He wanted to act now, which would be no ambush, but high time, noontime, his burning move.

The breeze kicked in, shaking the leaves. The sun worked the lunch hour near the apex of the sky. And the quiet stream rolled on. With Rio on his left, Games turned her way, his will in motion. He –

A voice interrupted him. A melancholic song. Games looked across the stream to where the melancholy came from.

No other part of the person was visible, just her sad music, which had the green look of leaves. The woman's voice filtered through the branches as trembling words, and then her body appeared to Games and Rio both.

She was in her fifties, perhaps, walking on the far bank. Her song, a made-up song, was in no hurry to settle, it had no need for ears. Saturday afternoon a quarter to twelve. The woman must've thought she was alone. When she saw Rianna and Games, she put a stop to her singing. She took her song in hand, tucking it under her arm. It had been a soft made-up song, and it came to nothing.

Don't stop because of us, called Games. It's nice.

The woman, thin and worn, smiled at them from across the creek, but didn't speak. Her hair was black, loose and short. There was some burden on her mind and in her body by the look of things. The light of her face was a weary light. The light of the sun-soaked trees was different. Upon the far bank grew a green patch of moss. The sky above was a blue warehouse of thought. And all the while, the stream streamed repetitively on.

The woman continued along the bank. After a bit, she untucked her tune from under her arm. She lifted the song to her lips and started singing again. The words, however, were difficult to make out because the woman by this time was far, and then farther. Finally, she was gone. Games and Rianna followed her departure among the maples and the river birches.

I feel bad we bothered her, said Rio, her eyes on the vanishing point. I think she wanted to be alone.

My mother used to think she was alone when she sang, said Games. I heard her though.

My mother knew she wasn't alone, said Ri. She sang to me, and to my sister. She'd sing in the kitchen and the garden and the bathroom. She...

Games waited for more.

I remember one birthday she gave me a song. It was the nicest present ever. But then she stopped.

What stopped?

I don't know if anything stopped. She just wasn't there anymore. I don't want to talk about it.

You don't have to talk about it, said Games. He went back to staring.

I mean, you can't expect things not to change, said Ri.

It's the nature of the world, agreed Games.

She didn't even smoke.

Your mother?

My dad tried everything. He made her eat macrobiotic. He took her to Germany and Mexico. By the end, he was making everything she ate. No meat. Lots of raw. I guess it was supposed to help. He did compresses and biography work with her. There was oil-dispersion hydrotherapy. And what's that plant you kiss under?

Crape myrtle? asked Games.

No. No. Mistletoe. That's it.

What's biography work? asked Games.

Trying to understand where you're from and how you came to be sick.

Games imagined a very ambiguous story.

I'm sorry, he said. Why didn't he know this? he thought. He didn't know much about her family.

No reason you should know, said Ri. It was only last year she died. Almost exactly a year ago in fact. She didn't even smoke. I already said that. Singers don't smoke. She was always so... I don't remember her sick, ever.

Games assumed it was lung cancer.

You were a nurse, said Games. That must've helped.

I don't want to be a nurse anymore, said Ri. It's not sick things I'm interested in. It's not what you do so you're no longer sick, but what you do so you're healthy that matters.

That's a subtle difference, said Games.

It's a world of difference, said Ri. People spend a lot of time focusing on what's wrong and very little time realizing what's right.

I think that's true, Games nodded. Yes, he nodded, but had he said it? There was the sound of the water rippling by, and the sound of his words reverberating inside him. Rianna was glad he understood.

You'll be a good teacher, said Games.

You never know.

There are things I do know, said Games. Maybe not

everything about plants, but other things. Yes.

Ri was glad, too, that he was so positive. After a moment, she said,

My mother had this quote I remember. She wrote it in calligraphy and put it in a frame next to her bed: *Life-threatening illness greatly intensifies love of life.* I'm sure that's true. But do you think a person needs the threat?

I don't know, said Games.

You just said you did know things.

You're right, remembered Games. Seems to me you can open your heart at every moment. No threat needed.

Ri looked at Games, who followed the stream with his eyes. *At every moment* – that's what he had said. It's a lot of opening, she thought. A great, expanding heart, if it opens more each moment. Of course the heart didn't always have to open far. Sometimes just inches was all that was needed.

You never talk about your parents, Rianna said, at last. It was the first bit of information you've ever given – about your mother singing for no one.

That's because I don't have much to say.

Are they together? asked Ri.

No.

Where do they live?

I don't know.

Are they alive?

The word echoed inside Games. Alive alive. He didn't answer. His noontime mind, alive alive, filled with memories mixed with stream mixed with light mixed with leaves.

You've got to know something? said Rio.

Maybe I do, said Games. It feels unimportant. I might be wrong. I never met my father, but my mother calls me on my birthdays. That's about it. She used to sing when I was young. Now that I think, maybe some of it was for me. Songs in the car. One about swallowing a fly.

There was an old lady who swallowed a fly, sang Rio, softly. I don't know why she swallowed that fly.

My mother was like that woman who just went past, said Games. Off in the woods, keeping to herself. Her hair wasn't short. It was black, though. I remember it pulled back and handfuls going in her face. She'd sweep the hair off, but it'd come right back again. She had uncontrollable hair. Mostly she sang when she thought I wasn't there.

But you *were* there.

Yep, said Games. Maybe that woman we saw is my mother.

She didn't look like you, said Rio.

No, said Games.

She had a nice voice, though, remembered Ri. Singing's good for you. It's a nice thing to give someone. I'll probably have children someday just so I can give them stuff.

Where'd that come from?

The stuff?

No, the children.

Well, Alex has two. I've got a niece and a nephew. I gave them both a cold once.

You're so generous, said Games.

She's a good mother, said Ri. And she's only three years older.

I'm three years older, said Games.

Not for long, and you're not a good mother, either.

Games nodded. He knew it was true. Some things he knew for sure. That Ri's birthday was coming, yes. Aunt Julia's birthday, too. And that he was no mother. For sure, for sure. What he didn't know was what he was good at. There had to be something. He had a voice coming out of him, a man's voice, he thought, but what was it trying to tell him?

The two of them waded a while in the music of the stream. It was a symphony. Hydrotherapy. A bright river of ripple and song. The stream cut through the woods, this world. It pulled things together. It tried to put them right. There were things on either side of the stream that found their ways to a meeting point. There were birds hiding somewhere in the leaves with the light. There was one fallen tree, broken in two. All things find joinery in the workroom of the heart, thought Games. It sounded pithy and rhythmical, that statement. A bit too sentimental, however.

Games wiped his hands in the dirt to remove the remains of ice cream.

How far is it to the wild columbine? asked Rio.

Not far. You ready to go?

She was.

Sorry if I'm a bit off today, said Ri. Like Prefect Paul.

You're never off, said Games.

They got up from the log, and the stream continued to run through the woods. Games put his arm around Rianna's shoulder in a slow half circle the way he'd wanted to some time ago. Rio leaned into Games, pressing herself to his side. It made his side, all sides, happy. It made him sing, and nobody heard. Though who can know for sure who's listening? And they swayed as they walked, June breeze through the trees. June trees through the breeze. Walking with ease. With ears to the trees. They music they listening they swaying they breeze. Together they June. They June together.

JUNE

Mothers

I am somebody's mother. Might be I'm that mother singing by the creek, the one who seemed troubled and whose children were nowhere in sight. Or Rianna's mother, with a song on her lips. It's possible I'm your own mother, Seffi, driving the car, strands of hair whispering down the side of her face. I'm not really sure whose mother I am. Maybe I'm Momm mother of Sok, or Naomi mother of Pearl. Could be I'm Olivia mother of Jessica, or Toinette mother of Vashon and Rams. There are many mothers to choose from – a long list of names: Rachel May June Julia. And there are scores of children, from August to March, for as long as it takes till we're familiar again. I'm gone from you now, but I was big with you once. Tremendous tummy back then, which told the world that you were approaching. Though for me there was no need for such a physical telling. It was absolute certainty, spiritual throughout.

Things must've looked good when I was pregnant, because some people said I had this wonderful glow they'd never seen before. I wanted to stand outside myself, in hopes I could catch a glimpse of that illuminated person. Then again, maybe I didn't want to see her at all. I had no history with the woman. Was, in fact, unfamiliar with the person I was becoming, and this despite all the books I'd read. My own mother said I couldn't fathom the change. She may've been right. Part of me was dissolving, and this was a concern, even if the part I was losing wasn't worth keeping.

People tend to hold on to old stuff. It's comforting. I get that. But why hold on to something that's had its time and is finished? The thing I eventually learned, the truth I want my children to trust, is that a greater *you* is always growing inside. It pushes the boundaries, increasing your world.

I knew little about this different me. My swollen breasts and advancing girth gave no clues. Yet, all the time, people would follow me with their eyes. They'd come up and talk, as if I was someone with a sign above me, and the sign read: *Welcome, one and all. Say whatever you have to say.* They must've felt a connection, even though I had nothing to do with their lives. It was in line at the bank, in the grocery, even pumping gas.

Let me do that for you?

Thanks, I'd say. I'm okay with it.

It's no problem, they'd say. The fumes, you know. And I'd let them have their way.

You'd think I would've felt like a princess with all the attention, but I shied away from the public. My experience with pregnancy needed to be intimate. It had to do with mostly me increasingly you. We were always together, you and I. I'd stand in the kitchen, all smiles. I'd sit in the tub, surrounded by water and the comfort of you. I'd pause on the stairs, and the wind of your being would blow my mind to a thousand good places. I'd hum by the sink and happily place my hands upon my stomach as stepping-stones to your world. I'd then look in the mirror and see me looking back at us both.

Later, I'd lie awake in bed, my husband lost to sleep. I'd stare at the dark ceiling, layer by layer peeling away protection, then get up and stand at the window, concerned for your well-being. I had no trouble turning on the worry. I'd want to talk. And you weren't there. I'd panic at the long stretches of stillness. I'd wonder if things would ever break free and be different, as after a long night when appear the first rays of sun. Ah, morning! When would it happen? I'd work myself up at that window, waiting for you, asking you things, getting no answers. Yet, I'd feel the reassuring nod of my head, and then sleep would call like a concerned girlfriend. I'd leave the window, returning to bed.

And I'd rise from my dreams, bright and early. Blueberries, bananas, chocolate milk. I'd walk and hum and cut up spinach with scissors. I'd stop at red lights, drive through greens, and press gently beyond my last days of work. At lunch sometimes I'd lean forward to listen to the conversations of other pregnant women sitting near my table at the cafe.

I hate this seat.

It's a terrible heat.

I'd like to die, it's so uncomfortable.

I want to lie on my stomach again.

I want my old stomach back.

I hate how I'm ugly.

I'd love her to shift.

I love when she kicks.

I love when she moves.

I'm in a daze because of this baby.

Crazy in love.

I'd move through the months in various styles. I'd finish my evening classes at the community college. Everything unknown was good to learn. I was young and vital, a sudden witness to life: a hand or a foot pressing within me. One turn at a time, a shift after dinner. One sudden kick from my constant companion. Was there too much lemon on that fish? I'd question. No good sweets for your dessert? I'd tease. But it wasn't as if you were an open book. So, what were you thinking when you went into hiding? You moved in ways I couldn't understand. And I wanted to understand what was happening inside me. Was it really not I, not I at all, not I even some, but somebody else so totally new, overwhelmingly near?

Every child is a new take on things, a fresh story on earth from some constant store. And what is that store, that steadfast star? What is that light and love from which all children come?

I continue to wonder about the place beyond conception, which is a spiritual place, which is the source of all life. I dipped into the store when I became pregnant. I tried to welcome love into my arms and my immaculate room. I struggled to know. Didn't have a clue what I was doing. I was paralyzed by the thought of an unknown person. Entering my. Yes, entering my life.

June summer wind crosses here, speaking through the

leaves. And I am somebody's mother beginning with yes. Yes – there is love to draw on, to nurture into a body. Yes – there is a wish for each particular family, a wish that someone will come to form in their home, that a child will be born. Yes – life on earth begins once more, through me. Yes – I try, each time, to do it right.

I am the representative of beginning. I am a mother working from the inside of life – accepting the spirit, providing the space for its growth on earth. I conceive all things and bring them to being. I reproduce on earth what is in heaven. I then nurse the body, tickle the feet, and shoo the flies. Holding tight to the hand, I watch for cars. Overly cautious, I then initiate our move, and quickly, quickly we cross the road. We walk ahead to the other side, to the world around, the great big place. It's a promising world, I say, and say it again and again as I coax a response, as I slide away, first with my palm, the fingers, finally the tips, growing ever more aware of inevitable release. And then, at last, the letting go.

~

June's a nice name, I think. I'll go with it. Even if it's got an old-timey ring, like out of the fifties. They don't name children June these days. Not anymore. Juna maybe. Or Jimmio. Jaimi. Josh. I knew a Juke, a Junco, and a Juneau, back in my life. I knew a Django and a Jules, but they came before I had children of my own.

I haven't always been a mother. I entered the world as a baby girl in Newton, MA. I just so happened to be at home when I was born, upstairs in a house full of music. A midwife to assist my birth. A bassinet alongside my parent's bed. I was happy at home, believe me. Faithful dogs, purring cats, and my loving parents who were very artistic.

When I was little, about the size of a small ukulele, Daddy put me outside with the early morning birds. Told me later, I sang along. And once, I remember it, Mamma Mia, with her Italian flair, painted my portrait as an evergreen tree: *Juniper*, she called the work of art, *Symphony of Love*. I was twelve then, and the living was easy. Rain and wind were lyrics for me, and the sun splashing on the window ledge made an inviting song.

So, later, when I went on the road and sang with a group, it was no surprise to anyone. What amazed me was that people would actually pay to hear me sing. Crazy, isn't it? I'd be out and about with Dominic and Nate. We'd jam and juke on small stages and in bars and clubs. We'd sing and wheel on fiddle and guitars, going till the wee hours, which were large times for us, then. We'd drink and smoke, rise wispy and disheveled, and sometimes fall. We were the jazzy response to Peter, Paul, and Mary. We were *Dominant June*. At first it was *Dominate*. *Dominate June*, which I had issues with. What person wants to be dominated? Not I.

Okay, I admit, both names made me smile, but our purpose was the music. I could pluck the high notes like cherries from the upper branches and soul out the lows like feet plodding the ground. It was various deals and terrible hours. It was occasional lovers, and thirds and fifths. It was out with the streetlights, the cities and towns. It was before I got married, pregnant, and settled. Before all of that, it was only myself. We'd go off and make music for money and fun. I'm telling you, voice was my instrument. It was my Tao, my way. Heart full of feeling and lungs lit with air. An open mouth, I'd say, is for delivering notes. A tongue with tones, too, is a virtue. Untangled is best: Sally Sue sells seashells on the sunny southern shore. New York is unique. Your Yorkshire's sure sweet. O Dee Eee Dee Bee Dee Bee. I Lie Lee Loo Lee Lay Lee Lo. I'd figure the rhythm to make it work. The music seemed to have no end.

Then, I met someone. Same old story, people might say. Man over takes. Now her life is done. But I didn't see it like that. My response to the world is to pay attention. To appreciate what comes and not miss opportunities. I'm my own judge, not someone else.

Ryan was a writer of documentary films, books, both. I was struck by his poise and undemanding presence. The first thing he gave me was a blade of grass, which felt to me like a promise kept from way back in time. We were both outside at some party, looking the exact same way through the windblown trees. He turned to me and said, "I've been carrying this around for a while. I think it belongs to you." He handed me the green blade. I took it. Nodded. Kept looking out. "Have I heard you somewhere, besides up there among those leaves?" he asked. Now, some might think that a terrible line, but it blew me away, though I tried not to show it.

Ryan wasn't much of a singer. Terrible singing voice. He was a teacher, though, but didn't try to teach me anything. I learned best on my own. We walked through fields where the cows grazed free and trekked in forests among mosses, ferns, the most amazing red and yellow mushrooms ever. And when we emerged from those woods, it was sky again and wide spaces, airplanes on high, gusts of wind. Ryan would wait until the wind had died, then he'd ask what I was thinking, and I'd tell him, and he'd stand there, smiling, a look of intrigue like I was telling him secrets of life, as if he'd never heard such ideas before.

Months later, he took me to Africa where I saw lives that were decimated. Where thirteen-year-old girls had been sold to fifty-five-year-old men as second or third wives. Where other girls had been raped and beaten and no one cared. Where the least of everything was abundant by far. There was mud in the rainy season and villages of mud-walled huts. Mosquitoes and famine and poverty, like always. And when the young girls got pregnant, these child-mothers were beaten by the jealous first wives, and if they weren't big enough, if their bodies weren't able to deliver, the girls tore up inside, and no one came to fix them. It just went on, seemingly by design. It brought me to tears. Ryan embraced me, rocking. No one came to turn any of it off.

> Famished the skies
> Dung sun after showers
> Anguished fields too dry
> Half birds sung out

These young mothers were rural and poor. They were women, too, just like me. It was the worst thing ever. Not that they were like me – I liked that part – but that any human life could be so disregarded. There was no importance to being a woman, not even a mother. A pregnant goat got more approval. A pregnant goat could actually contribute some wealth. Babies died, mothers festered, peopled looked away. And I asked myself, Why would a person look away? It made no sense to me, to turn from another life as if that were your most human choice.

> We come here to sing
> This branch our tree
> All leaves against the sky
> Together in the wind

And yet, if we live in a world where women are not recognized for all they conceive, they are missed and mis-taken, and so goes the spirit of life with our omission. If women are seen as part of only a toiling, material world, they are not as they might be – an image of soul. And if the Bible the Koran the Torah the Upanishads the Genome and Tradition make us unable to think for ourselves, then we have little say over what happens next. Which was my rant, my rave. Some version of song. I wanted to act with more effectual love.

And so...

I stood thinking. Distressed. I stood thinking.

So... Yes...

Haven't you ever, I one day asked Ryan, even you, wanted your life to be something more – some necessary beauty in your arms for once, the simple realization of all your hopes? I was not accusing him of privilege or thinking it hadn't been so. I was trying to make sense of things for others.

Go on, he said, because he liked my beginning, the sound of my voice, or the sense of things to come. So, I did, I went on:

Haven't you ever thought that others, of course, want the same? We're not so different, even though we try to be. There's a certain slant of life that cuts across everyone. I am part you and you are part me, and we'll both keep meeting for as long as it takes to be harmonious.

You're right, he said. We're in sympathy with each other.

That or antipathy. Actually, it's one big symphony.

And then, because Ryan always thought in large swatches of time, he described how he saw the grand picture: We, this world, all things and life, this universe itself, all universes and all of time play a role in that symphony as a single note. Life as we know it is one note completing itself. Maybe that note is AUM, the chalice of life on earth. It's everything together, for as long as it takes, just as you said. And you can even imagine it further – this one single note, this cup of everything, is no more than a bridge to the next note: *do* trying to finish so *re* can begin, which will take place some other time, some other world, some other quality of life. Who knows what that quality of life will be? But isn't it interesting? Isn't it our job to get there?

I guess, I said, if you want to imagine that far ahead. I'm more worried about the way we sound now, which isn't very good. It's no part of any note I wish to hear.

> And I'll suffer if you suffer
> Sing if you sing
> Wind of our being
> Lifts my limbs, loosens love

~

We went home, Ryan and I, my heart heavy with new music.

I remember hearing a lecture once. The speaker said, *Give a life some weight and there is the chance for that life to be felt by the world. See it as chaff and it'll blow away, unnoticed.* I heard those words not as lyrics but as song itself. The lecturer also said that it was only after society gave women the right to vote – in other words, only after society deemed them worthy – that women's health became an issue and maternal mortality a problem to solve.

What took so long? What good does it do the world for its individuals to be so selfish? I wasn't a mother, not yet, but I wondered it aloud after class one day. We had gathered outside, the teacher and some others, in the parking lot. It was

dark with streetlights. There was an argument about baseball,
whether it was good pitching or hitting that won a game. But
it was something else I was thinking, and I'd practiced the
speech in my head. I found a quiet moment between innings.

What makes it so easy to disregard each other? I asked.

You mean like, who cares about the fucking Yankees?

I mean, is it too idealistic to think every life is important? I
said.

Every life isn't important, said Mike with brown hair.
Many are a fucking waste of time. Pedophiles, rapists,
assholes, people who don't like the Red Sox.

This threw me for a loop, but I refocused on mothers.

The world is half full of mothers, myself and other women
included only potentially.

There you go, said another man who I didn't remember
seeing in class. You've got your mothers and your
motherfuckers.

I'm thinking, I said, how life gets inside you, not how you
get inside someone.

I heard a snicker, to which the man said: Everything's an
inside job.

Why did I go on? But I did:

Only about half the world has the luxury of –

What kind of curry?

Experiencing, up close, life growing inside them.

When I eat curry, it's lots of growling inside me.

Only a woman can create within herself that which is not
her, then set it free.

Somehow I'd finished my sentence. No one seemed to
care. Then someone did:

A man can write a book, he said. You don't have to be a
mother to be an artist.

I'm thinking of a real, pulsing body of life, I said. I just
wonder if many of the problems of the world are because,
mostly, it remains a man's world and men are not mothers
and don't have an intimate connection with another life?

A father has children.

Fathers tell stories. Mothers sing songs. It's all good, I
said. It's not a judgment.

That's exactly what it is.

I'm talking about how the world is arranged, I said. Women conceive things. They have babies and carry them to the world. It's easier to establish a sense of connection because life begins inside them, right there, with another human being, whereas for a man the sense of life is not obtained through the body, but through the mind. It makes all the difference in the world if something is really living inside you.

We're doomed then, if men can't do this, said the one who'd heard judgment.

No, we're just beginning to realize the importance of the female.

In the beginning was the word. That was a long time ago.

And I'm wondering now how that word got so lost, I said.

So, you blame me?

Not you.

But men.

I'm not blaming anyone.

Emily D. Did she ever have children?

Who? I asked.

Dickinson.

Not that I know of.

Interesting, isn't it? he said. And Virginia Woolf?

She had her problems, I said.

How about Harriet Tubman?

Harriet Tubman?

What kind of mother was she?

Gertie, I think, was her child, I said.

But, of course, Gertie was adopted, said the man who knew everything.

You're missing my point, I said. It's really not about women versus men, but…

Anna Jarvis, he went on. She wasn't a mother, but she invented Mother's Day. And Marilyn Monroe. How about good old Marilyn? he went on.

Only miscarriages, I think.

What about Simone Weil?

She died very young.

The Down syndrome girl, Leeba, I once met in Jerusalem? said this very worldly man.

She might not have children.

No, he said. You're probably right. And how about that flower painter, the photographer's wife?

Georgio –

Keeffe, he completed. She created lots out of herself, just like Stieglitz. They must've felt something moving inside them. But it wasn't children, was it?

No, I sighed. I was feeling assaulted.

Still, June Gardner Olivet – how'd he know my name? – she can say what she likes. He must've read my name off a paper.

I heard you sing three years ago, he explained.

Which made me remember that time of me. Sometimes it's difficult to keep yourself straight.

You had a good voice, he said.

Thanks, I said.

You had this song about oceans I liked a lot. And one about pigeons, but that was depressing.

It felt to me, in that parking lot, that we were now alone. Dark night. Streetlight shining. Cars reflecting. Keys in my grip. And he was my ghost. My ghost, but not me. And I wanted him to exit. I don't know why I had to stay.

Sorry, I said.

No need to be sorry, he subsided, before regaining momentum. You've got a moving voice now, too. Everyone says so. It's beautiful how you pin all the world's problems on men, just because, well, you're a mother, so connected with the way of life. No one outside your circle could ever experience it. Only the chosen few. Why, you've given birth to what, two, three, four of your own?

None as of yet, I conceded.

You sure it isn't more than none? asked my ghost. Not a brood or a clutch? said the dark parking lot.

I'm sure, I said, and walked away to find my car.

Some people are so annoying. I didn't want to talk anymore. Didn't want to study cruelty or nonsense anymore. I didn't want to sing, either, not as I once had sung. Not for the inconsistent pay. Not for all the riches in the world. Not for the art of it. Not for the entertainment. And especially not just for show. I wanted what was a different creation, as intimate with life as physically and spiritually possible. I wanted to begin with life – a blessing – and to bud with it. And I would know what it is that is everyone's origin. I would carry life's wishes out to the world.

~

I loved the sense of change inside me. Taking on responsibility. It must've been years, I must've been older. I remember the feeling as I stood at the edge of a field, near the trees. It was a field I knew, late spring early summer. The sun shone high. An untroublesome wind tickled the leaves. Shadows shrank to near nothing as the day grew warm.

I had grown, too, just as I'd wanted. Closer to things. Responsible, as I said, to a world of life outside me. I was bright and happy to be looking across that field, beside those trees, alone as it may've seemed. But I was not alone. Hello, I saw. Someone else came running. She took my hand and shook it. It rung like a bell.

Mommy, Mommy, come and see.

I went with my daughter and we bent to the ground. It was a baby bird, weak, without feathers, too young to fly. Somewhere up was its nest in the trees.

It's alive, isn't it? It's alive, Mommy. Do something.

But sometimes you don't know what to do. You'd like to do something good. You'd like to say something to make everything better. But all you've got is the cup of your hand for some dying bird and the chance to place the unfeathered body in the softly shaded grass. So that's what I did. Gently, gently. And we said a few words. Or I said them, mostly. Then I took my daughter by the hand, and together we walked off, as the sun began its descent and shadows rearranged themselves to the east, as the green leaves shook and I sought to explain things – life and death – to a teary child. And if it was not a satisfying explanation then at least maybe I showed a bit of empathy for her feelings. Or perhaps I sparked a brief understanding – how life works here, every day without tiring and without complaint. Because life never leaves, not even at death. And our job, what we must do, is to notice its measures, its rest, and its return. To pay attention.

To follow life's lead with our own good moves.

~

There's a universal mother who is part of us all. Each person, no matter who, is the nurturer of her or his own experiences on earth. Things grow inside. The inside increases. The outside to match it. The more we consider and the more we care, the larger grows the life within. Then eventually we must let what has grown come out. It has a right to its own time and place. Besides, who knows what light this new being might bring the world.

The good world opens, and it opens through the mother. Without some other growing inside me, I could never sense love. And without knowing that other, that person separate in the world, I could not work out the promise of love. That's what being a mother is all about, I think: sensing love, carrying it to term, and releasing that love to the world. It's not only about giving birth. Being a mother is also a doorway for love, which is a door that everyone, men and women both, can open. The door lets people in. It lets them out, freely. Luckily on earth, the door also includes a surrounding home. The home, of course, is a good place for love to be felt. It is a place in which there's singing in the morning, maybe a comfortable couch, and some fresh baked bread, which always is good.

That doorway, I hope, is who I was as a mother. I had two daughters, Alexo, short for Alexandria Olivet, and Rio, short for Rianna Olivet. I saw things through as best I could. I changed diapers. I drove cars. I made breakfast, lunch, and dinner, and then made it all over, for days and nights and days again. Fresh strawberries in the late spring. Apple cider donuts in the fall. I made love go as far as my voice would carry. I made love with my arms when the world wouldn't do.

A good world needs you present all the time. It's a lot of work and often no thanks. Sometimes I needed a moment near the trees to re-gather my courage. Of course, all I really did was stare at the moving limbs, the leaves. And then as if from the branches or from the far reaches of the universe something came into me, filling my heart with joy, which was like hearing the most beautiful song and wanting to sing it out. I was bursting then, like the old days, like the sun-through-the-cloud days. Oh, I was so happy for a while, and I knew this song would always be, even if I were to forget it for a moment.

And was I ever tired? Yes. Was I ever worried? Sure. It was sometimes so much worry and fret, being a mother, it made the world spin out of control, but I managed. And was I ever disappointed? Never in you, only in myself, and really only some in myself until I remembered again who I am. Not that I'm somebody great. What mother is ever good enough? I didn't have a book to explain things. I didn't have some voice telling me what to do. I was always a beginner and I'm still a beginner and a learner too for as long as it takes.

~

Red sun in the west sings sweet and low, like a chariot. The breeze goes green through the quieting leaves. I'm turning home now to be there for you – my love, my child, your self, your own. Whoever I am and whoever you are. Wherever I am and wherever you are. When the morning breaks or the evening upholds its colors. When the summer leaves quiver or the autumn leaves fall. When the night reigns over the world with its darkness, or the cherry sweet stars curve across the heavens and sing – I'm home. Home appears through the door that is opened by love. And through that door I am always there for you.

I am your paean, your mother, the first body around you, and your very first kiss. Hear me sing your praises. So good, you're bright, so very nice. You're like a plum, a turnover with cinnamon, a soothing hot bath. O, but it's getting late now and I'm almost out of words, nearly sung out. Hello, I call. Forever at last. I want you to hear all that is coming and all that is possible and all that is true. I want you to hear with your own ears, and mind with your mind. But my greatest hope is that you feel intimate with life, as if life is so close to you it shares your heart and your hands as you share its time. Share the time. All the life you have in time. You are the one to do it. You are the one who lives now and thinks for herself. Nothing but the best for you.

As you bring yourself full flower, I'm here with you still. As you sing to the world, I'm not so far off. And don't forget to clean the dishes.   Visit your sister.   Call your aunt. Remember all birthdays, not only your own. Say something nice or don't say anything at all. Go out on a limb. Help others out, too. Eat plenty of vegetables. Swallow your pride. Have a good sleep, seven eight hours, if possible. O, pleasant dreams, sweetie. And, please, say hello to the stars. Upload yourself into the mystery of love.   Then come down as sunlight to nourish the earth. I'll see you in the bright early morning, when the sky has fields of fresh joy to give. We'll sing joy together in the easy summertime, with the fish and the cotton and the sweet butterflies. O swing low. Sing low now. I'm almost gone. And aint it good to know you. Yes. Aint you just so good to know – my child, sunrise, my ever growing light.

SEVEN

Riding the songs. Taking their lead. Speeding and turning. Down the bumpy drive.

Games rolled then slowed finally broke to a stop. It was music from his head, mostly. Relentless lyrics and blues. He sat a few minutes, then turned off the engine. Almost two hours late. He listened to what played over and over inside. A couple old songs Ri liked: so far away, since you asked. Another his mother used to sing in the car years back. James Something. Taylor, was it? Games didn't want the songs. He breathed deeply so as to get the lyrics out of his body. Winter Spring Summer and Fall. Songbirds songbirds outside the car. He released a sigh. More of the same flooded in. He didn't want to think about it. Rather not feel this way, which was missing. Rather not be at work where he had to talk and think. He looked in the seat behind him. He twisted to look on the floor in the back. He'd lost something, let it slip from his grasp.

Looking often helps if you've lost something. Though, whatever Games lost, it wasn't there, not in the car, not in the air, not in the silence. Still, that's not the point. If something is missing – confidence, a tool, or even a person – if it's not where it should be, then something's amiss.

Too quiet in the car, not quiet enough in his head. *Amiss* – that's not a word Games often used. It popped in out of nowhere, like Ri's face at his door, like James Taylor, like songbirds, like.

A remix of thoughts. A brood of bad feelings. A clutter of useless information. A pile of scrap wood, there, out the window. Pieces discarded. Peace is discarded. A mess of whirs words work. Words often tried to tell Games things, hoping to inform or comfort or be meaningful to him. But sometimes they just kept him guessing. He looked through the windshield at the heavy gray sky and the dark green leaves of July, not quite ready to get out of the car.

Seven o'clock the previous evening. Games had sat at the table in his apartment, thinking about people who were dead. He couldn't stop the thought, as though it was an obsession. Ri's neighbor, Trudy, and Jonsey, the self-portrait. Ri's mother, of course, just over a year ago. She was someone Games had thought of, too, but had never met. June June. Now it was July. She liked to sing. She was a good mother. Her heart was in it.

There were other things also. Things that Rio had said. Days ago. In rooms together. In bed. In the car. She was missing now. Ri was missing and her mother, who was dead, had nothing useful to say. Games's own mother, too, speaking of mothers. He hadn't heard from his mother in a year and a half. She'd missed his last birthday, which had never happened before. She, too, was no help to him now.

Games sat in the car, hands off the wheel. Wherever Ri was, he didn't know. She could be dead in a ditch somewhere, for all he knew. She could be lost forever. Like his bike. Like his father. Like – He didn't even want to bring up his father, but there he was, just like that, in the car with him. Games turned away, to other thoughts. But his father came around the corner. So did Ri. A ghostly image of her face. At his door. At his table. Then she was gone. Gone and gone and where and gone. Into the trees, this nothingness sky.

Games last saw Ri five days ago. Past present future perfect. Everything had been good back then, five days ago. Friday. Her mouth did that special thing. Games had made balsamic tomato salad. He'd kissed her lips her mouth her neck her... Working his way. He was greedy for more.

More more more, Games said, working the fields, the furrows, the curve of her back.

More me or Mormon?

More you, the moron, he said.

That's mean, said Ri, turning from Games, leaving the window in her stead.

Evening through that dirty window. Games leaned to look down. A father with his boy crossed the street below. And when Games wasn't looking, Ri took off her clothes. Well, he was looking, but not at her, at those two on the sidewalk below. The father and son. The evening light. Of course, it's possible she never had her clothes on to begin with. But Games probably would've noticed that when she was eating her salad. Her balsamic tomatoes her red lips her…

Mmmm, sighed Games when he returned from the window, back to Rianna. Sorry I called you a moron.

Ri stood there. Soaringly beautiful. Accepting his apology. Five days ago. No more.

Games needed to see it, to say it again. Rio again. Her face and nakedness. That thing she does with her mouth. Her lips. Her back and forth, her belly and breasts. The float and curves of her beautiful flesh. Her all. Her verve. All her again. Allure again. To be sure. That he wasn't making things up.

Maybe he'd go home this evening, after work, and find… What? The hammer he'd lost. Oh, who cares about that? His confidence. His ease with the world. That things will work out. Because there it would be, just where he left it. And he'd take that confidence in hand, strike the world with it for good. And all the while, sitting across from him would be Ri. So near again. And she'd say, I told you you'd find it. And she'd be right. What is ever really lost if it's in you all along?

Though that doesn't speak to the fact of what is actually there in your hand. Because sometimes all you've got is some ghostly presence, which also is a physical absence. If what you want is not there with you as it should be, what good is it? When that's the case, you might sit in your car and stare at the sky, not knowing how to make meaning out of troubles and doubt and rock bottom feelings. Thick gray whatness, heavy with rain. And then lowering your eyes, there's this pile of scrap wood fit only for burning.

~

When Games called Ri on Saturday, Sunday, then three times on Monday, and yesterday, too, she didn't answer. He texted her. He even tried telepathy: *Games needs to talk. Pick up your phone.* And he thought of the joke where there's a guy writing and phoning and texting his girlfriend, and all the while she's standing beside him, quite touchable. So last night, that joke in mind, Games reached out, but he felt no one on either side, and no words came back to greet him when he spoke. He called Nat instead, Rio's roommate. Nat didn't know who he was at first. Then she did.

Just kidding, she said. You're that cute guy.

Coot guy, is what Games heard, which made him think of old Quincy Mesch.

Fruit guy, she corrected. I'm teasing, you know.

I don't work at Jakes anymore, said Games.

I still work at Indigos, said Nat.

The clothing store?

You ever listen to **sLiP nInE sIx**?

Is that a band?

All Raw. Awesome song. I dated the drummer.

Nice.

Not really, said Nat. He was totally into himself, you know –

Not really.

I'm moving to L.A. soon.

Games wanted to redirect the conversation.

Do you –

Okay. Wait. I've got to take this call.

Nat went deeper into debt. When she returned, she was no better at paying attention.

What? she asked.

Do you –

So, you should come to this party on Friday, she said. It'll be totally killer.

Nuclear?

Huh? said Nat.

What are you saying? asked Games.

Wait a minute.   Okay.

I'm trying to find Rio, said Games.

Why're you calling me, then? asked Nat. Did I see you at The Cave?

Was Ri at The Cave?

No. Why?

I can't find her, said Games.

She's strange, said Nat. Shit...

What is it?

What's what?

I thought you might know something, said Games. Where are you?

I'm here.

Here?

I don't know where she is, said Nat. I'm hardly ever myself.

You're not yourself.

I'm not here, said Nat.

You said you were.

Well, her stuff's here. She's not. I'm –   Nat went silent, distracted by something.

What is it? asked Games.

Shit, she said again. And again: Fucking asshole.

What is it?

I thought he took something of mind, said Nat.

Of mind?

What?

Did he?

Who?

Did he take something of yours?

What?

Never mind, said Games. What's her bed look like?

You want to see my bed? M'I in it? You're like a real flirt.

Can you just see if Ri's been sleeping there?

In my bed?

In hers, said Games.

Nat walked into Ri's bedroom to look. Games imagined the footsteps, the sound of her walking. He could see the hall, the door, the plants on the floor, the –

Nope.

What do you mean, nope?

It's a bed, she said. Empty.

Been slept in?

You mean that guy from that Arab country?

What? asked Games.

What did you ask? said Nat.

Has her bed been slept in?

I thought you said… Whoever he is?   You know the one. What's the name of that country? Jihad or –

What are you saying?

Doesn't look like it, said Nat. All tucked in like she always leaves it. She's so fucking perfect.

Okay. Thanks anyway.

Not like me. Mind's a mess.

Your bed is, you mean?

Why d'you keep asking about my bed? said Nat.

It's okay, said Games. Just wondered about Ri.

So, Friday, said Nat. Look for me. I'll text you the address. Oh, shit.

What is it?

Nothing.

Which was probably true.

~

Games got out of his car, still in his head. There may've been birds, but he didn't notice. The sky lay thick. Through it, nothing moved. Then tiny gnats. They swarmed around Games as he walked to the building site. He swept away the bugs.

Screaming, whining, beseeching, off. The sound of a saw crossed the quiet. The planking lay on the ground, ready to be cut and go up on the rafters. Reed pulled the saw through another piece of wood. Right on the mark. A high-pitched slice. A waft, aroma of fir wood. Games loved the smell of sawdust, of freshly cut lumber. The spinning blade ground to a halt. Reed looked up. Looked at his watch. Ten past nine. He loved wearing a watch, thinking it made him look professional.

You've arrived, he said.

Sorry I'm late.

Don't be sorry, he said. Be on time. It's the third time this week. What is it today?

Wednesday.

I mean the problem.

Games shrugged. He didn't want to speak.

Hey, gay man, called Foster from among the rafters. Couple hours more, you would've made it for lunch? This is half inch too long.

Grab it, said Reed to Games.

Games went to the wood. He brought the piece to Reed. Accept this peace, he wanted to say.

It's been a bad couple days, Games offered. It was the least he could do. Or was it the most?

Reed didn't seem interested.

Just let me know if there's something I should know.

There's nothing, said Games. I'll be here at seven tomorrow.

Good enough, said Reed. So, you ready to work?

Games stood, ready.

These things won't go up by themselves, said Reed.

Who ever said they would? thought Games.

I've got to rough-in the stairs, said Reed, leaving the saw. You okay with this? Take a half-inch off.

Sure, said Games. Maybe I should call the police, he thought.

What's that? said Reed.

Half-inch, repeated Games.

Reed went inside the unenclosed building. From the rafters, Foster called down.

Gay man, when you cut that, shoot it on up, then follow. I need you to pry something.

To buy, thought Games. Dubai something. Do pay. I need your toupee. To piss. To pray.

Games needed a hammer. He'd misplaced his own. Luckily, Reed had an extra one in his van.

Games cut the half-inch off and slid the long plank up, but he wasn't paying attention and the board jammed into

Foster's leg. He let out an aargh!!!!! with more exclamation than was needed.

Shit, man. You coulda –

Sorry, said Games. He was.

Just get the fuck up here.

Games found a hammer in the van and climbed the ladder to the roof.

You look like your nailer's on the blink, said Foster. If you know what I mean.

Not really, Games thought.

You coulda knocked me off, said Foster. I coulda fucking died. I'm not ready for that. You think I'm ready for that?

No.

Damn right, said Foster. Take this.

Games took the chisel.

Now drive it that end and pull back till both boards're tight.

He did.

Foster shot the wood with nails. Then he took the nail gun, pointed it at the sky, held the safety, and pulled the trigger once, twice, three times.

I hate clouds, he said.

The compressor clicked on, filling the world with loud, bossy clamor. Games didn't like the sound. He'd rather things were quiet.

Guy was here earlier said he knew you from somewhere, said Foster.

Who? asked Games.

Don't you mean where? said Foster. While you're up here, hold this tape. We'll get the next measures.

Games held the tail end of the tape. He looked at the sky. It was pure gray – an empty feeling. Luckily, though, there didn't seem to be any damage from the nails. Games looked back to the planking on the roof.

Old man or young? he asked.

What?

The man who knew me, what'd he look like?

He wasn't that.

Wasn't what?

Wasn't a man, said Foster. I said a kid.

You said a guy.

Well, a boy.

A boy, said Games. How old?

One-O-eight and a quarter. Seventy-two and three eighths. Make them proud. Two of each.

Games went down the ladder to cut. One-O-eight and a quarter. Seventy-two and three eighths. Pretty old for a boy, he thought.

The morning went on like that. Up and down, crossing the rafters, covering them. The inside was the ceiling, V grooved. The outside was a deck for twelve inches of rigid foam insulation. Shots from the nail gun. Screams from the saw. Every now and then the compressor kicked on. There was no other music at the site. Not the slightest wind. Usually there were tunes, the radio, something.

Fucking Weed forgot his machine, said Foster to undo the momentary quiet.

Games nodded.

No wonder you're off. Just doesn't feel right, does it?

No argument, thought Games.

She's gonna rain soon, said Foster.

Who is?

You wait, said Foster. And nothing to listen to but my own damn self. And you. Problem is, you don't say much.

Games tried to think of something. Trying didn't help. He asked:

So, what'd he look like?

Who?

The boy.

What boy?

The one who was asking about me.

Wasn't no boy asking about you, said Foster.

Okay. What's wrong now, Captain Literal? thought Games.

Like I said, explained Foster, he was poking around. His shirt was ripped, like the one you always wear. He looked a bit like you. That's all I meant. Had to tell him get the fuck out of my tools. You got a brother?

I don't think so.

Don't think so, said Foster. What kind of messed up

family you come from? I mean, mine's defunct, but –

Defunct?

At least I know what I've got, said Foster. I've got a sister and three brothers. Well, four, if you count Randy, which I don't usually on account of what happened with my truck.

What'd Randy do to your truck?

Didn't *do* anything. It's a long story.

Games did not ask again. Had no desire for a story just now. He cut more wood and shot it up, carefully. Sometimes he had to climb up Dubai. To pry.

~

By lunchtime, the east side of the roof was covered. The trees held still and the air hung heavy with expected rain. The three men sat in the glen behind the construction, eating lunch. This is where the wild columbine used to bloom. Looking now for the flower, not finding it, Games thought of Rio. His thoughts were in charge of him, not the other way around. His more all-embracing self wasn't leading the way, and the thoughts came across a bit hopeless.

Maybe that's how things work. If you're not in charge, you're taken for a ride. And whatever spins you spins you as it pleases. Or it might actually be that your perception, the way you look at things, is what takes place inside. So, if you see possibilities wherever you look, then your thoughts are of a viable, collaborative world. But if you see walls or abandonment or absence, if you see negativity, then the world is a dispiriting mess.

Games thought he should be more careful with how he looked at things. Maybe exercise some self-control. If his perceptions were bleak, he should shut down for a while, not spread that bleakness everywhere. Why add to the craziness? If Games saw Ri as done with him, it was an alienating thought. If he saw her lying dead in some ditch, had he not already killed her with such inconsideration? It was wrong of him to think that way.

Games waited for either Reed or Foster to agree with his wrongness. But they kept their distance, offering no alternative. Games wanted to be told a better truth. Or an accurate truth based not on his mood. He didn't want to lose Ri because he had killed her by thinking it was so. That was plain idiocy. It was unsustainable. He wanted to protect her from random disasters. And find meaning each moment in her company.

Because who would Games talk to if Rio wasn't there? Who would he sleep with, side with, wake with, walk with, grow with, make salads for? She was basil, sweet onion. She was wild carrot, laced in light – a perfect companion. Or a tomato plant, yes. Vine ripe, cherry red, sun gold. He couldn't get enough. And who other than she would tell Games about celestial gardening, about how the moon influences lettuce and eggplant? Who would ask him about offsides in hockey or wonder his favorite star?

Hockey star?

Not hockey.

Movie star?

No. Night star, she had asked him one night, not long ago. There're billions and billions to pick from.

Never thought about it before.

Then why not think now?

Yes, thought Games in the glen with nothing to eat. Reed and Foster were quiet, digging into their lunches. Now's a good time to think. So, he remembered the conversation a few days ago, with Rianna about stars. Friday night, just before she vanished. They'd just finished a late dinner. It was after ten. The first star that had come to mind was Sirius with its dim companion.

You can't pick that one, Rio had said.

Why? Is it yours?

It's not mine. But if that's you, then you're the lead and I'm the second fiddle.

I didn't know that's how it worked.

You don't know much about relationships, do you?

I'm...um...

No one's dumb, had said Ri.

I never said dumb.

Well, I don't want to be crumbs to you. Rianna played with sounds. And with him, too. She went on: Either I'm a dog or an insignificant white dwarf. Not a good plan.

Let's start over, Games had suggested.

Good idea, Ri had agreed.

Andromeda, then.

Chained to a rock. Is that you, or me?

You're the princess after she's free.

But it's a galaxy, Rianna had said. Not a star. And it's a shrub of the heath family.

Okay, Games then said. You be the galaxy. I'll be the shrub.

Rianna, it seemed, was considering this idea. Games watched her inwardness. He caught a glimpse of her mind, like a universe itself, forging the details.

Neither of us should be shrubs, she'd said. A shrub's too limited, especially when we're already pretty much human.

You, yes. Pretty human. Games had sounded like a caveman. Then he went on: I'm just a paltry one.

Don't you want to improve? Don't you want to grow to something more?

Games should have said yes, but he said nothing.

Don't you want to cross the field, Ri had suggested. Not be stuck in one place.

This is getting complicated, Games had said.

Rianna then took a moment to think about his words, or about complications, about galaxies and shrubs. There was a universe of things she might've been thinking. And then she answered,

Some things take time. We've got to work them through. No constraints.

No constraints.

This resonated for Games, as he sat in the glen, the sky more like rain every minute. Was he a constraint? Though throughout the conversation, Ri had been smiling, her eyes gleaming like stars themselves. No constraints in her eyes, Games told himself, trying to be optimistic.

Foster lay on the ground, his eyes closed. Reed leaned back, still enjoying his sandwich. He'd take a bite, and then hold the sandwich at arm's length, admiring it as if it were a fine cigar. He'd then take another bite to amaze his tongue. He'd chew, he'd swallow, he'd nod. His entire body was in on the act.

And Abe is his brother, Games thought, struck by the contrast of how Reed inhabited each task set before him, whereas Abe had difficulty committing one foot, left or right, to the first step.

Did Abe ever go to Alaska? Games asked.

What the fuck's on his mind, thinking like that?

I...

How the fuck's he going to make it work up there?

Games thought of some possible ways, but he didn't suggest them.

He's a fucking moron, just like his father, barked Reed.

Isn't he your father, too?

Doesn't matter whose father, said Reed. It matters what you do with your life. Don't avoid it. Don't fucking run away. I'm tired of telling the both of them how to live. Not my job.

Games looked for a way to close the floodgate. Luckily, Reed seemed more interested in his sandwich.

Man, this is good. Homemade bread, bacon, cheese, roast beef, avocado, exclamation point.

Bacon and beef, said Foster.

That's what I said.

It's overkill.

Fuck your road kill. You saying I don't know how to make a sandwich?

People say that one day we won't be eating food at all, said Foster. Not real food. There'll be a food printer and you'll print out the food you want to eat.

What do you mean, *print out*? asked Reed.

The food'll be in the ink. Inkjet food.

People are stupid, said Reed.

And there'll be apps to control sodium intake and how much sugar you eat.

Like I said. It's dumb.

Why?

Who wants to fucking eat ink? said Reed. You want to eat an ink porterhouse? You want to eat ink strawberries?

Leif Garbisch

He was talking to Games.
Me?
Yeah.
No, said Games.
Me neither. Nobody's going to do that.
Plus, began Foster, they say you'll be wearing glasses or contacts and all the information you want will be right there for you, like Internet for your eyes alone. You just have to blink to connect.
They're crazy, said Reed.
I saw this show, continued Foster. Houses won't be made of wood, and the walls'll be whatever color you want just by a click. And mirrors will tell you how you're feeling and help you find a date.
What date? asked Reed.
It's all coming, said Foster. You can't stop IT.
People are insane, said Reed. I love wood. Who doesn't love wood? You want to live in some Styrofoam house that clicks together like Legos?
Games looked up. Was he talking to him? But the question was rhetorical. He kept silent, which today was his way of saying something. The absence of his words was his presence at work today, the same way as the absence of Rio was her presence in him. Only – it should be that the truth of someone is what's most present, he thought. The actual, physical truth. He knew that physical presence was what he wanted, but what could he do to get it back? Look at the sky. Listen. Maybe there was something else he could do. He would figure it. He would –
A single raindrop fell. Then, after a moment, another. There was loud quiet in between the drops. Everything was about to crash.
Shit, said Reed.
Here comes the rain, said Foster.
Shit, Reed said again. We're going to lose another day. What is today anyway?
Wednesday.
No. The date. The date.
Thirteenth, said Foster.
Games listened to the date, the date. July thirteenth.

292

Julia's birthday, he remembered. A week and a half before Rianna's. He liked other people's birthdays. He always remembered. He'd have to call his aunt. He'd have to find something good to say. And the rain fell hard to make puddles and mud. Each man ran to put his tools away. Games returned the hammer. He covered the wood with a tarp.

Okay?

Okay, then.

See you tomorrow, said Games, his shirt getting soaked.

He waved goodbye.

~

Later, in his apartment, Games heard only the rain. The dark gray sky hoarded light, locked it away and wouldn't share. Six o'clock. No messages on his voice mail. Nothing. Games studied the silence, but found little else. The world was not talking to him. Or, he was not listening well.

He remembered hearing once that there are a thousand and one silences, each one carrying a different meaning. Like the silence of conception or the silence at death. Or the silence you give when someone asks if you liked *Silence of the Lambs* and you didn't like it but you know the person who asked you did, which is a different silence from the one you give if you liked the movie a lot and need a moment to gather your thoughts. Or what if someone asks what you dreamed last night, and you have to re-see the thing in your head before saying. Or if you wake up in the middle of the night and the room is an uncertain silence and you're alone with the dark. Or if when driving home you see a man who looks like he could be your father, you don't know why, but maybe because something put the thought of fathers in your head, and his shirt is ripped and he's walking the other way, and you wonder for a moment if it's even possible, if your father's still alive, that is. So, you look again. And he's gone. There's silence when he's gone. It's a certain questioning silence. That's all you know. And there's also the silence that comes from being so bothered by the idea of your existence that you don't want to talk. You just want to be wordless, thoughtless, an unspeakable you. Or the silence if you have nothing to add to the conversation, so you turn slightly and pretend to be interested in something far away. Or how about this silence: Let's say you're not in the mood to talk right now. You'd rather do nothing, just repeat a bunch of nonsense over and over in your head, but some duty tells you that you don't have that option. You've got to dredge yourself up from your inner slump. Got to give greetings to someone that maybe she can revive you. Call that person on the phone.

Games sighed. He found himself in the curious silence of duty. He did not dread the duty, nor was it forced upon him. The silence he experienced was the attentiveness needed just before he called Aunt Julia. Games gathered his thoughts, making a mental list of things to say.

> Happy Birthday.
> How's your back? Disc. Arthritis.
> Uncle Orro's research. Tennis.
> What's Peter doing?
> Michaela. Julliard. Viola. No.
> Cello. Cello. Cello.
> Cake and…

He began with a simple, Hello.
Hello, the voice returned.
Auntie Julia, it's me.
Of course it's you.
Happy birthday, Games said.
Oh, sweetie. It's so nice to hear your voice, said Julia.

There was something rich and warm, taken right from *The Joy of Cooking*. There was a hint of yeast and garlic. Smelled good. Looked delicious in Games's mind. Tasted real in his imagination, which seemed to send ideas to his nose and tongue. It was the way his aunt always spoke, her tender tending voice, that brought forth the food.

Still, something else about the meal was sad: Aunt J had to make it herself, even on her birthday. She sautéed and seasoned, she baked alone. Of course, she was used to it. Kids gone, and Orro lost to quantum uncertainty, thinking of Higgs boson and other God-supplanting particulars. Because even if Heisenberg had said that you change what you observe, Uncle Orro didn't want to change anything in his life, so he didn't observe too closely. Plus, he never cooked. Birthdays and meals and cleaning and children weren't his thing.

Are you making fresh bread to go with the children? asked Games.

Did you say children?

Chicken, corrected Games. Chicken Alfredo.

How could you tell?

I know what goes on there.

Games was quiet a moment, which was the seventh, or was it the eleventh type of quiet known to mankind. The disconnect felt awkward.

Is everything alright? asked Julia

Pretty good.

You sound sick, said Julia. Is it a migraine again?

I don't get them anymore, said Games.

Are you tired?

It's nothing.

What's nothing?

Didn't he just say *it* was nothing? Problem is, thought Games, *nothing* was another way of saying *something*. Maybe *it* needed explaining. Games didn't want to explain. He didn't really want to talk, especially not about himself or Ri. He'd made a list, hadn't he? Had he forgotten that already? Then he remembered something, but it was something else, not from the list.

Auntie J, I've got a question.

Okay.

Do you mind?

Mind?

I mean, it's your birthday. You've got the right to refuse all questions.

Now you've got me worried, she said.

No, said Games. It's nothing.

What is it, then?

Did you ever know my father? asked Games.

Know him?

I saw someone earlier, said Games. It made me think.

Who'd you see?

Was he such a terrible person? asked Games. Why would Mama... I mean, I could make things up in my mind. I don't want to make up anything untrue.

Where'd this come from?

It's just birthdays, said Games. I'm sitting here thinking about people.

There's a lot to think about people, said Aunt Julia, in a sympathetic tone.

Well, said Games. It's been sort of a bad week.

I'm sorry, said Aunt Julia.

No, said Games. I'm sorry. It's your birthday. I don't want to bring it down.

Oh, I don't care about my birthday. I do about you, though. Not him.

Not who? asked Games.

There is no him, as far as I'm concerned.

No hymn, said Games. What are you talking about?

Your father, said Aunt Julia. Isn't that what you asked me?

Yeah, began Games. I don't mean to... I can't undo the thought. Mama once told me he was dead. I wrote him off. Then I saw someone and. I don't know what I'm. My thoughts are all. It's.

Have you spoken to your mother lately? asked Julia.

Did he love my mother? Did she kill him?

Seffi! My God, no.

I don't mean on purpose, said Games. But it happens. A badly placed thought can do it.

Your mother's got her issues, but she couldn't kill a fly.

Did he kill himself, then?

Who?

Whoever he was, said Games. My father.

Does it matter to you who he is and what he did?

I don't know, said Games. Does anything matter?

Yes, said Julia, emphatically. My friend Lucia read this poem at book club. I like it.

> Everything matters
> Let none tell you different
> A world without meaning
> Just isn't. It isn't.

Okay. So?

So, what? she asked.

Did he? asked Games.

Aunt Julia was silent – the fourth kind, where you need a moment to think. Then she said: All I really know is... I know you. That's what I know. You came from your parents, but it's not who you are. I've never known anyone so much himself, so blessed with being, so good with others.

What's that mean?

You're an angel to all people. We're lucky to have you.

I don't feel lucky.

Maybe not today, maybe not tomorrow, but soon, said Aunt J. I see everything coming back for you. Everything. Even better than before.

It felt good to Games to hear those exact words. He looked at the window, dripping with rain.

I find that people who are most themselves have few troubles with the world, said Julia. They always see a way to make it work.

I have troubles, sometimes.

I'm sorry, sweetie. I know you do. Don't lose faith. You are overly thoughtful and kind.

Overly. That sounds bad.

Strike it, then. No more overly.

No more overly, thought Games. Just thoughtful and kind.

Not everyone calls on my birthday, said Julia. Only some, like you.

Some like it hot. Some like it cool.

I suppose you're right, said Aunt J.

I don't feel so good with others, said Games. Not right now.

There's always room for improvement, said Julia.

Games agreed.

I'm just feeling a bit down today.

Not on my birthday, you're not.

Okay, he said.

I've had a good day, said Aunt J. A really good day. I think we're actually going out to dinner.

This late?

I'm still waiting, aren't I? said Aunt Julia.

But you made dinner.

As a backup plan.

I'm sorry, said Games.

Everyone needs a plan B if plan A doesn't work out.

No, I mean I should be thinking more of you.

You are, said Julia.

So, how's your back?

Forget my back, said Aunt J. You are what you think. If I think of myself as arthritic, that's who I am. I don't want to be that person. I want to think for myself, not of myself. But of God and others.

Which made Games consider: His thinking lately had been a bit self-centered. Self-contained. Solitary. He had crippled himself with quiet. It was not a quiet of happy certainty. Not a quiet of mindfulness, either, where he felt absorbed in life. It was a quiet of disarray and discontent. Disarray, discontent, and such a disabling quiet that Games held his tongue all the more, because words just made the mess worse. Now was a messy quiet, a jumbled mind that no conversation could immediately clear.

Looking out the window, Games saw a far-off flash of lightning upon the evening gray. He waited for the sound. Waited. And.

Okay, he said, because it was all he could do.

Likely, he was a sick and troubled man, said Julia. Or, a thoughtless jerk.

Who?

Your father.

I know, said Games.

Maybe he was just like your mother, only different, speculated Julia.

How do you mean?

I mean, calling for help without any voice, said Julia.

My mother doesn't call.

Maybe she does, but without a voice, said his aunt.

I see what you mean, said Games.

You are your own person, said Julia.

I know, said Games. Just wanted to say happy birthday.

Then it came to Julia – something else.

You know, there is one thing I remember.

What?

Your mother said he was a fish.

My father, a fish.

Or that he liked to fish, said Aunt J. She called him a caveman, too.

A caveman? repeated Games.

What is it when you go into caves? said Julia.

Maybe she meant a lunkhead. A spelunking idiot.

No one's really an idiot, said Julia. Even at our worst, we all deserve forgiveness. None of us quite knows what we're doing.

It made Games think of Jesus, the fisherman, the way she said it. Hadn't Jesus said something similar once? Jesus Julia July, the thirteenth of summer. Still waiting for that thunder, and, yes, the joy of eating, to go out to dinner.

I knew you'd call, said Aunt Julia.

I almost forgot.

But you didn't, said Julia. You've never missed my birthday. Oh – here he is, now.

Who?

Orro.

Well, goodbye, said Games. Have a nice dinner.

Goodbye, said Aunt Julia. I…

But Games had already turned off his phone.

JULY

No Him

True! The world lies. It feeds it runs on lies. It opens its sluice gate and lies come in and lies go out. The world eats what it cooks in its sluicing days. It sucks it eats obsessively it lies. No stopping it. Can't imagine a more worthless place. Nothing keeping me here but some curse. I want to smash things. Want to total this world I don't even own. Fuck the world, and what I don't own. I am the world's traducer. It's a word I found in a pile of garbage. Am I the only one who knows this shit?

No one should be allowed to live here, only skeletons and stone. Instead there are human hurdles, real living people everywhere. Used to be I was good at leaping those, avoiding them mostly. It was alone with myself where I ran into trouble. I pissed into the wind to show I was someone. Then I was knocked from behind by that same wind when it swung for revenge. Followed by a kick in the teeth from the ones who wanted me to be their dog. They had it in for me. All of them. The demons who traveled invisibly, who mixed in my blood and my head. Eye grubs, ear weasels, fucking ticks. They burrowed in till I was the butt of their jokes. They lied in their lingos they didn't even care. Didn't care for me. I took it to heart all the lying, the half-baked ideas and hateful language, all inventions of me, not one song of praise but me as a mealworm, a disgusting meal for them to enjoy at will. For they…for them to eat…for they in their joy. They ate my heart. They ate. They ate my eyes, my ears. Me to the heart. They ate. They ate me, everything. Ate.

Till finally I was finished. Infinitely eaten. No reason to look for me now. It's nothing but indifferences. Maybe I'm here I'm nothing but shit. My own traducer. I like that word.

I don't know how or why I am this. They made me this. They make me do it.

But he's someone else.
A relief from them. Or if he's one of them, he's the trick. He came to me hours was it days, years ago. That smile of hopefulness slapped on him like a mask. I was run down wrung dry almost inert by the time he showed. Still he approached me, flirting like psychosis. I allowed him in, almost as far as Gin or Jack. He was real quiet, I hardly knew he was there. No air through the windows. No ice water either. The curtains were drawn to keep out the sun.

It was, in the end, the heat of the sun that made me leave for good. Not my kind of weather. I didn't have those fancy clothes to wick away the sweat. I frowned at the breaking clouds, packed what I needed, and cut loose. I thought I'd gone unnoticed, but because of the sun when I looked to my right, there was my boy at my side like a shadow, watching my every move, trying to figure his old man out.

You're tagging along? I said.

Guess so, he answered.

What for? I asked.

He was in no-talk mode, so I made the conversation happen just to show I wasn't all bad. Didn't even get from him the breeze of a nod about that, though. The rain had stopped, and the sun was a powerhouse up there on my left. Enough is enough. How many intolerable days do there have to be? How much taunting brightness good for nothing but showing me up? I was ready for some real shade.

There wasn't much relief, except for what's-his-name, who snuck up and attached himself to me. I could've said to him, *Not you again. Don't come at me with corrections. I don't need it — you coaxing me to stay, your saccharine shit.* Could've told him that, but just let him have his way. He doesn't need me telling him what to do. He's grown. And besides, if I give him hints along the way, he might learn something true about his old man.

Thing about my boy and me, we hardly ever knew one

another. I wasn't at his birth. We didn't spend a single day together. Except that one time. He came, a pimply reporter, knocking with pen and pad in hand, there for the scoop:

'Scuse me, sir, but I've got a couple questions I'd like to shoot your way, if it's convenient.

Why would it be convenient?

If you've got a moment.

This is bullshit. Bullfuckingshit. But you go ahead. Take your best shot, son.

The boy was thinking, back then, that he could know me by writing. He sat at his desk, lost to imagination. Shit, I don't know how he thought that would get him anywhere. His screwy mother must've put him up to it. Boy wanted to write an obit on me:

'Scuse me, sir?

What now.

They say you're dead. Is that the case?

Look at me. Do I look dead?

Not really, I guess.

You guess?

Well, no. I see you in my mind, a black and white picture. I hear you in my thoughts. I imagine you alive.

Then leave it at that, I tried to tell him. *Just leave,* I wanted to say. *I'm alive as I'll ever be. Least I think that I am. Let me check with my heart. Oh, wait. I aint got one according to the report, but that doesn't make me dead yet, does it?*

No, I s'pose it doesn't.

So, he went on to write. And it was a decent piece he wrote on me, not that I read it, but I got the gist. Dismissive, as was only fitting, but with other ingredients, too, such as hope and light. It ended with me walking off into the sunset, and who knows from there but maybe I'd come back a champion or saint or somebody less fucked-up. We never found out. The boy burned the paper in the oven, lit it with a match and let it flare up so he could forget about me.

He was a pimply-chinned kid back then, wasn't he? Sixteen what fifteen years old. What was he supposed to think? Now, he's twenty-eight. I'm sure his brain can cook things up better, with a tad more life experience. Problem is, the more experience you've got, the more *they* try and delete you from it. They chop you down, they spirit you away. Anything to make you disagreeable. Discord is the name of their group. Disconnect their only promise.

I'd warn him, if I could. They're everywhere. In wake and sleep. I mean, story has it, my boy's got distress. He's got a girl, likes to think so anyway, right pretty piece. Rio grand fuck, they tell me. They've got no sway over her. But she's run off, and now what do you want from me, I should ask him, knowing he won't answer. Don't whine about it. Let it be a lesson. Get over her. People don't tend to get along for more than a few hours if they're lucky. Till morning at most. Then it gets bitchy. Things are said, and cups chucked, chairs, wads of paper, books that who'll ever read and you're better off to throw them. Everything's better off just to leave: leave each other alone: leave for good. A law needs to pass allowing suicide. No one to tell you you can't do it. No other way but that. No one, thank you very much. No more people, no world.

And fuck, I had a girl once. Young once. Clear once. Sweetest meat as anyone. I've forgotten a lot of it now. No memory of sense. No sense in memory. If God ever gave me anything to live by, he took it away. Or they did. They're always telling me what's wrong with the world. Happy to say it. And I listen to them. I can't not listen to how they lay it out. Wish it were different, but it is what it is.

People are difficult, and women are the worst. Wish it could just've been their bodies. Bodies are easy, the tits and skin. I'm up for that. Hard tits soft tight ass is. The surface of things. Not their time or talk. Not saying I'm perfect. I'm just saying women are better with their shirts off, without all the shit they carry: emotions, lipstick, dumpload of words. They live in the past, don't get over it, it haunts them. Got no proper sense of memory, which is the same for me, and it hurts like hell if I think, so I don't. Like I say about days I say about women: *If they all were made of papier-mâché, I'd pass through them easy, then they'd biodegrade.*

My boy's persistent, though. I'll give him that. I don't know what he carries so important inside him that he's got to know things. That he's got to know me, too. I'd like to ask him why, but it would require that I give a shit. I've never been much for giving. Never been there for him, either, like I said. Like I said, don't even know his name, his birthday, nothing. So, it's his thing, I guess, his coming round, not mine.

~

Him picturing me back when he was fifteen, sixteen, that was an exercise for my boy. Everyone likes to practice on me. Shit, my father used to practice on me by rubbing my face in the ground if I so much as looked at his precious life sideways. Once when I forgot to flip his fucking ribs so they got all burnt on one side, he chucked them to the ground and shoved my face in the charred mess. Then he pulled me up, handed me some fresh ribs, and said, Cook em right this time. Practice makes perfect.

I never did see much improvement in him. He'd bat stones at me till I could snag them before they cracked my skull. Not bad, he'd laugh when the inning was over. Then, on a good day, he'd let me bleed his deer, and dress it, skin it too in four easy cuts. And, if I was real lucky, he'd take me out in his boat, throw me over with a lifejacket, and tell me to swim for shore.

I remember the outboard motoring away as I treaded water alone in Broad Creek. Best feeling ever. I swam not because of him but because it was one thing I was good at. I could've swum for miles without getting tired. I was like a fish without the schooling. A crab all by its sideways self. An oyster, sharp edges, lock-jaw, no pearl, soft on the inside somewhere. I remember my father standing on the mud when I swam up. He was all smiles, like I was his entertainment. He didn't even know how happy I was. And he hadn't done a thing to make it so. It was all me.

Out, he said.

I got out, myself. I wasn't afraid of him anymore.

Where's the goddamn lifejacket? That's thirty bucks you owe me, he said.

Who needs a lifejacket? I remember thinking.

Truth is, I took off on my own most days. I'd walk up to people's houses with cigarettes I'd stolen and fake gemstones for sale. Fourteen-year-old kid, trying to hustle.

Once a girl opened the door and she didn't have a shirt on. She was a bit older than me and her tits were the size of grapefruits with little red nipple seeds. I said, I like your earrings. They were silver and dangly. You want a diamond or emerald or Kool? I said. I showed her my stones. She didn't have any money, so I took a Coke she offered and stood just inside her door, sipping from the bottle. I had a boner showing through my pants and wanted to feel her up and she was mad that I didn't and said I had to go if I was going to be like that. Like what? I asked. A dumb ass, she said. Then we heard the back screen door slam. *Fenny,* her mother called. *Come grab these eggs.* I guess you could say that was all my time. She scrambled to get on her shirt, and I tipped my invisible hat and left. There was a dog growling at the brush as I went out the lane. Maybe a woodchuck or chipmunk or rabbit in there. Next thing I knew, the girl came running, her shirt on, shoes, everything. She gave me a Three Musketeers. I would've rather it had been an Almond Joy.

Later on, I was tired of hustling. I gave the business to Bird Neck. He was only twelve. Off I'd go by myself looking for bottles down in the mud alongside my friend, the water. Some bottles are worth a fortune, my uncle said. I found a clear one once, said 1889 on it. Found a blue one shape of a circle, with an engraved eagle about to set down. My father fucking smashed it when he was drunk. *The eagle has landed. The eagle has landed,* he shouted, a year before anyone knew what those words even meant. And I used to trespass, too. Didn't matter if there was a fence or gate. Sometimes men'd be building a new home or barn, and I'd stop and look up at the two fellows on the rafters, pounding nails, talking numbers like they were somehow bigger than they really were up there.

Hey you, one of them called down. Must've thought I was waiting on them. What're you doing in my shit? Must've thought I was stealing their tools, just because I was poking around.

Just looking for someone, I said.

Aint no one in my toolbox, he yelled. Who're you looking for?

Just some guy who works here, I said.

Which guy?

Didn't say he was a witch.

What did you say?

I might could tell if I remembered it better.

Might could?

Name's not Mike Wood. I told you, I don't remember it completely. It was more like Jimmy or Wayne or something.

You're barking up the wrong tree with those names, said the man on high.

It's a dog eat dog world, I told him.

Well, just see you stay out of my tools, the top man said.

Mind if I hang around and watch? Learn something?

Stay out of the way, you can.

And I picked up a hammer, then some real sharp chisel, brushing the bevel with my thumb.

Hey, what'd I just tell you? the bossy one barked, making to come after me like the devil himself. Put that the fuck down.

Sorry, I said, seeing the man, his horns coming out.

Thing is, I don't know if I really was sorry. I said the word, but it carried no weight. Thing about me is I don't know if I am sorry or happy or any of the shit I'm feeling, if I'm feeling anything at all. I do what I do because I have to. I am what I do. And no one else to care about, no one else to bother me with their rules.

~

Twelve years back when my boy came looking for me and buried me in words, he didn't see all there was to see. He didn't see how I, too, had been a boy in my own right, nothing to do with him, just me myself coming from the misery of birth, burning up out in the sun, no rest from it, no relief, just mixing with all the lies, diving deep, swimming round, and, eventually, stepping out of the creek, dripping wet, and then running for my life. He didn't see me as a real, separate person, but instead invented me to his liking so he could feel better. It only made him realize I'm not much to consider, which I don't claim I am, but I don't think it made him feel that better he was looking to feel. There wasn't one thing interesting he could find, because he didn't have any true information. He couldn't fill more than a paragraph or two in that first obit of me.

Thing is, who deserves a whole book anyway, let alone a chapter, if you really think about it? Is it some mass murderer who deserves the attention, just because he's such a dark and mysterious fellow? Or is it some governor, just because people voted for him and he accepted bribes from his brother-in-law's firm, and hooked up with Dessie-Lyn at La Vie every Friday afternoon? Or how about some CEO because he's got the green and his own personal cook and upside-down paintings of naked women in his bathroom? Or how about maybe some boy-loving priest with a back room for festivities? Now, there's the man who deserves volumes written on him. He's the best one for sure, a pure worthwhile human. But it's difficult to choose, isn't it?

Most everyone's a fucking disaster. I've made some bad decisions, but not as many as they'd have me think. They'd have me think it's everything about me is bad, but I won't let them have the last bite. I've got the one child, and I've only got one. No one can deny me some part in life. Sure, you'd think I'd know his name, but I'm bad with names. You'd think I would care, but I'm bad with consideration. Still, I didn't run off so much as was shoved by hands and kicked by the wind. I know there's probably a story floating around about a poor young mother Seffi and all the crosses she bore. But it was pretty damn mutual, I'd say. It was easy for us both to go. And you'd think I'd be sorry, but like I said, I don't spend much time with feelings. Besides, sorry runs so deep it's hard to find. Last thing I want to do is dredge the nagging thing out.

Problem is listening to your own shit day in day out. The wilderness talks to me, the terrible sun, the heavy hours, and then out of nowhere comes my boy, more weight around my neck. He doesn't know the burden he is. He thinks he's so light, but he isn't. I could've used less weight earlier, before I let my life be simmered down to a flavorless sauce. Before I went to that cave and did what I did. Another bad decision, they'd want me to admit.

Like hell I'll admit it. What the fuck's anyone know about

my life and how much better for the world if I'm not here? Maybe it's why my boy tagged along, not just another haunt, but so he could know, so he could hear firsthand of my demise. Of course, all he really wanted was to come in all high and mighty with his psychobabble so to turn the bad world good again: *Lift the veil and see the candle in your soul.* Wasn't going to happen for me.

People don't change. They suffer till they've had enough. That's my message for the world. Okay boys and girls, listen up: *God doesn't give a shit about you. Once you've exhausted all your days, you're done. Do what you can on your own, till you can't anymore. That's it. That's all the schooling you need. Class dismissed.*

~

There is something that torments me, though. That there could've been a better man lurking inside me. Why didn't he do more to get out? I'd like to've been someone I could've looked up to, a person who would've made good decisions for me. I'd like to've been somebody's real father, too. To've gone hiking once all the way to Trevor Mountain Lake up north, done some fishing, practiced survival skills for seven days straight, for two solid weeks maybe three even four in the great outdoors, alone together. I'd've been good at stuff like that. Could've shown my boy how to keep cool when it's burning hot, how to be real content with the night, how to fight off sickness, how to find water in the driest of places. All good stuff.

A father ought to teach his kid things. I wish I'd've been able to teach my boy about real trust, too. Real trust in someone, as opposed to just believing the best in him. True trust in a person comes after you've lost it. Trust appears when you think it most gone. That's what I wish I could've said to him: Take responsibility for your own damn life, and don't be such a fucking shadow of a son, hanging to my side because of some light in my soul that you imagine is there. Because I've never seen it. Or deserved it. Or even wanted.

I've always hated the sun the way it points me out. Larger and louder grows the sun. Smaller and silent go I. It goes on drinking until I'm drunk. It goes on drinking after I'm drunk. It goes on drinking without me. I wish I could wish things were otherwise, like a cool trust in someone different than me. Too late for otherwises, though. And where was my boy, back in time, when I could've really used him like a gun to shoot myself, or a different perspective? Where was he then? And where on earth ever was I?

~

I knew where I was. I kept heading there through the slow-cooking day. And when I arrived, it was as nondescript a place as I always thought it would be. A useless bit of field, just off the road. I saw immediately what I was seeking. A hole in the ground. In the middle of that useless field, there was a hole that led to a world inside the earth. The entrance was an open mouth with stony cold-sores and green on its lips, an ugly color.

I lowered myself in.

I wedged against the jagged walls of the cave. I sunk into the cool and hit rock bottom. And he, my boy I suppose, followed me, which was his own mistake, not mine.

Down in that hole, I saw his shadow alongside me. He was less than a shadow, more of a hint. I opened my pack to get at the flashlight, and sweeping its light I saw a gang of me milling about, a thousand monsters. They came free in that underworld. They held out their grimy, clawful hands as I brushed by. *Home at last at last at last,* they echoed as one. It was my fucking family playing games. But it wasn't a game I had any chance at winning. Then, those demons were gone, and we were alone, my boy and I, in my lethal chamber that emptied into the belly of the beast.

I headed down the shoot, a few lingering smells of the world above clinging to my clothes, before that world lost its grip and all I smelled was the mineral dank. I beamed my flashlight side to side, painting the scene. But the light was dying. Fucking batteries. And how was my body still with me, also? My boy, I mean. I felt for the pills in my pocket, rehearsing and rehearsing my bottle of gin down my throat, the opposite of words.

Ah, life, I spat. Aint you a trip? You limestone sentiment. I walked and stooped, crypt around, careful of my head. Sometimes the ceiling – crept not crypt – rung close like a pang, but it didn't make me feel tight, just hounded. I was harassed by unrelenting loneliness, which wasn't as bad as they wanted me to think. It was where I was meant to be. No one down there but myself and my flashlight with its two used almost useless D's. And I walked on, touring the passageways, stepping through water that soaked my shoes, up my pant legs, and into me.

I loved the water, even there. The moist road, the trickles, and the tongues of hell – the dark pools I stepped through. It almost made me want to. Almost made me wish to. Stop to turn some part of me free. Get out. Return. To free somebody I am. Some boy inside me. Somebody besides. To be that someone in the bright by the ocean with wind and fish and freshening waves. To stand for once with a clear view. What could be better than that? No more belittling nights with Jack and Gin in the ghettos, which only reminded me how like poverty I'd become.

Have you ever thought how to do it, though? With gas or gun or just by heading into the wilderness, day after day and deep into your absence till you're down as far as you can go. And what a relief it'll soon be. So, you sit on some rock and stare, no stars in the abyss, and the bears the wolves jump you and rip that last look from your face. Everything then pisses out of you, and the vultures who come later pick at your bones. And have you ever wondered what burden comes next? What disaster's after this?

Nobody answered my questions. I kept walking. Swigged a few pills in preparation. And when at last I looked up – it was the end of the road. Miracle of miracles. My miraculous lake.

Water gathered cool and deep. They named the pool of water deliverance. I had no problem with the name.

This was my place, my lake in the depths of the cave. Never thought I'd find it so easy. I squatted at the edge, lay down my flashlight, my bottle, took off my pack, took everything in. I thought I might fly. Was feeling it. Knew I would die there. I'd not go back. My flashlight dim as the future. It was almost out of glow. But I, I was bolder every moment. Rehearsal time was over. I was rich in this carved out place. The wealthiest I'd ever been. Butter sauce. Bacon fat. To be creamed deep. To dive, to swim, to end this stay. And

Something brushed past. Those demons again with enough shove to knock me off balance. They grabbed and tugged. Not a sound to their seizures. I was spun I was twisted like some devil's yarn. The better to play you with, I heard. And

A breeze escaped across the side of my face. I thought: If that was a bat, it was a bat who knows the ins and outs. And if it was my boy, he's leaving me, now. Good luck to you, I almost said. Or else I said: Good luck. Hope you find your way from here. Catch up with that girl upstairs. She's the real deal. Don't be like your old man. And

I gave him this picture as a parting gift: *Your father's face in an old black and white, found at the dump one day, picked up by some curious sorter, turned over in his hands, "he done died", all that was written there, nothing else to read or see, and so the thing's simply tossed back with the wine bottles, soda cans, and the torn magazines.* I gave him these words as well: *Get out of my way. Out of my space. Crack of thunder. Roll on.* And then

It was quiet again. That's all I'm saying. The most unsayable quiet. Couldn't get a word out because of the pressing quiet. I was wet with sweat. A few deep breaths. Death festivities all around me. And suddenly the light of my flashlight gave out. It was absolute. Certainty. Complete and utter. Over now. Nothing to see. I wiped my forehead. I rubbed my face dull, annulled it. Saw the black of the water. Felt it draw me in. To dive to digress no more. And I inched that way as I'd done all my life. No one to save me from the progression. There'd be no saving no saying no thinking no.

Nothing written of me in the paper. He who'd once written lines of my life, my –

Why wasn't he there? My boy. Why wasn't anyone there? I suppose I expected at least someone to care. No one came running at the eleventh hour, no Almond Joy or Three Musketeers. So, I stepped out of my body, drank the last of my gin and pills, lay down my life, and propped my dead light. I'm leaving for good, I said. Leaning, leaning. Over the water. I'm a wasted shot at living. Breathless mess. Hear me at least. Done failing. I'm falling. Do you.   Hear me. I'm

Stretched the words for as long as they'd go, thinner and thinner, till there was. Delicious death. Faced the water, could almost taste it to its quench. Only the water – over it, over. Off to the other – beneath, beneath. Head first down. Then shoulders, freedom, feet and soles.

I've come this way, I don't know how.

It's not too late, I hear. To turn. To see another way out.

I'm tired of doing it wrong, I say.

So, don't take the road you're always walking. You'll know you're not on it when you're no longer here. You'll be someone new.

What's that supposed to mean? There's nowhere else. I'm me as always, settling in. It's bedtime. Sleep time. Where's my fucking story? Once upon a time, I sink. Impossible to hear down here. My name's losing being. I never had a name. My being's losing light. Never had that, either. I see it happening while others watch from the sidelines. They're watching me drown. Just seeing it happen. People I don't even know who they are. They follow me down and look at their watches. Then they stop looking. Why? They turn and walk off as if now there's one less thing in the world is all. One less person. Show's over. And life goes on without me. Without him, they think. And that's okay, they all think. I'm watching them think it, whoever they've been and whoever they are. Leaving now. Murmurs now. Only murmurings of the world. The world grows dimmer and weaker until at long last no more, and the thing the only thing I can barely sense is one trivial hint of human decency. Only he's not so trivial. One lightening bug, a firefly. He's still here for me. Only I'm afraid to go there, I don't know why. It's moves I've never made before. I've never moved toward anyone ever. I'm slow afraid, I can't lift a finger, my eyes, my. Sore afraid, I can no longer breathe. This water I can't. Breathe this water. I'm almost done. It's things I've never thought to think. No thought. Just can't. I can't. I

What. A mistake! Take me back. Please. Take me ba –

EIGHT

Flash of light, then it was gone. Thunder broke upon the sky, rolled on. Late night August storm.

Games awoke and lay in bed. He stared at the dark ceiling, then lowered his eyes to the far corner of the room before resting his gaze upon the opened window. Enough quiet, enough stillness, enough sleep for the moment. Water of life poured from the sky, and the wind, like hundreds of voices, spoke all around.

Games was alone, three o'clock in the morning. It was a free-for-all, a breach of the peace out there. The manic rain knocked hard on the glass of Games's double-hung window. The open half, however, allowed the wetness into the room. Water collected on the sill and dampened the floor as Games lay in bed, motivated not to get up and close the window but instead to listen to the patter and chatter of the rain, and the thrilling wishes of air that passed through his room.

Vitality, drive, enthusiasm, he thought. It's a good way to be. To be passionate for something, how this storm is passionate.

Games didn't mind that the rain and wind entered his room uninvited, nor did he mind its wild playfulness so oblivious to his presence. It was the storm's spirited energy, not its arrogance, that interested Games, maybe not such a happy occurrence for those who would have preferred to sleep through the night, but for Games, who was seemingly unbothered by his sudden wakefulness, why argue with it? Rule #3 in the *Book of Acceptance*:

> Be not troubled by things that interrupt you –
> the things you can do nothing to stop.

Games didn't see the thunder and rain as rude or disturbing, because their intentions were simply uninhibited expression. Which made him think he should be more like the storm. It wasn't happening, though, not since Rianna had left some twenty days ago. Since then, he'd kept mostly to himself, with his unresolved feelings in an airtight box. Maybe that irresolution is why he woke, nothing to do with the thunder or the battering rain, more to do with his own debris, like loose washers and nuts rattling inside him, clinking tortuously against his skull.

It was really a lot of chaos in the world sometimes. Unavoidable problems to think about. Not only personal relationships, either. There was tyranny terrorism poverty homelessness, miserable nakedness, too. Well, not all nakedness was wretched, some was good, but it was the desolate part of nakedness that bothered Games, the part about being vulnerable and uncared for, a life that was barely considered. Everyone needs consideration, he thought. Declaration #18 in the *Book of Assertions*:

> If you are left to yourself with nothing and no one,
> you may seem free and unencumbered.
> However, true freedom and well-being
> find a better source in others.

Games thought about this assertion as he lay in bed, surrounded by darkness. It sounded both philosophical and pop-psychological. He didn't know which was worse – to sound like a philosopher or a cliché.

Another flash, another crack of thunder shook the room. Games was trying, depth of night, roused from sleep, to connect with the world. There were, in fact, many unsettling problems, most of which were not personal to Games: rape murder war hostility, violence toward children toward women toward animals toward one another, cruelty of any kind and all disregard of human dignity, bullying coercion oppression harassment. The list could go on: manipulation of others and of the earth itself, separation from nature, aloneness in life, suicidal thoughts, suffering days, deep-seated fears, miscommunication, no one to listen to, no one to speak with, the many disparate pieces of the earth down to and including the kingdom of atoms, the sub-kingdom of particles, disturbances, uncertainties. And the list didn't stop there. There were failed rights, bad health care provisions, unpursuable happiness, an utter lack of inner security, no concern for the truth. It was the darkest of times, the bleakest of houses, and the dickens in the details that made things seem bad. It was the hole, the pit, the wound, the depression, and what fills that depression – dark gray clouds and the heaviest of hearts.

It was a deluge out there. In the bedroom, as well. Wind over rooftops. The rain beat on. Games heard a siren from somewhere far. But nothing, he thought, nothing's really wrong until I attach that "wrong" label. Option #9 in the *Book of Choices*:

> Better not to think of right or wrong. Better to think things are the only possible way they can be at this moment. It isn't fate, just the current arrangement, given the world as it is. It's a diseased world maybe, unhealthy yes, unrealized sure, imperfect no doubt. And the way to make a difference is to reject nothing, but instead to cooperate left and right, and work through. See everything with a creative mind.

Yes, thought Games. The way to make a difference is to be as much like creation as possible. The more like creation, the closer I am to everything. And the closer I am, the closer I can move my thinking, right up against this storm for example, deep into any situation, even to the brink of despair, then the more likely I can break through and make room for –   He stopped his thought, but it would not be finished. For love, he concluded. There's got to be that. Room for love. A bigger place in me. Something that's never been before, where I can see at last what needs to happen. And it's not about wishful thinking, and it's not about magic, but what's true and truly beautiful. It's about Ri. Ri again. Here again. Here she is and here I am, and no matter the millions of details, the thing to run with is love.

The floor was dark, scattered with clothes, a book, his hammer, two pencils, and one plant lying on its side in a cracked pot, having been blown that way by the wind – and all of it, all of it now getting wet. The storm continued, unrelentingly. The deep night solicited Games's attention. He could lie in bed, philosophic, uncreative, or he could do something to move forward.

Hermes, he thought, because of the book he was reading. Patron of people who have something to say, breaker of boundaries, bringer of stuff that's good. Her and me. From me to... He would compose his thoughts and those thoughts would be a bridge. From me to Rianna, from Rianna to me.

THIS IS NO STORY
in three breezy pieces

First day of August, a storm blew through. It was three in the morning. Driving rain. Large smacking drops. Whipping wind. Limbs scraping the windowpanes. Sirens on and off. And on again.

Three sounds, however, stood out from the rest. First, it was a potted plant, struck by the wind. The pot fell to the floor with a regretful CRASH. Plant and pot were a gift for Ri, and the container cracked on impact, sending rich organic soil everywhere. The storm then blew the sound of that misfortune for miles.

Heidi Bond heard the crash as she went into the liquor store for her lottery fix, early in the a.m. BAM – like gunshot it was, which got her attention. She'd never get a winning ticket after a sound like that. Later in the morning, Malachi Rhodes heard a slightly different version while sitting in the bathroom with his wife's Victorious Egret catalogue and its feature photo spread of the highly successful string quartet, The Wrens. Malachi, who played the viola, thought his wife had slammed the front door, which made him worry that she was angry with him. She was often angry, and mostly with him, but, lucky for Malachi, this sound did not concern his wife or her anger. He returned to the catalogue, obsessing over a picture of women dressed scantily as doves, lounging among the cedars.

The second sound of note began just before sunrise, about a quarter past five, to be exact. The storm had blown a sheet right off its bed. Nothing anyone could've done about it. The sheet sailed through the air, flapping as it flew. Sounded much like a bird – a very large bird. A pterodactyl, perhaps. Sister Mary Delano sighted the sheet as she sipped her morning tea. Ginger tea, as there was no chamomile.

Finally, as for that third sound, the storm took a newly released CD of cello music, Bela Bartok and Zemlinsky, lifted it from the shelf and carried it far into the country. The CD landed with a gentle "shwop" on the bank of a stream – an intriguing find beside the red trillium, near a large blue rock, just out of reach of the rushing, purling waters. There were sounds trapped in that CD and others trapped under the rock. If someone had lifted the CD, it would've been no more than a curiosity. Though, had the same person lifted the blue rock, it would've let loose a swarm of hullabaloos resulting in a tremendous ruckus.

~

The rain had stopped about a quarter to five, and the wind eased midmorning between ten and eleven. The sun shone brightly above the trees. Sounds continued to spread across this first August day. What a scorcher to begin the month. There had been no relief from the storm, which was a bit of bad luck.

Still, there were many good things that shaped the day. A beautiful light-haired woman, for instance. She stood, now twenty-six years old. Strands of her hair, some the color of cream, others of hay, tickled her face. Liking her was easy, no matter the anxiety she may've caused. Liking her erased all problems. If she had a name, she kept it secret.

Secrets, it seemed, were her thing at the moment. So many questions. For example: What brought this woman here not long after her birthday? And why was she standing so perfectly still in the glare of the midmorning sun, not saying a word? She was far from her apartment in the city, that's for sure, seemingly engrossed in the hum of summer and the buzz of bees near flowers. There were lots of flowers with bees, and ripples that both looked and sounded like words in the stream nearby.

And then from behind the scenes, in its own surprising way, came a different sound, which was the rustling sound of a man who brushed his hand through the wildflower. He was the young woman's boyfriend, or at least he thought he was. He thought she had a good ear for hearing, which is why he brushed the flowers to get her attention. He thought, in fact, that she had the absolute best ear ever, and that she was the most beautiful, most kissable, most holdable, most luminous person. *Luminous* being a word he liked. She was a lightening bug, a maidenhair fern, Queen Anne's lace with the sun shining through. He could've gone on for hours, describing. The point is – she was nearby, and that made him very happy.

He did wish, however, she would turn his way and talk to him, because her voice would've been a welcome relief, having been away for a while. But she was in the zone at the moment, which meant in her own world. When she was in the zone, she was so focused that he, her boyfriend, didn't want to disturb her. He wasn't in the zone, so what could he add to her concentration? When she was in the zone, the world was intuitive riches, and she was trying to load up on all the good stuff. When she was in the zone, she wasn't always available to him. Lucky for the man, however, the moment he passed his hand through the flowers it opened a door out of the zone. The woman turned her head. She saw his face, and they smiled at one another.

I was thinking of you, she said at last.

You were not.

Yes, I was. Where've you been hiding?

Me hiding! he said. Me!

Yes, you. I've been home for a while. Since, well, not too long after my birthday. You haven't called.

Of course, I called, he said. I texted, I mused, I even tried –

You texted a moose? No wonder it didn't get through.

Telepathy, he finished. I even tried that. You never answered. Where've you been?

I've always been right here, she said.

This field, by this stream, in the glare of the sun?

Well, not here exactly. But not far, either. You know what I mean.

Not really, said the boyfriend. But he did love hearing her again, no matter how long it had been, no matter how far apart she was from him, no matter that he'd missed her birthday, which was a week ago. Everything was okay now.

What've you been doing? he asked.

I've been listening for things, she said.

Have you found the things you've been listening for?

Some. It's interesting. If I move ten feet this way or that, everything I hear is different.

That is interesting, he said.

And if I stand right here and tune it in, there's this woman, twenty-six miles off or twenty-six years, who's yelling screaming berating tearing into her boyfriend.

She's a thesaurus.

She's got every right in the book.

Why's that?

Because he forgot it was her birthday, she said.

I didn't forget, he said, reassuringly. It was last week. The twenty-fourth. I got you something.

What is it? she said.

He stood beside her, August first today. Sun climbing high. Brightness, breathing. Seeing her light.

Something green, he said. And growing.

MONEY!!!!! Oh, the girlfriend was very excited, overly so as in a stylized scene. I simply can't wait to spend it on lots and lots and lots of stuff.

It's not money, he said. And her spirits f

                                    e
                                    l
                                    l
                            like   a   brick

through air.

Then, because it was all in fun, she told him some flower names, and her spirits lifted again. These names happened to be of flowers they both stood among. Chicory, asters, black-eyed Susans, wild carrot. And there was a common mullein, tall in the distance. Look, she said. He did look, but what exactly was he looking at? He wasn't so good with plants.

Then she told him about her sister in Maryland who she'd been visiting for these two and a half weeks.

Three weeks, he corrected.

No, she said. I told you. I got back a few days ago.

The flowers in Maryland, some had been the same and others different. She told of the two chairs, also, that she and her sister had sat on back home. The chairs were out by the broken fence and the honeysuckle. And when the girlfriend said *honeysuckle*, when she followed the word with that special thing she does with her mouth, it was the exact tone and look that he needed. The boyfriend knew then that she was home, and not home away home, but home with him home. It was better than good. It was everything seamless again. Not one wound, not one scar. It was something in how she held the word out to him like a make-up gift. *Honeysuckle*. It was the sound from her mouth, the sweetness of her lips, faithfulness in her hand, and trust in his.

I'm sorry, she said, reaching out, taking his arm, his fingers, his palm. I'm stupid. I –

Nobody's stupid, he said.

I won't do it again. Her touch was like harmony after so many discordant days.

I just needed time to think about some things without having to say them to anyone, not even my sister, not even me, not even you. I should've told you, though.

You just did, he said. Everything's okay. It's always okay.

No, it's not. I was wrong.

There's plenty of time.

To be wrong? she asked.

To think and then say things, said the boyfriend. For us both to do what we have to do, he suggested. And to do things better. What else is the world for?

Things done better. This made both of them think. The world is for something. Might as well be that the something is something better.

They were black metal chairs, she told him at last. With curved seats. They'd been my mother's favorites.

Sounds as if you like those chairs, too, he said.

I do, she said. There're a million things I like.

The boyfriend heard this and hoped that he stood somehow apart from them all. Then he thought, No, she can have them as she wants. She can like things however she likes them. As long as I'm somewhere.

You are, she said.

Am what? he asked.

First in line.

After allowing that to sink in, the girlfriend told of a friend of her sister's, a young mother dying of cancer.

Things are bad, she said. There's nothing left to be done for her. She's gone into hospice, thirty-six years old. Glioblastoma multiforme on the left occipital-parietal lobe.

Very aggressive growth. I couldn't just leave. I felt I had to stay. I was there for a reason.

There's always some reason, he said. I mean –

It's hard to see sometimes, said the girlfriend. She's so young with a child and everything – everything to look forward to, and she won't get to see it.

She might, said the boyfriend.

No, said the girl.

They both were quiet for a moment in the midmorning glare, leaning slightly toward one another, listening to the babble of the stream and everything – everything nearby, everything in the distance, everything to look forward to.

It bothers me so much, about Marjanna, she said to him.

Medjoo –

There's nothing I can do for the world, sometimes. I'm no help at all.

That's not true, said the boyfriend. Help is what you do best. Borrow my eyes. See for yourself.

I knew you'd say that. Well, not the part about your eyes. Why do I feel I've got to pay attention to your words?

It was then that the girlfriend mentioned Hermes.

Herman?

Hermes, messenger god, she repeated.

I know Hermes, said the boyfriend, because he'd been reading a book. And when he was young he'd read others. And his mother had told stories. There were certain gods who stirred thoughts in him. Zeus, Poseidon, Aphrodite. He felt the buzz of ideas, as of a fly trying to remind him of things.

Then later that night, when he was alone, he reread the parts in his book about Hermes. Hermes was born deep in a cave in utmost peace. His mother was Maia. His middle names were Wit and Charm. He was also the guide of souls on the way to Hades. Nothing wrong with that. There were other things, too, such as how merry and precocious he was as a child, and things to do with cows and fruit and building relations. Plus, most everyone was fond of him.

You're a bit like him, she said, back near the stream. She was piling stones, one on another, when she said it.

Like who?

Hermes, she said. Weren't you listening?

Of course he was listening, he was just thinking of something else at the moment.

So, what was her name again?

Hermes?

No. Your sister's friend.

Marjanna, she told him. She is so sweet and kind, creative.

Like Medjools. That's what it sounds like.

Medjool dates? What are you saying?

He shook his head, not wanting to play.

You see the best in everyone, he said.

It makes me very sad, said the girlfriend.

To see the best?

When a life is lost.

It can't be lost if you see it.

Then I don't mean lost, she said. I don't know what I mean.

I'm not making fun. About Medjool dates, I mean. Just, I like that name. Marjanna.

Hmm, she said, reaching for more stones to pile on. She seemed to be slipping, withdrawing again. The boyfriend wanted to say his girlfriend's name, to remind her of herself and where she was. In this field, with these flowers, this sun, with him. But he didn't.

Then she told him that the best time of day to instill courage in a person's mood is early morning when her spirit is nearest her body, and the day hasn't brought in distractions.

I'll remember that, he said.

But if the morning's not available, anytime will do.

The boyfriend reached over and put a hand on her back as she continued to build with the stones.

Any pick-up lines that you prefer? he asked.

Ones used on me have included: Is that a mirror in your pocket, or do I just see myself in your pants? Or, who could forget: What's your sign? Dangerous curves ahead?

Those are good, he agreed.

And he wondered if she meant to pile the stones so high. It was becoming a landmark, what she did. Like a cairn. And did she mean to wipe away her sweat with the back of her hand when it dripped from her face and neck? Did she mean to explain herself to him by not saying much on the subject of her absence? Because, that subject was the elephant in the field here. Still, what mattered most was simply being with her again, among the flowers, looking into her hickory eyes.

Chicory, she said, not in a corrective way, just to be sure that he meant blue.

That's what I meant, he said. Chicory.

What especially interested him was that she wasn't transparent, though sometimes he wished she were a bit more clear.

There's a light in August like no other month, said the girl.

I read a book by him once.

August Strindberg?

William Faulkner, said the boyfriend.

The girlfriend nodded, said nothing, flushed red with sun.

You're dripping hot, he said, looking at her brow and cheek and neck.

She suggested they find some shade. So, they did. He followed her the way sound follows lightning, the way clearing follows storm. He went with her under the green green trees onto the banks of the creek.

There's another of my birthday presents up there, she said, giving nod to the leaves.

Everything green is for you, he agreed.

Even mold?

Mold can be useful.

Still, I feel bad, she said as they sat in the shade, near the water. Bad for not telling you things.

Don't worry about it, he said.

It's not what you think. You think I went away from you.

I... Yes.

You guess, she said.

Yes, he said. Well, I thought you were missing. I called the police.

You did?

Yes, he said.

Well, was I?

Were you what? he asked.

Missing.

The boyfriend didn't want to talk about it anymore.

You don't have to explain yourself, he told her.

Life can be very intense for me sometimes, said the young

woman. I'm just learning to see it, to cooperate with it better.

You always cooperate, he said.

Maybe that's the problem, she said. There's so much wrong, and I realize I have to accept that, too. The good comes easy, but the bad takes work to make it right. I'm far too positive when it comes to this world.

Are you sure about that? he joked.

I was, said the girlfriend. And then you. You throw me off balance.

Like with those pick-up lines I used.

Was it you who used them? she asked.

I hope so, he said. The light through the leaves dappled his skin. A patch of dirt, not very wide, separated them.

You look different to me, he said.

Growing up, I was a brat to my sister, the girlfriend said. We're opposites, really.

I doubt you were a brat.

And my family, you know, is super important to me. I want to be there for my father and my sister and...

She didn't say who else. Two weeks ago, the boyfriend thought for sure there was someone. As the *Book of Connections/Disconnections* puts it on page 27:

> Arrows are shot and hearts are missed as much as they are
> pierced. People love who they love, and you can't change that.

But now, in the shade, he thought only of her thinking again about him. Each moment is a relationship being created. It's a work of art done with others. The colors of a painting work side by side. One person sits here looking there, another sits there looking here.

The girlfriend reached into the nearby grasses. She tore loose a blade.

Listen, she said.

She put the blade of grass to her lips and whistled a song.

What's that? asked the boyfriend.

A blade of grass, she said.

No, the song.

It's by Bartok, she said. A folksong. I was listening to a CD I found by the stream.

You found that CD?

Yep.

I like it, he told her, speaking of the grass notes.

I can do better with a stick, she said.

She picked up a piece of branch that lay in the dirt between them, strumming it like a guitar. And someone might think he just imagined the tune, that no recognizable melody could possibly have come from that stick. But it would've been wrong to think that way, to doubt so deeply. Because there was music in the branch. There was music in the air. There was the watery world rolling beside them. There were rays of light descending through the good green leaves. Everything seemed important and beautiful – how he, the boyfriend, was thinking clearly, how he saw her in this light, how gently she held the wood, how it touched her breasts, tantalizingly close, and how she put her fingers on its bark, making chords with her left hand and plucking with her right.

I'm not playing games, she said. Not playing games with you.

I know, he said. So, what's that piece? It sounds familiar.

Water Music.

I remember it from my Aunt Julia. She'd listen to classical music while she cooked. It wasn't guitar, though. A symphony, I think.

I'll play some Segovia, said the young woman. The Spaniard.

He listened to her play a Spanish waltz. Then Spanish moss. Finally, Spanish rice with onions. Smells were in the air, conversations and food, time and space, things coming together. It was easy for her, as if she took the world into her heart and spoke with it.

Nice, he said, when she'd finished.

I need more time with things, she said.

I thought it sounded good.

I mean, to see the bigger picture.

That's a lot to do all at once, he said.

That's why I haven't been here, the girlfriend finally explained. I needed time to myself for a moment. Of course, it wasn't all to myself. It was with my sister, too. And with Marjanna, and that was sad. She's only thirty-six. A husband, a kid, and she's such a good artist.

I like her name, the boyfriend said.

Sad thing is, she won't get to…

To what?

Paint again.

You never know, said the boyfriend.

Or watch her son grow up.

You never know what's going to happen, he finished. There's plenty of time if your picture of time goes on, if life evolves the way it's meant to.

The young woman drew a picture in the dirt with her branch, and the young man followed her marks. It was a picture of time, a picture to express what was going on inside. It was lines and no discernable form. It was ripples on the creek, it was rivers in the mud, and insect trails through the dust of the earth, it was inspirations of light coming endlessly down. And then he looked up from the picture she drew. And when he looked up –

~

Games was back in his room, as happens sometimes. The rain had ended. It remained mostly dark, just a hint of morning in the air, and still a bit windy. What time? he wondered. Had he fallen asleep?

Sometimes you feel better and don't know why. Sometimes after a storm, the floor is wet and stuff lies scattered – papers, books, pottery, clumps of soil, and a vibrant tomato plant. It was all there on the floor with his hammer, his tape measure, and his pencils, waiting for work on Monday.

But today was Saturday, the start of the weekend. Games knew by the feel of the air it was going to be a hot one. Not much relief, after the storm. Though the best relief was that he knew where Rianna was, because she'd called him earlier and they'd briefly talked, which was about time. And he knew now, 5:00 a.m., that she was asleep in her room, maybe dreaming. Not far away. So, he'd get out of bed soon. He'd had enough sleep. He'd call Rianna, early, because she was up by 6:00, and he'd say something light and breezy to ease her out of bed, to help encourage her in case her mood was a bit off. Because who knows what it had been like for her, those nearly three weeks. And who knows why she'd been gone so long? But he, if he could help himself, wouldn't bring that up.

For now, Games was alone, still somewhat dazed by the dark. In the east, however, there was a beginning glow from an unburdened sky. It was a charge, a cheer to him, even though he didn't yet see that glow, as he had no window to the east. So, he'd get out of bed and put on a shirt. Not the ripped one, another. He'd wipe the west window ledge, because of the rain. Wipe the floor, too. And he'd pick up the potted plant, repair it with super glue, pack in the dirt, prepare it to bring to Rianna later this morning.

Soon it was coming, the first word of the sun. After the first, the second, then the third, the fourth. And Games would see more clearly the highs and the lows, the fars and the nears, the shifting momentums that make a day. The constant support behind it all.

MARJANNA IN AUGUST

My husband is everything to me. My child my boy is everything as well. They should be back soon, and then you'll see for yourself how wonderful they are. I haven't talked with them for a while, which troubles me. I think they might be lost, and this burdens my soul. Still, I do know how lucky I am to have them in my thoughts. It's just that words, even metaphorical ones, don't come close to expressing my feelings. The world, as well, I can only begin to describe how much it means, even now.

I started off slow, but complete with health and security. My mother's cooking was magic, I never got sick, and my father let me ride on his shoulders. In my life I was the beneficiary of so much love and attention, as if there had been a fund set up for me alone, a foundation full of greetings and smiles and doors to go through that steadily increased my time and space. It was a fund also of plants, animals, people, sunlight and rain, amazing bones I found in the woods, a nautilus shell where there should never've been one, and stones, perfect for holding, with lines of quartz running through.

I'm survived, on earth, by that love and attention. The same love lives there still, bound by its duty to nurture all physical life, and bring forth the earth's incredible beauty. Truly, I mean it, I'm glad for that. My gladness extends beyond me, beyond even joy. It seeks to make others its recipient, too.

~

Sure sure, I don't really know who I am anymore. Or, perhaps I should say *who I was*. I don't consider it a problem because I know other things now. I know life doesn't stop with death. This new understanding sheds some irrefutable light yet does little to direct my soul. The continuance of life brings only more questions. Mostly I ask: What took place? Was I really someone on the earth? How did I do on a scale of one to ten? A five or better?

A person wants to be better than a five. A person wants to be someone, doesn't she? I think so. At least she wants to be enough of someone to leave a mark, even if only small. The trail of a periwinkle across shoreline rocks is one such mark, a very delicate line as I remember it. Perhaps the mark one leaves is shallow footprints, soon to be washed away by the waves, or something like the splats of raindrops on the soil, whose moisture is quietly absorbed. Volume doesn't matter. If the mark represents a real presence, it cannot be effaced by the weathering effects of time.

Of course, no one would want her mark to be harmful, like a slap to the face or a scourge to the land or a ball and chain to someone else's soul. Nor should the mark be mere details and formulas for how the world may be used for profit. Rather, in my distant and humble opinion, the mark, at its very least, should appear as a single brushstroke of one's own creation, and this mark must live beyond its doubts and confusions and carry with it the goodness of life in both color and form.

I don't mean to sound dogmatic or judgmental. I'm really only judging myself. My mother gave birth to me, which made all the difference to my life. And I say now, however long it's been since my death: What did I give of myself back there? I consumed, I know, and I passed things by unnoticing. Did I work through my wrongs the way the sun, warming through the atmosphere, illuminates the leaves? The months were my being, which was spring green amazement, August summer light, deep winter reflections, and melancholia, too, as a damp drizzly November gray day in the soul. I lived through the months. Did I live beyond them? Did I love even once? I really don't know.

~

Moments ago – or maybe much longer – I was having difficulty adjusting. I was broken off, a bite-sized piece of bread from the loaf. I felt like one of those detached elbows, the oxbow lake of a river I remember seeing in books. I was having trouble remembering the stations of my life. And then, as I was on my way, just after death, I was struck by a voice in the distance as of someone asking for me. Asking quietly after. How things were going. That sort of thing. Wondering about my family and connections. It made me feel good to be considered, not for myself alone, but for all that I touched along the way. He came toward me in words of the world I'd left behind. I suppose his job was to help sort through things or to carry me across, but after approaching out of the darkness, all he did was listen.

Strange thing is, I didn't really know him. I'd never heard or seen the man before. He's the boyfriend of a friend's sister, or so the story goes. That makes him sound like a stranger to me. The description also makes him seem more complicated than he is. If I knew his name, it would make things easier. I suppose I could call him Otto the Blue. But better to call him Sudden Lee. Sudden Lee was the name of a turtle my son and I saw one day. I can picture that turtle on the lawn. The sun was just peeking. It was a humid August morning. We, my son and I, were both up early. And out of the blue – suddenly, a turtle.

Come with me, I said to my boy as I ran in the house. You've got to see this.

He looked up at me. I sprung and re-sprung like a bungee. I whirled like leaves in the wind.

Hurry, hurry, I joked. We'll miss it.

We ran outside to where I'd seen the turtle on the grass, and we stood together above the incredible creature. It hid its head. We were frightening, I suppose. And if you're frightening, bring it down. We squatted in the grass so as not to overwhelm our new reptile friend.

Where'd he come from? asked my son.

The water.

He walked all the way up here?

She. I think it's a she, I said. Yes, she did.

Why?

Who knows? I said. Isn't she beautiful? If you could see

her swim, you'd...

What? asked my son. As the turtle just sat there.

You'd see how she really moves.

~

Everything interests me. The dabs of life I see and the ones I can only stroke with my imagination. There's also the unknown I like to think about. It's the painting that hides under the masterpiece. Scrape away the surface. There're layers of meaning, and I'm somewhere in the mix. I've lived a wish and wonder-filled life, with knowledge of rivers, with conversations of turtles, and with shadows at poise and play upon face after face in the early morning light. I've primed and painted and've had my share of mishaps and re-workings. Plenty of re-workings, I'm sure. Just, it was never me alone. Hardly alone. Even when I felt remote or removed, I was not alone. There was a world around me. There was my husband and my son, my family, my teachers, my friends, as many friends as fit in the palm of my mind, where I held where I hold them so dear like cerulean blue. I can't explain the color, only that it's an intense feeling of friendship, as with my one closest friend. She has a sister who has a boyfriend and the boyfriend is...Otto, is...Sudden, is... It's all part, I want to say art, of some bigger picture.

And now being dead. I don't know what to make of things. Don't get me wrong – I am not sad. Please, don't think I'm sad just because I lost a bit of time on the earth, or that I won't get to paint anymore canvases of the shore and old discarded boats. No more crab pots and canvasback ducks just beyond the spartina in the late summer haze. I'm not sad for myself. I'm really not. There's plenty more time, I promise.

I'm sad for my husband and my child, though. They should be home soon. I'm sad for all of those friends who've written such moving remembrances. I'm sorry I can't think of their names or thank them personally. I'm sad for my mother who gave birth to me and for my father who was as selfless as water and gave me an endless appreciation of life. What child is supposed to die before her parents? I think it was I, which makes me uneasy. And I'm not sad or upset for the turtle, because what does she care about me? She cares for her eggs and about getting enough to eat. She lives her best by letting things be, except for those plants she's got to rip and swallow. Oh, what am I saying? Maybe even the turtle cares for me some, in some other world, in some secret way I don't yet know. You see, I'm still trying to understand this life – the immensity of it, woven throughout. What on earth would make me ever stop?

It's true. And yes, I am sad for whoever might miss me simply because they'd gotten used to my being around. It's like that grape juice stain on the rug and that pile of bricks by the toolshed. Some things seem like they've been there forever. You look away, you look back days later – the stain hasn't moved, the bricks are still there. You get to depend on them. Weeds grow around the pile, making things messy, but you can deal with the mess because those bricks are not moving. No time to move them. It's hard to picture life without them. The sun shines on their red backs, and the rains fall upon their rough skins. Mice might even make a home in their heap. And you know, not just in your heart you know it, but also in your eyes, that those bricks are the reason for many good things. It would be wrong if they were gone. They are there as a collection of creation, a mess of meaning. They are there if you need them. They remind you of home.

And then, all of a sudden. What can I say? The earth spins through the years until, one day, you look up, and whatever it is you've so gotten used to is no longer there. How did it happen? Nobody said it could change. Yet when you look up, there are no bricks anymore, no stain on the rug, no her on earth. There's no her any longer. What happened to her? You look in the fields, by the creek, in the squelch of the mud. You look in her room, by her easel where she used to stand. You stand alone by that easel, not wanting to move, beside the greens and the blues and the unfinished love still at work on the canvas. She's simply not there.

Okay, maybe I am a bit sad for myself, as well. But it's only because I'm simply not there. Nobody, however, needs my sadness. They need my exuberance and joy. They need that constant. They need that grace. They need to think of me as water, now taking on a new form. They need a ray of light to come through the window and help them witness the truth of things. That's what they need. That's what everyone needs. And it's what I need, too. Grace of water. Rays of truth. Such grace would help me to welcome the light, so I might see better what somewhere much deeper I already know.

~

I met her by the produce, Alexandra Olivet. She's the friend I mentioned earlier. I liked her right off the bat. She was picking out strawberries, which had to be organic. Her mother died of cancer – not the same cancer as mine, but cancer nevertheless. Her mother's cancer was in her lungs, mine all in the head. Better to say the brain, not head. I didn't imagine the sickness, did I? That would've been a strange cause of death. I can see it now:

How'd she go?

Incurable bout of imagination, I fear. Fancy Cancer, that's how they've labeled it.

So, no one could stop the visions from spreading?

Took over her entire body, what I was told. Engulfed her in pictures you wouldn't believe. Crazy images twisted her inside out. And now. Now she's dead.

Anyway. That's one way of looking at it.

I don't get the point of sickness. Though, perhaps I do. The *I Ching* says: *The earth in its devotion carries all things good and evil, without exception.* And the way I see it, our bodies are the same. They contain all sickness and health, just as the universe does. It's all a matter of balance, to keep things running smoothly. It's about a heart that welcomes each season, and lungs that give and receive like a doorway. So, what brings imbalance to the universe? What brought it to my body?

When I was young, I'd stand out back and look at the stars. I was what was out there. My body, all galaxies and planets.

It was meteors and nebulae and the black spaces between the hanging lights. I felt entirely at home, with both light and darkness, with the known and the unknown. There was a good balance, when I was young.

But it didn't last. One adolescent day I took myself down. I stopped being together and started seeing things in pieces, which is natural, I think. I myself was one piece, everything else another. Nothing felt whole anymore. But it was okay. It had to happen. You've got to break off in order to build your life. The breaking, however, brought disquiet into me, which lasted for years. I didn't know what to do with the disquiet. I let it flirt with my thinking and play games with my intellect. I called my separateness me. But it was just the fool of me. And maybe that was the start of my sickness.

I'm not saying I gave myself cancer, though maybe it is what I'm saying. Maybe it was my own stupidity that brought about my demise. Unless it was simply too much stress, too little zinc, a slight miscalculation in my cells, a toxic overload perhaps, or not enough sex. I remember reading that last one in some pop magazine. But the sex one wasn't me. No need to say more.

There was, however, this man told me once that if I would face up to my sins, I'd get better. His voice was thin as shale. I should've broken and crumbled his words in my hand. Turned them to dust. But I didn't break anything. I just nodded. Is sex a sin? I asked. He put up his hand as if to hush me or bless me or both. Before I could stop him, he was quoting the Bible.

Another person told me to surround myself with an aura of light and see my being as its beautiful center. She was from Russia, said I needed to be still and accepting. I didn't want to do any of that, not to surround myself with an aura or to see myself as a beautiful hub or as a house of passive acceptance. I wanted to live as lovingly as possible. I wanted to paint my watercolors and watch my son play baseball. I wanted to listen to the Bach honed by my husband, listen to the rhythm of our heartbeats when talking, our orgasms when making love, and then early in the morning the alarm going off. Five fifty-five. I didn't want to die. So, how can a person avoid what's lurking to kill her? There must be time-tested methods to gain strength of body and soul. I'm no doctor. At least, I never studied cures. I wanted only to make some kind of splash in the world.

Anyway, Alex. Let me explain. She has two children and is herself a few years younger than I. We formed a nice friendship, which began at the produce. I prefer to call our friendship a chord, because my husband is a musician. He studied at the conservatory and practices every morning. He played Bach for me so the cancer would pause to listen. It may've worked some. He took me to radiation. He gave me baths and, at the end, even brushed my teeth. There is no better man in the world than he. And our friendship, Alex's and mine, came partly because of my cancer, and partly because we both love to swim, but mostly because of my husband, who encouraged me in everything I ever wanted to do.

During our encounter in the produce, Alex and I decided to enter the eight-mile swim for *WWE*, which stands for: *Water Water Everywhere*, or maybe it's *Everyone*, an organization whose cause is healthy drinking water for the entire planet. I don't consider myself an activist, but I do like to swim. Besides that similar enjoyment, Alex and I both have boys. Her oldest and my only are six now. My son, Theo, was named after Theodor Schwenk. Theo was also the name of Van Gogh's nice brother, but my son was named after Schwenk, the author of *Sensitive Chaos*, which I read while I was pregnant. And what a perfect pregnancy it was. I still feel, even now, Theo's thoughtful life growing inside me.

Theo, my son, was born late April when the shad bushes bloom. I always liked those white flowers. On the other hand, I also remember eating shad roe when I was young, which I hated – all those slimy little eggs. Ugh and ugh! I filled my napkin as much as I could, and then emptied it into the dog bowl – yummy stuff for our golden retriever.

Theo's not much like a shad, not the fish, at least. He's no water boy. Doesn't even like taking a bath, and that's okay with me. I never believed in pushing a child to be other than who he rightfully is. I don't mean he didn't have to take a bath. I wasn't a mother like that. He had a bath almost every night. I just mean, if he doesn't like swimming, if water's not his thing, I'm not going to force it.

~

Now I wish to give a picture. I don't mean a drawing, even though I like to draw. I mean something a person can see inside, which begins as an imagination and then grows, if lucky, into something essential, much like water.

Here goes: It's an August morning, early. I don't remember the year. I'm a young woman, healthy. The sky's a slowly opening flower of light, as the sun, which hasn't quite risen yet, sends its preview from just below the horizon. Humidity, however, already fills the air.

I live by the wide creek with my parents. Temporarily, we've all agreed. Though we love each other, it's only temporary. Not our love, that's not temporary, but living in my parent's home is. Let's just say I've got to get my feet back on the ground. My mother is a big fan of the ground. She enjoys her garden, but she hates August because it's always "hot as the dickens" and her dresses stick to her body as if she's made of glue. I think that's funny – both her saying: "hot as the dickens," and my imagination of her as glue.

Few are awake this early in the morning. Mostly the watermen, out making noise with their boats, puttering around, trolling for crabs. I stand watching it all from the kitchen window. Then the sun pokes its crown in the east. It is stray rays of light at first like loose, unruly hairs. I catch a glimpse of the source of brightness as I put on my suit. I'm off to swim in the calm, perfect water.

Water is my thing. It takes on both the shape of whatever it fills and the colors of all that is near. It doesn't mind changing, either. It goes with the flow. Holds stuff. Supports stuff. Dissolves stuff, too. Sugar, for instance, dissolves in water. Baking soda, yeast, stress, and woe. Water gleams with the light. Its job is to serve life. Doesn't matter if it's murky either, water still glows from within like a happy thought because of all it might do to re-freshen the world. And doesn't even matter to me its briny taste in my mouth. We all need salt. Water's got spice, it's got zest, along with fun stories and facts. Sure, sharks live in water. Eels. Jellyfish, too. But I'm not bothered by the nettles. I put Vaseline on my face as protection from their stinging tentacles. I wear a black body suit I received in exchange for a painting. It was a small painting of geese, wings wide, coming in for a landing. The body suit has a retail value of 75 dollars. It fits snuggly, and I enter the water slowly, like entering a temple.

God, it's beautiful out today. So calm. And peaceful. I hear the music from the crabber's boat. It's Bozy Blades, a familiar captain. He loves his country rock. His skin, after years of exposure to the sun, has turned to a warm brown leather almost. I pause as I arrive beside his white boat.

Out for a swim, girlie, he says to me. And it's how he says it that makes me love him this moment, looking up at his weather-worn face.

The water's great, I tell him.

Used to be it was cleaner.

I don't mind, I say.

The music behind him trebles through the air, catching on a few low flying gulls. I bob up and down in no hurry to leave.

Got to keep moving, says Bozy. He always has so few words. So much work, I guess. He's such a likeable soul.

Have a nice day, I say back.

Arright, he says. You do the same.

And I swim on past Bozy's boat, and past the sign that reads: *YOU ARE RESPONSIBLE FOR YOUR WAKE.* I swim past the buoy, red right return. I'm in the middle of the channel, going across. I'm heading for the bay, but I won't go there. I'm not that brave. I swing to the right and head west. I put my head down and reach with my arms. Stroke stroke breath. Stroke stroke breath. My legs barely kicking. Stroke stroke breath. I'm in the zone is where I am.

Not far's this island I've been to before. Herons nest there. I swim and think of those great blue birds. I don't hear a thing outside of me. Maybe a whisper at my ear, which is the tiniest splash. Maybe the morning in my mind, but that's just a thought. I count my strokes. I pace myself. There's rhythm and movement out in the water. One two three. One two

three. Life freedom fraternity. Life freedom fraternity. One
two three. One two three. There's no one but me, and I don't
much count. I mean, I count numbers, but I don't count, not
here, not as "the most important thing" to consider. Maybe
one thing to consider, sure. A member of it all. What a
good world it is to be part of, dissolved in, and living with.
My heart contains the world. The world's heart includes all
of me, even my missteps, even my strokes. One two three.
One two – And then I stop. I don't know why. It's nothing
wrong. No worries.

Still, there's often something getting in the way of a good
feeling. I don't know what it could be, however. I look
around. I'm over halfway to the island, sort of hugging the
shore. By the look of the sun inching up the east, I've been
swimming almost an hour. A small breeze comes to ripple the
water. Then I hear the splash of oars, and see a small green
boat heading my way.

It's a picture right out of a romance novel, maybe as seen
on the cover. It's some guy in his rowboat without a shirt. I
don't know what to do. I see his muscular back. He doesn't
see me. I'm in his way, I'm a log. I'm in his way, debris. How
could he possibly know I'm here? But he does. He slows his
boat alongside, pulls in his oars. I wait for him to become a
voice.

Morning, he says, like there's nothing odd.

Immediately, immediately, I like his sound. And that
nothing is odd. And his face – that he's smiling. So nice to
see. He's young like me. More beautiful, I think. Hot sun in
the sky, cool water holding me up.

If I keep heading the way I'm heading, he asks, will I get to
Royal Oak?

What?

Royal Oak, he repeats.

What's Royal Oak? I say as I tread water.

There's trouble in town, he says, like he's some sheriff. I'm
making my way there to help out. I've got a green boat and
plenty of ideas.

What trouble, I think? What good's a green boat? Is he
making fun?

I don't think there is any Royal Oak around here, I tell this guy.

Oh, there's a Royal Oak alright, he says. It's a real rural place, full of restrictive rules.

And lots of alliteration, I bet.

You think I'm making it up? he says.

Well. Water fills my mouth. I spit it out.

I've come all this way to get directions, and you think I'm making fun.

Sorry, I say.

Legend has it there's a mermaid in these waters, says this guy, staring right at me. I don't look away. Are you the mermaid I've heard stories of?

No.

That's too bad. I've always wanted to meet a mermaid.

Sorry, I tell him. You're out of luck.

I'm always out of something. Last night, it was toothpaste. This morning, it was bed.

Well, as long as you've got your health, I say. And then I think: What a stupid thing to have said. But he doesn't seem to be bothered.

Ever since I read the book *The Animal Family*, I've wanted to meet one, says the boat guy.

One what?

A mermaid, like you.

Oh, I say. I know that book. It's my mother's favorite. But I'm not –

I look at him looking at me. I wonder if he's for real.

Are you a hunter? I ask.

No way. Are you serious? I'd never hunt.

Why not?

I love animals, he says. Don't you?

Yes.

There you go.

But when he says this I think, I'm not going anywhere. I just bob and wait and try real hard to be a mermaid for him, even though I'm not.

Do you live alone? I ask.

I've got a dog.

What kind?

What's this, the Spanish Inquisition? he says.

I bob a bit more, holding my own. My arms are wings. They're full of water. Why do people say that? I ask. But he just shrugs, like it's one more mystery of the world. I ask on:

So, what's the trouble in real rural Royal Oak?

Royal Oak, he says. Never heard of the place. You want to grab onto my boat for a moment? You look tired.

I'm not tired, I say.

I've never seen someone swimming like this.

Like what?

Out here.

I do it sometimes, I say, reaching for his boat.

There you go.

There I go, I repeat. What's that supposed to mean?

I'm Demetrius. What's your name?

Demetrius, that's a funny name, I say.

You can call me Meter. I don't know her yet, but I'd like to Meter, he jokes.

Meet who?

I don't know yet, he says. Just someone.

Well, good luck, I say. And then we go quiet. A few small waves slap the boat's hull. I guess. Guess I should keep going.

How can you keep going? he asks. Going can't be kept.

It takes me a moment to get what he's just said. And then it must be that I smile, because all I feel's this flood of happiness, which has to go somewhere. It has to come out. And it's all that he needs as proof that I like him.

Mind if I tag along? he asks. Wherever you're going? I could shadow you, if the sun is right, or spot you if you need some extra cash.

I'm okay, I say.

Still, I think it's my calling. Maybe I'll discover something, like your name.

Sorry, I remember. It's Marjanna.

That's a nice name, he tells me.

But you're not headed the way I am.

Doesn't matter. Things turn. I can turn, too. It's easy. Let go for a minute.

I let go of his boat and he turns it around, just like that, carefully so as not to bonk me.

I sort of feel responsible, he says. Now that I've met you. What if you don't make it?

Oh, I'll make it, I say, holding onto his boat again.

I know. But still. I saw a floating log on my way out. It may've been a shark or a gator.

There're no sharks or gators here.

Maybe not. But why take a chance?

I like taking chances, I say.

And there it was again, his beautiful smile.

What if I promise not to get in your way? It's not every day I meet a mermaid.

I'm not a mermaid, I say.

I don't know that yet, he tells me flat out. I haven't seen all of you, have I?

Which sounds sort of racy, but it also sounds sweet. I'm not afraid of this man. Not one bit. I feel odd and even, light and dark, together in pieces, entirely home.

The water ripples at my shoulders. It washes my feet. The sky is big and blue. It's all over the place. And I see him smiling. It's a whole body smile, a bit of soul, too. It touches my eyes and my heart. It enters my lungs. It goes as deep as I know. Then I release his smile like breath, hoping it will return. And it does. There's the sun on his face, and my wet, wonderful world is gleaming. Our first conversation and all that is to come. I'm happy in this world, and nothing nothing nothing nothing will diminish my happiness or weaken my bond.

Okay, I say, after only the slightest pause.

So I swim, I swim on. And he follows alongside like protection.

~

That's it, for now. That's the picture I want everyone to see. It's not my legacy, not much of a mark, I know, but it has been caught like a lump in my throat. I had to get it out.

The morning I met Demetri, I was alive and able and was going somewhere, even if I didn't know it. I wasn't just following another person. I was leading the way. And I wasn't alone. Hardly alone. How could I ever have been alone with the universe in my heart? And how can I ever be alone, now, with my soul that knows the presence, the ever-presence of others?

Green green, his boat in the water. Stroke stroke, his oars, my arms going through. I in my black suit, maybe a mermaid, making my way. My face is wet and my hands are free. There is no rush or rust in my limbs, no disquiet in my thoughts or cancer in my imagination. None. I have so much energy, you wouldn't believe. I have much space, much room, and many wishes to grow.

But life isn't all about me. I swear it isn't. When my boy and my husband return, I want them to know where things stand: never in the way, I hope, but in rhythms with a living world, with our undulating, incoming outgoing world. And I want them to know that I hear them always. That I roll with their voices. I wave in return.

> You asked me why I had to die.
> You looked out the window
> to the water. My soul
>
> was silent. It was all I could say.
> Forgive me, my love. Let me
>
> hand you an aster, some chicory
> sky. The tide, if you look
> is low, is changing, bringing
>
> more life

No matter where I am, no matter what disguises I wear, I will be a room with a table and chairs, iced tea in glasses, a lamp for when it's dark. I'll welcome all words, easy and hard, for it has been others who have welcomed me on the way and who welcome me still.

And it is something outside of me I long to say now, I long to say soon, I long to say when – something just over there, but within easy reach. And this is it: You must fill your heart with love and let that love go to the world. You must let it walk past the easel with those drips of paint, past the kitchen with the summer berries, past the vase on the ledge, its withering blooms, and out the door. Let that love walk on the grass where Otto the Blue, where Sudden Lee crawled. Let it look at the bricks, let it lean toward the water. Let it weave through the marsh grass and swim as it pleases. Let it warm as sun let it cool as rain let it be as tears and starlight, too. Let that love go as far as it can, even farther. And there you will find it and it will find you. As I release my hold.   As I float   away

NINE

Why do people get married? Ri asked Games, driving to the wedding of her cousin Dreama to the graphic artist Cade.

You mean, why not just live together?

Why not simply be in the world, no official attachments, but with friends and family as it pleases?

As it pleases, Games repeated. What's that mean?

If you're happy together, why complicate it with marriage?

Rianna took the last sip of water, looked at the now-empty bottle, and laid it on the floor behind the passenger seat where it would roll and chime with the other used bottles for the remainder of the trip.

I'll take a sip of that water, Games said.

Too late, said Rio. She knew he'd been watching her finish the bottle, waiting for the most unpromising moment to ask for a drink.

That's why people get married, said Games.

To be denied, said Rio.

No, said Games. To share what's most essential. Water's one thing. There are other important things.

Why do you need marriage for that?

Well, you need time and space in order to share things with each other.

So, marriage is time and space, said Ri.

It's a bottomless pit. That's why people get out when there's a chance, while there's still hope.

I'm serious, said Ri. What's essential to share, besides water?

Games thought about things people measure out for one another.

Bathroom time, he said. If you've got only one in the house. Thoughts and feelings, too. Those are essential.

What if you're a private person?

If you want privacy, began Games. Well, why would you want to get married? You'd be saying, Hey, do you want to marry me, because I don't want to spend any time with you?

Mmm hmm, Rianna agreed. People are too smart to let that happen.

Now you're being sarcastic.

So, what if some guy did get married, said Ri. And then learned, as the secret slowly leaked, that the person he married, she's a real mess?

What's the mess?

She's leading a double life, said Ri.

Like that girl, that girl in Tennessee?

Not her, not her, said Ri. This girl, the one we're talking about. She's got one lover in Europe and a husband in Portland with a kid named Dirk who lives with the guy's parents.

Dirt?

Dirk, Ri repeated. With a K.

That's not essential, said Games. It's drama.

A kid's not essential?

Well, maybe the kid. But – I don't know what we're talking about anymore. Who is this girl?

Exactly, said Ri. She's so secretive. Who knows where she came from? Who knows where she's going? Is she even going to be home for dinner tonight? She never shares stuff with her husband in Portland. Just wants to travel alone.

It's too confusing, said Games.

Because she obscures things, reminded Rianna. I told you, she's like that. There are men who love her all over the world. And a kid she's abandoned with people in Portland.

Why are they important?

In Portland. Portland, I said. And the truth is, she might even worship llamas or maybe she's a piece-packing member of the NBA. My bet's that she's a government operative.

The NBA?

What?

You said peace-packing member of the NBA.

NRA. And I didn't say peace. I said piece.

Well, you can't know all the trivial details about someone, Games asserted. Not when you're married. Maybe not ever.

But that's not –

What if two people get married, interrupted Rio, and one of them is crazy?

Who's the crazy one? asked Games.

Say the wife is crazy.

Why's she always get to be things? complained Games. Why not the guy?

Okay, the husband, then. He's the crazy one.

How can you tell?

Things he does, said Ri. Weird things. Never brushes his hair. Obsesses about every little word. Has to have his way. Drives like a maniac.

That's not crazy, said Games. And it's nothing essential. Craziness like that is just quirks. I mean, look at Mozart.

You mean, listen?

Games meant, think about. Think about Mozart.

Or van Gogh, he suggested. He painted in swirls. And Paul Dirac. Ferdinand, Dick Kleen, Charlotte. They all had quirks.

You know a lot of people.

Ferdinand's a cow. Charlotte's a spider.

So, if one of them dies? Rianna said. Is the relationship over?

They're all already dead, said Games.

I'm not talking about Dick Kleen and them, said Ri. The husband and wife.

Games had forgotten what they were talking about. Rianna watched him, trying to read his thoughts.

So? she asked

I... I'm. Tell me what you think.

I think what's essential is invisible to the eye. Rianna went on. That's what the little prince said. But I also think that what's invisible is knowable. And I think what is knowable can be shared. So, I guess I think what's essential can be shared, as long as you can know it. And, once you hold something in your heart – a relationship, for example – you can never stop knowing it. Ever.

A lot of thought went into that, said Games.

Rianna had more:

The thing about marriage, though. Anyone can get

married, but to stick with it takes practice.

Practice? Games didn't like the word.

Work, then.

Like a job, work? Like toil?

Not a job. A joy, said Ri. Marriage takes joy.

A joint? Games asked, though he knew what she'd said.

No drugs for me, said Rio.

You're my drug, he teased.

Your drudge?

My adage, he corrected. The be all and end all. The buck stops here.

You mean we can stop this charade once and for all? said Rio.

I think we should, said Games.

Because I'm so done with you, said Ri.

No, *I'm* done, said Games.

I've had it up to here, said Ri, raising her hands to her brow.

And I've had it up to here, said Games, touching the roof of the car, knocking it twice, three times, as if the sound added to his years and years of bitterness and frustration. God, the agony of living like this. It was driving him mad. All her sideways thoughts. All her backwards emotions.

How dare you make that sound, said Ri. How dare you drive angry.

He did it again, just to be obstinate. He knocked the roof. He stepped on the gas. And then he did it again, to prove a point.

You're a maniac, like I already said.

I'm not the maniac. You're insane.

Is this what we've come to? said Rio, calming. No kind words any longer. Look at us. Look at us.

I don't want to, said Games, fixing his eyes upon the road ahead.

Look at us, she repeated, shaking her head, playing the part. What brought us to this lowly place?

You stole that line from a movie, said Games.

Just answer the question, said Rio.

Life, said Games, resignedly. Inferior words. Hanging together too often.

A good hanging is better than a bad marriage, said Ri. We should consider ourselves lucky.

Lucky we're not married, said Games.

Thank God, said Rio.

Thank the Lord, said Games.

Lord God Almighty.

The Man Upstairs.

Do you always have to have the last word? said Ri.

I do.

~

What's your cousin's name again?

Dreama, said Ri.

Sometime between mile two hundred ninety and mile three hundred they had patched things up.

And your older cousin, the one who lives in that place?

Camphill?

That's it.

He's Luke, said Ri.

And your father? Games asked, trying to remember, to put it all securely in his head so that when he arrived at the scene he'd be ready.

Ryan, she said. You've met him already.

Games remembered the hike in January, but he'd forgotten the name.

It's Mr. Olivet to you. *Sir* is mandatory, during casual conversation. *Your Excellency*, when you have something important to present, like wine or a dissertation.

That's very helpful, said Games.

Stop worrying about it.

Games told himself to stop. He didn't say this to Rianna. To her he said:

Who gets married in September?

I've always liked September, said Ri.

That's why you'll be a good teacher, said Games.

They drove on, looking for a certain road, or, more specifically, a certain dilapidated building in a field just before the road. The building was the thing.

What kind of ceremony did you say it is? asked Games.

Friends.

What do you mean, friends?

It's Quaker, said Ri.

What's that?

They don't need a priest to mediate.

No priest?

I don't think so. Everyone's quiet, waiting for God or maybe it's Christ to speak to them.

So, no one's going to talk at this ceremony? asked Games.

I don't know. I think they may've written their own vows.

I can write those, too, said Games. AEIOU and sometimes Y.

It's a crying shame no one's snatched you up, said Ri.

Games watched the road, the late morning traffic, a passing car, the sun. It's a crying shame. He said nothing.

You're like a prime catch for someone out fishing, Ri continued.

I've never been fishing.

I went fishing once, said Ri. With my grandpa.

Where?

On the Choptank River.

Choptank. That's a funny name. Did you catch something?

A puffer fish or balloon fish. It wasn't any good. We threw it back.

Get rid of the bad ones, said Games. There're plenty more fish in the sea.

Rianna looked at the passing field – a sea of grasses, flowers.

There's a pond there, I think, she said, at last.

Is there going to be alcohol? asked Games.

Did you take up drinking?

At least tell me there's going to be cake.

~

Games was getting hungry. They'd been driving six hours south, since six in the morning. The same time zone. Six plus six was twelve. So, why'd the clock say one? When would they get there, meandering through the countryside like this, the noonish sun in the bluest sky? He was glad to be with Rianna again.

Egads.

Games turned to see what.

Just something she saw, but as they got nearer, it wasn't what she'd thought.

Never mind, she said. I thought it was a lion in that yard.

Turned out it was an upturned wheelbarrow, yellow with a brown tarp bunched on the wheel.

A lion would've been nice, said Games. Still, he was glad for whatever came about. He was happy to be out with Rianna. He was glad not to be working for Reed anymore. He was happy for Ri, too, how she'd been lucky to find work. She had good karma with work. He needed some of that. Games needed a good job, a better job, a more meaningful one.

You must be happy about your job, he said.

Where'd that come from?

The lion, said Games.

I didn't think I'd get the call, said Ri. I really want to teach in a Waldorf school, or maybe in a charter. This is good.

A what kind of school?

Charter.

No, the other.

Waldorf, repeated Ri.

Like the salad? asked Games.

Is there a Waldorf salad?

Grapes and walnuts and lettuce, I think.

There's a Waldorf, Maryland, said Ri. I went to a Waldorf school. I know I told you.

Games nodded, sure that she'd said it. He'd look up Waldorf later, if he remembered the name. Think salad. There was Maryland also in the salad. Mayonnaise, he meant. Mayo and walnuts. Think walnuts. Walden. Waldorf Pond. Maybe fish in the pond. Fish, family, friends. Quaker Oats. Quaker. He'd look that up, too. Right now he was thinking about other things.

It's weird, I heard about your father from Quincy Mesch before he died. I didn't know you then.

Papa used to be his student, said Ri.

I know, said Games. So, you going to leave me alone at this wedding, go talk with your people?

Everyone's going to love you, said Ri. And if they don't, well, you'll suffer and I'll suffer right alongside.

I don't suffer fools kindly, said Games.

Are you calling me a fool?

I'm going to take some classes at the community college, said Games. Going to finish my degree. I might need some help with trig. That's all I'm saying.

Rianna looked at him, soothingly.

You don't have to impress anyone, she said. Just be yourself.

Games glanced at Ri. The side of her face held a soft light that ruled his mind, commanding his eyes to return to it again and again. The shirt on her breasts was tantalizing form. The architect of her body must've been a –

You don't need any help, said Ri.

Everyone needs help.

Cousins and aunt agents.

What?

Cosines, I mean. And tangents.

It's tricky, said Games.

Okay, said Ri.

Okay, what.

Okay, I'll help you with trig. And then she remembered. Then she looked out.

Uh oh, she said.

What is it?

We missed the turn. It's like a mile back.

What can we do? said Games.

If you keep going, things will only get worse. They always do. This is a total disaster.

Games stopped the car on the side of the road. He didn't want things to get worse. He had to think. There had to be something. But before he could figure what to do, Rianna, egads, leaned over and kissed him on the lips. He didn't see it coming, but there it was, for crying out loud. They kissed for a while on the side of the road as, one by one by one, three cars passed by and the sun neared the apex in the late summer sky. There were tall grasses in the ditch beside the soybean field. No lions or wolves or bears or fishes. There was the idling engine and junk on the backseat, books and a rope and a CD of Mozart. There was an hour to go before the ceremony.

Am I your inamorata? asked Rianna.

I don't know what that means. You are my core data. You're in my Corolla.

I'm nothing but a car date to you, said Ri. She noticed the clock.

This can't be true.

What?

Shit, it's one already, she cried.

That's an hour fast, said Games. Remember?

Why don't you just set it right?

I like to be early.

Well, we're going to be late if we just sit here, said Rio.

Games turned from her. He turned the car around. He knew just what to do and did it.

I'm not sure I want your help with trig, he said. You get distracted too easily.

I can do better, said Ri. Give me a chance.

~

Five minutes later they arrived at the house of Dreama's parents. It was an old brick house with beige trim and a cut green lawn, a swing set, a left-leaning basketball hoop, trees and everything. There were orange mums growing in raised cedar beds and some blue wildflowers waving in the distance. A slight breeze sidled up close. Quietly, the air passed by a tent, fluttering the flaps. The tent had been set up on the side for the caterers. There were about seventy-five, eighty chairs, front and center. There was a pond beyond the chairs, cattails at one edge of the pond, and a small green float alone in the middle. Definitely fish in the pond, as sometimes they jumped, and a lawnmower left out, which was the only real blemish. A dog ran free and a boy ran after. Three hawklike birds floated on the tall, still sky. Two clothespins left lonesome hung either side on a line. One bench by itself with nobody on it. And lots of people milling, dressed in light colors and hats.

Games shook hands with everyone he met. He reintroduced himself to Ryan and shook his hand, too, sir. Yes, sir. He did, sir. Your Excellency, I've got something to discuss. No. No wine to give. And no dissertation. But, yes, sir. Very important, sir. Games met Dreama and Cade and Caleb and Alex. He shook all their hands, egads. He met Mrs. Reardon, who didn't see well without her glasses, and old Mr. Dugdale with only half his teeth. He met Jonathan Something and his sister Jenny or Wendy who kept her hand close to her mouth as she spoke. And there were Dreama's parents and the parents of Cade. There were apparently others and quite a few children. One child was Tinny though he may've been Timmy. One child was crying and that's all that she was. One child had blond hair the color of milkweed fluff. One child went fishing and fell in the pond. And the hawklike birds all left the sky. The dog, now leashed to a stake, was barking. The minute hand circled and circled the clock, getting closer and closer and – It's good of you to come, someone said, stepping forward. Good of you to make the effort. It's no problem, Games said. It was a nice drive.

And so, the kids were married just after two. They said their vowels with bright, starry eyes. People sat still in the afternoon light. A poem was read about taking it slow. About you and me and the lively air. About waking and learning and what there is to know. The food was okay. The cake was all right. The bride looked pretty in her large white hat. The guy taking pictures seemed twelve, thirteen years old. Some people drank and drank, with little effect. A number told stories, a few cracked jokes, and one old man, at least eighty by the look of his wrinkles, posed a riddle whose answer was – what else? – love. Ri had gotten it. Games had not.

Then, just after five, Rianna was tugged aside by her sister. Alex took Ri by the arm and quietly guided. Rianna looked over to Games. It wasn't a problem, though. He was comfortable by now. He'd shaken most everyone's hands, for crying out loud. He could enter any conversation and share a joke or a riddle. He could talk with whoever or simply go off by himself and look around, which is what he decided to do.

Games walked to the pond where the same eight-year-old girl fished who'd fallen in earlier. Instead of shoes, she had bare feet on. And her dress, now dry, was likely a new one. When Games came close, the wind gusted so as to cover the girl's face with her hair.

Catch anything?

Not yet, said the girl, sweeping away the hair and tucking it. She pulled the string from the water to show him. On the end she had tied a tiny chunk of chicken.

Do fish like chicken?

I do, said the girl, popping a piece from her pocket into her mouth.

I bet you swim, too.

I'm a good swimmer, said the girl.

I'll be over on the bench, said Games. Let me know when you get something.

Okay.

Games walked to the bench.

Mind if I sit? he said.

There was a man on the bench. The man, a bit older than Games, made extra room and Games sat beside him.

Is that your daughter?

Yes, said the man. That's Phoebe. She flies headfirst into everything. My boy, Andreas. He's the one taking pictures.

Is he thirteen?

Twelve and three quarters, said the man. Feeb's just past eight.

She enjoys fishing, said Games.

She likes to feed them, said the man. Truth is, egads! she does what she wants.

What did you say?

She likes to hold them in her hand, just long enough to feel them living, and then let them go.

Better alive than dead, said Games

No matter the route. We end in joy.

What's that? said Games, confused.

What else to say? We end in joy, repeated the man. It's another poem by Roethke.

Games still didn't understand.

It's "The Moment," said the man. He's the one who wrote

"The Waking."

Oh, said Games, less confused now.

The poem that Ellie Baines read during the ceremony. "I wake to sleep, and take my waking slow."

Now Games remembered.

I'm Ryder, said the man.

A writer?

I wish. It's Ryder. Like a horse rider. Or a proviso.

I'm Games. Not James. I'm not much of a provider at the moment.

Don't shortchange yourself, said Ryder. I know who you are. Rianna used to babysit years back.

The two shook hands. Ryder's grip was firm, and he held Games's hand long enough to show the grip meant more than greeting. A wish for friendship, perhaps. Or some pressing need. Games was the first to release, and his hand, now lighter, resonated with blood. The two men watched Phoebe at the pond. She reloaded her string with a piece of meat, and cast it.

I remember losing it once, said Ry.

You lost a fish?

Nothing about fish, said Ryder. My cool's what I lost. It was with Drey. We were camping, one of those father-son bonding things, just the two of us out for five days alone and he did something stupid on day three that cost us a bunch of food I'd collected. I said things. I was hungry, angry. I threw words like stones. I kicked the ground as if I meant it to be him. I'd had a bad day, was sore all over. I called him names that weren't his own. Stupid things a person says. There was nothing I could do to stop myself from ranting and railing, and then I saw him crying and there was nothing I could do to take it back. He'd just turned ten about three months earlier. Ten's young, but you understand things at ten. I think I may have always had a temper. I can't remember exact details, just the demon in the room.

Demon?

Mood, if you prefer, said Ryder. I hope you won't think that I was a terrible person.

Why would I? said Games.

You never know, said Ryder. My temper used to find its

way out of me when I was stressed, but that time, there with my boy, was the first time I ever saw it for real.

Sometimes you have to see things to change them, said Games.

There was this ugly person standing beside me, coercing the worst from me, laughing at my inability to overcome.

What do you mean, overcome? asked Games.

Do it better. You've got different selves inside you. Different routes you can take. One is small and is subject to bad influences and temptations. Another is a larger self who acts on his own and is more who you want to be. I couldn't overcome that smaller self, but I wouldn't let it happen again. Never again. I'm bigger than that, I thought. I wasn't going to be that small person ever again. All people have their personal weaknesses, don't you think? And we all have our moments of strength and seeing.

I bet Drey doesn't remember a thing about it, said Games, wondering why he was privy to this narrative.

Oh, he remembers, said Ryder. Why do you think he doesn't like camping?

I don't know, said Games. Maybe he likes other things more.

You're right about that, said Ryder. He likes baseball.

There you go, said Games.

Hockey. Photography. Chemistry. Girls.

Games followed the list of likes.

So, I bought him his first camera, began Ryder. One that uses film, because then he could develop.

Ryder paused to see if Games got it.

Develop, right. That's pretty good.

So, I took him on a work trip with me. I was with Ryan and we were filming up and down the coast. I don't remember what it was about. Do you remember what it was?

No, said Games, wondering why he would remember something he never even knew had happened.

I was on the camera, said Ryder. Who was doing sound? I should remember that. I remember other things. I remember being on a roof once, taking off shingles, looking out. Does anyone else remember that? I know Andreas likes the water better than the woods, just like Phoebe. That was, what, four months ago? The filming, I mean. I took him out of school. You can be too rigid about things sometimes. School, you know. Or whether to eat all your vegetables. To keep your room clean. I remember Camille used to be rigid about sleep training when the kids were babies. They'd cry and cry, but we couldn't touch them. It's better to have a flexible mind, I think. A person, it's true, can be too light and cavalier with the world, I know. I'm not saying to be careless. A person can be too much this, too much that, too much just almost anything. But you can never be too close. Connected, I mean. In fact, it wouldn't surprise me if after you died you were to ask yourself: Hey, you'd ask. Are you satisfied? Satisfied? you'd say back, sort of confused. Satisfied how? Then you'd take a moment and spell it out for yourself: Think you could've done more? Think you could've reached out farther? Think you could've moved closer to the people of this world? you'd ask. And you'd consider the questions coming from yourself to you, but you wouldn't have to consider very long. The sad answer would be that you are disappointed in yourself. Yes, you'd say. For sure, you'd say. I could've done a million things better, closer. I could've done a million things to be more involved.

Ryder put his hand on Games's shoulder, as if to confirm his presence or to act upon what he'd just said. Games felt the touch. He tried to picture Andreas with his camera. The boy was somewhere up the hill, with the others. Games couldn't quite fix him in his mind. Instead, he looked at Phoebe fishing. It was easy to see what was right in front of him. Light took her body, it took the pond, it took the trees, the greens, and the sky. Games didn't know if it was actually true that the light took things. Why would light take them? Where would it take them? Better to say that it found things and shared itself with them: Light traveled invisibly without much on its mind, not much to see, and then, stepping into its way – a planet or a pond, a stick or an arm, which prompted the light to come out of hiding, to share itself on that thing, where it would say hello in its bright, nonjudgmental voice. Hello, the light would say, touching whatever. Nice to meet you.

Games watched the light discover the earth. He heard

some birds, a distant song. A singsong voice. He heard a name being called from above, as if from the sky, or from clouds drifting in. Phoebe. Drifting in. Phoebe. There were no clouds. No threat of rain. No gods, egads, for crying out loud. No, the voice came from up near the house. A woman's voice descending the slope, calling.

Phoebe, come up here. Get away from the pond.

It was, Games figured, Phoebe's mother. As she neared the oblivious girl, the mother looked over at the bench and saw Games sitting there. She stopped running to her girl and went his way instead.

I'm sorry, she said, approaching the bench. I didn't see you there. You were probably watching her, weren't you?

Yes, said Games. We both were.

Both? said the woman, whose name was…

Games knew the name. He'd just heard it. He had met her earlier, near the lawn mower.

Camille, right?

Yes.

She seems happy enough, said Games, speaking of Phoebe.

She already fell in once today, said her mother. She's so effin stubborn. Does what she wants. I'm just… Worried, I guess. So worried, you know.

Games didn't know, but maybe he should have. There were still many things to learn about others.

Games waited for Ryder to say something. Maybe it would be words to ease his wife's mind, to help her through what seemed like a difficult time. Maybe it would be a wordless expression. Ryder might simply stand from the bench, take his wife's hand, and together they'd walk to Phoebe, silently, separately, though it would be abundantly clear: We go through so much together. We rise and fall, we get up again. Always again. Don't worry. We fight we make up we try to see the good in each other, the hope in our children, the joy of living on this earth each changing hour.

But none of that happened because Ryder was no longer there to get up. No one sat beside Games on the bench. It was Camille the mother cooling her mind, Phoebe the fisher casting her string, and Games the watcher keeping still. All else was the evening light that settled on things, that shared itself, that did not take, but offered a beautiful view of the world.

The house up above. Blue flowers at the fringes. That old mower by the bush. People hugging, kissing, saying goodbye. Everything glowed. Be yourself, said the light. You with me now and I with you always. We are nothing without one another, no matter the end of days.

Because the light was leaving slow. Goodbye goodbye. Like a slug slow, like a turtle. Games on the bench heard the slowness of light. He saw the light go. A fine way to end this wedding, he thought. And it was. Illuminating, though maybe a bit sad as well. Goodbye, Games heard. Goodbye, September day. Goodbye with all my heart, my loves. Watching Camille and Phoebe walk up the hill toward the house. And what felt like a hand, still pressing his shoulder.

SEPTEMBER

Ryder

Amazing! He took my hand. *Shared* is better to say than *took*. He sat with me on the bench and we both watched Phoebe fish for her elusive minnows. The blue flower was chicory off in the distance. Nearby, there was some wild thyme. Then they left, Camille and Phoebe. He left, too. Games, that is. Drove home late with Rianna, and the next day looked up Waldorf salad and Waldorf schools. He found a description of the man, Rudolf Steiner, who had written a book, *How to Know Higher Worlds*. When Games said the title aloud, there came a light inside both himself and me. Wind arose, like sudden peach-blossom flowers. I saw the words he spoke not in my mind but dancing in the field as if they were living. The words spun green among foliage and turned blue under the sky. They echoed yellow yellow through the grasses. I liked the sound, the picture, too, which was a picture of my innermost emotions. I felt alive again, ready to push forward. Later, when Games went to sleep and he no longer imagined me, my sense of the living earth stopped, too. The wind subsided. The colors disappeared. And I. I wanted all the more that everything continue.

The title of that book, *How to Know Higher Worlds*, sounded familiar to Games. He puzzled whether somebody years back had given him the book. He could almost see the experience again. I know what that's like – the brink of remembering. Then, he looked up Roethke and found "The Waking." He found "The Moment." "The Far Field." He found "Wish for a Young Wife." He looked me up, Ryder Walker Callahan, finding only references through other people's work and lives. There had to be something more to my time on earth.

When he sat with me by the pond, watching Phoebe,

Games had found inside himself my happiness along with a load of my unfulfilled ambition. It's curious how any part of me could've become part of Games. Maybe I'd helped put it there – that happiness and potential.

Honey-like joy surrounded us that evening, there for the tasting. Birds circled above where we sat. Flowers praised the late sun with their colors. The earth spun on, continuing creation. It was good of Games to find me out. He then held me like a milkweed pod and pulled the seeds loose, watching as those seeds drifted off in the September cool.

~

I don't know why I came back as I did on the wedding day. For the happy faces of people and the colors of the earth, I think. Don't know why I ended up on that bench, either. I suppose it was the exact place I needed to be. I wanted to see Camille once more and hold her. Hold her, yes. I hadn't planned it, how to hold her, but my desire brought me within inches. I wanted to hold Phoebe and Andreas, as well. The enormous promise of their lives. The last I'll know of my children is that late summer wedding. They are wonderlands and inspirariums if ever there were.

I didn't mean to leave my wife and children. I meant to be a good father, a good husband, a good person to all. Better than this. To give my attention. To grow and be better. Everyone is someone better than they think they are. Bull thistle, loosestrife, wood aster blossoms. Everyone is a flower in the light of the sun and, if lucky, in the eyes of others. And as I spoke with Games on the bench I saw that undying need as well: to not let go of my better self, but to hold to some possible bloom among all the beauty of the world.

~

I remember this: Being a kid, black and white in every photograph because my father had a low opinion of color. He believed in rising early and tackling the day hard. He believed in other things, too. He believed that only fools suffer.

When I was young, the morning rose outside my window, unfurling its petals. Hour by hour, I'd walk my small world, run with it, play with it, getting a grip. I was learning stuff by touch and go, by tripping and falling, by tasting the different fruits and candies, and by feeling the details of the earth so to discover what was what.

In time, the world became a much larger experience. It was not my experience alone, but a mutual one. I picked a stone from the ground and the stone touched me back with its smoothness. I tossed it in a puddle and the water rippled in return. I remember holding a frog one spring, and that frog, I knew, was living. The green squish, the pulse of existence, made its mark on me before I set it free. Later, I leaned against the rough bark of a willow tree in summer. I felt the autumn wind uncomb my hair. Then, as the year ended, I sat on the frozen winter ground, late in the afternoon. Earth slept beneath me, and above – a light blue sky.

Another day, after reading Whitman, after Roethke in eleventh grade, things began to make an even larger sense. More than mere sensations that were to do with as I pleased, all things came to me out of their own free will, each opening my mind to its entire being. Thus, I could know the world thanks to this giving nature, and I could know nothing of substance unless I accepted the gift. Each particular had a great, perhaps even wishful, say – the sun on my arms, the wind through my hair, a leaf that landed upon my chest as I lay, looking up. I felt the warmth pass through my shirt. It coursed through my body like blood. The warmth, the wish, then found my heart, a welcoming place in the making.

When I noticed that all things gave themselves to me through this touch, I could by conscious acts begin to build my life on earth with these endless bridges. Whatever I held communed with me through my skin, into my blood my body my mind myself, wanting desperately to connect and be known. Because, as I see it, with everything of the earth there is an urgency to be discovered. And there is some eternal relationship we've let dissolve to near nothing. Yet I remain confident that everyone and everything is invisible inviolable family longing to be recognized at last.

Hello you.

Hey there friend.

Where're you hiding yourself? my young and playful mind would say to the stick to the clouds to the stars early night.

I'm not hiding – always right here.

Whoever you are, I'd say unhearing, stick in hand, stars in sight after the clouds move off. *I'd ask you such questions, if you were here. I'd see how you are. You wouldn't believe the things we'd talk about.*

It's nothing about belief. You just don't quite know.

I just didn't quite know. That's it exactly. But I see things more clearly now.

I remember spotting a baby bird, once, dead on the sidewalk. It's a familiar story. I was a boy then, eight, nine in my rubber boots. I saw it first, my mother at my side. We bent to the bird. The pieces of its broken blue shell lay nearby. I did not hesitate. I picked the bird from the ground and held it in my hand. It was cool and limp. It was soft, unfinished. It was flightlessly still. I wasn't sad so much as disbelieving this was possible. I'd held baby chicks before, squirmy kittens, old toads. I'd held wriggling worms. Yet here was a creature who'd lost all life. I wanted to be a magician and make the bird wake in my hand and fly off. I could not see my mother or hear the exactness of her sympathy and comfort. I could only see what I was unable to do. Then my mother moved my hand with hers. We lay the small gray mass in the grass with the leaves and twigs. Later that night I heard my father kick closed the fridge, hiss open his beer, and belt:

It was a bird for fucksake. Not a week's work down the crapper with nothing to show.

But John, he's –

He's what? Is he going to get my money from Clay? Why do you have to coddle him? Fuck that. Welcome to this shitty world.

It's not that, John, you –

High time he learns that there's no good without a bad underlying it. Things live and things die. Get over it. I hate people who mope about in melancholy. There's no time to waste with goddamn sentiment. Get on with the day. Figure it out. Don't let the world have its way with you.

Ah. Well played. I'm glad I overheard the tough, so

touching love. And softly I went to sleep in the sweet and holy dark, which was no match for the comforting mood of my father.

Thus, I remember growing. I held pencils and forks. I held my pocketknife. I held grapes in my mouth. I remember quite well the hand of Gra-gra, my stubborn, steady grandmother who lived with us at the end of her days. I was twelve, thirteen. Her hand was gray and spotted. It looked cold and dead, but she moved it so I'd know she was still very much alive. She took my hand in hers and gently squeezed, which felt like being squeezed by a handful of bones. She carried my hand to her chest and spoke. I don't remember what she said. There were wrinkles on her face. The skeleton beneath her skin was trying to make its way out. The blood that bore her being from her heart to every muscle and cell sighed as it came around once more, so tired from its thankless work. Though I shouldn't say thankless. Not thankless. No. Gra-gra was the first one I knew who appreciated everything. Much of her was in that grip, including gratitude, including joy. She did not let me go until I was informed by her touch.

You've got it, then? she said.

What's that, Gra-gra?

You've got what I can give you, she told me.

I don't know what you mean, I said.

But she didn't tell me. Instead, a few minutes passed and her hand went limp. I saw she'd fallen asleep. Nothing else, just sleep. I eased out the room to more vibrant things.

Later, when I was in the tenth grade, I remember holding a mirror. We had to write a poem about an object. So, I traveled in the mirror to meet all the faces lost. All the versions of myself I'd been before. My younger sister, Brette, sat in my room, watching. She was always in my room, looking at something or listening to her music. She was half my age, but twice as brave. She sat nearby, though not in the mirror. The journey into the mirror saw me going back through the years, losing grip on my self-expression one face at a time. Then, just this side of birth, when I was most afraid of what the oblivion before me might bring, I turned around. Ah, baby. I stayed there for a moment, wondering about that tiny person lying in the bassinet. Breath and being and who I might someday be. The return journey saw me slowly becoming more myself, growing in mass and muscle, walking in nature, taking hundreds of photographs of water and sunsets, entering high school, kissing Stacy under the streetlight and Emma by her back door, then pausing at the person – me – mirror in hand, staring into his eyes, which were my eyes, too. Journey complete. My elbow slipped off the edge of the table, and the image went tumbling. I heard my sister laugh.

What are you doing? she said. You look like you're on drugs.

I turned the mirror on her. She stuck out her tongue.

And I remember holding mud scraped from my boots and my wet socks that I pulled from my feet. I once held blood from a bad cut, too. It dripped from my finger onto my palm, and I stared at the rich red substance until I found enough sense to wrap the wound with a dishrag. I was no doctor, no medic, but I could make do. I was nobody special, really. Just a guy with a sister in a colorful world – a person who didn't know what to do with his youth.

Soon, I was fresh out of high school, pimples on my face. Freedom was the best thing I had going for me. She, Freedom, was the most beautiful experience I'd ever seen, even more beautiful than goldenrod. She was uninhibited in her nakedness, and she determined herself by going as she pleased. I went with her. There was great comfort in the moment. Great confidence, too. Youthful conviction. I dreamed of all the paths I could take, all the journeys I would make. I might go anywhere, do anything. I was an asset, for sure, someone to take into account. Not an *ass-head* as my friend, Avery, would kid. A possible asset, at least. Odds were ten to one good.

So, I remember this that happened when I wasn't looking. I threw some chunk of concrete as far as I could, not caring where it landed, not paying attention to the ripples for once. I remember, then, holding nothing. It all happened so fast, just as my father had warned. There was some purpose to meet, along the road somewhere. In the city after dropping out of college. In the pub after pointless work. In bed late at night after the last toke, looking out. There was something to see, but I was in no mood to look for it. I lay there, holding nothing, not even thinking. And my mindlessness like relentless waves only eroded me further.

Everything I've been saying's been the rise and fall of my soul. There were tempests and equanimity. There were sunrises, sunsets, clouds, and rain. There were punches thrown at the walls, if I remember correctly. I see the fervor repeat before me. I relive the confusion.

And then I arrive at Camille. I remember Camille, like the sun after clouds, like the opening of a field. I came upon her first at the Easton Film Festival, beside the Japanese maple. What I mean is that I brushed against her by accident, knocking her down.

The first thing I did was to knock Camille – to knock you down. You, yes you. I'm sorry about that. I remember the feeling of her when we first laid eyes. Startled yet smiling. Then I helped her up. I held her hand and pulled her toward me. A beautiful image. And I knew at once, in that touch and pull, I knew the return of myself. Its invisible presence had never really left me. Nothing had left me. There was a hidden guidance I'd not taken to heart. I'm not saying I'd been waiting for Camille to stir my soul. I'm not saying it wouldn't have happened without her. Though I did wake up with her perfect touch, that's what I am saying. I wasn't dreaming of what I needed to do anymore. I was beginning.

~

The press and prints of my fingers upon you. I remember holding your breasts, more full and pertinent than the idea of freedom, holding them in my two hands, and taking them into me, to my lips and mouth. Oh, the love stories I could tell – Arabian nights, American nights, molding them, kneading and transforming them 1001 times in my living art.

But I was no artist, really. Wasn't a maker of worlds. Still, I formed a life with you. I allowed your eyes, your breasts, to transform me by their magic. Your body breathing in and out, the rise and fall of light, and the curves of skin I cradled and craved. You read to my body, I read to yours. We fit, one into the other, like minutes into hours, months into years.

And I remember this, not long after Camille: holding a baby boy who was naked Andreas. It was a different nakedness than I'd ever felt before. It was someone new and tender and welcome. It was a boy with all his days ahead, all his might to come. This was my son, and I listened for his supporting angels the way I always listened for the bird songs in spring and the color shifts in September. I felt a hint of truth enter me. It was early morning light upon first awaking and opening my eyes. And this light I could hold in my hands.

I remember, too: holding a girl who was Phoebe. She was less weight though no less life. My two hands were under her entire body, resonating. I listened through my hands and am still listening. I never wanted to put her down. Because I was selfish. Terribly selfish. Since, I have learned some to let go of that self. I don't know when I somewhat learned it. I'm learning it still.

I remember a story written by Andreas. He wrote it recently, not long before I died. The papers rested in my hands, flat and smooth as a windless pond, crinkling as I read them one by one. I don't remember the plot exactly. "The Magic Camera and the Sea," it was called. I held those inkjet, inexperienced words. When I put the story down, my mind was a mix of amazing images.

I remember holding loads of things I can't fully recall – all bits of the world, all bites in my mouth taken from apples and peaches, all things tasted and studied, chosen somehow. How did I choose? I held the ground in my hands, and crumbled it. There was a handful of rain once I took from a puddle, and a turtle from the road I moved to the side. There were eggs cradled by my fingers, bike handlebars, and, one time, maybe more, a hot cup of oolong tea that I shifted between my palms to keep that cup from burning my skin.

And as would happen sometimes, there were words I held in my mouth. I couldn't keep holding, so I spit them out. I should've held my tongue, you might think, because the words were ugly. But because they were ugly, I spit. They were mean, and I'm sorry. They were insensitive words. Senseless, really. They were loud, rash words. It was wrong. They didn't seem to break much, those words, when they fell upon others, but there are always things afterward to fix.

How deeply I should've remembered the holy all. What happened that I lost hold? I wanted things beautiful, what was I doing? I remember a fist now and then, and pounding the sheetrock. I remember racing around and throwing things out. There were bad days for sure, and I don't know why. I didn't really want to be rid of things, did I? I didn't want to be angry. There was nothing to be afraid of. I wanted to be clear. And to be closer. To hold everything always. In a welcoming heart.

Which reminds me. Once, on some assignment, listening to the ocean waves crashing in front, I felt an amazing release. It was as if I were my most creative self for a moment. The sky was blue and not one person was on the beach, but there was singing all around, and the stone I'd thrown so long ago had broken into a multitude of pieces that were grains of sand. I took a handful of sand and let it rest in my palm.

What a good earth it is to provide for us – all the means of life and each new moment when I may if I might, may know what has come to me. Each grain, each gift, my wife and my children, wave after wave, song upon song, flower by flower. I hold you each. I feel all life. Andreas and Phoebe. Camille, my heart. And though I'm bound to what's living, though it's hard to let go, I watch now as that handful of sand I once held sifts through my fingers.

~

I have wondered at times what makes the world order itself out of chaos. I have wished to know what lives behind the surface of our lives. If I could peel back that surface, making the underlying truth visible, then I would see the eternal structure of things. I would see what really holds us together. And if ever I had such a view, I'd rest assured.

As for now, I don't know anything greater than this: holding one moment in the palm of my hand. Which is your hand in mine, when I think back upon it. Your hand, Camille. Your soft, your actual, your certain hand in mine. Where is this moment in me as I speak? It's there by the Japanese maple as I lift you off the ground. There are grasses by the pond off in the distance. And we are light together, strong. Strong together, trees. Trees together, full of change. Change together, we are leaves tinged with orange. September flowers, we are goldenrod. Goldenrod, we are fields for miles. For miles for ever, we are love that I hold. That I hold without failure. Beautiful miles of love.

I remember your every ounce, your press and pulse, and I remember it now with gratefulness. I hold your hand like that very first time. I take you in through what is equivalent to skin and find you real inside me, which is outside me here, all the universe I'm seeing, the life and togetherness yes, the truth like a magnet, a light for my being, much greater life without a doubt in you and me, in this keep and simplest touch.

~

Camille, you blew me away once. I blow away now. I think I must have died just recently. Let me explain:

I was up on the roof not long ago, replacing some shingles. I was holding to something with my right hand. An airplane passed over. I looked up, looked out, a gust of wind, and then I was gone. I fell, I think. I felt the failure in my body. I felt it in my heart. I don't know if it was the fault of my feet, my hands, myself, the loose wind, or the plane overhead that shattered the equilibrium. But I'm sorry I wasn't more alert and careful. I never meant to lose my grip. I never meant to let go so thoughtlessly. I never meant to fall or to be far off. I never meant to take myself away from you.

~

The flowers are feelings
this time of year.

The temperature is perfect and the air inspires light. The place is free and primed for creation. God breathe the moment. God breathe the world. What is it about the act of breath that makes me think God?

I am an artist somewhere inside me. That's what I am when I'm most at home. I'm in love now, too. That's what I am with you, Camille, in my soul. I hold your hand. I cannot let go. I can't let go because I can't let go what is already free. I'm only beginning to understand the idea.

Milla, you are the freest, the prettiest, most beautiful person hands down, and Drey and Feeb the best children ever that the world could know, and I, just now, am one joyous life full of riches. It is sweet, sweet joy, just so much joy. I float with joy as if a seed upon the wind, and my thoughts are colors of late summer flowers. And the thing I most want is to hold life for real, to do it again. Not as a tree or a flower. Not even a lion. But to do it myself, only more myself. To do it again.

I want to do it again, not this again, something close to this, though, and closer to you, closer to everyone and everything. I want to do my life with as much light as possible, and let the shadows fall where they may and words not be wrongful. I will be I, you will be you, and each difference will be how we've grown from here. There is more to come. I feel it coming. In my heart my hands my body our world. We are keyed into unlocking ourselves – our secret will be out. We are at length to be together in every light and shade. And I. I will put it right some day. As for now, hold fringed gentian up to the heavens own blue, and to everything of the earth, give love.

TEN

You tune into people, said Rio to Games.

She released her hand from his, and once again they stood apart.

I turn into them? Is that what you said?

Tune, repeated Rio, trying to be serious. Maybe it's the wrong phrase.

Tune them out. Is that better?

Yes. More what I was thinking, agreed Ri, sarcastically.

It varies, said Games.

What varies?

Involvement does. Same as for you. What connection you feel. Sometimes it's strong, sometimes weak.

So, it depends on receptivity, said Ri.

Or presents. Games held forth his bag so she'd get his pun. He had four gifts to deliver to his aunt, uncle, and cousins. His best presence, however, was with Rianna.

Problem is, he was leaving her now, going off for a few days. She might joke how his greatest gift was just that – to leave her. It was like a(h) final(ly,) goodbye.(!)

Games wondered sometimes where he really stood with Rianna. In harmony. In tuitive. In love. Or less soulfully linked – simply next to her, beside his car. In the October light with breeze sliding across the rooftops. In the very middle of the month, the 16th, to be exact. Most leaves on the trees were oranges, yellows, were shades of red. Some leaves had fallen and lay on the ground, while others remained green upon their branches. If Games thought about it, everything made sense. The world continued to unfold and he and Rianna were comfortable with it, unfolding along.

They stood together alongside his car. Games was ready with his small bag of clothes and a smaller bag of presence. Four o'clock in the afternoon. Quite pretty, Ri's face with the sun shining on it. Seeing her made it difficult to leave.

What's that flower, said Games. The one poets write about?

Roses? Tulips? Fringed gentian?

Not those. The one that never fades.

Amaranth, said Ri, like a botanical encyclopedia.

I could look at you forever, said Games.

You'd have to close your eyes to sleep.

I read about a man who never slept, said Games.

Who?

A man.

I don't believe you, said Ri. A man has a name.

It's true, said Games. Travis. Travis Beauregard.

How do you remember his name so easily when you barely remember mine?

It's a mystery, Rose. I mean Rianna. Thing is, Travis is short for Traviss with two s's, which was his real name. He never slept his entire life. They called him the Watchman of Wichita. They called him Captain Wake. They called him Mr. Sleepless.

Games stood there smiling at these names and his story.

Don't you have to go? said Rio. That's go with one *g*.

I guess.

What are you waiting for? she asked, trying to sound mean.

Games didn't know. There were clouds from the north and the temperature was falling. If he got in the car and left, he knew Ri would melt into the past and blend with history, recoverable only in memory or in some documentary film about young teachers in America. How was it possible to keep her with him? As if on cue, Rio handed him something.

I almost forgot.

It was an intriguing beginning.

Remember Camille from the wedding last month?

Games was bad with names.

She had two kids, Andreas and Phoebe.

Still nothing.

Her husband had recently died after falling off their roof.

Oh, yeah, said Games.

Her son took this picture of us, said Rio. I just got it

yesterday and made a copy for your wallet.

Games looked at the 2x3 photo. In it, he and Ri were side by side, almost touching, just as it was here. There was nice light in the photo. It was well composed. Andreas had talent, and only thirteen.

You're smiling, said Games.

So are you.

Does this mean we're an item? he asked.

There it is, on paper, said Rio.

Games put the photo in his wallet. He radiated calm and received the same. Good receptivity. Rio leaned into Games and he kissed her. There was little else he wanted to do. He reached with his hand and felt her cheek and neck. He kissed her until her leaning grew awkward, until a siren sounded, until it was time to let go. Who determined it was time? Nothing was written. There was no manual.

An old man walked past, on the other side of the street, glancing their way with voyeuristic interest. Games and Rianna noticed him when they eased apart. The old man looked away, and Games got in his car. He rolled down the window.

Goodbye, he said.

Goodbye, she said.

I love you, he said.

I love you, she said.

The sky is green, he said, just to see what would happen.

The sky is blue, she said, proving she wasn't a parrot.

Games gave Rio the rev of the engine and an empty bottle from the backseat so it wouldn't roll and make noise. Then, with his arm reaching out, he drove off, waving. In his mirror he could see Rianna, without the rev but with the bottle and the afternoon light. He continued to glance back, until turning left onto Taylor erased her body – a slow curve of deletion. Yet, in his mind Games could find Rianna, there for the asking, more powerful than fusion, than any matter or magic. He didn't even need the photo, but it was a nice thing to have in case his mind went blank.

~

Games drove on the highway and then off at exit four. He passed farms and fields. He passed the old paper plant and businesses with strange names, such as Ev-Lan Inc., Simplex Industrial, and Multicorp. He swung past the college green and headed down the hill. People in pairs, Friday evening. He pulled over to the side, a half-mile from his aunt and uncle's white house, his old home.

A young woman with hair spilling out of her helmet sped past on her BMW, going way too fast. She swerved to avoid something in the road. Games didn't see what it was the driver chose to miss. Instead, he was struck by changes in town. Buildings he used to know had been remodeled. The sidewalks were undergoing repairs. There appeared strange new people at every corner, new construction at the school, a new traffic pattern on Market Street, and a mural supporting locally grown agriculture that Games had never seen before.

Games drove on, arriving at his aunt's as the sun disappeared from the sky. He came in bearing gifts. One for Aunt Julia, all smiles. One for Uncle Orro, not yet home. One for Peter, in Seattle. And one for Michaela, also visiting for the weekend.

God bless you, said Aunt J. I'm so happy to see you.

Any effort Games put forth was always more than she expected of him. She'd made a dinner of lentil soup and sour cream muffins. Michaela had sliced some apples and cheese. She'd squeezed lemon on the apple slices to keep them fresh. The three of them waited for Orro. They waited some more, Julia telling them about the accident over near Two Buttons Diner. Classical music soft in the background, the windows gone dark. No one knew how long it would be.

By eight-thirty, Julia, Michaela, and Games were too hungry and ate without Orro. Julia said a short grace. *We praise you, Lord, and thank you for this food and all the bounty that comes of your love. Amen.* The grace repeated in fragments inside Games. *All the bounty that comes. Praises and thanks, Lord. You lord.*

Who was this Lord who his aunt praised and thanked? Games didn't have much respect for such a being if He required attention and demanded praise. Just do what you have to do, and don't ask for anything in return, Games thought. He looked around to see if the Lord was sitting in the room, angered by Games's profanity, or verily smiling upon it. If God were there, Games figured He could take a joke. But Games didn't see God, which was a shame, he thought. Would've been interesting. The Lord could've had some soup, even though it needed more salt. The muffins and apples and cheese, however, were near perfect. God could've gorged on muffins, as much as to stuff Him. And verily, He would've said unto all, Now, I am pleased.

Quarter to ten, Uncle Orro came through the door. First, he'd had a late meeting with a student. Next, he'd narrowly avoided an accident when, making a left turn onto Rosendale, this motorcycle came out of nowhere and barely avoided striking the side of his car, which was discombobulating at the time, but now he was over it. Then he'd had dinner with Godine and a friend of Godine's. Hadn't he told Julia in the morning? Apparently not. He kissed his wife on her forehead and apologized for his misdemeanor. Had he known about Games and Michaela, he'd've changed his plans. But, of course, no one tells him anything, which was more hyperbole than truth.

Orro poured himself a glass of red wine and sat with his daughter and nephew in the well-lit kitchen. They talked about Godine and Godine's friend from Cairo. They talked about work and Games's part-time studies toward becoming a teacher.

A teacher?

Yes.

Why would you want to teach? asked Orro. Why not do the very things you wish to teach others to do?

I can do them already, said Games. I'm pretty good at reading, for one. Spelling's a breaze. I mean, breeze.

Yes, well. People, I've found, are unteachable and for the most part uneducated. Which makes for disappointment for me as a professor. And yet, at the same time, it's a more accurate view of the world. What can I tell you?

Games could think of nothing. Michaela shifted positions in her chair. Julia, at the sink, continued to scrub dried lentils from the bottom of bowls. Then, when Julia had finished washing and came to the table, they all talked about the change of weather, which morphed into a discussion of the observable universe. It was talk of stars, event horizons, and all possible worlds that were out there, parallel universes with anti-time and anti-space and anti-light and anti –

Don't say it, said Orro. He knew Games well enough to hear *anti-pasta* in his nephew's mind. Uncle O took a long sip of wine. During the lull in the conversation, Games remembered and went to get something.

It's not my birthday, said Professor O, when Games handed him his present.

Open it, Papa, said Michaela. Be nice.

He did his opening act, which was to pull the thing from its paper bag. He tried to be nice.

What's this? said Uncle O.

It's called a book? said Games. A recent invention.

Catching the Light. Zajonc. I have this book on a shelf. It's old.

Sorry, said Games.

Good thing I haven't read it, said Orro. Now, I suppose I have to. You've given me a task.

A tasket, said Michaela.

Ah, to be buried in it.

A tisket a tasket, corrected Michaela. I didn't say casket.

And thus, life ticks on, said Orro.

Rianna thought you'd like it, said Games.

Who's Rianna?

I've told you, said Games. A friend.

A girlfriend. Yes, I remember. Another recent invention, it seems.

She likes to read to me.

I thought you said you were good at reading.

I'm also good at listening to her.

Ah, said Uncle Orro. The first ingredient of a lasting relationship: Listening to her. I give all young men this bit of advice.

You'd like her, said Games. She loves plants and science.

Kepler wrote well on the planets. Feynman on physics. Gould, Dawkins, Asimov – all good science writers. Jaimi Dean-Beckett is doing great work with genes. Genes are the thing of the moment, along with Higgs boson. There's a gene to determine each outcome. Rather thrilling, I think.

James Dean? asked Games.

I doubt he determined much of anything, besides a good pose for the cameras.

Maybe so. But what name did you say?

Jaimi, with genes, said Orro. It's a crying shame how minds are deteriorating these days. Too many are infected by primitive tribal superstitions, interest in the occult, metaphysical beliefs, that sort of thing. My advice is to be material so your material is relevant. Most books have no beneficiary effect upon people, as a student of mine once put it, totally by accident, I think. Beneficiary. I couldn't agree more. What did you think?

About what? asked Games.

This book.

I like light, said Games. There's more to everything than meets the I.

I hope that wasn't a pun.

More to everything than meets what we see, then. To be more clear.

More clear, repeated the professor. Yes, well. Far too much feeble-mindedness these days, if you ask me. Though perhaps you're not asking, are you? It's what technology is for, to clear up what's going on. Make it *more clear*, as you might say. We scientists envision the need for a tool. The tool is made. We use it to measure. And we come to know what this universe has got in its pockets.

Coming from a man who won't carry a cell phone, said Michaela.

I don't like phones, said Orro. But that's just my hang-up, no pun intended. Then he continued where he'd left off: We'll get to the bottom of the universe someday, even if only to recognize that it's an endless pit. We're only at the edge of the life explosion. We're making our way. There's always something greater to discover. Thank the human mind for science.

It's not just more technology we need, said Games.

You've got something better? asked Orro.

There's no machine of the world that will measure anything outside the world itself, said Games. There's no technology that will discover God, for example.

Orro looked stunned.

Where'd God come from?

A grace I heard at dinner.

A grave, more like it, said Orro. Why bring the sterile concept back to life?

I'm talking figuratively, said Games.

Leave the old magician in his grave or grace, if you will – that's where he belongs. We have our own powers now to decode the mysteries of the universe. We will someday know ourselves by what we make and what we measure and what we do and whatnot.

What I mean, said Games, is that the material world will only reveal more of itself and only prove more of itself alone.

And what is greater than that? asked Orro.

Music's greater, said Michaela. Love is.

Both reducible to physical and chemical components, said the professor. To the function of fields. To the Core Theory. To the inner workings of the brain, to keep my terms understandable. I don't mean to take the colors from the rainbow. I, too, enjoy a beautiful sky. I, too, love Bach. It's the truth of how things are put together I'm after. Not the gleam in the eye, but the reflective properties of that eye. It's the makeup of stars and viruses, of this chair, my genes, and of the whole human body that excites me to tears.

But don't you think, said Games, that to know the truth, our thinking's got to reach life not only where it manifests in matter but also in how it speaks to the heart? We can think in different terms – terms unmeasurable by a machine.

What terms do you propose?

Metaphor is one way where thoughts can breach the unknown. Another is meditation. Another, attention.

New Age gibberish, said the professor. And improper English, too. The word is *immeasurable*. But you didn't come here for correction.

Be nice, Papa, said Michaela.

Forgive an old teacher his vicious red pen. I used to think the mystics may have had something to offer, but that was back when I was young. Didn't I try to point you in the right direction?

You did try, said Games.

Without success?

You were a good teacher.

Undergraduates don't know a thing these days, said Orro. If I were still with them in 101, I'd have to unlearn from their brains all the myths they've latched onto. Hardly worth my time. Each person believes his ideas must be correct. Why else would he have them? I'm actually saddened by the whole business of education from the ground up.

What would make you happier? asked Games.

To write, said Uncle O. Like everyone else. Make my millions. Have my good fortune, too. And travel more, with Julia of course. Where are we going some day?

Australia for you, said Julia. Italy for me.

See how concisely she says things. I could speak for hours and still not say anything so clear and compact as: Australia for you. Italy for me. It's something I should work on. But back to your question: Everyone's got his perspective, something to add to the mix. All such geniuses, aren't they? Well, the universe doesn't care one way or the other what you or I think. Atoms don't care. Genes don't care. And why's that? Because the universe doesn't think. It doesn't act from any hidden will or agenda. It doesn't know me from you from Julia and her God. And I don't mean any disrespect to the parochial consciousness. My consciousness is no better. But the thing is, the universe doesn't play games, no pun intended. It just is, and the more you figure it out, the farther along you get in this fascinating business between birth and death.

Business?

Adventure, if you prefer. But you've got to know the rules by which things work and not invent your own to satisfy desires.

Do you know the rules? asked Games.

I know the ones that work on me.

Such as?

The rule of sleep is one, said Orro.

He got up from his chair, feeling tired from a long day and a narrow escape.

Then he remembered:

We shall not cease from exploration
And the end of all our exploring
Will be to arrive where we started
And know the place for the first time.

T.S. Eliot, he explained. 1942. Someday we will know this world – that is the scientist's credo for as long as there's one more step to take.

You could take that quote in a different way, said Games. That it takes new and different thinking to open doors, otherwise you're just walking down the endless hallway with blinders on. Besides, Eliot was religious, wasn't he?

So was Emma, said Professor Orro.

Who's Emma?

Darwin's wife, said Orro. He had to be careful how he spoke around her, not to offend her sensibilities. How sad for them both that she would not travel with him. The point is, the human mind must travel on. It does not want to be stuck. It has a universe to explore and no one can stop it, not even God.

Why would God wish to stop the mind? asked Michaela.

Exactly. *Exactly*, repeated Orro, with emphasis. But God's a persistent idea. His very presence, even as a myth, keeps people down. What person could possibly think alongside a true God? If the myth were true, no one would have a chance. That's what the myth-believers say to themselves, and so they stop thinking. Get rid of the old magician, and human thought will rule as it should. Keep him around, and everything suffers. But that's just me talking too much.

So, maybe God sacrificed Himself, said Games. So people would have a chance.

Took his own life, said Orro, considering. To give man room to grow. You should write his obituary the way you did for that paper. You did that once, didn't you? Some small-time rag.

I did, said Games.

Put the issue to rest then, once and for all, said Orro.

But some people might not want to read an obituary of

God, chimed in Michaela, as if to nudge her father.

Orro remembered. He had to be careful how he spoke around his wife.

Yes, well… he began. This could go on all night. And speaking of night, I've got to follow those rules of mine. Who is it who said, Sleep is mankind's equalizer?

No one knew because no one had heard that quote before, but everyone agreed that it had to be someone.

Well, good night, he said. Don't mean to be rude.

Uncle Orro left the kitchen, taking his quarter glass of wine. Michaela, Aunt Julia, and Games remained seated. The book lay where it had been placed on the table beside the lamp.

He's tired, said Julia after watching her husband go. There's a lot on his mind these days. University people pushing for him to retire. Do you want some tea?

Sure, said Games.

Kaely?

Yes.

Julia put on the pot and returned.

Where'd you get the Chagall print? Aunt Julia asked, reminded by seeing the gift where she'd leaned it against the wall. Fiddler on the roof.

Print! exclaimed Games. It's the original.

Did you steal it?

I wouldn't call it stealing. You can take it back to the museum when you're finished.

I like his purple coat, said Aunt Julia. And his green face.

Classical music in the house, said Games. It made me think of you.

Kaely plays the cello so beautifully, said her mother.

I know, said Games. How's it going?

You know, said Michaela.

But he didn't know.

I'm not as good as I thought I was, she said. There're others who are so much better.

But you like it, said Games.

I guess. Thanks for the CD.

Rianna found it by the side of a stream.

That's an interesting place to find music, said Michaela.

It is, said Games, which reminded him. There's this book I used to have years back. What'd you do with the stuff in my room?

What book? asked Aunt J.

I don't remember exactly. Something about other worlds by the guy, what's his name, who began Waldorf schools.

You mean that tea man who built schools in Pakistan? asked Julia.

No, no. This was some book written a hundred years ago. Someone gave it to me and then she died.

Noelle Bestmartin? asked Julia.

That's right, said Games, surprised she remembered.

I put all your things in a box in the attic. It's got your name on it.

All my stuff in one box.

It's a large box.

I'll look, said Games.

And later he would, but for the moment he sat.

Do you think God's an old magician? asked Games.

That's just your uncle talking, said Julia.

Yes, but what do you think?

I think I'm not close enough to Him, not close enough yet to know what to think.

So, God's alive for you? asked Games.

I certainly hope so, but it's not up to me, is it?

Of course it's up to you, Mama, said Michaela. You can think on your own. You can have a thought. You don't always have to wait to know.

Sometimes patience is the best route, said Julia.

It's not about patience, said Michaela. It's about thinking for yourself. Don't you think God needs you? God wants you to be confident.

I don't know what God wants, said Julia. I have to be patient. We know a lot about patience, don't we, Games?

What do you mean?

Your mother.

It made Games sigh.

I didn't want to trouble you. It's just…

There was a long pause and Games knew something was up.

She called and we spoke, began his aunt. It was two days ago. I knew you were coming, so I wondered what to do.

You weren't going to tell me? asked Games.

I was waiting, said Aunt Julia. For the right moment.

Is she coming here? asked Games.

Here? Heavens no. She wanted your address.

Okay, said Games. I guess I didn't even know if she was still...whatever. Alive.

Neither did I. But it seems she is.

Okay, said Games. So, you gave her my address.

I did.

Did she say anything else?

She asked what I was reading.

At least you know it wasn't some imposter.

His aunt nodded and may've said something under her breath as well. A blessing in disguise, an inaudible prayer.

So, are you? asked Games. Reading anything?

I'm liking Tolstoy at the moment.

That must've made her happy.

Who?

My mother.

It did, said Julia. But then she had to go and hung up.

Games got up. He, too, would go.

I think I'll look in the attic for that book.

He poured his nearly full cup of tea in the sink, then he left. Julia neatened what had gone awry in the room.

You shouldn't've brought it up, said Michaela.

But she called, said Julia. I had to tell him.

Well, she is his mother, said Michaela.

Which was true.

~

The following evening, six o'clock, Games and Michaela walked home on a quiet road in town. Houses with pumpkins. Houses with corn-husk figures and living black cats. Games looked left, Michaela right. They both would leave the following day. Games had found his book, *How to Know Higher Worlds*, among other childhood possessions, had read most of it that night. Michaela appeared troubled when

Games turned her way. Where the trouble had come from, and how it had worked its way to her appearance, he did not know. When out of the blue – the startling scream of a ghost, and the shrill, electronic laughter of a Halloween witch.

Haaaa hahahahaha.

What's the matter? asked Games soothingly, after they'd gotten beyond the trouble.

Oh, nothing.

They walked on, cousins, curious frights, almost home. It had to be something. More decorations – skeletons and goblins. One jack-o-lantern, glowing from within.

I think I should leave the conservatory.

Just like that?

Yes. But I won't, she said. What would I do? I'm not very good.

Not very good at what? Games wanted to ask. As he walked with Kaela, he pictured her playing the cello. It was a clear memory from years back, living at home. She would bow the music, be the music, oblivious to everything else, swaying gently side to side in her chair as if the notes were wind blowing through her, tilting her in every direction, always guiding her back. What Games remembered most was her playing. But now, he pictured Kaela placing her bow down and leaving, walking away without a sound. There was a chair in an empty room with a cello leaning on its arm. No music, no wind, no side to side swaying. It doesn't always work to make music. Though, maybe, thought Games, Michaela just needed to push through.

Sometimes you've got to push through, said Games.

Yeah, said Michaela, but there was no enthusiasm behind her word.

You're good, said Games. You just need to push yourself to find it out. Or maybe not. Don't push, I mean. You've got to know when to push and when to let go.

That's not very helpful.

It wasn't, Games admitted to himself. He went back and forth thinking what would be helpful, pushing or not pushing. And as he continued in this waffly way, he heard the rumble of a motorcycle approaching from behind. He hated the sound. He wished it would go past and be gone already, but the bike seemed to be following them, menacing, taunting, coercing him to –

Games turned to look. The machine kept its slow pace, and the helmeted driver hid her face behind a tinted shield. Games stopped walking, Kaela too. The bike pulled alongside. The rider nodded. She turned off her bike, removed her helmet.

Games? Is it you? I thought it was you.

She was right, it was Games. But who was she? Someone's older sister. The someone had been a friend in high school. He'd had an older sister: Lazy, Lenni, Laura, what? Jahvion was the friend. Games remembered that much.

Lenni? he chose.

Lena, she corrected.

Lena, sorry. Nice bike.

Oh, I don't know.

What don't you know?

You remember me, don't you?

Yes, said Games. This is my cousin.

I know Michaela, said Lena. Hi.

She shook hands with them both.

Michaela was surprised.

I always shake hands, Lena said.

But Michaela had been surprised that Lena had known her.

I know everyone in this town, said Lena.

Why?

Why?

I mean, how's that possible? said Michaela.

I like it here, said Lena. I like the people.

A car went by, a bit too close.

The people, yes, said Lena. Not always what they do.

Games had heard *appealing mess* for *the people, yes*, and was trying to make sense of this as Lena pulled to the side, providing more room for the exchange of news: Javi had moved away years ago. Her parents were divorced. Her sister –

Sister? said Games.

Cheyenne.

I didn't know there was another sister, said Games.

Another. Another. Lena had to think about this word *another*, because from her perspective there was only the one.

She's seventeen now. Has special needs.

What's her name again?

Cheyenne.

What's the matter with her?

I don't think anything's the matter.

I mean…

Just a bit handicapped, began Lena. But we're all that way.

All handicapped? said Games.

Sure. You might not see it, but we are. Shy's got three fingers on her left hand, no fingers on her right. That's easy to see. But she holds her hand out to shake, just like you or me. And when she hugs, no one does it better. It's full of love. She's this beautiful child who'll never grow up. I've got to be here for her, you know.

Games didn't know, but he nodded as if he did.

Lena was teaching eighth-grade math, coaching cross-country, staying close by. She went on and on about the boys and girls in her class – the thoughtful things they did, the anxiety they caused her. And besides Lena's students and her sister, Cheyenne, besides running, living here, and some guy whose name kept coming into the mix, she loved to ride her bike.

I take it to school. My kids love it. How cool am I to ride a bike? Nice BMW, quiet ride, though it's got some problem now, helmet always, obey the rules, hand signals in town, never go too fast, drive responsibly, no drinking – ever.

Never too fast?

Well, said Lena. Don't tell on me. Don't tell my kids. Chris rides, too. But he's been sick with something catching. Man, it's good to see you, G. You look the same, only better. Then looking at Michaela she asked, How's the Big Apple for you?

School?

I wouldn't call Juilliard a school.

Okay, I guess.

I heard you play once at the Avalon, a couple years ago. Remember?

I remember my mistakes, said Michaela.

You're the only one, said Lena.

She looked at the sky as if it were a clock. Or a voice, calling her attention.

I've got to go, she said.

Okay, said Games. Nice seeing you again.

I don't talk to Javi much. He's in Seattle.

Seattle, nodded Games, not speaking it. The word filled a quiet pause.

Say hello, Games said at last. Though, how could she do it if they didn't talk much?

Lena, however, had put on her helmet and didn't hear the order. She started her bike, let it roar, and with a wave she was gone.

~

Sunday morning. Games bought the *Times* for his uncle. He made lasagna, French bread, and, together with Michaela, a chocolate cake, icing to come, for his aunt, so when she returned from church she wouldn't have to cook. He finished his book – *How to Know Higher Worlds*. Was rereading it already, underlining certain lines. *An unshakeable trust in the good powers of existence.* That line jumped off the page. Underlining it made it stay. Games liked it when words jumped, and he liked it when they stayed in his mind. He trusted his words.

Games told Michaela, after she put the cake in the oven, that he thought she should stay in school. He didn't know why she should stay, maybe because he was going back to school himself, or because he thought she'd regret leaving. She was young and there was plenty of time to change but now was the time to persist. He didn't say all that to her, though somehow it was there in his voice, even if the only thing out of his mouth was: I think you should stay.

I know, said Kaela. I will. But part of me just wants to go to the woods like Thoreau, build a house all by myself, using only materials I reclaim.

Why a house?

A tiny one with a view. A room, really. I could live there

and people could use it when I'm not around. Lots of people need a place.

Makes sense to me, said Games.

He liked his old home where he could visit. He liked thoughtful Michaela. He liked his kind aunt. He liked his uncle and his uncle's friend, Vin Raines, Orro's doubles partner in tennis. He liked having met Lena and picturing her eighth-grade kids as described to him, picturing Jahvion, too, at least as much as he could remember of his old friend, now living in Seattle where Peter lived. He liked the Goth who sold him the Sunday *Times*, whose mangled tattoo on his forearm mended in a heart further up, and he liked the very old man from behind whose white hair resembled a burst of milkweed in the sun. And later, walking on, there was more that Games liked. He liked those girls he saw with their mother, all three of them dressed in red, and the forty-something woman who sold Michaela the train ticket and called her honey and was curious about her tuba, even though it was really a cello, and said she had a brother who played the banjo, and Kaela nodded and the woman nodded back, handing her the ticket. There was so much to like. The day was unshakably good.

Michaela carried her cello and boarded the train. Games watched the train leave the station. Then there was the young guy on the bicycle who zipped past Games as he walked to his aunt and uncle's house, and the boy with the hat on backward, and the father with a baby in a frontpack, the baby, too, round and brown, squished tight with fat legs protruding – tiny tiny feet and sock-covered toes. He liked these people, yes, just as Lena had liked them all. Why shouldn't he like them? They didn't demand his attention, they didn't ask to be liked, but they deserved it. Games had plenty of appreciation to give. He could easily like who he saw and fill his soul with their available light.

Games's mood was particularly accommodating. Especially today, nothing could bother him. All was good, the eighteenth of October as he walked to his aunt's. He entered the house, almost four-thirty. The afternoon had run its course quickly, it seemed. There was music on the radio, a soft, fulfilling Brahms.

Hello.

Games went to the kitchen. The light in the house had the sweet smell of cake and the gleam of lasagna, melted cheese. Games saw his aunt's sweater on the peg, her bag on the table. She entered the kitchen empty-handed.

Did that go well? she asked.

Yes, he said. Back to New York.

And she was okay?

Everything's good.

But Games had to leave now, too. So, where was Orro? Still playing tennis, I'm sure, said Julia. Will it be difficult having the house empty again? I'm used to it, she said. And when were they going to New Zealand? Or was it Australia? This January, next January, some January. It'll be a January trip, I'm certain. The Australian Open is in Melbourne, she said. Then what about Italy? It'll happen sometime, Julia assumed. Luckily for now there was lasagna and bread and a great chocolate cake.

I want to put icing on it, said Games.

I don't want any icing. Too sweet.

Games nodded. He went to get his bag. Returned to the kitchen.

I've put some food together for you and Rianna, said Aunt J. When do I get to meet her?

You didn't have to do that.

I want to meet her.

I mean the food.

We can't eat all this food, said Julia.

Games took what was given: bread and lasagna. He took a slice of cake for Ri and one for himself, preserved in a glass container, no worries about the icing. He stood ready, leaning toward the door, but hesitant, as if there was something else he had to do before he left. Sunlight streamed through the west window and struck the wall. The house was a refuge from things that happened in the world. Inside, it was a place to do very little, to be quiet, to reflect and be still. Difficult, difficult to break away. Necessary, necessary. So, go but don't break. Stay true. Head over to the wall as to a shelf with books, take down the light and hold it in your palms. Say thank you for what you take. Maybe God is watching, longing for what you do. Say thank you before leaving. Thank you, Auntie J. And then carry the light with you. Walk out the door.

~

Games hadn't gone far out of town when, sun in his eyes, he saw a deer streak across a field. He followed the deer until it was out of sight. Moments later he saw her – not her the deer but what's her name. She was around the curve on County Route 3, after the abandoned inn. Such an untraveled road this time of day, and there she was, standing just off the pavement with her bike, waiting. Games pulled alongside. Lena. Lena.

Everything alright? he asked.

No, said Lena.

What is it?

Something's wrong.

With your bike?

Oh, you know, she said. That bike.

But Games didn't know.

If I put it beside the tree over there, will you take me to Olanna?

What's Olanna?

It's not too far.

What's there?

Chris, said Lena.

Sure. How far is it?

Three, four miles the way you're going. It won't take long. It's not out of your way.

It's not a problem, said Games. I just didn't know.

Now you do.

Yep. Everything's good.

Games got out of the car to help. Lena, already ahead, escorted her bike to the tree. She dropped it there without concern. The bike looked like a lost cause at the trunk of the tree, as if crippled and unloved.

What do I care? Tree doesn't care. All these orange leaves about to drop. Damn thing doesn't work anymore.

The tree? asked Games.

Lena turned, and there stood Games beside her. She hadn't known he'd followed.

Not the tree, she said. The bike. No one's going to take the piece of junk.

I thought you liked it, said Games.

Not anymore, I don't.

They returned to the car without speaking, got in, and drove away. The sky watched from the distance, broken by streaks of clouds. Keep it together. Stay true, stay true. But Lena began to cry.

What is it? asked Games, slowing.

She didn't answer. How could she, crying? It wasn't sobs. More a bluesy almost inaudible lament. Internal bleeding, as if the soul could bleed. Sadness filled the car, becoming temporarily the only air Games and Lena had to breathe. Games wanted to pull over, open the door.

Keep going, said Lena. Don't listen to me.

She composed herself. Immediately healed. Her crying simply wasn't there anymore.

Sorry.

It's okay, said Games, who watched the road and waited for an additional explanation.

I never did want to get married, Lena said at last. Didn't want kids of my own, either. I've got Cheyenne. We're enough for each other. Besides, I just wanted to teach. I love to teach. I just wanted to go my own way with life. You know, figure the form as I went along, not give my plot away too soon, be helpful though, and do something worthy around here.

Games knew exactly what she meant.

But you're not married, are you? he asked.

He was always pushing for it, said Lena of Chris. I'm not saying he was insisting. He's almost five years older. Has his own picture of things. Always wanted to have kids. A family. Someone to throw a baseball to. To take fishing. A boy, a girl to have in photos on the mantle. Shit like that. Someone to read to at night. One fish two fish, good night moon fish, all the king's horses and all the king's men. But one family is enough for me.

Games didn't know which family she meant.

A family is not... Well, for me it's not... I've just got to be who I am. It's not for me, is all – marriage, kids. I don't mean to be selfish. That's not selfish, is it?

No.

I just didn't want to do it, said Lena. A family life isn't for everyone. It doesn't have to be for everyone. I leave it to others. I take nothing from those who don't give.

The last line seemed out of place to Games.

I demand nothing from others, she clarified. It's everyone's own business what they can give.

Games listened to Lena, but what was she telling him? He hardly even knew this woman, who was, what, thirty-one, thirty-two, who was someone he remembered only in passing, who lived nearby in Olanna, and was now in his car, the low sun so brightly pressing her to speak that it was difficult to see precisely.

Turn left up here, she said.

Maybe things'll change for you, said Games.

No, said Lena. What's done is done.

You never know.

Just past that kind of raggedy looking fence, she directed. I'm sad for Cheyenne. How will she ever make sense of things?

What things?

She gives her life for the sake of others. What about me?

I'm sure she loves you, too, said Games.

That's not what I'm saying. I'm telling you flat out that whatever ever happened, it was all about me. That's the wrong way to be. How stupid was I.

Everyone needs help sometimes.

You still don't get it. What did I do with my life? I can't make it work now.

Come on. What's this all about? asked Games, whose driving had slowed to the pace of walking. It's just a damn bike.

Who cares about the bike? said Lena.

That's what I'm saying. You'll see. Everything's going to be okay.

Yeah, well... You know I didn't do it on purpose. There was a deer.

Games remembered the deer.

I know. I saw.

I really did love teaching, said Lena. I just didn't realize how much till now. Okay, stop up here. Not too close. Here, here. Before... Okay. I could have given more. I recognize it now. A person, she wants to do like the stars and dance with life, circle and shine, to increase beauty if she can. Like you said, everyone needs help sometimes.

You see, said Games, thinking she was already feeling better about herself.

Yes, said Lena.

They both stared ahead. Looking at –

That's Chris, talking on his cell by the door.

Games saw him, too.

Is that his bike in the drive?

He's got a Harley.

Can he get your bike? asked Games.

He might. He will. His dad's got a truck. Chris does tile work, you know. Wants to start his own company.

Games didn't know that.

Okay, said Lena. So, I'll just get out slowly.

It sounded strange how she said it, as if she didn't want to startle Games.

I don't want him to see me with you. He's real jealous, you know.

Okay. But...

Don't worry. He's not that observant. You just never can predict how someone will take something until it happens. You can guess at it, but when it actually happens... People respond how they respond.

There's nothing to respond to, said Games.

There's always some response. I was going to break up anyway, but still.

Games watched the man move in the yard.

He seems troubled about something, the way he's pacing.

Probably trying to call me, said Lena. I was supposed to be here an hour ago. Something's always wrong, isn't it? If I could've given him my all, I would've. But there's Shy. Besides, I just love teaching so much, you know.

Games did know that. Lena was like someone he knew

very well. Doing good for the world.

She got out of the car, neither thanking nor looking back. She snuck around the bushes, then under the tree with its orange leaves clinging. She went around back and out of sight. Strange thing was, she didn't go to Chris. And what happened to her helmet? Or why hadn't her cell phone rung, if Chris had called it? She didn't have them with her, thought Games. Helmet, phone. Which was odd. And what was the cut on Lena's face that he now saw when thinking about her, the red wound he was suddenly remembering? And there was something else, too, about her black leather jacket. It was ripped across the chest, the fabric flapping. For a minute, Games pictured that Lena had been sitting with him, her jacket torn open, her belly and one of her breasts exposed, which one was it, and blood like a prop, a Halloween gag, and he hadn't even said a thing, hadn't thought about it till now. He'd been so oblivious. But, then – the sun, he remembered. There was that brightness. The light playing tricks. It was all very strange what the sun could do to the mind sometimes.

Games watched Chris stuff his phone into his pocket and go inside. He continued to stare at the now empty yard for a moment. A Harley by itself. Too bad about her bike. Then Games backed his car into the neighbor's drive to turn around, feeling as though he was sneaking away, as if he'd done something illegal or immoral. But he'd done nothing wrong. He'd visited his aunt. He'd brought them all gifts. He'd talked to Michaela. He'd made lasagna. He'd accepted food. He'd said thank you to Julia. He'd even helped Lena after her bike broke down.

Games looked at the drying, browning plants in the ditch. Autumn flowers now losing their blooms. Things are born, he thought. They are given a small package of time to use on the earth. Doesn't matter how the package is wrapped, doesn't matter if it's got a ribbon and a bow. All that matters is that when the contents are depleted, the plant dies. Things are here, then gone. How far is gone? It can't be completely. Can't be for good.

Games remembered about seeds. He sat in his car and watched a gleam in the field, off in the distance. Seeds, he thought, allow the life to return. And not just return but to grow on, gleam on, and not just gleam the same as before, but maybe even to transform into something brighter. And that's just the body. What of the soul, the spirit, the mind? There's something to see beyond the body, to learn…a…bout –

A police siren interrupted his thought. The car sped by. Lucky for Games he was still in the driveway. The vehicle had Olanna Police written in blue. It was a blur, the car, and its sound was unevenly spaced. What was that term? The Doppler effect. Doppler, October, Olanna, life-cycle. Games had already learned a few things about… The world. The earth. How things work. He knew of seeds – sesame, poppy, pumpkin. He knew some basic trig. He knew that sound traveled in waves and that it was faster to travel light, without burdensome possessions. There were red shifts, blue jays, rose-wine skies, and browning leaves. Yes, there was a dying world all around him. But there was something else, too. Games loved the dying world. He loved the living world more. Mostly, he looked for a world with purpose. He found it in ditches, in fields, in family, in strangers. And happiness, yes. He loved that, too. He wanted to gather happiness in his arms and hold it out, to watch it progress. And he wanted to move, of course. To move happiness with Rianna. Further and further. To know Rianna more, better than any small picture in his wallet, better than any bloom in the ditch or gleam in the distance that only teased his eye. Why did any of it have to remain unknown or unacknowledged? All truth could be seen here and now. It could be held for sure if you were perceptive enough, if harmonious with –

Games glance up the road and down. Why was he here? For these thoughts, these plants, this sky? Sitting in his car, off the road, out of the way, he couldn't remember, and then maybe he did. That tree with orange leaves still clinging. Streaks of clouds. Evening light. He was trying to be helpful, harmonious with life. He turned to the small house and whoever was inside and whoever wasn't. One bike in the drive, the other not.

And Games knew where he was going, at least at this moment he did. With the matter of the police car now miles away, he just wanted to get there – get home, start working on personal things, to make them real. No mystery this moment.

Mostly an unbidden truth that fired his will and enlightened his soul. And he wanted to know more about this truth, but then maybe he did. Which was not just his positive spin, it was his unshakeable trust in the good at the root of all life.

OCTOBER

Lena

It's weird not riding my bike any longer. No leaning with the curves or blazing trails on a Sunday afternoon. The call of the road is something I miss, that easy voice talking no troubles, unearthing no problems, just letting me be. It was fiercely freeing. But now I'm growing my appreciation for larger things. And it's not even spring.

The geese are going south with their all-day songs of autumn – first period, second period, and third. Planning period, fourth, before lunch. Those birds have so much talk inside them, and I give them my ear. It's time now to carve pumpkins, press apples, and taste fresh cider donuts that are glutinously sweet. It's a variable wind through the colorful leaves. I am x, I am a times whatever I c. How cool it is to be the wind blowing far afield, and yet to remain in place, upon our earth, kept here momentarily by my heart.

~

It was strange running into Games and Michaela as I did. Strange, too, meeting him on the road out of town with my bike totally busted, my jacket and shirt torn, my head with its fringe of blood, and my left arm mangled. Maybe it was because of the low sun in his eyes, but I don't think he suspected anything. He took me to Chris, dropped me off, and then he left. I wasn't really sure where he was going. I never asked. Games didn't live here any longer. People move on. I get it.

I remember seeing that book on his back seat, though, *How to Know Higher Worlds*, and it made me think: What world am I in if it isn't this? If I'm not in Cheyenne's world, if I'm not in

Games's and Michaela's, if not Chris's or Javi's or my parents' worlds any longer, then where am I? And if I'm no longer with my eighth-grade kids, or Ms. Joyner, "if you can't beat her, join her," from across the hall, if principal Will Gibson is not in my new world, the custodian, Curt, and Cheyenne again, Cheyenne, and those kids again. O kids, orchids. Because mostly Cheyenne and each one of my kids. Something about my experience was making me sad. I think it was how the earth had been snatched from under my feet, and how Cheyenne and my kids had vanished like trails of smoke upon the sky. Though how could I say that, with everyone dancing and shaking and chattering inside me?

There are some real good ones in the bunch. All of them are good, but there are a few who are prime candidates to make it in this world – your future leaders, scientists, inventors, whatever. But there's more to someone than her occupation. Why not just be a plain good person? Like Yoshia, Otto, and Wyatt. Then there's Scarlet Tanager. Who can forget a name like that? Scarlet's a whiz at probability. She told me in September that the probability of my dying in the next five hundred years was 0.9. I think she was making the number of years large so I'd feel close to immortal. When I asked her what's the probability of my dying tomorrow, she looked at me hard. Don't even talk like that, Ms. B, she said. I felt bad for having upset her. Some of my kids are super sensitive. They put up a good front, but I see their vulnerabilities. The world they live in is difficult. It's amazing they don't break down at the drop of a hat, go crazy. Amazing they don't cry more often. Still, I hope they'll all remember the fun we had, especially with pi:

No matter how fat you're getting, I once explained, no matter how full you are or how tediously sweet the filling, you've got to keep going with your pi. There's always more pi.

What's your favorite? asked Scarlet.

First, it was key lime. When I was back in my element.

What was your element?

Elementary school, I clarified. My second favorite – peach. Third blackberry, fourth pumpkin, fifth shepherd's, sixth American. I always liked that song from way back in the seventies, which was before I was even born. Bye, Bye Miss American Pi. And on and on. By twelve I became irrational. It was tooth and nail pie. It was blood, sweat, and tears. It was God, this pie is boring pie. At fourteen, I began to think outside the circle. Not to brag, but I memorized the digits to 755, which was the number of home runs that Hank Aaron hit. Still, it was far from the record of over 67,000 – digits, that is. Not home runs.

Who's Hank Aaron?

Who's Hank Aaron! Hammerin Hank. I met him once, I explained, at the Baseball Hall of Fame. Cooperstown, New York. I wasn't irrational yet. I was ten years old. Played on the boy's team, Bradley's Overhead Doors and Skylights.

I played on Swift Electric, said Brendan

You had it easy, I said. Try putting Bradley's Overhead Doors and Skylights on a Little League uniform. They opted for Skylights as the one and only word. Not bad. I was good as any boy on the team.

What about Hank Aaron? somebody asked.

He was the nicest.

You say that about everyone, said Scarlet.

I don't know about that. Mr. Aaron grew up in the south, picking cotton. It was difficult work. It made his hands real strong so he could hit all his homeruns. When he shook my hand, I could feel his strength. It was more than muscle. It was heart, too.

The heart's a muscle, said Brendan again.

Not the heart I'm talking about, I said. He gave me his autograph and a tip on how to hit a curveball.

I don't think my kids were impressed. So, I stopped my story there.

~

Everyone was always nice to me, my whole life. I even include Traci Wright, who was a bully at first, at least in the fourth grade, not after seventh. One day, she held me down on the playground and called me a whore, whatever that was, and forced me to say it. Say it. Say, I'm a whore, her breath in my face like what she'd eaten for breakfast. Say it. Say it. I'm a little white trash whore. I tried not to listen, looking right past her Cap'n Crunch sounds and smell to the blue and white houses across the way, the tangle of trees and electric lines. Lions, I called them. Power lions.

Later, I asked my mom about whores. A horse? she said, not looking up from her sewing. Not a horse, a whore, I said, but she was distracted by buttonholes and just said it was a large number of people, either that or a lot of stuff you keep hidden away, which didn't make any sense. So, I asked my dad, who had excellent hearing. He couldn't lie or fudge things, not even a bit, and never for his children. He told me what a whore really was.

Who cares, I said later. Said it to Javi, building with Legos. Traci's just mean, I told him out loud. Which was true, but what could he do, being only seven. Seems he must've done something, though, because Traci wasn't around after that. She wasn't in school for almost three years. Then she came back in seventh grade with real short hair and a different personality, at least toward me. She wasn't mean anymore, just left me alone. I'd like to think it's because she softened, but more likely it was just how I let, or didn't let, the world affect me.

I had no interest in games people played or in getting the upper hand. I had no time for cruelty, either. Plus, Cheyenne had recently been born, and I wanted to hold her, no matter what anyone said, no matter how difficult she was. She was someone special. And I remember thinking: If you focus your eyes in just the right way, you can see the good and not the mistakes in each person. Yeah, I suppose I may've thought that, but mostly I was just interested in sports, and in running away from my small hick town.

~

I was a girl with my head in the clouds. In one ear out the other. Things moved along, not much in the way of planning. There were hints now and then of perception, but also a fair share of apprehension. There was college after high school, flirting with things, with people, too. Never washed my face or faced up to things, just partied and hung, just did what I did.

I squeezed into spots left at the table. I drank shots of tequila and rolled with guys. I lay on the grass by the old stone wall, awakened by a nudge, then up and stretched. Up up up from the bed of the earth. Let's go, let's go. I had no patience.

In that way, somewhat, I moved my life. There were warm nights with stars. There were trees in their winter beauty and empty roads flooded with sun. And I went as I pleased, shedding my skin like a snake, financing my study abroad by picking grapes and working as a nanny. I lived green and wild, had no complaints. And I was no whore, no way, but my body went galloping galloping galloping, and if I drove myself crazy, it's because I drove without stopping. It must've looked like it was all about me, and maybe it was, but really it wasn't. Because how could that be the case if I wasn't much there?

So, I returned home in time, partly to find a place of my own, and partly because I never could get my younger sister out of my head. She was sweet and kind and everything whole – whole person, whole human being, even if something was wrong with how she came into the world. She didn't have all her fingers, her head was too large, and her legs didn't much work to support her. She got real sick sometimes. It was her liver, her lungs, her heart, who knows. For some, it would've been too much. I remember my mother saying, She'll never be more than a child stuck inside a broken body. But it is what it is.

When I came back, I came to teach. And I came to be with Cheyenne, too. I came home to take her out, like a date. To get to know her. She was the absolute nicest, the best person ever, even if she didn't say much. She planted her feet hard on the earth, when someone was holding her. First things first, she wanted to grow. So, I taught her to hold a worm, then how to lay it gently down. I taught her how to break sticks to let the music snap out, and how to purposefully spill a handful of seeds.

Not all in a pile, I said. Let's do it one by one. You hold, I'll place.

I taught her leaf shapes. I taught her plant names and flower smells. She sat in the garden behind the house in spring and patted seedlings into the ground. I filled her room with lilac cuttings. I stuck a cactus by her bedside and tomatoes on the sill. I put pictures of marigolds and forget-me-nots in her head. She loved her plants, so I loved them, too. Green thumb, my sister. I always thought, no matter her special needs, she could work in a nursery someday, or in a garden somehow, or a greenhouse somewhere. If someone would give her the chance when she got older, she could do it better than most.

~

I stood one morning with Cheyenne in our mother's house after Dad had left. I kept my sister from falling with my arms. There we were, an ordinary day, nicely balanced. The back wall rang with early light. Bells in my head, like at school almost. Only, it was Saturday. I wasn't at the blackboard scratching numbers or dredging my kids for a response. I wasn't moving from desk to desk, pressing on through the riffs of groans and sighs. I was with my girl and my head was clear, which is why, I suppose, the playful light on the back wall chimed.

The show was beautiful to see, to listen to, standing with Cheyenne. It was the life of my sister I knew at once, the way truth can resound and you never even asked for it. Never suspected it was there. I saw Cheyenne's grace and sacrifice. I saw the magnitude of her offering, shaky and imperfect as it was. I saw her individuality giving itself like blood to a depleted world. I saw genius in her limbs, there for the leasing. She was twelve, not yet half my age, but she was actually ten times smarter in her crippled body, a hundred times wiser than I. The light rocked upon the wall. It climbed there with its shadows and shapes that were buffeted about as if wind was loose in the room. And I saw many things that morning, light I could count on, details I'd not noticed before. It was a list of reasons for our world, all good. I read the list –

Cheyenne and shadows and sunlight and family and me. Why was I on the list? No one was there to explain it.

~

Once, a few years later, I came into Shy's room with folded laundry. I quickly put the shirts on the bed, at her feet. She shook my hand, first things first. I leaned in, and she gave me the softest most generous big Everest hug.

You hug like a mountain, I told her.

At last she let go, and after the words sank in, she said:

I am.

You're a mountain? I teased.

I can go real big.

What do you mean, go?

Just watch. I can do it.

Okay, I told her.

Cheyenne's body from the bed to the wheelchair needed support. I began to lift.

Lena, she said. Today I can dance. Not today. Now.

And I knew she wanted me to help her dance before she went to the chair.

Can you show me? I said.

Of course, she could. I stood behind, holding her up, offering support. She moved her arms in loops and curves. It was treetops in the wind. It was sailboat masts on a jaunty sea. It was a dance that sprang from the music inside her – water from some unknown source that made a river before my eyes. An ocean, even. A great current, a flow – that's what I'm saying. Such flowing feeling, you wouldn't believe. Her legs were weak, but I could see their efforts to kick the way dancers kick and bend the way dancers bend and leap the way dancers leap. I knew that Shy pictured she was dancing perfection.

And I understood something then that I'd missed in my twenty-eight impertinent years. Holding Cheyenne, I witnessed that there is a person inside each of us who wishes to be free. Not free to simply do as she pleases, not free to live without purpose. Rather, there is a guiding desire, and maybe it's unconscious, to show and say, or to try to show and try to

say, one's true self on earth. And whether or not we let that
greatness out, it is up to us and ever up to us, and it is always
our time to do it now. Not sometime later today, not
sometime tomorrow, but now. And I saw the movements in
her thoughts. I saw the thoughts in my imagination move
easy. For a moment with Cheyenne, I didn't feel guilty for
having strong limbs that moved to my will. I didn't feel guilty
either for having the possibility of freedom in my thinking life.
I felt privileged to be here. I had a duty to hold Cheyenne and
others, and all the while holding to also let go. It was a duty
and not an obligation. An opportunity really to share myself
with my sister. And, yes, to have growing appreciation, too.
In Shy's green leaps, her yellow turns. In her brown hair and
wild flowering mind, I woke from my sleep to see the two of
us dancing with all of life.

And then she stopped in my arms, fell limp. She grew
absent. It was over. Not over over. Not finished. Though
nothing more was said, and Shy never danced again that I was
part of. It had been, however, a sudden door for me – an
openness I could not have found alone. And I'd have to work,
to work well with my life. I knew I'd have to overcome walls
of doubt to keep that openness from closing.

~

Fact is, we all actually know more than we think we know.
We know it somewhere inside ourselves. However, it's so
damn difficult to know it here and now, out in the open.
That's the very thing, without the expletive, I always told my
kids, and they'd hold me to it, the literalists that they are.

You know I know how to factor, someone (Adrian, likely)
would say. I know it inside real good. I just chose not to
know it last night because I didn't have time. Or, then there
was this: It's real easy to see now that the answer is $(3x - 1)$
$(x + 6)$, Haley would complain when she saw my correction on
her test. You can't mark it wrong, though. You know that I
know it somewhere, just like you said.

Still, you have to get to your knowing, I explained. Prove
it to yourself. You can't just tell me it's possible. I mean, I'm

here to help. But you are the key.

I told them this just the other day. It seemed to confuse them more. So, I went a different route:

Of all the students in this school, you're the set that complements me most.

You know, Ms. B, said Brendan. You shouldn't let our praises go to your head.

Complements not compliments, I clarified. I don't mean I'm good. I mean you are.

Yeah. Tell me something I don't already know. Brendan again.

You're all complex numbers with good imaginations, I said. And properties of equality. You're all such perfect cubes and right angles.

I gave this a moment to sink in.

So, Ms. B, if we're so perfect, asked Jenny Burns, why do we have to know this shit?

This what?

Yeah, said Ava. If we're angels, why do we sit in school all day?

But you don't sit. Not even for forty-three minutes at a stretch.

It's boring to sit.

Still, I always ask you nicely.

Yeah, you do ask nice.

So, we agreed to agree about most things. And our arguments ended. Because I was right, and they were each right, too. Still, some got low C's on the midterm. A few of them D's. But – and I hope they hear me as I say this now – no worries, no irretrievable failures. The world is going to be okay, and each of you will be okay, I promise. Every life has absolute value. But things aren't given to you. You've got to work for what you want and what you need. And when you have what you need for yourself, don't just keep it inside like a prized possession. Don't hoard it. Don't horse around. Give it to others like a ride they could use to help them get somewhere, too. The thing I most want you to learn this year – a life of giving. Each one of us is a gift that opens. Words come out sometimes, nice helpful words right out of the mouth. A number of balloons magically rise from the soul.

Birds, stars, and maybe even a handful of chocolate. Have some. For sure. What's mine is yours.

~

Walking in the dark at Jeffries Pond, going slow with Cheyenne. It could've been a week ago. It could've been last night for all I know. Was anyone else there? No one I could see. Summer was over. It was autumn air. We were bundled in coats, up to the stars. I walked with my arms around Cheyenne. She was so light and easy to move. I mean easy to carry. I mean easy to love. I mean my hands and feet knew what to do. I mean it was work, good work, well worth it.

Lena?

Yes.

I'm tired.

It's just a little more. Can you do it?

She stared at me, then down to the ground. I knew she had things to say. Don't hold back.

What is it? I asked.

Lena?

Yes.

What time is it?

I don't have a watch.

Is it too late?

I shook my head.

It's still early, I said.

It's early late.

That's right, I said.

It's real pretty out, she said. I like it.

I know.

Are we lost?

No, I said.

I don't want to be lost.

We're not lost, I assured her.

I wanted her to get out, to see everything she was made of – stars and galaxies, planets, too. There was the night sky with its constellations and formative space. It was a painted ceiling, all portraits of her family, mine. I wanted Cheyenne to know the wholeness of herself. How unlimited she could feel.

A revelation, maybe: part earth, part heaven, part hidden, part light. A falling star struck the sky like a match. Then it went out.

Where did it go?

I don't know, I said.

I wanted to have something good to say. I just stood there, however, waiting for the hiddenness to stop and for something to pop.

Is it coming back?

I don't think so, I said.

I felt bad for saying No, but didn't want to lie. Wanted to do better with my telling, though. I can always do better. There was a cool breath of wind to the night as long as we were moving. When we stopped, the breath stopped, too. We sat on the gray dock that reached onto Jeffries Pond. I on Shy's right side, holding her steady.

You see, I said. Isn't it nice? It's so quiet and –

Lena?

Yes.

Are you going to leave?

Why would I do that?

You could just go away.

Never, I said. And there I felt I'd told a lie. Dumb dumb dumb. Shy was smart. I thought about the falling star. And so I said this: You remember that star we saw – the one that shot across the sky? I can see it again if I look in my head.

It's a lot of stars, said Shy, not hearing me right.

It's billions, I agreed.

What's billions? she asked

A lot of stars, I said.

Who's that one?

I don't know.

Who's that one? she pointed.

I don't know her name, either.

I held Cheyenne's body with my own, offering support. Her independence on earth had been sacrificed so that others could move with opening arms and others could see with widening eyes and others could think with loving thoughts. I knew it was for love that the earth was here for us. I knew it was for love that the good and the bad, the highs and the lows all happened in life. I knew it was for love that I was alive. I knew I knew I knew – so little, really.

There was more to Cheyenne than met the eye, and there was me trying to see her better. But how? I wanted Cheyenne to feel what it was to be the universe. I wanted her to see what was inside her, to see and become the wonder of space. It was a vastness of herself. It was a picture this night. I wanted her to have the picture of herself on the dock, looking at a sky full of stars, and herself full of stars, those stars peeking through. I wanted her picture to be of the clear light of herself, and... I wanted it, too. For myself. That picture. Before everything was gone.

~

The pond was slow, casual water. Branches with their last listless leaves hung along the banks. Those branches hid the leaves among the dark, they hid the colors upon the dark, they hid their thoughts within the dark. Other things hid as well. No mice no cats no bears no one. No moon either to be seen. Where was the moon? It was something Cheyenne wanted. Her good, night moon. It was a book she loved.

Is the moon up there?

It's not out tonight, I said.

But look, she pointed. Is the moon coming there?

It's coming sometime.

Now?

I don't know.

There?

Maybe.

Maybe there? she asked, pointing.

Well...

There?

I thought about the moon. I tried to see. In my mind, in the sky. The universe, my heart, my eyes, my –

Where is the moon now? Shy asked.

I didn't know for sure. I couldn't give her the moon. I could not find it.

I like the moon, said Shy.

Me, too, I said. Let's wait for a minute.

I wanted to make it happen for her, picturing out in world what I knew she held inside. Cheyenne had the moon inside her, so that's what I wanted her to see, as real as us sitting on the dock, as real as the stars overhead. In the night was the moon, and the moon was with God and God was the moon and anyone could see it if they just knew how to look. You don't have to wait forever, I thought. You don't have to be afraid of telling the story. You don't have to have everything perfectly composed. You don't have to be able to say the sphere with precision. You don't have to be an astronomer or anyone special, like a saint or a weatherman or a professional dancer. You just have to think about it differently. Expand your thinking into love. You have to look with love at what lives around you, at all the great things that you can know.

Cheyenne, I said.

She looked at me.

It's the moon, I said, pointing.

Where?

There.

And I described it to her, a fantastic moon in the sky: It's a big round light with a face. It's a fat glowing body with a face like Buddha.

What's that?

Buddha's a real good person.

There's a person in the moon, said Cheyenne. And it wasn't a question.

A good person. And there's a song coming from the moon if you listen with your right ear, and a story if you listen with your left ear.

Cheyenne tilted her head to the left, to the right, trying to shake loose what was in.

And a good sense of humor to boot, I said.

The moon wears boots?

No boots, tonight. It isn't raining. But there's a faint ring around it. Do you see? The moon scatters its light like seeds all over the water.

Shy looked hard for the seeds.

Or like diamonds, I said. Tiny sparkly diamonds all over the water.

Real diamonds? she asked.

Sure they're real. Why not?

Why not? repeated Cheyenne. I like diamonds.

Diamonds are hard to find, I said. And when you do –

They're here, said Shy. They're everywhere. I see them on the water.

What luck, I said. We're as lucky as can be. We get to see the moon tonight and diamonds and everything. What luck.

What luck the moon, said Cheyenne. I luck it.

You luck it?

I luck the moon. The moon I luck.

She thought it was funny to luck the moon. Not lick it or like it or love. Good luck. Lucky moon.

Lucky me, said Cheyenne. Do you luck the moon?

Yes, I said. I luck it a lot.

And I looked out far. And luck filled the sky. The sky was luck, the world was light. It was easy to lift, such a likable world. I lifted the world high in the unclouded night. I could bear it, I could. There was nothing that was too much for me. There was nothing I could not take on. I took on time, in the clear of my eyes. I filled my time with courage, which was mine to give and Cheyenne's to receive, to add to the already great store of her own.

Oh, Cheyenne,
my sister luck.

Where did we go from there? You and me both in the light of the moon. We moved from the dock, the sparkle, the diamonds, unafraid of what would be next. Nor am I afraid now of how I will grow. I remember us at the water's edge. I remember us on the wise moon ride, inspired. So lucky I am to have been there with you, to've timed my life that I could know the world with you, that we could pull things from hiding and see them with our hearts. And so lucky I am because there are great things in store, which is more than luck. It's how I'll be and what I will do. And it's how you'll be and what you will do: running, dancing through the ever-opening door. Shouting, shouting: Look at me, look at me. Look at me now. I can do it. I can do it. No problem. I can.

ELEVEN

You think you're in luck and maybe you are. Having traveled all night, you wake. The floor is strewn with spiritual adventures. Look and remember, good fortune lies everywhere.

You've got your old job back at the Jake, and the weather is near perfect. Feel and see. There are many colorful birds that fly overhead like whirlwind leaves. Sure, there's a minor problem with your car, but it's better to walk anyway. Besides, it's a beautiful morning, which makes it your moment to shine. You are optimistic, your hair looks good, and your face like the eastern sky takes on light. There's a twenty in your pocket – what a surprise! You're happy so happy you feel like singing: Hello sun, hello birds, hello people, sidewalk, trash. And what's more, you're the eleventh customer at Rev, and that's the number they're looking for. You hit the mark, and you weren't even aiming. You get a free bagel and a shirt with a rabbit logo. Oh, and another thing: Remember that 97 percent you received on Professor Kowalski's most difficult exam? You made it through, just like Ri said you would. On your way home last night, she hugged you for your brain and brawn, the two of you walking with the moon like a smile in the western sky. The smarter you are, the more money you'll make. For me. For me to spend, she'd teased, walking over the bridge just before it collapsed in your mind. You sure caught a break with that bridge last night. But don't think like that, not now, not this fine morning. Don't imagine collapse. Don't conjure the tragic. It's just a warning, this time. No fine for you, no ticket. Because what a great day. Say it. You and Rianna together – that's what's important, no matter how much money either of you make. You're both here for real. You're both here for free. No charge today. And the bank stays open much longer on Wednesdays, handing out hundreds to those in love. You'll have to go after work to collect your loot. What luck for you, on account of Rianna. And the best is still to come. No lie. Look under the cap. You've won. Nothing to lose, like meaning. Everything to gain, but weight. Things, you sense, are going your way. No need even to check when crossing the street. Still, why push your luck? Look left and right and left again, just to be certain. Think good thoughts so the nourishing work of those thoughts can be done in the world. Be good to your luck and it will be good to you.

~

The evening of the same day, Games jumped to his feet, said to Ri:

I'm off to buy a lottery ticket.

A fool and his mother, my money always said.

Even your mix-ups can't bring me down.

Just wait.

For what?

Things always change, said Ri. They shift and reshape themselves.

I thought you were an eternal optimist.

What's wrong with what I said?

If you're saying that things will get worse –

I never said that.

What did you say?

Just, you've got to be ready.

You mean when things turn bad, said Games.

When they turn whatever, said Ri. Doesn't have to be worse. Don't you know the fable about the crow?

What crow?

Your mother never told you about the crow and the boy?

What crow? What boy?

A boy, began Ri, woke up happy. There was the sun and everything. He couldn't find his shoes, but it didn't matter. He had a crisp apple instead of sausage for breakfast. Less fatty. More dietary fiber. When outside, the grass tickled his feet. It gave him goosebumps. An acorn fell on his head, and it made him laugh. He played a naming game with a tree and hide-and-seek with the sun. Even his drunken father stumbling past made him smile. There's nothing like this place, he said. He held out his happiness for the world to see. There in his left hand like a shining gem. That's when the crow swooped down and stole it.

Stole what?

The boy's happiness, said Ri. After that, it was gone.

And you think I'm that boy, said Games.

Things like to change, said Ri. That's all. You've got to go with the flow.

So, what'd the boy do after the crow?

He held out his other hand as a fist at first. Sure, he was pissed. Then something inside the boy made him open his fist. You can see where this is going.

Not really, said Games.

There on his palm was… Are you ready for it?

I am.

Was self-determination, said Ri.

Hmm, said Games.

Hmm! That's all you've got to say.

Games liked the picture of the boy with self-determination in his hand. Self-determination might be an improvement on happiness. Which means that sometimes things can go from good to even better. The last days of October, for example, the air was sweet. Then on November the seventh, Games got a raise at work out of the blue. He got A's on all three exams toward the middle of the month. In fact, through much of November, No Wonder, as Ri called it, there was not one bad day to bring Games down. Thirty days hath September. April, June, and No Wonder.

~

Just before Thanksgiving, Rianna came by late after parent-teacher meetings. Her coat was open, revealing another layer.

Sorry I kept you, she said.

No problem, said Games.

He'd made his famous lasagna and a salad with organic pears from the reject bin at work.

Everything's good, he added.

Everything?

Her question, the tone of Ri's voice, made Games doubt.

The food's delicious, she said. Thanks.

They sat, middle of their meal, forks and knives in motion, and a magazine open to a picture of some remote mountain lake Games hoped to visit one day. He showed Ri another picture taken somewhere in Patagonia.

I like that view, said Rianna. Do you think –

They heard a thud outside the door.

I'd like to –

And three knocks that followed.

Who's that? said Games.

Why do people say *Who's that* when they hear a knock? asked Ri.

Because they're surprised, said Games, who was himself surprised to hear the knock. He pushed back his chair. It's just a reaction.

It's knee jerk and dumb.

You think? said Games, hearing her words as Steve Jerkindum, whoever he was.

It's got to be someone, said Ri.

Games opened the door. But it was no one he could see, only books in a box, and a blue envelope on top. He heard footsteps descending the three flights of stairs. He heard the front door to the apartment house open and close.

I'll be right back, he called to Rio.

Games ran down the stairs, pulled open the door. Out on the street, almost nine-thirty now, he scanned every direction. A car went by. He watched it go. The sky was starless because of clouds. It seemed to Games just then that his good luck might be slipping away.

Damn, he said, and went back to his room.

Damn, Games repeated, which was strange to hear, as he never cursed. Rianna was looking through the books: Essays by Montaigne and Emerson. *Sensitive Chaos.* A biography of Yeats. Of Frederick Douglass. *Great Expectations* by Dickens. *To Kill a Mockingbird* by Harper Lee. *The Phenomenon of Man. The Meaning of Love. The Epic of Gilgamesh. A Child's Christmas in Wales. Ozma of Oz. The Book of Psalms.* Paintings of Turner and Chagall. *The Book of Constellations. Goodnight Moon. Gift from the Sea. The Joy of Cooking. The Animal Family. Of Mice and Men. Paradiso* by Dante. *D'Aulaires' Book of Greek Myths. Thousand and One Nights,* a collection. *Thousand and One Puns.* Poems by Poe. By Dickinson. By Roethke. Cummings. Brooks. *Ferdinand. Charlotte's Web. The Little Prince.* All books well worn. Nothing contemporary. Rianna gave Games the envelope to open. On the index card inside, the message read: *I will rise and go now, and go to Innisfree. Which is my lake. With no one but me. And you shall be here, inextinguishable of life. For I am a dreamer, yet you shall decide. Have confidence in your ability.* Along with three hundred sixty-five dollars to represent days, and one piece of a seashell for who knows why.

~

The final days of November, Games kept his eyes open, looking for his mother. He thought he saw her once in the market, at the end of the cereal aisle. Then there was the woman on the bus, as the bus drove by – her, too. After his Perspectives in Education class, Games heard footsteps following him to his car. He turned to see, but it was someone else. There was an older woman once, leaning against a pole with a bag on her shoulder – late forties, about the right age. And soon after, another woman in a long black coat with disheveled black hair. Yet with all these possibilities, it was never a match.

Still, Games knew his mother was out there, somewhere. He didn't know what she looked like now. Maybe her hair had gone gray, or she wore glasses, had gained weight, and walked with a limp. Games doubted these changes, even if it had been almost twenty years since he'd seen her. Which added to 7,300 dollars, not a measly 365. More, if you took in leap years. Rianna said it concerned her some about his mother because it seemed such odd behavior, but Games said there was nothing to worry about.

Nothing? asked Rio.

Her question made Games reflect.

Not for *your* safety, said Ri. For her well-being.

She's always taken care of herself, said Games. It's what

she does best.

Maybe you're right. But still.

Games considered the strangeness of the situation. Sure, his mother could look after herself. But why didn't she step forward, stop all her hiding, see her son, and meet Rianna? Games could make dinner for the three of them. He wasn't ashamed of his cooking. He wasn't ashamed of his life. He wasn't ashamed of her, not of any –

Maybe she's ashamed, Ri interrupted.

Her words caught Games off guard.

Maybe she thinks you'd be disappointed.

Okay, said Games. A little. I don't understand why she is the way she is. But really, I'm only disappointed that she stays away. It's important to…

To what?

To, I don't know. To –

There are things sometimes a person just can't do, suggested Ri. There's a door she can't open, words she can't say.

Well, she could work at it better, said Games. She's always had a more compelling urge to keep her life to herself.

~

The book-drop experience made Games want to be present and accountable, not the opposite, which to him meant remote or missing. Life on earth is far from an isolation event, he thought. Far from… Face it. What better thing was there than to live well in the world, to cooperate with it, and to love Rianna all the more? He could – yes, he – could stand up and prove it. He could show what cooperation means. Games wasn't ashamed of anything, really. He wasn't afraid to try something new.

On Friday, Games let Ri know what he'd been thinking. He walked into the room, words prepared. He'd worked it all out. He'd been thinking. Been thinking they. He'd been thinking they should.

Spit it out.

Live together, said Games.

But I like my place, said Rio. Especially now that Nat's not there. Rianna was folding squares of paper into cranes. The cranes were blue, gold, and black so far.

It was just a thought, said Games. He noticed one crane had stripes, which was odd for a crane.

And even though it had been a difficult day at school, with kids bouncing off the walls, and the principal in a grumpy mood, Rianna took in the thought. She held it a moment, like holding that drawing of fish, twenty-seven of them, swimming and flying and sitting at desks, given to her by a student. That was a generous picture, and Games's idea was a generous thought. Rianna reimagined his words to see how they might fit with the picture of her independence.

You wouldn't have to change how you do things, said Games.

Change is good, said Ri.

But I like you how you are.

Games stood beside himself in thought, which was a brief though noticeable separation. *Cranes with stripes. Paper cranes. Crease lines. The folds, the making of a life.*

It's me who needs to be different, he said. I see all these templates. Many mirrors, each containing a possible me. There's no one true reflection.

I don't know what mirrors you're talking about. Ri looked around, to prove her words. She knew of none in his entire apartment, not even in his bathroom, which may have been the reason she didn't want to live with him.

It's a metaphor, said Games.

Ah. A metaphor.

I've got no good picture of my life at the moment. It's just temporary.

Your life is temporary?

No. This mood.

Ri felt bad. She went to Games. She stood beside him, leaning in, supportive.

I don't care about mirrors, she said.

Just feeling a bit...

Unsure, suggested Ri.

No way to stop the feeling, said Games. It won't be long.

I know, said Ri, standing tall, looking at Games. It's just around the corner. Easy to see.

What's easy?

You're easy, said Ri. To know. This amazing creative generous person. I see it all the time. I look forward to you, like spring. The restorative feeling of flowing water. Light coming through the window. You're poetry.

Ease and poetry don't go together. People are afraid of poems.

Not of you, though. You're light in the mind, easy to see.

So, I'm light and easy, teased Games, picking on the words. In your eyes, I'm a simpleton.

You don't weigh that much, said Rio. A simple one seventy at most.

It took Games a moment, and then he smiled. The play on words. A *simple ton*. Ri was quick, was sharp, she cut beautiful lines, her body her mind, like a well-honed chisel. He wanted to touch her to see if she'd draw his blood, if red drops would wake him, if he'd come to his senses without further delay.

What is it? she asked.

Nothing, said Games. Waiting for things. I'm tired of waiting. But it's just a mood. No problem. I'm not going anywhere.

By which he meant that he was sticking around, accepting, strengthening, and that Ri could do as she needed, to work out her own equanimity, to move in or not.

I remember the first time I saw you, said Ri. On the mountain.

You mean in the parking lot below, said Games.

No. I mean on top of the mountain.

Games thought back to that January day on Mount Everett. The view from the peak. Not a leaf on those branches. No bears. No snakes. One bird floating way far, way high, upon a light, way-blue sky. The winter sun was heading down, leaving no trail as it went.

Ashes in the air, reminded Rio

I liked Quincy Mesch, said Games.

There you were, Rio recalled. In a reflective mood. No problem, like now.

You were the problem up there. You walked too fast.

Later, you showed up at the nursing home, reminded Ri.

Following me, like a stalker. After that, in your car. After that, in person. After that, in my head.

Your bed. I liked that.

Head, I said. But head bed – what's the difference? And now you're here. Ri brought her hand to her chest, tapping it, as if to place Games there, as if to say he was everything inside her. Games picked up on the metaphor, but said nothing. I can't get rid of you, Ri finished.

Like an annoying pest, said Games.

There are poisons for that, said Ri.

I'm hiring a taster. Going to watch my back.

How can you? You don't have any mirrors.

We're not talking about my apartment, said Games. We're talking about your heart.

They both thought about this. Apartments with and without mirrors. Hearts with and without pests and poisonous thoughts. It was lots of problems to solve. The night was still early, however. Black and white in the one-lamp room. All they needed was a bit more time. Maybe some wine for romance, for changing the mood. Though Games didn't drink.

Would you move in here if I bought a mirror?

Rio considered it. I'll have to think.

Why would you have to drink?

Think, not drink.

Maybe you should go with the flow, said Games. I was lucky you were there to begin with. Remember that day on the mountain?

I just reminded you of it, said Ri. It was nothing to do with luck.

Then it was all about timing, said Games.

Not timing either. More to do with paying attention to every moment and doing what's right. Like it was fate but it wasn't fate, it was... It –

Games's phone chirped, thus ending Ri's search. A text from Hardy wanting Games to take his shift at the market, Saturday afternoon, which was tomorrow.

I don't want to do it.

Then don't.

I could use the extra money so I can hire the taster.

Come with me instead, said Rio
Where're you going?
Visiting.
Who?
Dove.
Who's Dove?
In the hospital, said Ri. I told you before. You never listen,
which she knew wasn't true.

Dove in the hospital. Games had to think. Then he
remembered it some. She was the girl in Rianna's sixth-grade
class who was hit by a car when crossing the street with her
mother. When was that? It was... It – He was tired of
thinking just now. Tired of things that didn't make sense. He
was tired of people being hurt and being sick and dying, and
then there he was, having to figure it out and make it right.
Everything was always on him. To unshatter the mess. To re-
invoke life. Or, maybe he just had to remember it better. He
sighed and the memory came back to him.

That was, what, a month ago.

No, said Ri. Little over a week. Right around the time
your mother dropped by.

Games pictured his mother, who was more of a myth to
him now. And, yes, he would like to see her. Help if he
could. Which *her* was he thinking about – Dove or his
mother? It was important to feel connected to life, thought
Games. Not just be a spontaneous visitor. But an intentional
one. Not an accidental person, but undeniable in the world
and essential to others. Confident, too. In every decision.
Dove. Yes. Of course, he remembered.

Is she better? he asked.

I think so, said Ri.

That's good, he said. I'll go.

~

Rianna and Games entered the hospital room with its stifling
brightness, relieved only by the window, the world outside.
A nurse walked past the open door. The ones in the room
shook hands and hugged. Visitors: Games, Ri, and Dove's
mother sat near the bed. Dove, the student, the patient,

shifted positions.

Everyone who's anyone's been in here, said Dove.

In your room? asked Rianna.

No. The hospital.

Dove had a drip going in. But soon she'd be out of this place. She looked warm and cheerful.

Like there was some important government guy born here, said Dove. And a princess or something. And that actor who won an Oscar. His child got sick and almost died. You know, the one with the hair that makes him look like a rocker.

Not really, said Ri.

And a hockey player from the Red Sox came the other day, talking to kids. That's what they told me.

Did he talk to you?

No. Grandpa was here and Aunt Jacqueline and Uncle Cole and my cousin Kelsey who plays bass with the Red Ivy Trio.

She's your cousin? said Ri.

My brother's here, too.

I don't like the sound of that, said Rianna. She knew about Benjy's muscular dystrophy.

Benjy's not well, said Dove's mother. It's both my children in one hospital.

What's going on?

Of course, you know he's got Duchenne.

Rianna nodded. She'd read Dove's stories. Had learned the details during parent-teacher conferences.

Now, he's got pneumonia. Some respiratory infection. His heart's acting up. Everything at once, you know. It happens. One moment we're grateful for our lives together, grateful for moving and breathing and never giving up. One moment Dove and I are walking to the hospital to visit. The next moment this.

The *this* she referred to was the car accident.

It's all bad timing. I just thank God it wasn't too serious.

I'm fine, said Dove. I want to go home.

I bet, said Ri.

I don't get it, said Dove.

What don't you get?

They won't let me even visit my own brother.

Hospitals have their rules, said Rio.

She could see that this wasn't a satisfactory explanation.

You'll be home soon, Rio reminded. Benjy, too. You know, I don't really remember. How old is he?

Eighteen next month, said the mother.

Rianna calculated the lifespan. Five, ten more years if he was lucky. But now with the infection. The trouble with his heart... Dove's mother sat beside her daughter, holding her hand. The girl was bruised, but her voice was strong. Her leg was broken in three places. She had broken ribs and lacerations. Looking much better, though.

I brought you some extra math to do, began Rianna.

Ms. O. You're joking, right?

Yes, said Ri.

You're the best teacher ever.

Thank you.

Yola said maybe tomorrow, said Dove.

Who's Yola?

A nurse. I think I want to be a doctor when I grow up, said Dove.

Not a teacher.

No way. Nothing against you, Ms. O. Maybe I could cure MD.

I was a nurse once, you know, said Rianna.

No way. And you didn't like it?

Not enough.

I don't like it in here, either, said Dove. I like it outside.

They all looked to the window.

Then why do you want to be a doctor? asked Rio

To keep people out of hospitals. I'd be one of those doctors who works without laws.

Without borders, you mean, said her mother.

I wasn't even born in a hospital. Right, Mama?

You were born at home, said her mother. Benjy, too. Luckily, Dove doesn't carry. Neither do I. It was a spiteful mutation, but – welcome to Holland.

These last words dropped on the floor like a heavy weight. Their meaning was a confusing thud, then silence. What did anything have to do with Holland? Dove was the first to respond to the silence. She looked at Games, sitting behind her teacher.

I like your boyfriend, she said.

How do you know he's my boyfriend?

Because he doesn't talk. You do all the talking, and he looks at you like he's interested. That's like my dad.

That makes me feel sort of bad, said Ri. I'm not that way, am I?

She's really not, said Games, leaning forward. She must especially like talking to you. She never talks to me.

I like to talk, said Dove. And sing. And move. And lots of stuff.

How can you stand to be in here? asked Games.

I can't stand. Don't you see my legs?

Dove, said her mother.

He asked.

I did ask, said Games.

You see? said Dove. This place makes you crazy.

It's supposed to make you well, said Games.

We went camping last summer, said Dove. That was so much better. Where was it?

Yosemite.

Yosemite, repeated Dove. Papa would call, Yo, Semite, if I got too far off, exploring. Yo, Semite. Get back here.

We're Jewish, explained Dove's mother.

I'm sorry about your brother, said Games. What's Duchenne? I've heard of muscular dystrophy.

Duchenne muscular dystrophy, said Dove's mother. It's all one thing. There's a defective gene for this protein in his muscles. They just deteriorate. To be honest, it's a simple problem but not a very simple cure. He's got the most beautiful mind.

Like that movie, said Dove. Only a different problem.

I saw it, said Games. It was good.

And he loves to swim, said Dove. Papa goes out with him almost every day.

You can swim with Duchenne? asked Games. It was more of a question for Dove's mother.

It's good to move, and the water helps, she said. He hasn't been able to for a while, being in the hospital.

You going to get married? asked Dove.

Dove, said her mother.

Well?

Married? Me? said Games, as if it was the farthest thing from his mind. I've got stuff to do with my life, places to go, mirrors to buy. I've got to promote my book, my career.

Benjy wants to write a book about nothing to do with MD. He's got all these opinions about everything. What did you write?

Actually, nothing yet. Problem is, if you're married, you're stuck inside, washing dishes, watching TV, and talking about your day. There's little chance to write.

I don't watch much TV, said Dove. I don't ever want to get married. I want to go to Africa and India and the tip of South America. Maybe I'll get married some day.

Me too, said Games. Maybe.

I think everyone should be happy, said Dove. I want Benjy to be happy. I love him so much. And Papa and Mama.

How about yourself? asked Games.

Why not? Even the person who hit me with her car. I don't want her to be sad or go to jail.

It was just an accident, said her mother. She won't go to jail.

She gave me this painting she painted.

Dove pointed it out, leaning on a chair near the wall. It was a painting of a dove in a tree and a dove on the ground and a dove in the blue-green sky and a dove in someone's purple hand. A family of doves. Four doves. The sun made a playful ribbon of light. The moon was holding itself in its own two hands. It was morning and night, both. It was summer winter spring and fall. It didn't look like November, even though that's what the painting was called: *November Love*.

I like it, said Games.

I want to be a painter, too, said Dove.

A doctor, a painter, a traveler, a singer... Games was making a list.

And someone who climbs all the mountains in the world.

Wow, said Games.

And – who is it who does everything herself and doesn't need help?

A do-it-yourselfer?

I don't know, maybe, said Dove.

Or a hermit?

Isn't that a kind of crab?

It's someone who lives alone, said Games, and doesn't need people and is afraid sometimes even of her own family.

That's not me, said Dove. I don't want to be a hermit.

And not a teacher, either, reminded Rianna.

Sorry, Ms. O.

You've got to be yourself, said Ri. Open your own doors. That's what I tell all my kids.

Which somehow made Dove think of Benjy.

What I like about Benjy, he lets you know what he thinks. I'm like that, too.

It's good to voice your opinion, said Ri.

So, why'd the guy with Duchenne want to go to the seafood restaurant? asked Dove.

Why?

He heard they had mussels. And there's another one he told me, but I can't remember.

The one about the light snow, said Dove's mother.

What one about snow?

Maybe it was something else, said her mother.

You going to say hello to Benjy when you leave? asked Dove.

I don't know, said Ri. Should we?

You've got to, said Dove. You can't just come by and not see him. Everyone likes visitors.

Okay, said Ri.

Okay.

Okay.

So, when they left Dove, that's what they did. Rianna and Games went to see Benjy.

~

Two days later, the last of November, Benjy died. Rianna told Games when he came to pick her up after school. It was cold outside. They drove to the river and walked on the path in the late afternoon. The days were growing so short, it was hard for them to hold the light. The sun, by this time, had almost dropped from the sky. Clouds in the distance, accompanying the sun. Geese in the distance, migrating on high.

I was thinking, began Rianna.

Games's phone chirped. It was a text from Hardy wanting Games to cover for him on Tuesday.

You going to do it?

I don't know. I need the money. But I've got a lot of reading to do.

He returned a text, saying, Okay.

All those books from your mother?

Those, too, said Games. You've probably finished the ones you took.

Gift from the Sea was easy, said Rio. I'm still reading *The Phenomenon of Man*.

My mother never read to me, said Games. But she told stories. All the Greek myths. Other things.

I wish I could meet your mother.

You had your chance.

We could talk about books and what you were like as a little boy.

I was never a little boy, said Games.

I thought you told me you were.

I was making stuff up. This is the extent of me, what you see now.

You live in the moment, said Rianna. Now and Zen.

I've got to work on my memory, said Games. Every night, I think backward to the beginning of the day.

I do that, said Ri.

Since when?

I told you before.

I don't remember, teased Games.

They stood at the river, staring at the imperceptible flow: the late colors on the surface, the fish at different depths, the journey to sea, and the sea itself somewhere far. Things were ongoing, traveling to some end. Then the whole business would start over again. A day would return as a clear blue sky. The sky would then fill with clouds. The clouds would be heavy with rain from the oceans. The rain would fall to the earth and find its way to the river, this river. And the river would go to the sea again, speaking softly, assertively, and always offering clues with its voice. What did the river want to say now? At this moment, there was the cold, a few orange clouds, and a soft, distant hum. A lullaby without words. Games and Rianna stood bundled, listening.

Maybe he's here, watching us, said Ri.

Who?

Benjy. I feel somebody's presence. Maybe it's your mother.

Games turned from the river and waved, just in case.

I wish she'd just show up or call and tell me where she is. I could go the rest of my life not knowing.

Leave it alone, said Ri.

Leave her alone, you mean.

I mean, don't fight it, said Ri. You'll just waste energy on a futile cause. It is what it is.

I bet she'd like to meet you, though, said Games. She'd like you, I know. You'd get along. You'd get her to talk.

What, she doesn't like talking? asked Rio.

Games tried to remember what his mother was like. He could see her sitting across from him in a diner once. He could almost make out her face. He could see her back, as she sat at the table at Aunt Julia's house. He could see her from the side next to some blackberry bushes. He could see her lying on her back at some beach. He could see her in a car, slumped at the wheel, resting her head. Then he, Games, got in the car and she started to drive. There she was, just staring ahead, not talking, not listening to the radio or him, driving and driving far down the road, wherever. After that she was gone, no trail. Games suddenly remembered:

You were about to say what you were thinking, he reminded Ri.

I was?

Yes. Don't you remember?

No.

Yes.

Maybe it was about Benjy and Dove, said Ri. It's sad to think about.

Maybe, thought Games, but he didn't think that was it. It

was about himself and her, for sure.

She'll be back after Christmas, said Rio.

Who? asked Games.

Dove. In class.

I like her, Games said. I liked her brother.

I think they were good for each other, said Ri.

If I ever have a girl, I'll give her a bird's name, said Games.

Yellow-bellied Flycatcher, suggested Ri.

Cedar Waxwing, said Games.

Arctic Loon.

Tufted Titmouse.

Kittiwake, said Ri.

Not bad, said Games. Or Starling. Or Vireo. Remember Vireo? Or plain old Gull. Just Gull. Hey, Gull. Gulliver for a boy.

The Dalai Lama once told me to look at things from all angles. You're sure to find something positive that way.

Did he really say that?

He did.

To you?

Well, I was in a field of cows, but I think it was to me. Why wouldn't it be?

Games could think of no reason why not, as he and Rianna walked side by side, against the flow of the river. Was living meant to be a constant battle where you had to test your strength against the current? And what was that current anyway? Did each human, in his own walk, oppose the rightful drift and dance of life itself? There is a struggle, then a weakening of forces, and eventual loss – inevitable death. And yet, as the Dalai Lama suggested to Ri: Anything looked at one way can also be looked at another. Nothing is negative from all points of view. Struggle in life opens the door for sympathies to visit, and sympathies make way for better, more compassionate understanding.

Now, I remember what I was thinking, said Ri.

What? asked Games. He knew what she was going to say, which was: It wasn't right for her, going on like this. She wanted to turn around. She wanted to go with the flow, her own flow, to open the door, make way for other people and different experiences. She wanted, most of all, to be free.

Time alone, time to think. She wanted her independence. She wanted her old life back, her blossoming self again, her unburdened soul. No more of this wallowing. No more.

I want to learn to fly, said Ri.

Fly?

You know, a plane. Will you go up with me?

When?

Well, not now. Sometime after I've learned. Would you feel safe? I mean, with me?

Of course he would. He'd feel safe, he always did. He wasn't afraid. Life was no problem. Life was good. It would always work out. Confidence. Confidence. You shall decide. And trust. Trust in your ability to read the world as it's written. To move it to heart. To be moved, too. To not make things up, but know the truth, and say it. Hear it speaking like a river, a current, the flow of existence. Hear the truth, all the beauty in it. There's ample beauty in what the truth has to say. Hear it and say it yourself. Here and now and –

Sure, said Games. I mean, yes. Yes.

NOVEMBER

Benjy and Dove

Who doesn't miss out on things in his life? Name someone. I'm not alone in all the stuff I didn't get to experience, let alone have. But why go there? Let me tell you the good things I scored, just like everyone else.

Air is one. Water definitely, blue like my eyes. And who on earth doesn't have gravity? Okay, balloons fight against it, but that's because gravity's such a weighty thing and balloons want to be light and easy. Light and easy – yeah. And, I mean, who doesn't know the sun almost every day? That's air, water, gravity, sun. Even a blind person gets his share of sun. The sun might seem hidden for a blind person if you think about it, but if you think differently about it, the sun's got less to do with your eyes, more to do with your insight. And along the same line, who doesn't get a taste of the truth wherever they go? So, air, water, gravity, sun, and the truth. The truth is out in the world in a million story lines. Sometimes there are plots that make you uncomfortable, so you turn away. Like it's hard to read poetry or stuff loaded with sadness. Easier to read sex and horror and science fiction. It's hard to go up to some homeless guy, easier to approach a bed of roses.

I had things in my life that no one else got to have. It was my private hoard. When I told that to my sister once, she thought I said *whore,* which made us laugh. I wish, I said. We'd joke around and have fun with words and the world. Doesn't mean I didn't get sad sometimes. Sadness was part of my personal whore, I mean hoard. It was a sadness I thought no one else could possibly share. Though maybe everyone, when feeling like shit, would say the same. Then one day my mother said: *Don't let your sadness get the better of you.* So I asked: *What's the better of me?* She told me it was a good question, and then didn't answer it. I didn't get angry with her, but maybe I should've, just to show I wasn't done thinking about it.

But, back to my thesis: There's been tons of wealth in my life, stuff I can't even remember. There was being happy about my days and the people inside them. And then there was being sad. There was even room for anger, which was all about my fears. Those fears still live in me, even if I don't live in the world like I used to. Thinking about it now, I feel bad. I'm afraid I've lost out on everything. I'm afraid even now of not being heard or seen how I really am.

Sorry, but for a moment, that's the room I'm in. I'm angry with myself. I'm angry with others. I'm openly angry at life, because what has it ever done but make things difficult, because what does it care, because seems to me it doesn't. That's how I feel. But don't let life know I said that. It wouldn't understand why I'm complaining. It'd be like: *You don't know what you're saying. When have I ever stood in your way?* And me: *Let's not argue about it.* And back to life: *Who's arguing? Just be yourself and don't complain.* And me again: *What do you think I'm trying to do?* And life: *Sounds like you're complaining.* And me: *Why don't you go screw yourself and not so much others?* I mean it's not like I don't have things...blablabla...to complain about... blablabla... Once you open the door to your feelings, it's a hard one to close.

The way I see it, anger is starving. That's what it is – it's a starving thing whose only food is anger. So, it feeds itself with itself, which only makes it more starving, increasing its need for that one-note diet. It's actually sort of sad. Makes you feel sorry for anger and how small and limited it is in life. If anger wants to change, it's got to do so because of a bigger picture. Or a healthier diet. Something healthier and more true replaces its appetite. And it's not voracious anymore. I like that word. Anger sort of calms and cools and can experience other things. Friends can give a truer picture to anger. A window looking out to the world, or a sister, say, who's always there to help. Parents, too. Good parents take your anger and digest it for you when you can't. Life does the same if you don't get into a pointless argument with it. Life's got the bigger picture, and it's got stamina to take your temper. Life chews your anger and swallows it and works it inside. Then out it comes not as shit but as sunlight. How does that work!? Well it does. I've seen.

Thing is, if it's anger all the time, it's too much for anyone. No person, no matter how saintly, and not life either, no matter how it plays the martyr, can take someone's anger all day and night. Not the best parent in the world, not the greatest actor, no way. If it's anger all the time, it's shit and it stays shit. No one wants shit. Do you want shit? I never did. What people want is lightness of being. You know, like the balloon. And also what they want is love, which is a way of looking at the world that opens your eyes to what's actually going on. Maybe that sounds sappy sentimental, but it's not like I haven't thought about it. It's not like I just made it up this very minute. I think about things lots. I feel them, too. I call love *sunlight* sometimes. I call it *cool water to swim in on a really hot day*. I call it *hard ground to wheel on*. I call it *someone who hears me and I'm not even talking*. I call love *yesterday in the hospital when I knew it was done. It, done*. I mean my time in the world. And I call love *life. My life, specifically*. I call it *the day I was born*.

But now I'm angry, just for a moment. It's not like it's who I am or who I was in the world. Ask anyone. I kept it positive, mostly. Now I'm a bit pissed though because everything's gone and it happened so fast and others get to go on for longer. Even others with Duchenne go much longer than I got to go. I wanted to go at least till... Well, for as long as... Shit, I don't know.

Seventeen's nothing. Others aren't so limited. They get to drive their own cars all the way to the Pacific Ocean if they want. They run up and down stairs and still have time to write books full of birds and opinions and maybe a good snowstorm, if they have it in them. But not me, not that I don't have a snowstorm in me. I just got swept off before I was ready, got tossed out of service before I'd even had a chance to be more than "The Duchenne Kid." And that's not a joke. No joking now. The chair and the brace are gone, the leaves and trees are gone, the pool water's gone, and I'm gone, too. Seems there isn't much left of me besides these words written by some guy I hardly know. What's his fucking name? Rhymes with lame. What'd you think of your blue-eyed boy now, mister? Him and his girlfriend. They stood like movie stars in the hospital room with Papa. All of them talking. Me, like a blob. Me, leaning back. Me, relearning to breathe. Knowing in my heart how fucked I was. I guess I should thank him, though. If he's doing this like a benefit for me, the least I could do is say thanks.

I'd rather he's doing it for himself. People always did things for me when what I wanted was to do for myself. Maybe that was selfish and I should've understood that that's what MD was really about: Letting myself be carried by others. I don't know. A person still wants to do himself. And I never did all the stuff I wanted. Swimming in the ocean is one. Going to college. Driving free.

My friend, Ottom – not Autumn, that sounds like a girl's name, but Otto with an *m* – he made a movie about a guy driving a car. It was this guy in his car. Most every shot was him driving. You saw the guy get in the car. Then you saw him from behind his ear and all the places he was going. At the end he got out of the car and stood under some trees. The trees were green and blowing in the wind. It was summer. Then the leaves turned colors. And the colors fell and lay scattered on the ground. Then there were bare branches that dissolved to branches with snow. First, blue sky came through the black and white branches. Then it was red sky, followed by a whole bunch of stars.

I liked his movie. He had to be patient to work it through. The only sound was the radio sometimes talking, sometimes singing metal, sometimes playing classical, and then the engine alone, and the leaves in the wind, and the stars just hanging out together. Ottom made it for me, he said. There was my name, listed as the producer. The name turned colors, then it broke apart and the letters went everywhere. It was the closest I ever got to driving or having a real job or…

And I never had sex, either. No matter my whore. And never once kissed a girl other than my mother and sister, or felt some girlfriend's body what she's like without clothes. Can only imagine what it's like – a naked boob. Ottom said it's like a small balloon. But it could be a big one. He needs to make a film about it. I read in some poem a boob's like cupping your hand against the wind when you're driving and sticking out your arm. I can't even say I know what that's like. And what are other things, too? Climbing trees with your bare feet and sliding into home after rounding the bases. It's just words and pictures in my head. It's what other people do.

I don't even know what the actual world is like anymore, not really. Rotting apples, flying geese. Maybe it's still cold in that place, at least the place where I used to live. The daylight's fizzling away in my hometown, instead of my muscles any longer. So, what else is new? People are sad that I'm gone, I guess. I'm Buffalo Bill Ben, my sister once said. Used to / ride a watersmooth-silver / stallion. She liked that poem, the one where he's dead. But not me dying, she didn't like that.

Mostly I'm mad that it's over. I'm mad at myself for feeling how I do and that I can't get past it. I can't get past the labels. I'm MD. Weakness and isn'ts. I'm the doctor visits. I'm the meds, the chair. I'm Mama's worries and Papa's liftings and Dove's pushing me smooth. I'm the fucking body I hated sometimes. Hocus pocus, it didn't get better. It was the body I had and it did nothing wrong. So, why go on being mad? Why hate any longer?

Hate is something that controls you. It leads you down its stupid destructive path. Look at things differently and you build yourself up. You can walk on your own. Can be smart with life. It's a million can-do's that lead to is's. And suddenly, you're not angry anymore. You can be who you are, just like anyone else. Look at things differently, and the hate drops off and you decide. You decide how much better things are going to be from this moment forward. From this moment forward, you carry yourself. You take your life onward.

~

I don't understand how, but I definitely move easier now. Maybe it's my mind or maybe it's the real me: There's flow. Like I'm dreaming. It's fantastic. You don't need muscles.

437

You don't need a chair. All you need is will. Or whatever it is that gets your move going. Light moves because of it – whatever *it* is. Thoughts move, no thanks to muscles. Muscles are mostly shellfish / totally selfish when it's all about them. They're not your life. The brain, not either. Muscles and brain are there to assist you. They're there to work for you. Muscles and brain are not who you are. So, who do they work for? That's what I want to know.

What's happening now is that the door's been nudged opened and I'm like everyone else for once. Though it's wrong that I said that, because no one is really like anyone else. Also because I'm not ashamed that I had MD. We worked okay together. It had a few wise things to add to my life. I'd never say it took me away from myself, just like cancer doesn't steal the person. MD added perspective and a few unexpected details to my piece. My piece. Strange composition. Like I'm a symphony. Like every human being is. A symphony longing for attention. My father once told me that. And who even knows all the instruments or hears every note? Not me. I've got work to do at listening better.

I suppose there's been a symphony of me from the very beginning, which is harmonious to say. Still, there were days I was pissed at the walls put in my way. Which was total discord, you know. Every day it was something, and many days that something made it hard to keep smiling. But what else to do? Mama beside me at the bathroom sink, at the kitchen table, Papa with his poems, with his encouragement at the pool and everywhere, and then Dove next to me like you wouldn't believe. Well, believe what you want, but I must've always known the better truth even if I didn't act with it all the time.

One time, I remember. There in my room. Dove, her smiling face, so close I couldn't hide. *Buffalo Bill's defunct.* She'd come in all bouncy saying those words. Said, *Buffalo Bill's Defunct*, because of that Cummings poem that Papa'd just been reading to her. *Defunct. Defunct.* She always had to say what was in her head. Why wouldn't she? Why wouldn't anyone? And why would I have wanted to hide? I didn't want to hide. She didn't know what defunct even meant. Said it from memory, smiling like it was the funniest thing ever. Onetwothreefourfive. Her voice brought me out, no problem. Justlikethat.

And the thought of her brings me out now even further. Dove coming into the room. Standing there. Or is it here? Reciting, like I'm audience. Bright-eyed and playful. She's part me, I'm part of her life. So close, I want to make it as real as it feels, as true as it is:

Dove at my side

I

remember her being born. A total little baby. Not crying much, though. Just taking things in. Growing. She was going one way, I the other. She stepping forward, I slipping back. But that's not the thing about her I want to say, not the thing about me either. I mean –

The more open you are, not pissed or complaining, but listening for the truth in the world and in others, then the more you're educating your own ears. Teaching them about that symphony, I guess. Then you can know things from the inside out. Secret things are told to you, and you don't even have to ask. It's okay to ask, but listening's more important. And not listening in your headphones, not in your own stillness, but listening active, putting your ear right up against stuff and wanting to get there, really there, not being afraid to move that way. It's like Papa once said to me: *You've got to move even closer when things are within reach.* Yeah. Moving is everything.

~

Dove is here for me now. I'm her big brother and she's my big heart. Sure, they say that it's my heart that's enlarged, but she's the one, really. She wheels me down the street, across the way, over the smooth and onto the bumpy ground. If rain comes on us, we'll be cold and wet. If the chair falls over, we'll pick it up together and move on. It's going to be okay. Everything's going to be okay. This day is. This rocky route. This tree is.

Perfect, says Dove.

What's perfect? I ask.

This tree, says Dove. Weren't you listening?

Hey. A little respect for your elders.

Maybe I'll respect you, if you start standing up for yourself more, she says.

It's a running joke. Or, I should say, a wheeling one.

Dove stops pushing when we come to the perfect tree. It grows alongside a large red barn. I've heard stories of this barn.

How'd you find it? I ask.

There's this guy and his girlfriend, says Dove. She's my teacher, Ms. Ri.

Misery?

You know who they are. They told me where to look.

It's great, I tell her.

You up for it?

For what?

To climb, silly?

Are you kidding? I say. I've been ready since forever.

Wow. What was it like back then?

I don't want to talk about the past, I tell her.

So, we consider what's here: the branches of the tree, which are great for climbing; the tree itself that's ideally situated next to the roof of the barn; and ah, that roof – the pinnacle. Dove's so ambitious. I like that about her. She hears of something and decides it's something for her. She sees the opportunity and seizes it. Sees and seizes. Carpe diem. The ridge of the barn will present a view of the world. A view is an opening. Who knows to what, but there it is like a door you can go through. Dove does what it takes to get where she needs to be. And I'm here with her, doing the same.

We'll be able to see where the sun goes down, she says.

Sounds good.

Looks good, you mean.

Right.

We'll see for a million zillion miles, Dove tells me.

She loves to climb. It's how she is. I think I'll like it, too, as long as I can pause now and then to enjoy myself. Dove takes the lead, putting her hand on the first branch. She encourages me to follow, because there's no question whether I can do it or not. With her I can do anything. With her I'm more me than me alone. There's no sad body, no disability, there's only yes.

So, you coming? she asks.

Sure, I say. I mean, yes.

You're not worried?

What – me worried? I'm annoyed she even thinks it. You're not afraid, are you? I ask.

I aint no fraidy cat, says Dove, and she pulls herself up the tree. I pull myself behind her fast. Justlikethat. The branches are even more perfect than I imagined before climbing. She jumps to the roof of the barn. No problem.

You with me?

Right here, I say. And I am.

She's like a cat, not fraidy, a fearless tiger I'd say, or a mountain goat maybe. Easy as pie. No questions asked. She reaches the peak. No one to blame if she slips and falls. No one to blame, not me or the universe or the cedar shingles. Not the geese flying south, honking like crazy. Everything's on her. And she does it.

You like it? she says.

I'm good.

She moves along the peak to this cupola thing.

Got to climb this, she tells me. It'll make all the difference.

I'll stay here, I say. Looks kind of rickety.

I guess I'm not as brave as my sister, but that's okay. I don't have to be her. She climbs right up that cupola thing, as high as can be, as broken as it is. I really don't think there would be room for me anyway. And now she starts surveying so I can picture it, too. I can picture her words.

It's the town that way, she points. The river over there. And the school parking lot and the Little League field with nobody on it.

Why would they be? Baseball's over.

But I like baseball, she says.

Baseball's okay, I agree. Too much standing around.

And there're squirrels getting nuts, and two bicycle riders. Over this way's trees as far as I can see and what looks like the ocean way in the distance.

No way you see that far.

Yes, I do.

What color?

Blue.

Unbelievable blue or achievable blue?

Huh?

What kind of blue?

Just blue, she says.

Are the waves any good?

Doesn't look like waves. It's real smooth.

Is it the Atlantic? The Arctic? The Indian?

What Indians? I told you, it's the ocean.

That's okay, I tell her. What else do you see?

There's the road going to the city. Look where I'm pointing.

I see, I say.

It's got lots of cars, maybe thirty or fifty. And over there's a few deer looking for food.

A feuder! What's his feud about?

Dove looks down on me like I'm crazy.

How many deer? I ask.

Like three, she explains.

Oh deer. That's some odor.

They're out of the woods. They're trying to cross.

Don't worry, I tell my sister. They'll make it.

And there's some dad tossing a football to his son. You see any of it?

Now that you say it, I do. What else? I ask.

Winter's coming just over the hills. You can see him.

Him?

He's got a long white beard. He's trying to sneak.

What about snow? I ask. That's what I want. A real big snowstorm.

I don't see any, she says. Not yet.

The days are getting shorter, I say.

But we're so tall, she tells me. Like we're giants up here. We're like God.

Does God stand on the top of barns?

Sometimes, says Dove. Looking at the world.

Yeah, and maybe He gets mad and throws curses down on all the people messing up in life. Take that, you stupid humans.

No way, says Dove. He's not mean. God doesn't do stuff like that.

Might, if He's mad.

Why'd He be mad? He knows people have problems. He doesn't hate or cuss. He loves what He sees.

You're probably right, I say. And I look around. November evening spreads far and wide. Some guy riding a bike like I wish I was riding. There's a girl cycling with him, like I wish there was someone alongside of me. I'm not saying there isn't. I'm just wishing something different, is all.

It's true, I say. Easy for the world to be beautiful. Not so easy for people. But I don't know if she hears me. I look upon the world, out from my heart. And the trees are trees and the road's a road and that last ray of light doesn't want to leave. I can tell that it doesn't. Just wants to stay. The light lingers in the fields, on Dove, and with me. It's trying to hold here a bit longer, just to do some extra work. And who can blame it? Look around. There're lots of things that need more attention in order to really see them.

I don't believe it, says Dove. There's XXXX and OOOO. They're looking for us.

What did you say? I wasn't listening.

Mama and Papa, she repeats.

Do they see us, you think? I ask.

I don't know. Can you do that whistle thing with your fingers?

No.

Dove keeps watching. She doesn't say a word.

What about we wave, I say.

Which we do, we wave, and immediately they wave back. Waves travel in both directions. They don't crash in the middle where it's empty, where it's no one. Instead, all the waves come together in me.

Do you think they're worried? I ask, holding waves.

What's to worry?

Maybe they're angry we're out and didn't say why.

Why'd they be angry? says Dove. They love us. Can't you see?

Of course, I see. I see, I hear, I know it's true. Still, you can be mad sometimes, because of what happens in life. You can be confused and afraid. But what are you afraid of, really? No fall could destroy you. And, besides, there's so much that's uplifting – don't you remember? Of course, maybe you do remember and that's why you're bothered. You can be disappointed about things, can't you. You can be torn-up sad when everything's over, when it's a wrap and someone's turned off the lights. Sayonara. Because you might think to yourself, you might wonder: What was the reason for anything, really? Then, in your own good time you work it out with life. You do what you've got to. You do the thing you're supposed to do. You carry on like a long, open view. And off you go – a brave ship, an explorer – to become... Whatever. But definitely become.

~

> That's it for me, onetwothree
> This defunct blue-eyed boy
> Is growing dark. I'm ready to go

Goodbye my body. Goodbye red barn. Goodbye gravity. And Goodbye trees. My friend Ottom, thanks for it all. Warm Mama Strong Papa and Dove, my sister heart. Couldn't've done anything without all of you. And goodbye Nurse Air, Nurse Water, and Doctor Sun. Goodbye to the boobs I never touched. Plus everyone, everyone with your warm coats on, your hats, your scarves, and your walking shoes. Going places. Doing things. Here's to you, places. Here's to you, things. Unforgettable earth. I don't know what else to say. So long.

And now, at last, and for whatever it's worth, I am light. Am happy. Am weightless. Off to whatever's just over the horizon. I'm freewheeling easy up the road. And who would believe it, but I'm running true.

TWELVE

The earth goes back 4.6 billion years. A hostile place at first. No roads, no schools, no indoor plumbing. It was a vast reservoir of warmth, however, suggesting something bigger in the works.

Slowly, then, a world with water and atmosphere. It rained a lot, which helped with the metabolism of the planet, though the storms put a damper on the prospect of outings. Yet, maybe life could find a home here. Nothing is ever perfect, but something acceptable – well, that's another matter. Humankind studied the place from a distance. The first humans even went so far as to buy a ticket, but remained cautious, standing by, waiting for less troubled times, or at least a more suitable room for the reception.

And the earth spun on, showing all sides. Basalt and granite continents separated from the one great ocean. There were bacteria and algae, jellyfish, fungi, worms, and spiders. Human life inched closer. An entire hill covered itself with ferns. There were dinosaurs, butterflies, mice, and large, unappreciated flowers.

Then, one day, just after sunrise – a sonorous acclamation. The eastern field was set as if ready for a picnic. Precious metals rang like a million tolling bells, leaves sang green notes, and birds settled in bushes to keep the sky free of clutter. It was an ideal place, beside the slow river, ideal for a new story, for kicking back to listen. Among the clouds appeared enough blue to knit a shirt, and the air contained the odd but appealing scent of freshly cut grass. And lo, the human spirit plunged in, incandescent from the journey.

What a mysterious creature, arriving without fanfare. No telling the sex of this first human, either. Though to keep the story rolling, picture a man leading the way, as men often bulldoze into things. And he was something to behold, this man, though no one held him. He was something to see, though no one else saw. He was someone alone, but lucky for him aloneness hadn't been discovered yet. And as evening approached, he looked to his left and there was another, dipping her hand in the river and straightening her back as the low sun poured light upon her. She shook the light from her skin and her long hair went flying. She then turned to face the man. It was good of him to find her. Or of her to find him – whatever.

What an imaginative time it was to begin with. Fish, showing their ties to both sun and moon, flashed gold and silver in the river. Birds pulsed by, drunk on wind. And the first two people sat quietly, satisfied by all they saw. Rising then from their dreaminess, they walked wherever it pleased them to walk.

No words passed between the two as they moved. They asked nothing of life beyond a supply of food and water to match their needs, plus enough fronds and flowers to weave into fabric. He, the man, built fires and worked his hands around pieces of wood. And she, the woman, distinguished herself with her native wit and good looks. There were times, however, she questioned the strange habits of the man, such as throwing stones into still water to watch the splash or sneaking up on small creatures as if he could catch them. But she kept her bemusement to herself.

It wasn't long, though, before both the man and the woman got to thinking. It was a decent enough place to be, they thought, because of all the musical insects and the abundance of places to sleep. Still, there came days when things seemed to fall a bit short. Was there nothing else to this world besides long stretches of light followed by extended darkness and then occasional rain that left puddles and mud, such mud that sucked and squelched, that caked the skin? There had to be something more, maybe a curiosity hidden in the thicket – a secret stash of red berries or a bicycle that some thief had placed there.

Sometimes, when the mood was right, the man and woman touched one another simply to be different. At first it was a slight nudge or an indelicate bump for no reason. With the unearthing of passion, however, systematic touching became all the rage on earth. One afternoon, the hands of both the man and woman got the better of them. Those hands traveled over each other's flesh as if to organize it. It was a very pleasant feeling, and their hearts beat fast, as if they both were at the edge of a cliff, seeing the fall and sensing the fear, prepared to fly even without wings.

This feeling was a start of something new – the sense of being connected to another, to all things outside. Yet with this sense came increased uneasiness. There were feelings that grew as interior language. A whirlwind of questions with no discernable way to explain. Until, at last, the man and woman learned to speak outwardly what burned inside. It was good to loosen those first words, though this only paved the way for dissatisfying conversations. With talk, it seemed, nothing was simple any longer. Disquiet and inner confusion blurted out.

What do you call that? asked the woman one morning, pointing to the sun.

That I call good, said the man. And he walked away, because he'd didn't want to get caught in some heated discussion. Then in the afternoon of the same day, or maybe months later, the woman had another question:

What do you call this? She handed the man a cold and motionless winged creature she'd found beneath a tree.

This, he sighed, rolling it in his hand, feeling no flight. *This* is not what it is. So, it must be what it is not.

Is it good? asked the woman.

To call this good, well… Behold the work of mystery. This is what it is not. Therefore, it is not what it is.

You talk in circles and riddles, said the woman. Everything should be straight and clear.

Maybe you're right, said the man.

I am right. You've got to unravel the truth from the mystery. Then come out and say it with confidence.

Easier said than done, said the man. Things aren't always as they seem. He then threw the creature up, naming it bird, whereupon it flew away.

The world seemed unfathomable the more it was spoken. It was difficult even to figure the most obvious things – the height of the many-storied trees, for example, or the number of paces to the hill nearest the setting sun, or how to best prepare meat to bring forth its flavor. Sometimes the man and the woman thought it better to be vegetarians, even vegans, as a show of appreciation to the life they were given. But, given by whom, that was the question. And besides, the taste of animal flesh was exceedingly good.

They kept at their lives from morning until night, trying to work out the right thing to do, not knowing for sure. They grew older, grew up, grew into. They grew more earthly, barely aware of changes in their being. And after much time the first two humans became three humans and the three became five, then the five became eight, then thirteen, twenty-one, thirty-four, fifty-five, and on and on all thanks to Fibonacci, until they amounted to a very large number indeed. If some of the number went away, so be it. No one knew where, and only a few paid even the slightest attention. And when additional humans appeared and were pressed for details as to where they came from or what their reason was for being here, the newcomers provided no information, like highly trained POWs.

So, the earth wove its way through dark and light, and humans sprung like weeds through the cracks. Sometimes a person would be heard sobbing among the wild mint. Other times, a stranger would appear floating upon the surface of the lake, looking like a lily pad, only face down, and not one human did much to interfere with the floater or retrieve his body or feel sorrow. Everything, simply, was an occurrence to witness, which is to say that very little thought was given. True, a handful of people painted with berry ink to express their ideas, but most just looked to the sky and waited. When would come water? they wondered. When would come food? When again would burst that roar from above, the terrifying explosion that before shook the land? And when, when would it happen, a clarifying voice like the warm good feeling of the sun on a cool and windless day? A voice, they wondered, saying what to do and why.

Before too long, however, or maybe it was after a while, the door to better understanding finally appeared. No one knew the time was ripe, yet there came a day, the twelfth day of the new moon after the season of the first honeying. The sky shone particularly clear that day, and there it was – the door. A two-paneled oak portal with a shiny brass knob. And the door itself called out like this: *You. Hey. You. Yes, you. You're in this place and this place is good, but things have got to change. Consciousness evolves – that's all I'm saying. Don't just stand there like a lump and let things happen around you. Time to be a part of it all. To push forward.*

As it happened, a young man passed in front of the door the very moment it spoke those words. He was out hunting for mushrooms to go with his honey when he heard what he heard, which at first he thought was birdsong. Call it fate or call it a heightened sense of his surroundings – something made the young man stop. He recognized the opportunity and turned the knob, easing the door open. There, on the other side, sat Death, though the young man didn't know him as Death. And Death looked up, startled from his book, a cup of hot tea steaming beside him.

It's Oolong, said Death.

Come again?

Oolong tea. I'm a stickler for precision.

Who are you? asked the man.

Death. Haven't you been listening? The one and only. And you are?

Just me, like always.

You sound a bit disappointed.

I haven't found any mushrooms.

So, you'd like things to be different, said Death. You'd like to grow into someone new. And at the same time, you'd like to remember where you've come from and how you are like the universe itself.

I don't know about all that, said the man. I just want mushrooms.

You need to figure it out, though.

The mushrooms?

If that's all you want.

Death laid his book to the side, and amended his greeting with a smile.

We can skip further chitchat, he said, jumping to his feet. I do, however, appreciate you opening your mind to me.

What is ur-mind?

Thanks, too, for the world, said Death, ignoring the mishearing.

What world is that?

Your world, of course, which is our world now.

But I came to you. I came through your door. Where have I come?

It's not my door you opened. You are where you've always been, and now so am I.

And it was true. There was no new world with a chair and book. There was no sign of any door. There was only the same world as before, only different because of Death.

Things are going to be better now, said Death. You'll see.

I wasn't aware they were bad, said the man.

That's because your eyes were closed. Now they're open. You're still adjusting.

The man saw trees and branches. He saw leaves and needles and fragments of sky.

What matters most is that you don't think badly of me, said Death. Do you think badly?

I don't see why I would, said the man. You seem like a decent fellow.

Well you wouldn't, just yet, think badly of me. However, you might someday. So, please remember.

Remember what?

Not to.

Not to remember?

Not to think badly, said Death. It's not my fault what happens on earth. And it's not my fault what you think of me. You're the one opening and closing doors. You're the one who thinks or doesn't.

Okay, said the man, who, looking again, could find no door.

Okay, said Death. And the two shook hands. There are some good ones in the glen if you follow the path to my left.

Doors? asked the man.

Mushrooms, said Death. Then he turned and walked right, into the world, his face full of promise, excited to introduce himself to anyone and everyone, intending to help all people get on with life, even if very few of them would invite him for tea and even if none would want to accept his offer.

~

The earth endures death. Trees and rocks and fish endure death. And all human life upon the earth endures death, as well. Is it even imaginable – a time or material world where there is no death? The imagination itself eventually succumbs to the withering process.

Here, people die each day, deeply troubled. They die untroubled, too. They die at the top of their games. At the base of mountains. At the end of their ropes. At sea, at home, at work, at war. Sometimes, if lucky, they die at peace. They die in cities and towns, impoverished and in parks, in every imaginable scenario, inside and out. They die to get what they are missing, die to get a taste of some savory food. They die of thirst and of hunger. They die to hear and to know. They die to discover new things and to tell secrets they've been holding inside. They try to ward off death, but they just can't do it. They drink coffee and stay up all night, thinking of ways to get death to back off, but death needs to visit. He's doing his job, no harm intended. Still, people drink green tea, eat fresh organic bread and mangoes, plenty of turmeric. They go to psychics and gurus. They go to doctors and priests. And death comes like an offer that none can refuse.

And the people die, young and old, leaving behind what they've collected – shells from the beach and chipped wooden frames with photos of husbands and children, mothers and aunts. The people die by the roadside, by the river, by the hundreds each minute. They die by the thousands each day, and by the will of God, which makes it easier for some to accept the loss. People die by guns going off in their very own faces, by being hit over the head with tire irons and baseball bats. They die by drowning in bathtubs, by falling off bridges, off rooftops, off horses, down stairs, down holes, by falling asleep and not waking up. Some people die before seven a.m. Some people die before seven years old. They die, kick the bucket, and don't come back, no matter what's said or done. No matter the magic, black or white. No matter what's dreamed of or wished for – that party is finished, the individuality done.

It is inevitable to die and endless the ways people do it. You might think that people come to the earth just to die, but that would be a pessimistic way to look at things, as though life, as the song goes, is but a dream, with nothing to hold onto. Thinking that life on earth amounts only to death would be like reading a story that has taken you days, weeks even, to complete and has offered you many new places and much to consider, and yet despite all your time and apparent effort, you've thought nothing the whole journey, heard only the flip of pages, and then at the end, with the final clap of the book, you look up and say: "Hmm. Did something just happen? Hey, what's that over there?"

There must be some response to life on the earth other than a resounding personal silence, as death turns from the bedside, leaves the room, and walks on. Of course, that assumes a meaningful relationship between each person and his life. It assumes there is a connection, a friend in life, someone who cares. Which, according to legend, is true. Life is interested in what you think and do, has hope for you. Sees promise in your time on the planet. Even offers up a most intimate promise, if you can hear.

There's a promise to each person originating before birth. You'd think you'd remember this promise, but your memory for such cosmic stuff comes in whispers at best. A quarter way through life, wind reminds you of the promise, but it's difficult to make out the words when you're young. Then halfway along, it is birdsongs and curious light, or the cool feel of sand sifting through your fingers – these and other things bring you to your senses. There is something that's out there, that you need to remember.

I promise, it begins.

And maybe you look up.

I promise that I am with you.

Come again.

The promise starts fresh, so you might better hear: *Call me I. I unfinished. I with life. I am your ongoing I. And I promise that I'm with you always, even after death. In fact, death is the route upon the earth to understanding that I exist at all. Life and I stand together while you, on earth, live through your days. And you return to me, death after death, until you know that I am here. You return to me at death, in order to learn that you must work on earth with the weather and the colors, bright and drab, with the mosquitos and hummingbirds, the heartaches and the riches, to arrive more fully at me. It's a matter of spiritual understanding.*

And I promise you a long and meandering adventure. I promise you relationships and places that you'll take to heart or perhaps ones you will leave behind. I make no judgments about what you do. Though, if you ask, I'll provide suggestions. I could promise you the moon or the stars or some otherworldly cliché, but the earth is all you really need. It serves as a home for the body and a school for the soul.

And I promise that if one day you hear my promise coming through the branches, you will stop in your tracks. You will be held in place by the ground where you stand, listened to by the breeze you listen to, and seen by the very light you see reflecting off trees. You will, in a sense, feel yourself known and loved and needed. And if you pay attention to this new understanding, you will hear the first notes of a higher world, notes that contain my promise. When you hear those notes, you may hope for more. You may even listen intently, look and think: "What's really going on here? Is there more to life than meets the eye?" *But if you do not stop when you hear the promise, if your heart is full of habit and your mind locked by routine, you'll likely proceed without further awareness — simply the world as is, under the sun and stars. Nothing new. No wonders to open you because of your tightly sealed mind. And that should be an unfortunate feeling, if it happens that way, though you won't be bothered because you will not notice your deficiency at all.*

And that's a promise, too: Your relationship with life is up to you. For no matter how much I tell you that life has meaning and is good and that I continue with life beyond the range of death, if you are uninterested to know what's behind the curtain, then the world will remain confirmed by your opinion, which is a confining thought that has little to do with the evolving truth.

No matter. I give you a promise of days and nights and a living trajectory even through death. This trajectory is what makes for meaning. But why is there aim to begin with? Where does it lead? And how long till we're there? Fair questions, all. And it'd be nice if I had the answers, but I am as much a part of the questions as are you. Together we are a door now and then of our very own openness, an openness that leads to a new way of seeing. And when you love this world (its winter trees), *when you love the sky* (now muffled by gray), *when you love the side of someone's face in its subtle light, when you love* (her. Here. Turning her way) *even if your love is barely enough to secure these things, I promise you it's a good place to begin.*

~

You're just standing there, said Rianna.

He was – looking at the sky, thinking about birth and death and the mysterious promise of life.

Aren't you going to shut the door?

Yes, said Games.

He went back and pushed the car door closed, didn't lock it. Then Games and Ri headed up the mountain trail. Warm air from the south collided with cold from the north. Soon there would be snow, but for the moment the world lay still, and the sky was a smooth gray lid to seal in thoughts.

I want to tell you something, said Rianna after walking briskly at first, then slowing on the path, almost stopping, almost.

It's not mine, I promise, said Games.

What's not yours?

The baby, said Games.

What baby?

I thought you were going to tell me you're pregnant.

And you want it to be someone else's? said Ri.

She was right. Games needed to think before he spoke.

It isn't, is it? he asked.

Isn't what?

Someone else's?

What are you talking about?

The baby. Games caressed the word, as if to show his gentleness with such a vulnerable thing. To show he'd be a good father.

There is no baby, said Rianna.

None?

No.

Games felt a rush of disappointment. Birth would've been another thing entirely, a new world to live in. Perhaps he was ready for it. He could see himself having children. Telling them stories. Showing them leaves, leaves shaken by the wind. Showing them the moon changing night after night in the sky. He could see himself being a father. He could see –

You had names picked out, didn't you?

Geezer and Baklava, Games told her.

I hate those names, said Ri.

She was right again. Geezer was too old and Baklava too sweet. They continued through the woods. Roots of trees. Loose stones. Fallen leaves. The time had almost come to say.

Can you be serious a minute?

Yes, said Games.

I was out last night with Chrissy.

Drinking?

No.

Alcohol's not good for the baby, said Games.

You promised, said Rio.

I'm sorry, Games said. And he was.

So, this guy comes up to us –

A guy and a goat walk into a bar, thought Games. The goat –

Tries his lame pickup lines, Ri continued. At first I thought he was going for Chrissy. But when I looked over, she was talking to some other guy.

What bar?

Spotty Pepper.

Games nodded. He didn't like drinking, never hung out in bars much anymore.

He wanted to go clubbing, said Ri.

Games resisted the urge to make a reference to baby seals, which would've proved him weak-minded and also would've brought up the baby thing again. He bit his cheek to keep from wrong speech. If he had any hope of making this work, he had to control his urges.

Did you go? he asked.

No.

Did you want to?

Want?

Is that the wrong word? asked Games.

Nothing wrong with the word, said Rianna. It's the wrong intonation.

You do what you want, said Games, smoothing his intonation. That's all I meant.

See, that's the thing, said Rio

What thing?

You think I don't care about anyone but me.

I didn't say that. I'd never say that.

It's what you think, said Ri.

No.

Yes.

Games paused on the path, which was beginning to ascend more steeply. Rianna, up ahead, stopped and turned.

I think all you do is care about others, said Games, who knew that most her wishes were ultimately wishes for the world. But maybe now he'd have to adjust his voice so she'd better hear his thoughts. He'd have to stop messing around when a clear mind was needed. He would be a good place for Rianna, a fine field for planting her own thoughts and feelings. He'd be sun and rain, be rain and sun for her. No matter it was winter he would help to grow what she gave him and not allow it to die on some frozen ground. Not kill it either. Never kill her intentions or her thoughts.

I know you care, Games continued. It was the first thing I knew about you. It's so obvious, I take it for granted. Don't listen to me. You were saying.

I wanted to be somewhere else, said Ri, keeping her distance.

Games nodded, as if to show his full attention in the quiet gesture.

Out of there, Ri continued. But Chrissy was drunk, and the guy she was talking to was a real creep.

How about your guy?

He wasn't my guy.

I know, said Games, stepping closer. I just mean... Why are you telling me this?

It's difficult for me, said Rianna. I'm trying to make sense of something.

You always make sense. Just not now, which is unusual.

I mean sense of –

Look, it doesn't matter, said Games, trying to ease her.

Of course it matters.

Well, a little, said Games. I mean, if you wanted to go with him.

Which I didn't. It's not even about him, is it?

I don't know, said Games.

The two continued, side by side, up the mountain. Afternoon light filtered grayly through the leafless limbs.

It's not, said Ri. In a certain sense it is all about me, but not this me.

There's nothing wrong with you, said Games. Not this you or any you.

Why can't there be something wrong with me? said Ri. Of course there's something wrong. If nothing's wrong, how can I ever make it right?

If nothing's wrong, you don't need to make it right.

That's not how things work, said Ri. I walk through life with myself each day, and if I'm lucky I see her – a girl going out, going to work, going to bars, if only sometimes, a girl being propositioned by a jerk, a girl who's not empty and not separate from life, but one who's also not taking things to heart, not because everything's got to be serious, I know it's not all serious, but because why not meet each moment with…

Rianna went quiet. The ceiling, painted gray with clouds. The paint, still wet, dripped streaks on the sky. The trees, stiff multistoried spectators, stood waiting. Each moment. Waiting. To meet each moment with –

I was going to choose love, said Ri. I stopped myself in time.

A missed opportunity, said Games. I always want to hear what's on your mind.

Ri liked him saying this.

Games guided Rianna along the trail, nudging her to the left at the fork.

This way, he said, pointing to where the path temporarily leveled. Ri followed, and thinking became a bit easier for her, as if the air had been cleared.

There was this amazing truth for me last night, she said at

last. It fell onto the table in a splash of light, right next to the pretzels.

You mean like a sign?

An epiphany, actually, said Rianna. Big time. But if I use words to explain it, it all disappears.

What disappears?

Ri shook her head. Words – they seem to destroy what I felt.

Games knew Rianna would find the right words. If he didn't interrupt. If he walked with complete confidence in her. If his interest didn't waver.

It's... I'm... Ri was making her way. She looked where the path was going. She –

There's someone up ahead, she said assuredly. New and ready. But I'm standing back here and I don't want to stand back anymore.

Am I keeping you back?

Rianna was talking about her experience the previous night. Games should've known this, and maybe he did. She wasn't talking about him. She was talking about herself. She was talking about the found light on the table next to the pretzels, which was a sense of something important in her life. Call it *Epiphany*. Call it a *Higher Self*. Call it *Thinking about Purpose*. Call it a *Path to Love*. Call it –

A door opened to me, said Ri. Talk about opportunities! There was a great storm coming through the door. I knew the storm was blowing me to pieces. And I was okay with that. The pieces, you know. And no one else saw the door or felt that storm. I saw the opening, knew what was coming, felt it breaking me. This shattering storm. Trying to bring me to my senses, actually. Which would be difficult. I knew going through would be something hard for me to do. And I knew it would bring peace in the end, not pieces. It would bring a great feeling of life. And not just a feeling. My whole existence would be different. It was out there, through that door, after the uproar: more receptivity, more recognition of beauty in all that I meet, more gratitude really. Gratitude like what a seed has for soil, like what a bird has for the air, like... Unlike anything I could imagine. I didn't imagine it. I knew I could do it. Had it in me. Had to, had to go.

Games loved this door. He wanted it also.

Then I heard the door close, and I couldn't find it again. You'd've thought I would've been sad. But I wasn't sad. I was suddenly happy, like the faces of parents when their child arrives at the airport and they see her after a year of separation. The door was behind me. I'd just stepped through. And in contrast, this guy stood in front of me, trying to pick me up, which was also a door open for me, but there was a stagnant, backward feeling to going through that door. That door opened into the exact same room with crumpled napkins, stale light, and the smell of beer. There was no light there. No way. It was all very small life and uninspiring. And when that ugly door closed, I wanted to hide from it and not let it ever call to me again.

You've got no foot in that backward door, said Games. Tell the first door. Keep telling it.

He glanced at Ri, who looked strangely triumphant, and there wasn't even any sun shining on her. He couldn't stop looking: to the path, then back to Ri. To the path, then back to –

When do we come to the top? she asked.

Games didn't answer. It was better to let Ri do the talking, since she was on a roll.

You mentioned a baby, she said at last. It's as if I've conceived something. Or remembered it. As if it's always been there, and now – There's suddenly this peppermint in my pocket and –

A measly peppermint? said Games.

Sometimes they're really good, said Ri. There's got to be stuff I'm doing inside constantly – conceiving, building. Stuff I don't even know.

It's true, said Games. You're encouraging yourself.

Ri thought about this, and nodded.

So one day, say, I reach into my pocket and there it is – the peppermint. I bring it out and look at it. How'd it get there, I wonder? Maybe it's always been there. But the thing is, I look at it differently because of all my inner encouragement, like you said. It's not a measly peppermint. It's a jewel. Lit in a way it's never been lit before, and I see it at last. It's more than a jewel really, it's the entire universe, full of growth and purpose. It's everything about me and about life, all in that simple candy. I see stars and planets. I see the past and the future earth. I see where I've come from and where I have to go, and I remember at once – it's all in that candy – who I am and who I'm meant to be. This is my baby, the beginning of me. There's no going back. I'm here

> like the sun
> that holds the world
> in its light never leaving
> to take a break always
> assisting the weeds
> as much as the roses
> the heart as much
> as the eye

They had stopped walking without even knowing it.

Say that last part again, said Games, leaning in. He thought it sounded like poetry.

The words aren't really that important, said Ri. I just know that the bar is not who I am any longer.

You've crossed the bar, said Games.

I'm not dead.

Is that what that means? Don't listen to me. But what do you do, go a couple times a month with Chrissy or Nat?

Not Nat.

Whoever, said Games. It's just to have fun.

I'm not saying I'd never go out again, said Rianna. Don't think I'm a saint. But all at once there's someone back there who's not me anymore. Someone here is.

You're a different person, said Games. I've always known that.

I didn't know it, said Ri. Now I do. It feels I'm free, and I wasn't even expecting it.

You watched yourself give birth to yourself. And who knew you were pregnant?

Yeah, maybe. And why after that would I want to waste time with someone I'm not? I want to spend time with who I'm becoming. I want... Don't say it.

You're very becoming, said Games.

You've got no willpower, said Rio.

You set me up, said Games. I couldn't resist.

They started to walk again. The trail wound through the woods, inclining toward the cold, gray sky. It lined itself with words that settled upon its surface, as if the trees were still dropping leaves and these leaves were thoughts and the thoughts burst into language at the slightest touch.

It's okay to go out with friends, said Games. To relax, you know.

This is relaxing, said Ri.

What's this? asked Games.

This, repeated Rio, looking around, then looking at Games. There's a new life breaking out of me.

I'm not quite sure what was so bad about the old one.

Rianna thought for a moment.

Nothing was bad, she said. How could she say this better? It's all good.

You're a butterfly. From a chrysalis.

No, said Rio. But I am happy.

You're always happy, said Games. Even when you're not. You were born happy, like one of those sweet-natured girls from the south.

I don't know those girls. But I am beginning to see something.

See what?

What this world is, said Ri. It's a physical ship on a spiritual sea. There's nowhere to come from and nowhere to go without understanding the spirit that conveys all things.

Games liked what she said. He walked with the words, which echoed inside him, tapping his chest like heartbeat, playing through his mind like soft piano notes. Bach, Brahms, pianissimo. Ri pressed on:

Someone could spend years writing a book of herself, Rianna began. Say, a simple love story. It's funny how love starts out as the best of everything: beautiful skin, fun times, unlimited kissing – a paradise of sorts. There are pictures taken at the shore and even more kissing in the shade, on the train, behind the trees, laid out on the kitchen table.

I like where this is going, said Games.

It's not going there, said Ri. It's going somewhere

different. Because one day heaven closes its gates. It can't stay open all hours. Love becomes earthbound and begins to erode. Individualities flare up as arguments. *You* forgot to call about that thing. Well, *you* forgot to remind me. Crimes and recriminations. Love shows cracks and other signs of weakness, because really it can't do all the work on its own. It's up to the people to make love a success. And what do people really know about love? They haven't given it much thought, just been running on passion and presets. And so that simple love story begins to deteriorate from word to word because the love wasn't built but expected as a God-given right. And if things are just expected and not worked for, how true can they really be? Or, maybe, how real can they truly be? That's a better way to say it.

Games struggled with the distinction, but gave up, as Ri continued her story.

So, what it comes to is this: The main character trudges on, growing more and more disillusioned, not knowing why she's so unhappy, no matter her three kids, no matter her new kitchen table. And then one day, maybe she's forty, maybe forty-five, she pulls into the driveway, stays there, stays put, not getting out of her car. Something prevents her from moving. She looks at the trees and the sky behind the trees, and the sky looks back, not even sympathetic, just poking through the branches without saying a thing. But she, the hero, has something to say. It's a lot to say, really. She opens her mouth and out comes a thought and the thought is a bluebird, a surprising bluebird: Wow, she says. To think I've wasted my time till now.

Wasted it how? asked Games.

Without understanding what was inside her. Or by not thinking it necessary to come to some terms with life.

But she understands now, said Games. I mean, the person whose story it is.

All I'm saying, said Rianna, is that a lot of stories would end right there, looking at the sky with trees, seeing a bluebird flying through.

It is a nice ending, said Games.

Not for me, said Ri. It's actually the exact time to begin the story. I don't want to end in self-awareness. I want to begin with it. That's the story I want to be. Why spend all the time in old skin, when new skin is who I really am?

Like the ugly duckling.

If that's how you see me, said Ri.

I see you that way, I see you this way, said Games. I like all your skin.

You're too predictable, said Ri.

New skin used skin, offered Games. Light green and blue skin. And who knows what it'll look like in thirty years, but I'll like it even more.

I just wanted you to know, said Ri.

Games was confused. He did know. He knew Rianna could never sit still. He knew she carried the world into her heart, not wanting to change it, but wanting to hear its correspondence with what was inside her already. She wanted to know the world alive and well and growing into something good.

I feel change like a new sun in me, said Ri.

Babies, thought Games. Babies again. Sons and daughters. Kid goats. He looked at the thick clouds through the bare, unmoving limbs. He was interested in Rianna's every thought, not his own punning ones.

Don't you feel the warmth of the sun? asked Ri.

Usually.

And the stars. I know you like them.

At night, said Games. Taking them slow.

There's an outside of life, said Ri. An inside, too. I'm tired of a world whose inside's ignored. I'm tired of a world that's got nothing better to be because it's not given the chance. That's not how the world really is. That ignored world's a half-world. It's meaningless. I'm not going to be part of a meaningless world anymore.

When did you ever live there? asked Games.

Well, I'm here now. A world where if we don't become closer, we don't see it.

Closer to what?

Each other, for one. Who knows what else?

This is nothing new, said Games, happy however to hear the thought expressed. It's always been your way.

No way, said Ri. It feels new to me.

Games shook his head.

You're just catching up with who you already are.

I didn't like where I was last night, said Ri. Didn't like that person.

Okay, said Games. He said the word gently, let it sink, sing deep.

And as if the word was magic, everything became okay. Ri okay and Games okay, the mountain path and air okay. And they came okay to a small bridge okay that crossed an alright stream. And there they paused a moment before going up the steep, narrower slope.

I told Kaan I was getting married, said Rio.

The guy's name was Con?

Yeah.

But you're not getting married, said Games.

It was just a thought, said Ri. I thought other things, too. That you –

Don't bring me into it, said Games. I was home, reading. It's my alibi, and I'm sticking to it.

Yeah, but I'm a better witness, said Rio. You were in my mind the whole time. I can prove it.

How?

Well, I could if I wanted. What I was going to say, though, was that I thought about something you'd be interested in. I thought about mothers.

What about mothers?

What they do to conceive life, said Ri. I saw Dove's mother the other day. She came by my classroom, her eyes were red from crying. She was trying to hide it. She didn't want me to know. I get it, but why not? What's the matter with crying? What's wrong with knowing someone is sad? And later, I saw this old woman with white hair who made me think of your mother, how she might be one day. She saw me looking and looked away. She didn't want me to see. But what's wrong with seeing, with being seen? And then there was the photo of my own mother on my shelf. I saw her looking back at me, watching me from the frame, beside *The Metamorphosis of Plants*. Or maybe it was from somewhere else in the room, because there were eyes in everything. And I stood there, taking it in.

I wish I knew your mother, said Games.

You know her more than you think. People seem to grow in you like you're healthy soil. Still, she always looks the same in that picture, even though I think she's fading a bit. I don't mean that I'm losing her. More that she's moving on and I'm learning to see her better. I think she's still someone, just not so much June Gardner Olivet anymore. I mean, not only my memories. I know, instead, that she's out there, rebuilding a life. Something's slipping away. Something even better is coming in. Everything's a living flow, if you can just see it that way. Like Daddy's documentary on the sea. It's a living work of art, like the water itself.

I liked that movie, said Games, walking again, starting up the steep part of the climb. Did you ever tell him I liked it?

Yes. He's going to do one on bees.

Honey, bees are sweet, said Games.

Did you just call me Honey?

You're crazy, said Games. Why would I say that?

Ri stopped. She looked around. Maybe she was crazy. Where were they anyway?

Did we miss the fork?

No, said Games. That was a mile ago. Maybe more. Unlike someone, I've been paying attention.

~

It was the mountain they'd climbed almost a year ago, when Quincy Mesch's family scattered his ashes. The same mountain today, only different: cloudy with possible snow in the late afternoon. Cows in the chilly pastures, honeybees sleeping. And soon, a long, unobstructed view of the valley. Only two people climbed the mountain this day, both of them having come their separate ways, and still to come – a billion zillion new steps from here. School was done. Christmas soon. Games would be going to see his aunt and uncle, Michaela and Peter. Tomorrow, Rianna would leave to visit her sister and father in Baltimore.

Whatever happened to Abe? asked Ri as they neared the top of the mountain.

Alaska.

Don't ask me. Atelier, that's what you need to say.

Atelier. I'll tell you, thought Games. That was bad, he said.

Ba dah boom. Ba dah boom. I'm here all week, said Ri.

Give me something better.

Rianna came up with one.

My ticket says: It takes two to Tonga.

That's the best you've got?

She had more.

You can lead a horse to water, but what about a pencil?

What about it?

It should never be lead, said Ri. But graphite or charcoal.

How about the plumbing? asked Games. And the paint on the windowsill?

Get the lead out, agreed Rianna.

She took the lead, walking ahead unburdened, and Games had to go fast to keep up. He thought about Con. Hesitated to ask.

So… What happened with your boy, Con?

Rianna slowed her pace to explain.

He came loaded with fake marijuana.

What's fake marijuana?

Spitfire, Devil Juice. It's potpourri. He called it "pot" pourri. I don't know what happens when you smoke it.

What a fraud, said Games.

He showed me his tattoo of honeysuckle creeping up his arm, turning into barbed wire on his bicep.

Nice.

The problem was, he thought it was a rosebush.

He thought his bicep was a rosebush?

The honeysuckle, said Ri. I mean, who thinks honeysuckle is a rosebush, and there it is, all over your arm?

Who names their kid Con? said Games.

Seems to me, a person should know something about the world he belongs to, said Ri.

Do we belong to the world?

We belong in it, said Ri. At least you should know what you put on your body.

He's a con artist, said Games. Trying to fool you.

No one's going to fool me, said Ri.

Games held that thought. He took it as a challenge. Down the road a ways maybe he'd have some fun.

~

Left, right, center. Three great distances from the top of Mount Everett – as far as the eye could see. There lay the densely clouded graphite sky and the long, unfettered views to the north, to the south, and straight on west. The firs with their needles, the deciduous nudes.

It was cold up there, too. December twenty-first dressed in Saturday gray. Light wind, birdless limbs, and 100 percent chance of snow. Ri showed very little skin, a scarf around her neck. Games wore a hat and gloves. He wrapped himself in pictures of the world. He then took twelve steps, counted them out, to stand beside Ri, who had separated herself for a moment.

Fine Swedish finish sweet sexy delicious mimosa the most. What was he thinking? The most. You're the most. Beautiful person, he should've said, but instead said: Everything you do is all right with me.

Not everything.

That's where you're wrong, said Games.

You see, Ri told him. I've made a mistake already.

How could he have fallen for that?

Rianna continued: Say you're on a mountain and it starts to snow and the snow makes it so you can't see a thing, not even your own hand. And there's a plane overhead, not far overhead, and you hear it circling, tipping its wings to rip apart the clouds and stop the snow. So, you look and look. And how long till it works? How long before you see what's right in front all along?

The plane? said Games.

No. Not the plane. The plane's a metaphor.

Metaphor, metaphor. Where had Games heard this before? A metaphor for what? he asked.

For clearing the head, said Ri. I don't know. That's the problem.

You're overthinking it, said Games. Let things work out as they do.

You should be a counselor, with all your platitudes. You could walk up to people on the street. You know, straighten them out with a few honest words.

Like a crook? said Games.

The bird?

Not a rook. A crooked person.

You mean someone bent out of shape? said Ri.

What's got you all twisted? I'd say to the guy. Work out your kinkiness.

That's not very understanding, said Ri.

Okay. Then: Here's a wrench, I'd say. Do what you can. When it comes down to it, you've got to fix yourself.

You're talking about me, aren't you? said Ri.

You are a bit kinky.

Maybe I need some counseling.

No.

But I have this great insight, then I don't just go with it, said Ri. What's wrong with me that I don't trust what I know?

Nothing's wrong, said Games. You're working it out. It takes time. Takes work.

What if, one day, it's too hard to keep working things out? Changing moods, you know. Clear head, cloudy head. And I give up?

You. No way. Give up. Don't have it in you. But if things feel a bit rocky, I'll help. Buy you some ice cream, or maybe some more time. How about that? Same way you always help me.

Rianna kept her sights on a rising trail of smoke miles away.

Ice cream?

Sure, said Games. I've heard stories of people like you.

What stories?

Stories of caring people. Like you and Ursula.

Who's Ursula?

Everyone knows Ursula, began Games. It was beautiful on the fen where she was born. The changing tides, the fog, the green marsh for as far as the eye could see. Her parents loved her every minute of the day. They played hide and seek among the patens and Juncus and river birches. They pointed out the moon and red-winged blackbirds. They made her laugh.

Then one day, a cold stormy day, Ursula's parents left early to get food and a new toy for their daughter. "Keep the fire burning," they said. "We'll be back by three with a pleasant surprise." But three came and left. They never returned. It wasn't pleasant at all. What did Ursula know about time? What did she know about lost parents? She was seven and knew only timeless happiness. So, she was taken to the institute to learn hard truths. There are lots of details I've got to leave out, but it was eleven lonely years, let me tell you. At eighteen, Ursula left the institute to join the real world. She took to the streets with her only possession – a book of matches. Still, she knew better than to say her life had come to nothing.

You can't just leave her out on the street with some matches, said Ri.

Well, it wasn't long, continued Games, before Ursula met some homeless people sitting by the dumpster behind The Pretzel Barn. It was an uninspiring place, and the dumpster was empty. Look up, she told them. But when they did, the sky was full of storm clouds. A blizzard was on its way. "No good. No good," said one homeless man. So, Ursula led her friends to a place she knew about under the old railroad bridge down by the river. There they shivered, waiting out the storm. At least they weren't buried in snow. Ursula used her matches to strike up conversations. None of the conversations lasted very long. Most in fact turned into monologues given by her new friends. The monologues sounded like wind across the fen from when Ursula was little, which made for memories of better times. There has to be something I'm missing, she said to herself, thinking over her life. For some reason, I suppose, I've come to this.

Rianna waited for Games to finish his story. Yet, no more was coming.

You're not stopping there, she said.

I thought I'd give Ursula some time to figure it out on her own.

Seems to me, she needs something to keep her warm.

Have some faith in her, said Games. Ursula's an excellent thinker. She knows what to do.

Sometimes a person can think too much, said Ri. Overthinking, you know.

Maybe you're right. That's why Ursula looked to her friends by the river. She didn't know why things happened the way they did in her life, but maybe that didn't matter just now. Here I am, she thought. She stood with the river in front, as it flowed to the sea. She stood with her homeless family, as they tried to stay warm. She stood with the sharp wind that stung her cheeks. She stood upon the earth, surrounded by angels.

I bet she liked that there were angels, said Ri.

She did. And she stood with the clouds above and that train whistle in the distance, too, and with the looks from strangers driving by in their fancy heated cars. She stood with memories of happier times, and with presentiments of a future where all would be well. You see, there was a lot that Ursula was connected to. She just had to see it, and then she did. She also understood that she could make her connections stronger with empathy. You can't go wrong with empathy, she thought. And that in a nutshell is what Ursula was about. She brought the world into herself one degree at a time and gave it her undivided attention. And if she were to die right there, by the river without warmth, so she'd die. And if she were to live in the hearts of others, so she'd live. The end.

The end, exclaimed Ri. You'd just let her die out there?

She's not going to die, said Games. She'll figure it out.

You could at least give her a blanket. Or get those drivers in their fancy heated cars to pitch in and build a shelter. They've got the money, I'm sure. Start a collection. A foundation. Get the mayor involved.

Have faith in what's going to happen, said Games. Ursula's a lot like you. She's not going to be broken. She'll never stop trying.

Still, you could make things easier for her.

You mean like how the superhero, Woebegone Woman, helps others?

Now, you're just making things up.

No. Woebegone Woman. You and Ursula are a lot like her, too. She can make anyone happy just by standing near.

Because she's so sad? said Rianna.

Woebegone. Be gone all woe. That's what Games meant. Not woeful.

You don't mean that Ursula and I are sad and miserable, said Ri.

No, said Games. I mean the opposite.

He was looking at Rianna, thinking of light. Make light of nothing. See light in it all. He looked at her cheeks, and he looked at her eyes. He held out his words for Rianna the way he always hoped to hold them, so as never to let her down.

I mean that you are someone who makes people more themselves, said Games. It's happening to me like it's happening for you. It'll happen for others – Dove, Con, Fiona, Marcus, you name it. All students, everyone you touch. You are the best possible teacher.

That's nice of you to say, said Ri. It's reassuring.

Maybe it is, thought Games, not saying this. He and Rianna looked at the view, unspeaking. Games continued his reassuring thought inside himself. For himself, to himself, not sharing it with Ri: Maybe yes. Okay. It's reassuring to know that what you do best might also help others in their lives. It's reassuring to know that life is a family and a promise for good, and that whatever comes up in days...well, you can handle it. You can take it on. It's reassuring to hold that truth. Because it's not always the feeling, is it? The world turns. Feelings change like seasons. It'll happen for sure, time and again, that the intensity of life will increase and pile upon you like so much garbage. Even the dust that settles on your shoes will add to your charge. Where'd all this weight come from? you'll ask. Maybe the burden is overwhelming sadness or fear. Maybe it is overwhelming information, like the devil in every detail that discourages you. Well, that's just how it is on earth sometimes. No one gives you a manual. You receive no guidebook on your birthday. It's up to you how you see the world.

Hmm, said Rianna, out of the blue, or out of the gray of the sky.

What is it? said Games.

The view here – a good friend. So all-around uplifting.

There you go, thought Games. Say it. Let it be known. The olive round view. The highs and lows of you. What's true.

~

Rianna and Games stood at the summit
looking over the edge.

It was months ago now, almost a year. Somewhere down there lay Quincy Mesch's ashes. *My flesh was burned, but I did not mind.* Somewhere in the earth were the littered remains of his body, many of its molecules having been ingested by worms. *My flesh was eaten, I did not know.* Or taken up in plant life, or slowly having filtered through the mineral world. *Laid out bare as ashes, I rose like a phoenix. I reappeared.*

So, where was he now? What is left of anyone after the body is gone? There are memories, of course, for as long as they last. And personal items too painful to toss – a set of carving knives, a favorite torn shirt, a hand-pressed columbine flower, a handwritten note. The art of artists and inventions of inventors persist in the world. Sometimes there's even a message on the phone that no one can erase. But what about the movement that calls itself I? There's courage in I. It is a courage that people on earth can remember and never let slip into oblivion. It is a courage, in fact, that wants to persist in itself and with itself, as if saying: *I am given life on earth for a reason, and that reason does not stop at death. There's duty to the earth that is impossible to delete. I am someone who helps create the body to begin with. Death has no claim on my being.*

Reaching out to a nearby tree, Games broke off a dead branch. He listened to the snap. He stooped on his haunches and drew in the dirt.

Life never stops renewing itself, renewing connections. If strings and atoms and molecules and minerals keep going, why not the life itself, which is more essential?

What's that mean, though – more essential? thought Games. He stopped scribbling. One might think that the building blocks of life are the primary elements. That, however, is true only on the physical level. There are other ways to look at life, other ways to understand its presence upon the earth.

Life came first, said Games to himself, staring at the squiggly lines he'd made with his stick. It created the materials it needed to get itself moving, and not the other way around with matter coming first followed by a by-product of life. And what's more, continued Games in thought. Even before life, there was the motivator love. Love the motivator, the way a wish sparks the will. I wish to live in the world with you. I wish to say you are beautiful. I wish to kiss you, and then, if I move my wish forward, I do.

What are you thinking? asked Ri.

What gets things moving, said Games.

Wind, said Rianna.

Why wind?

Okay, spin, she suggested.

What spin?

The rotating earth.

Why's it always something from science?

Art then, said Rio, who could've come up with a hundred more motivators. Like the spin of a story. Or inspiration.

She studied the lines Games drew in the dirt. The image swirled like a van Gogh. It read like words trying to make sense of the world.

There's no art here, said Games.

How about birth? said Ri. And, no, I'm not having a baby.

Games drew stick figures of a mother and child. He put in the sun, with rays of light that were scratches upon the ground.

Everyone says birth, said Games.

Because it's a good place to start, said Rio.

Games tried to picture babies he'd known. There was one who always came in the store with her mother. The mother's name was Ursula. Ursula, Ursula. That's where his earlier story came from.

What's her name? asked Ri, looking.

Who?

The kid you've drawn.

A guy and a goat went into a bar, thought Games. The

goat was a kid. The kid's name…

I don't know, he said.   He made a move with his stick as if –

Don't x the baby out, said Rianna.

I wasn't, said Games. It's not like I'm God.

Is that what God does? Exes things out?

Games didn't know what God did. But he, himself, added another stick figure and drew long dashes after all three people. It was hieroglyphs to indicate they were moving and had important things to do. The picture was a family: Mother, father, and kid daughter nameless. There was a sun in the sky. Rays of light spreading out. Waves coming in from the eastern ocean. That sort of thing. Ri leaned closer, looking over his shoulder to read. She knew what he was drawing because it was about the two of them.

I remember being up here a year ago, she said.

Games remained hunched to the ground. He'd already been remembering. He remembered some more: Dalai Lama conversations. First words with Ri. Last words for Quincy Mesch. Thoughts passing through about Death.

Digging his stick into the dirt, Games heard the range of life and the rhyming though unruling ways of Death. He thought he heard Quincy Mesch say that Death had no claim on his being. In fact, maybe Death serves life, as a representative, he heard. A teacher, even.

Games imagined Death politely moving things off the floor so no one would trip. He pictured Death wishing to be helpful. Who notices this good nature of Death? All it gets is fear and disrespect. Yet Death is no monster, despite that it does come like a thief to steal people away before they're done. When someone dies, his life appears before him as an unfinished house. There are piles of lumber, screws, and nails scattered about, and he says to himself: *I was just about to rough-in the stairs, order the windows, and put on the shingles. Look at this mess. What's going to happen to me now that I'm gone?* No one wishes to be taken away before the roof is shingled, and all he has to say for himself is sawdust everywhere and piles of sheetrock lying in wait.

And so how to overcome death on earth, and flow with life not fold away? This question persisted from somewhere in

Games, somewhere way back, as if at his birth it had been etched in his name. But the question also persisted from somewhere in his future, which was a confusing thought. Games couldn't see the future, but the question of overcoming death streamed back to him from a time when he and others close to his heart would irredeemably die. He would die. Rianna would die. Children, yes children would die. All plants, all creatures that have life would die. The planet would die. How then to go on, experiencing so much loss?

Games sat on his haunches on top of Mount Everett, Rianna beside him, snow coming soon. He drew no more in the dirt. His stick dug in. Stuck in the cold ground. Some thought of overcoming death – but how, and why, and...

Do you. Do you want. Do you...

Games didn't know why it was important to know. He couldn't stop the waves from coming. Past present future here. And he remembered something Rianna had said. *The earth is a physical ship on a spiritual sea. There's nowhere to come from and nowhere to go without understanding the spirit that conveys all things.* You overcome death by understanding that there is a spiritual support to things and that human life contains the promise of figuring it out. You figure it out in the workroom of love, which is the human on earth with all that's around him, with all that he meets. There are sleepy trees and hidden flowers, there are birds in the bushes and children not yet born with names undecided, there are millions of good people and plants and clouds to appreciate. You can overcome death on earth by your appreciation of life, by your relationship with everything, by tending to love for as long as it takes.

Do you want. Do you want something...

Games almost heard. And then he did.

Do you want something hot to drink? asked Ri.

Games looked up. Rianna was studying the stillness of his stick and his unfinished sketch. Here he stooped – too much thinking, not enough art, not enough act.

Something hot, he heard. To drink. And he wanted to say, *Someone, you mean?* Not to drink, not to dream about either, but to talk with for real, to reach with his hands and feel her warmth.

I've got hot chocolate, said Rianna. She took the thermos from her backpack. They shared the cup, the steam, and the friendly view. This afternoon of the shortest day. Neither Games nor Ri had a ruler or a watch, nothing to measure with, and their cell phones were useless this side of the mountain. Some high hawk took notes in the distance. Some low rising smoke from an invisible fire. Some burning left to do. Some how.

~

Games and Rianna stayed at this peak till their hands were cold, till the sky came within inches, and it started to snow. It was only a few flakes at first, nothing to worry about. There was plenty of time to get where they were going. They watched the small, dry snowflakes fall straight and true. It was late afternoon, it was nothing to question, nothing more to think about. Snow filtered down, increasing the world. What more to say? Do what you can to increase your connections.

Games reached over and pressed into Ri. He gently kissed her lips. Sweetly then passionately, so that if some stranger had been passing by, he'd likely have paused, a bit embarrassed by the show but unable to divert his gaze. Not bad, the stranger would say inside, and then continue on his way without asking for details. What greater details would he need besides these two people on top of the world? Not bad, he'd mouth in passing.

And *not bad*, Games would hear in his blood, in his eyes closed to excess, in his body pressing to be the kiss alone. *Not bad*, Games would hear, but *good's* more like it. *Beautiful* is even better, which was Games's feeling on this mountain. It was his thought when seeing Rianna's face. And it was the earth as seen from up high. The winter uninterfering sun. Some welling spirit within the clouds. The hawk now gone. The silent other birds and sleepy multistoried trees. All things beautiful. That sort of thing.

In essence the world is good if only you know it. Or if you don't, maybe somebody else does (a stranger passing by) and can tell how to get where you need to be. There are lots of people on the earth, most of them helpful, most of them kind, all of them family, even the troubled ones, the passing ones, the absent ones even.

And when Games and Rianna walked down the mountain, they navigated the descent by memory and feel, because their eyes were looking inside, upon one another, and their minds were still on the story, The Kiss. Three four five o'clock by the time they... Hearing the snow around them fall. Five-thirty by the time they reached the car. The day had passed quick. The base of the mountain – why so soon? It could've gone on. Everything, everything, the walk the world, like this forever. It could've lasted lots longer and no one would've complained. Not Rianna or Games or the accompanying trees.

Gray dome up above. Half an inch of white on the road. Before they were born, Games and Rianna both pictured this time. They pictured this place. They watched the picture develop as a promise in their souls. It was an awesome view from the top and a long though not long enough kiss coming down. It was a moment to be made by walking together. Before they were born, there was a budding thought about this time. The color of that thought would've been difficult to describe, but the shape of that thought was ubiquitous light. Before they were born, Rianna and Games each saw themselves on earth. They saw they each would walk and ride and climb and descend. Bodies in movement from place to place. And all along there would be words, given and received, to help them through. There would be words and hands and trees and birds and. They'd feel the snowflakes like a million falling stars. Games, Rianna, in their long ago pictures of this moment, saw a promising idea composed of light, which was for each of them a foundation of support. And that picture, that timeless view back before they were born, was much like the picture now at the base of the mountain. Only this – their timely walk up and down the mountain, their arrival at the car – was something they could shiver and be warm with. This was something they could experience together on earth. They could touch it as skin, as a matter of living fact. They could hear the world whisper through the sleepy trees. They could get in the car and drive with careful slowness through the snow. They could wake in the morning and remember.

Standing together at the foot of the mountain, watching the cautious traffic pass. No wind. No hurry. No sense of loss. Just here. With plenty of time. Life like a ship. On a bed. On a sea. On its current of love. All the branches singing stillness. All the evening's graceful close. Gray sky loose with falling snow. And each new day to come.

Little Bird

DECEMBER

Let's go for a walk. And I do. Up the road, away from home. Off the road, out of view. The air is cold. The night, clear and peaceful. Winter, which is here to stay, has been establishing itself for many days. Its roots were surface tendrils at first waiting to dig in, like a film of ice upon a pond, dreaming of skaters. And now that the roots have dug, they reach deep into the land, hushing it with a chilling grip, slowly putting my neighborhood world to sleep. Yet I do not sleep. And thoughts don't sleep. They stir the air as do the gently turning stars above, leaving impressions. I read these thoughts to see what's what.

Here's to beginnings,
sincerity, awareness, and finding doors in perception through which, if I'm lucky enough to travel, I may experience what some call mystical things and others call nonsense, but I call meetings with life. I hold my hand open to the night sky for support and confirmation. I present it as a gesture of my mood. There's nothing in my palm. No problems. No complications. Well, receptivity and welcome are two things in my palm, but they take up no space, and the stars don't object to what I offer.

I've been here before, in settings like this, alone with these stars many times in the past. It's a slow rearrangement up there, never the same sky twice, always a slightly different drift and a variation to the story. But the gist is familiar and I am at home. I know that what I see of this vast presentation is not meant to be a mystery to me. In fact, somewhere in my being, I've always known the universe's openness and its disdain for disguise, as if our cosmos were etched upon my soul at the beginning of time so that now when I meet it again, it is with the possibility of recognition. I nod my head and smile.

Hey, friend, I say.

Hello, sweetie, says the sky.

I like your constancy.

Like Jell-O, is it?

Not your consistency, I say. How you're inviolable, almost hallowed.

Allowed to what?

You're here for me, for everyone, I say, trying to form my words to precision.

Oh, says the sky.

My life is no better than anyone else's, I say. But still you –

I know, says the sky.

And I've made nothing up, either.

Nothing?

A name or two. Maybe a detail turned here or there to drive home a point.

What point is that? asks the sky.

I close my eyes to the sky, keep quiet. I tell myself that I don't have to answer. The sky knows well enough what's in my heart. It's just giving me a hard time. But the sky's not the reason I'm out walking on this winter night. These stars, planets, and galaxies are not what I wish to say. As remarkable as they are, there's something more compelling on the way. There's going to be a birth – that's the thing. The news of the day is a child in the wings. I can almost see her. She remains off stage the way the moon hangs out just below the horizon, ready to rise, or how the leaves hold themselves in, bursting to bud when spring comes near.

The child itching to arrive is my first grandchild. She demands in her easygoing way to be here, and I'm happy for that. Hers is a sincere demand, just as the night sky is sincere in its approach, just as the earth is sincere in its honest lines and colors, in its straightforward works of a natural world. I stand here and wait with an open hand that is a gesture mostly in my mind, whereas my actual hands both dangle, one at each side, the fingertips of my left brushing my leg, and the tips of my right numb in the cold.

Of course, it doesn't matter so much about my hands. It doesn't change a thing how chilled the night air. What matters more is the mystery of life becoming known. Already
I have put a ladder on top of the mountain and climbed many of its inexhaustible rungs. I have gathered hints and winds. I've gathered scraps of debris. I've come to several surprises along the way, not to mention countless doubts. And occasionally, too, I've arrived at some wordless insight, where things are clear and I wasn't even expecting it.

Once, years back, for example, when our son Tory died, I paused for a while on my climb. I looked for answers among the clouds and leaves, in the stones at my feet. I looked for a change in the world and saw instead consoling light. What a window that was, what a soothing difference, discovered first by my grief then widened by my attention. I ought to be able to convey the meaning that that light brought me. But it was a private experience. Not a word made its way out.

The two deaths, in fact, that are closest to me are the ones I've felt most powerless to convey. To begin, I want to be clear that our son died doing what made him happy. He was helping others, carrying aid and supplies when the bridge collapsed. Did the world ever recognize how selfless Tory was? Unfazed by requirements of life, he was never afraid to take charge and spread wealth, which was nothing about money and all about compassion. I really should tell his story, as his short time on earth gave relevance to the idea of awakening consciousness that becomes acts of love. And maybe I will someday. Maybe I'll tell who he was. But for now, even at this late hour, I can't seem to do it, and Tory our youngest remains quiet inside me, so powerfully quiet as trees full of wind with the sound turned off.

Tory died before his sun had risen to noon. Bright midmorning, light in his eyes. And we felt it, Ri and I. We knew he was gone. We rested our hands in our laps, our eyes on the ground. And I went off alone, lay myself down on a soft moment of grass just up the slope, off the path. I hung out with the tear-soaked clouds and changing light. And I did not lose hope, not then, and will never lose it, I swear.

Then later, when Ri was taken from me, I fell long and hard and didn't look up until I heard birds admonish me in my despondency. *You idiot,* said the birds. *You said you'd never lose hope. You swore it, even. You had us believing.* But they were wrong, those birds. They weren't patient enough to wait out my mood. Don't deny me my feelings, I wanted to shout. *Just give me a moment,* I said softly instead. *Let things fall. Let my tears collect on the earth. Let them soak in and work the ground. Let them nourish this world like rain like sun like seeds like... And I promise I promise I'll. I'll do it better. I'll. I'll show you hope. I'll find the way to know that what's missing is here, continuing to grow, still working for our earth.* I said those words back to the birds, my friends. I looked up and I said it and knew it was true.

So that even with Rianna and how she died without asking me almost a year ago, I was not down for long, because ultimately I'm a climber. I will not give up. It's an unwavering duty to life I feel – to respect life's laws and support its weights and wishes, and I'll continue each day with Tory on my shoulders, with Ri in my heart. Star lights, star heights, as far as I can climb tonight, for as long as I stay true to your voices, no matter how quiet or sadly incomplete. I will never not have you with me. I will learn from you wherever you are.

And there you have it, no oversight but insight: I see no other way to live than to work love as if it's the only job. And the one boss is myself, some better self, way up ahead calling back to me: *Games, Games, is that the best you can do? You think by saying the word "love" you've completed your work.* But really I don't think that. I see no end to what I must do. And Rianna, who feels the same, might spell it out soon, if I'm patient. I know what she's like.

We watch together what is happening upon this world. We watch through the darkness for signs of the birth – might be a car going by, flashing its high beams for this reason alone. Of course, the sign might be something more subtle – a bicycle rider pedaling through the dark, or a winter goose dimly stated upon the night sky. Truth is, Ri and I help each other to see things better. We always have. And I've noticed that if I walk in this world with one hand warming another person and the other hand receiving her light, I am no longer sleepy, but increasingly awake, balancing happiness with sorrow, sorrow with joy, joy with disquiet, and then always and inevitably the resounding light. So that now I nearly tip with wonder at the approach of our grandchild.

~

Luckily, everything has been prepared well for the birth. All towels and washcloths, all blankets and bed sheets, are fresh. Ice has been crushed and put into cups. Diapers are folded, stored in the cherry cabinet with the carved heart on the door, a cabinet I made and a heart I carved. The floor was just recently vacuumed. The bathroom is spotlessly clean. There are meals that have been prepared with so much affection that they might easily come to life right there in their dishes, singing and dancing, clowning around – potatoes gone wild and impassioned lasagna. Unfortunately, that playfulness doesn't happen. Instead, those meals sit in the freezer, quiet on shelves, ready to be warmed in the oven and eaten. It's such good food, whose greatest wish is to nourish. The house on the inside is ready.

And there's a light at the front door to welcome all visitors. There's a path to the light and a figure on the path who might well be an angel. I don't know if she's an angel. She is helpful and kind. I've never met an angel, so what can I say? I wonder about things, though. No harm in that. I ask myself, too, if there is God, because there's plenty of room in the world for God, especially God who keeps to himself, just out of sight in the shadow of the barn, or just out of mind behind my words.

No matter – angel no angel, God no God – it's a perfect night for a new person on earth. Who better to be that person than you, whoever you are? There's your birth with its unfolding story on the way. Might be tonight. Might be tomorrow: December the twenty-fifth. I'm not pushing for a specific time. It's nothing biblical I'm after, not that familiar narrative everyone knows. This birth will be one of a kind, no matter its time, and I'm as happy as the million stars that glint and gleam and ride the sky, turning to find the perfect arrangement for you, longing to see who on earth you'll be.

Each life continues a mystery unveiled in time and then again in time and at length in love. Why should I worry? I do not worry. I walk outside and I pause just beyond Twin Berry Farm. I shift and remain. Imperceptibly I shiver, ready to unfold further, to unbind my every measure, and, if able, to let what is most immortal speak. The tension is good. I see intention coming well to the world. I see trees brush black the night. I see an arc of constellations, and some of their names are lost to space, yet many remain known to me.

~

Of course, it's all going to be fine. The birth, I mean. I've got no worries. Though I won't deny that I'm sailing a highly charged sea of anticipation, enjoying my own ride, as well. It's just a first grandchild is different from a first child of one's own. With the birth of your own child, you've got no distance from the drama. You are caught in the middle, and all that's around you is one pregnant thought. You are inundated with baby names and blankets and concerns about preeclampsia. What else can you see? With the birth of your own child, your first, you don't have time, maybe not even the desire, to think what it all means. You are not much imagining how life unfolds, but how the newborn's going to change things and whether you can manage. The mysterious nature of birth isn't so much alive with your first child. Instead, you're running anxious and cautious, your ear to the heartbeat, feeling the kicks. You are overwhelmed and dazed, attentive, unsure.

And I, just outside of that narrative, stand calm, open to what comes. This is my first grandchild, and my schedule is free for wonder. I have the whole night sky to take her in. The experience entrances me, enhances me, too. She is a miracle to begin with, and I am a witness. Here, I've got more space in my days for thinking and more quiet in my life for feeling. I allow this new person to approach me so I can know her even before the trees or the sun, know her how she'll mesh with the earth, how she'll grow like spring flowers, and how easy it will be to love her.

Whereas, with my first child, there was a whirlwind of excitement and lots to do. My first child was the change I'd been waiting for, and when she arrived, she arrived – just like that. I quickly stopped pacing and started adjusting. And did I handle change well? I soon found out. And did I accept the newcomer or did I fight for my old self? And with my other two children – it was more of the same. With all three, I had to get used to it quick. I had to brave the air of an entirely new world. Or else, if I couldn't breathe, if I suffocated, it was because, perhaps, I resented the change. But who wants to stay the same? I ask. And who wishes even an ounce of resentment in his heart? Not I.

~

I remember being thirty and becoming a father the first time. That was life-changing. The opposite of resentment. It was a feeling at once of the justness of life.

I remember something else that was life-changing, too. I was twenty-eight, almost twenty-nine at the time, making my way home soon after Christmas, a few months before I married Ri. It was night, the end of December, almost like now, only saturated with snow. The roads were dangerously slick. Not many cars and not a single star, that's for sure. I drove, mesmerized by the flakes that glinted across my headlights. Occasional vehicles – one apparition from the dark and then another – went by on the icy road.

Then out of that same darkness, out of the near and snowy night, a car skidded my way. Either I didn't realize my danger, or it was simply too late to do anything about it. The car's high beams paralyzed my mind with inevitable collision. I took in those blurry beams of light – nothing to think, nothing to say. I smelled rich, confusing coffee that tangled the air. There was little else I did but brace myself for the impact. Flashes of my days layered me unanswerably, that if I climbed up and through those layers, would I get out? And if I dug in deeply, would I be protected? It happened so fast, I had no time to figure or act.

My muscles contracted, and my hands gripped the wheel

tight. But, thanks to the luck that was with me there, the troubled car slid past. And it kept on careening till it dove headfirst into the ditch, slammed into a pole, and came to a stop. That couldn't be good. Immediately, I pulled to the side and turned off the ignition. I ran through the snow in that uncompactable darkness.

Be okay, be okay, be okay, I panted.

I got to the car quick and looked inside. It was a mother and three kids, the children all shaken and panicky. Steaming coffee dampened the dash. I helped the children out. One two three, and there was the mother, scanning and touching, assuring herself of each child with her hands and words. Everyone accounted for. No one too badly hurt. Scrapes and bruises and the oldest girl upset because her brother's leg was bleeding and she wanted the blood to stop. Madison or Addison, I don't remember her name now. It's all right, I told her. I wrapped the boy's leg with one of my shirts. All the children, I think, had the name of a different president, and their mother, with such unwavering confidence, spoke to each child by his or her name, holding each face in her hands, clearly telling the child what to do and how very brave, how very safe, repeating firmly and lovingly: *We're all safe now. It'll be okay. We're safe. We're here. Everything's okay. Listen. Listen. It's going to be fine.* She looked then at me, and I could see she was grateful for my presence. I put forth my hand, and maybe I touched her. I know I said something. Words can seem empty, though. Then I called the police. Better use of my words. I was grateful, too, for all that goes well in life. I was grateful for the best in each of us that is there for the saying, that is there for the hearing, and that is there for the giving – no need to ask.

Standing in that snow on the side of the road with that gratitude and awareness, I knew sufficient relief to last a lifetime. At first, only that: release from harm, and a lifetime to breathe. And as if it wasn't enough, there landed such sweetness of snow on my face and arms. A gentle sweetness in that biting cold. Whereupon it struck me – a further thought perhaps conceived at the moment – that there was something much greater going on, something that approached me, confiding as confidence. I joined with the confidence, and we embraced as friends. I knew at once the correctness of things. It was a holistic understanding that appeared, if only briefly, in such a changeable world. I knew in my heart that the accident should be: fortunes, misfortunes, and every moment should be, the mother, the children, their hugs should be, and I should be and Rianna and I and a family should be, the earth well rounded and the snow so deep, the cold, the winter, the slippery road should be, care should be given, help when needed, and love most of all, then spring, of course, the spring should be, melt and mud and new growth should be, young birds and insects and a change from this, a change to that, a beneficent change, and stars the stars should be coming soon should be, out of the dark should be light should be, a familiar, fresh life each day should be, a feeling of wonder and a longing to know more.

And it was not only that those things should be, but also that they were. Conceived in me that night beside the battered car in the falling snow – intentional life. Briefly, it coursed like blood through my body to warm me. Purposeful life, life that was meant to take shape the way it did, life that moved me and that I might move, that anyone could move. It was life I participated in and perhaps, with some thoughtful intentions of my own, could make new.

I was young then, standing and waiting for the ambulance and police. I had no other place to be, was in no hurry to head my way. So, I stood near, spoke some, a bit louder than the snow, and I absorbed the remaining night, the huddled figures in the dark, and this promising universe with its light. There was no real home just yet for me, only hope and the constant flakes that covered the world so that when I woke in the morning and looked out, all would appear fresh and peaceful, not seeming in need of much work, though I would know that work was needed – on every road and in everyone. Roads always need work, don't they? And they are not alone in the improvements that are needed. The whole world seeks funds, prepares for the future, longs for improvements that are due, sometimes long overdue.

The snow fell quietly wherever I looked that night. It filled the ditches and covered all tracks. It fell on the roof of the crippled car. It fell at my feet and upon the tree-unseeable distance. It fell and would not stop no matter how much I looked. It fell no matter how far or long or deep. And I was lifted by the earth around. I grew not in inches but in acres of heart, and looked not inside but everywhere out.

And it was clear to me at that moment, as it is clear forever now, that all of life is not so much a mystery as it is a constant act of love, and I am the actor, not a pretender, but a doer and a force of my own responsibility. I am but I to fill whatever space I'm in, the way the stars fill the night sky, the way snow fills the cracks, the way you, soon you, whoever you are, fill my mind as I hear you come close.

Come close, my grandchild. Come close, this life. And I will come closer still. For I cannot wait for love to happen. I have to bring it to life with my self. And let all that is be is of love. And your heart let it be for the giving and the good.

~

I was still young, eight, nine, when I last saw my mother. I don't remember my father at all. I used to imagine brothers and sisters in everyone I saw. Why not everyone is my family, I thought. I would do things together in my mind with those siblings. We'd catch fireflies or hike trails, pick up stones to toss at cans or swim in the ocean waves all day. This was not an obsession, but an unrestrictive way to approach the world. And then I'd bob in bed at night, as if the bed were the waves and I the waves and the night itself such endless waves, and before I knew it, I'd be asleep.

When I awoke the next morning, the house would be waveless, no difference to the place, no mother, no father, no sisters or brothers, water water nowhere near, but sunlight poured through the window often, and I became a bit more myself by seeing the sunrise and feeling its clarity. At first it was an innate sense of something other. Later, I held to the opinion of a spiritual dimension that exceeded, perhaps, this world alone, never to deny our world or even outdo it, but rather as somewhere to extend my being, as something to think toward. It is a thought and a place still taking shape, one I confuse with words.

Yet one thing that is certain: Slowly, my brothers and

sisters became less inside me, more mixed with the world like everything else. Apart from me, distanced. Separate – that's what things became, and I don't mean it in a bad way. I mean, they, those imagined people, all people in fact, all trees and birds, cars and pavement, stars and sun and even light itself – everything broke from me at some teenage year, and I was alone. Not in loneliness alone, because there were many people nearby, and there was a natural world and a world of man-made things, too. But if I was ever to know anything other than myself as an island, if I was in fact to rediscover my relationship with everything, it was up to me to cross the water and join the world out of my own imperative. By making an effort, by longing to know first who was nearby and then who was afar, my family increased and the world along with it.

~

My whole life, I think, has been longing to know. Each month's a new chapter in my self-education, but it is all on the way toward seeing beyond myself. The thing is, I'm not so very great to think about, really. I'm nothing like the characters in the *Canterbury Tales* or Dickens. I'm not like the souls in *The Divine Comedy*, nothing so amazing as this dark night with stars or the birth of some child who'll add interest to life.

And I've watched the light fall from the sky and rise from the earth. I've seen that light illuminate the passing time. And I've been amazed at the layers of life I've witnessed in my sixty good years. Sometimes it's been a difficult telling, sometimes the sadness has seemed unbearable, but there is nothing I would change, nothing other than a change in how much deeper I might feel, and in how much wider I might think, in how much closer I would be to others and to you.

Games... Games...

Yes?

I've been waiting outside for a while.

Sorry.

Don't be sorry. Thanks for the light.

I thought I was just talking to myself.

No you didn't. You've been calling me all night. Everyone can hear. Hoping I'd say something to interrupt your soliloquy.

Not to interrupt.

To make it ring true, then.

Maybe.

Why were you so certain I'd come?

Because our grandchild is near. You wouldn't want to miss it.

But Games.

Yes?

How now brown cow? What I mean is, how do you know if it's really me?

The world sure is interesting. Thing is, you can welcome all life as if it is a person, as if it's someone you love, but you can't take life into your hands as a physical body. You can't hold its round face between your palms and kiss it on the mouth like you used to your wife, a long sad year ago. There's no mouth to life that I've ever seen. No face either. Hours together, though. Hours at the table. Hours on the road. Lots of good laughs. Some tears.

I'm looking at a star move across the sky. I mean, how can a star move like that? Astronomers in their observatories must be going crazy trying to figure it. Poets looking up must be rhythmically intrigued. Me, I'm just pleased, following along. I lay my eyes upon the sky, as if the sky is flesh and my eyes are hands. I follow the movement from right to left, deeper and deeper. It's solace to my fingers, music to my soul. And I think to myself: What is it? What is it not? Not an airplane or comet, no way. And not some lost thought looking for home. It's a visit tonight from out of the heart.

~

I've heard that a person continues to exist in a place even after she's left it. I'm sure there's some truth to that. Nobody knows every rule of existence. There's a presence of mind and there's a presence of life all around me. In winter, especially, when there're lights in houses across the valley, when there're lights that travel across the universe from other worlds, when I am in no hurry to be anywhere else, I receive messages to make me think, maybe even to answer. It would be wrong to stand here and say nothing.

So, these thoughts of mine, these words, these letters, these epistles I send into space as my way of corresponding. My longing to know. But as Rio used to say: *Stop your drawn-out rambles. See clear.* She'd set me straight by putting her hand on my shoulder or her focusing lens to my thoughts. *Games,* she'd say. *Come on. You're looking right through it.* And she used to bring me other things, too, besides her grounding sense. Gifts out of the blue: origami animals that I'd give to my seventh-grade class, burdock root to roast, a dandelion clock to blow. And now these stars and the coming birth. Not everything is from Ri, of course. Though I like to think it is.

Rianna, in her time on earth, had a way with people that would soothe their minds, like shade in hot July. Annelli, for example, our firstborn daughter, would be upset about some dried-up worm on the pavement. She'd pick up that worm and carry it to the weeds, as if death needed to be out of sight. But Rio would say, Let me see that worm. So, Annelli would return and place it in her mother's palm, and then Nell and I would stand, prepared for a miracle. We waited, we were certain. Expecting that the worm would start wriggling again.

Games...   Games...

What?

This isn't about me, you know.

I look at the night sky. The dark with light sky. The stars with voice. I wish I were as uninhibited as she. I wish –

Games, did you hear me?

I know, I say. It's just –

And it's not about us, says Ri.

I didn't say *us,* I said *just.*

And it's not so much just about you, either, says Ri.

You're right. I've been thinking that lately.

I can hear, she says.

You can hear me? I ask.

Everyone can hear you. Your thoughts are louder than dragons.

What makes you say dragons?

Thinking about children, I guess. Childhood. Imagination. My father's dragon. I like dragons.

Your father had a dragon?

It's a book, I think, says Ri.

I know what she means about thinking. There's so much to think. I wish I'd do it better.

Your thoughts aren't bad, says Ri, reassuringly.

Not bad? Only that? Only – Not bad?

You want them to be beautiful, don't you?

Sure, I say. Who wouldn't want that?

Okay, says Rianna.

Okay what?

Okay. Let them be beautiful.

Easier said than done, I think. But I keep my eyes up. Keep my mind open, trying to make beautiful what I do. To see it happen inside and out. Bluebells in winter. Cheeks red with blush.

Nice, says Ri.

There's no privacy, anywhere, I complain.

I told you, your thoughts are loud. Besides, you know you like talking to me.

I do, I say. It's just I miss the details. The soft and the warm. All the good stuff.

And I wait for her to give me something – a hand with a leaf in it, or a list of all she's been up to.

No matter, I say. My life is part you, and you are part me. Our presences are interwoven.

Didn't Whitman say that? asks Ri. About all people.

I don't know what man said it. I'm saying it now. About you. We help each other to understand.

Understand what? asks Rianna.

Trigonometry, the names of flowers, why people die when it's all about life.

What's all about life?

The stars, the earth. You name the thing, I'll say it's living.

Dirt, says Ri.

Living.

Colors.

Living.

Words.

Words are trying to get back to life, I say.

Is that why people die? asks Rianna. So they can get back to life?

I don't want to talk about it with you.

What do you want to talk about?

Anything else. Everything else, I say. But, Ri, you're not really here, are you?

I can't believe you're asking me that.

You're the one who brought it up earlier.

No, she says. I just wondered how you knew it was me.

It is, isn't it?

Yes.

That's all I need to know, I told her. It's such a free gift, as that handout you sometimes get at a party.

Since when do you have to pay for a gift? says Ri. The very nature of a gift is that it's for free.

I guess that's right, I say.

It is, she says. But it's just for a bit more that I can hang out, working for the world like this. I'm almost out of words.

Out of work?

Words, she says, a bit annoyed. Not work.

I don't want you to be out of words. I miss your way with them.

Rianna takes a moment to respond:

Still – you do recognize me, don't you? she says. I can't hear my voice, but I hope I sound like me. And my hair, you remember my hair? I always thought I had pretty good hair. It never hurt anyone. It never robbed a bank.

Looking at the late December sky full of stars, I don't have to try. Yes, she is beautiful, I see. As beautiful as I have ever seen. More beautiful than I have ever seen, she is. Yes, very. Blond, very. Round her face is. Wisps of light. Very becoming. And I see her blush.

Why do you do that? she asks.

I'm sorry, I say. And then I say what's on my mind: When

Tory died, you were alive. We found courage in each other. We overcame his death together. Of course, he didn't really need our help, did he? But when you died...

We were no longer together? says Ri, unsure. We could find no courage?

I didn't say that. But I, on my own, had to do something. Death did not take you away, it gave me the opportunity to know your life like never before. If I look for it in the right way, I can always find the life in anyone's story. I can keep it going, and it's not even me doing the keeping. I simply carry the truth the way arteries carry blood, the way a channel carries water.

You carried me to my bed when I'd lost all that weight and strength, says Ri.

That was a terrible diet, terrible workout program, I say.

I'm being serious, Games. Each chapter is something to bring you closer to life.

It's really just closer to you, I say. And if through you I know all of life, so much the better.

Are you almost there? she asks.

Nothing's so easy, I say. I might, however, be one step closer. I feel I've awoken a bit.

What did you wake to?

Shadows and light.

What's that supposed to mean?

That all things have many sides to them, even contrasting sides. The only way to understand the truth of the matter is to keep coming back to the matter and experiencing it again, only differently. We're all mixed up, trying to say ourselves clear. As for me, I'm feeling more whole lately.

Holier than thou? says Rianna, wondering if she heard me right.

She knows what she heard. She said it with a smile, which is a gesture that does a lot of good for me. I know she understands what I'm getting at. It's just...

What? says Rio.

I'll never get there, will I?

Never get where?

Where I want to be with you, I say.

Where is that?

We barely got out the door together. A mere beginning.

I wouldn't say that, says Ri. And whereas you say that nothing's so easy, I say that nothing's too difficult.

Nothing? I repeat, hoping to hear her adamant confirmation, plus examples. I wait, looking at the stars. Nothing? I say it again, watching Orion – one bright and serious hope. You can think of nothing that is too much for a person to take? Not one thing? And of course, I'm thinking of losing her. But silence is Ri's only response. And all that I can put into that silence, every possibility that floods into its space, convinces me she is right.

She's going to be my grandchild, too, says Rianna after the pause. I've followed her conception. I care about her even if I'm not there. I want so much to be there. Can you even imagine my perspective?

I know, I say. But I don't really know.

And we lean upon each other in the quiet December night. Part of me wants her to be here so much I can't stand it. That's what I imagine. Us again, climbing mountains, seeing the big picture, coming down to earth in time, raising children without tragedy, waking in the morning to the song of birds, and, of course, that she never dies. Though I don't mean never, I just mean not when she did. I mean, why did she get sick and die when she did? I wrack my brain and wrench my thoughts and imagine resurrection so that when a person dies she goes on living without missing a beat.

And how stupid am I to be unable to endure a little missing? How stupid am I that after all this story and the many years to get here, I don't include death in the picture of life? That's how you overcome things. You overcome them by inclusion, not exclusion. You overcome others you've got a problem with by somehow including those others in your days. And you overcome all that is impossible to bear by finding a way to make it part of your story.

And I know I'm wrong to want what only I want, as if I am the decider of things on earth. As if my wishes rule. Besides, Rianna is here right now, so why not give her my full attention? Why spend time in dissertations? And if she wishes to leave, then I must accept her wishes. And if she's able to stay, I am grateful. It's her life to do with as she pleases. I can't interfere, I can only carry the tune.

It's the steadiest thing about you, I say.

What, my catchy jingle?

No.   And I tell her: That you care so much about everything. You care so much that you rearrange your schedule to be here.

Well, there was a small window in my calendar.

Even your teasing, severe as it is, comes with light, I say. A million twinkling stars.   All I'm saying's that you care enough to spend time with people you can't really get to know.

You've got a narrow definition of "to know", she tells me.

I'm not talking about some great philosophical *Knowing*, however. I'm talking about Rianna interacting with living human beings right here on earth, which is difficult if you're dead. Of course I don't say this. I don't want to upset her. Doesn't matter, though. She hears me anyway.

You're right, says Ri. Still, I can't stop working for our world, not ever. The world is in me. It's in you. But like I said, it's not about me and what I know. And it's not about you and the people and details you hold inside. It's how you choose to convey this world that's important here.

~

And she's gone again. Or so it seems. I want to think of something funny to say, to bring her back. I can't just now. Just now I'm so deeply affected by everything. It would be wrong to joke.

So, let me be clear. Let me say it all again, only better: I see the world walking toward me. I take my life to the world. I don't interfere. There is my father, long gone. My mother, so long missing – I'm still waiting to learn what happened to her. Aunt Julia and Uncle Orro never did make it to Italy. There are people through the years I've come to know, and I've shared in their lives as if those lives were the air I breathe, and I thank them all. There is Quincy Mesch, who called me to his bedside way way back, who got me thinking of birds. And he was a teacher, too. And his wife died young, so comparably to Rianna. And he was sad and devoted to her the way I am devoted. But his life is his own, and he had three children and one of them killed himself, which is something that makes his story quite different from my own. And I shared my life with others, with Trudy Lynne, with Curtis Bridge, and with Benjy and Dove. And my children: Annelli our nest egg and Jacob our blue jay, both who are alive and well, and Tory who... It breaks my heart, so I ask Rianna, and she comes in to say it:

He died, Games. He's okay, you know. He died bringing tools to others so they could tend their lives, build, and be current. He's moving on.

Currents through water. Currents through air, I think to myself.

Our forward-thinking son, concludes Ri. Include him in your own good life.

I do, I say. I know who he is when I love him. Tory is the morning star rising. He's the red sun at night. He fills me with a heaven's length of hope. I know who each of my children is when I love them, which is slow and consistent going. All things take time and good things take more. For the moment, I see what I see and carry it grateful. Earth and people. Stars and space. Children all, evolving with life. And at the forefront of my mind is my beautiful Rio, who –

I'm right here, Games. Rattle oh ghost, wave oh ghost and be seen.

Don't say that, I tell her. I'm trying to explain things.

Well, I wish you wouldn't. It suggests a lack of confidence.

It's just –

It's not just, she says. You keep saying it's just. Your explanations are criminal. They ruin the mood.

Maybe you're right, Ri. Like always.

Not like always, she says, but here, yes. Then she re-says it. Not like always. But here, with you.

Okay, I say.

Just now, she says. Talking it over. This moment. I'm right.

It's true, I say. I can see it is.

~

So, I won't explain things to muddle the mood. The only one I can speak for is myself, and my mood is lighthearted, which means to me that light fills my heart. It's been a while since the mountain when Rianna Olivet and I first met almost thirty-three years ago. It's been a while since I've been to that mountain, but even if I stop going, it doesn't mean I don't still experience a part of me there.

And it's clear tonight, not one cloud I can see. It's not death either that I see. Death is in no way the impetus of life. Everyone knows what the impetus is. They're just afraid to say it. But I'm not afraid. Neither was Rianna, though she was more deliberate with her words. The word is love. That's it, as always. No one should be afraid to say love, as long as they know that saying does little to make it so.

That's what I'm thinking most right now. I'm thinking of love, and I'm thinking that my words are muddy representations. And yet I go on, because there's still work to do: It's not the face of suffering that unites all people, but the fact that all we do, all we can do, what we're meant for, is love. Love is the way out of all messes, the way to pay off debt to one another, the way to give thanks for this time on earth. Love is the only way to move forward. No matter how well, no matter how poorly – it's what I do and what I've been doing from the very beginning. As a separate matter, as a separate individual, I make various attempts to bring things together. Step by step, I move toward another as if by a hidden force, which is a spiritual force, which to celestial bodies is gravity, but to my way of thinking is love. And I'm nowhere near, am I? Still, I'm here, which is a good place. This is the place of becoming, so I've heard. And one day in the future, we'll look back on this time –

We?

~

I knew it. Rianna is here. Somewhere. I just heard her again. In the crisp cold December air. It's coming on the one-year anniversary of her death. Annelli was twenty-nine when her mother died. Now she's just past thirty and becoming a mother herself. She's having a baby, our first grandchild. It makes my heart sing and sink at once. I sing at the thought of an emerging new life and sink into wishing Ri were here to enjoy it. Sing and sink into. You. Into. Sing and...

I don't get over some things easily. I'm trying to see what she's doing now. I think of her hands planting seeds through the years. She'd pluck them and place them, she'd cover the seeds with earth, she'd cover the earth with life in her modest way. And I think of her feet, bare in the bed at night, or running with Tory and Jake to catch the wind. *Let's catch the wind.* The three of them'd run, arms wide and they'd bring their arms to their chests, hugging. *Now, let it go.* Then they'd spread their arms like wings of birds, and the wind would be free again. And I think of her feet walking toward me. I think and I see. And there she is, sun on her face. Sun. Sun. I'm facing the sun.

A simple meeting took place one day on the mountain. Which became commitment, immutable proof, bendable in wind, unbreakable over time, more vital than Ri sharing her days and her toothbrush with me, or me sharing my thoughts and my hammer with her. We became a world shaped by thousands of days. By ups and downs. The fasts and slows. Rain dripping from leaves as we passed by. And when we stopped walking, there came the even more quiet sound of our pure unbreakable involvement, like a child's heart as it beats with joy, or the song of a bud as it unites with its bloom.

Life feels infinite, and maybe it is. The feeling is like climbing to the top of our continuous Everett, opening our minds to the ever greater circumference of view, absorbing the expanse, and seeing, for the first time – what? No words. A seamless story. A melding puzzle. A waking thought. More than you and I could've dreamed on our own.

~

Which reminds me, I say.

Reminds you of what? asks Rianna.

I already have a story to tell our granddaughter when she's born. What do you think?

What's the story?

Once upon a time there was –

Oh, interrupts Ri. Don't tell that one.

You know it?

It's old and full of words.

Do you have something better?

Why's it have to be a story at all? she asks. Why not the truth?

I like stories, I say. Children like stories. I thought you did, too.

I do, says Rio. But I also like the truth.

Annelli, Jacob, and Tory liked my stories, I say.

They did, agrees Ri. There was the one about the red barn with its giblets and fairies.

Did you say giblets?

Goblets, I mean, says Ri. Goblins, whatever. And the one where the moon came back out of the western sky minutes after it had set. And the one where it rained syrup, which made a sweet, sticky river of Pancake Street.

I don't remember that last one.

I remember everything you've said.

And I remember lots about you, I say back. Like the times you went flying. First time you took me up.

What do you mean, up?

Into the air, I explain.

And how'd I do that? she asks.

In an airplane. Are you even listening?

I am listening, but I never did that.

Sure you did.

I never learned to fly, Games. You're making things up.

Why would I do that?

To please me, she says. So I can rest assured.

I swear it's true. You flew to the coast, to Kitty Hawk. We tipped to the Atlantic. We flew through clouds, broke into blue. Then we landed on a grass airstrip and got out.

Of an airplane?

Of course, an airplane.

I don't remember that, says Ri. Never thought I had it in me.

You've got a million other things in you that you don't even know. And what you haven't done yet, you're going to do. One day, you'll be bursting with exciting things to say, and the world had better be listening. The best is yet to come. You can count on it.

One two three, counts Rianna. Maybe you're right. I don't want you to get sidetracked, however. Don't grow old on me. Tell something current that comes your way.

Like a river or The Labrador?

Depends, she says. Black lab or yellow?

Why's the color so important?

Soul important, did you say?

So. So, I repeat.

What an indifferent answer, says Ri. So-so. I can't believe you'd say such a thing. Color expresses the innermost soul. Very exciting. Nothing so-so about that. You should see the colors I see.

I just want to tell a good story, I say as if to explain myself.

Tell it, then.

Rianna, I say. I say, Rianna.

What?

I'm not ready to answer her question. I color her name over and over inside my head, an innermost color, an endless adventure of curves and shades, a great plot with twists and turns. Rianna, Rio Grand, Ri, Ri-Annie. My sun rose, my indigo light, my yellow my red my orange carnelian.

What? she repeats, almost annoyed by my delay.

It's you at the moment, I tell her. You're what's running through me.

That's sweet, she says. But I thought we agreed that this isn't about me.

Why can't it be? I think. I don't say this out loud. Why can't this, all this, be an expression of my love? I don't say this either. Instead, I stare at my shoes, dark in the dark of night. And I wonder if Rianna, if all of this, is just a figment of my imagination. It would be disappointing if that is so. Heartbreaking to me. If her talk throughout my body is no more than the gentle, chilly breeze, if the familiar sound I hear is only what I make of her in my mind – how unfortunate that would be.

I heard all that, says Ri.

And I look back to the sky, wanting more.

Ri?

Yes.

I agree with you about most things.

Most?

What you said about stories, I mean. Most stories are interested only in themselves, in what they can do to stay alive and keep going, regardless of the life of their own characters, regardless of real truth in their plots.

You mean that most stories are selfish? she asks.

I think about this, and maybe it is what I mean, though it's not what I say. Instead, I say what I like about a story. I like when a story works hard to discover something it didn't know was there. I like when a story sees life with great and greater understanding. I like when a story represents the truth and its characters learn to overcome their confinements and are free.

Oh, Games. That's more like it.

More like what?

That's the story to tell, says Ri.

How's what I just said a story?

Plot it out, says Rianna. See where it leads.

It's stuck on you at the moment.

Don't let it be stuck. That's not like you, Games.

No, I agree. I've never felt stuck. There's always something on the horizon.

Like our granddaughter, says Ri.

I almost forgot, I say.

Don't forget. That's what I've learned from you. To live each moment as if it contains all of time. To live in time and timelessness, too. For one another.

I'm sorry if I'm keeping you, I say.

You can let go whenever. I'll be okay.

Did she really tell me to let her go? As if I would keep her against her will. As if I had some authority over her.

You've always had a captivating way about you, says Ri. Besides, it makes me happy to hear you. There's no distance between us. You don't allow meanness. You drive away wrong. And it's all because of your effort to see the spiritual truth of life. That's the best story ever, and it weaves through the world on the back of wind, in the light of stars, through the oceans on whales, and upon the skies as birds. Blue jays don't argue. Doves bring peace. And robins who die live on in the inextinguishable fires on their breasts.

My mother quoted that image, I say. Where's it from?

Everything you hear becomes you, says Ri. I become you. You become you. Strangers become you. Parents and sons and daughters become you. Grandchildren, too. Fir trees and snowfall and bird names become you. Movies of bike thieves and journals of war. The berries you pick and the flies you swallow and swat. Each thing you say is a share of your soul. But why? What good is it to share with others, to share yourself like this? Why not lie down on the cold winter ground and forget you're a part of anything else? Why wonder about humanity and interdependence? Don't give it a thought. Become like the outstretched crust of the earth. Live and die here, like an assortment of sticks, like the hardness of stone, where you've got no burden of others and no connection to me. Where there's only this to know: No clues, no interests, no cares, no concerns.

I can't do that, I say.

I know, says Ri.

And I know how intimately she knows it about me. What's more, I know what she is going to add:

You're a conduit of spirit. You're a pathway for your soul and others. Everyone and everything is part of the flow. Can you do it for all of time? Can you say it even more?

I can, I say.

Good, she says.

Is it good? I ask. And I wait.

I wait for Ri's answer, but her language is lost to me. So, I take the hiatus to picture what comes in her place. The earth and its people. The birds she spoke of and the trees I darkly see. There are inextinguishable fires everywhere, and I wonder what's up with the flames. And what's up with these pictures that arrive inside? My mind shuffles the pictures: Midwinter snow settling on trees, summer thunderstorms coming over the hills, and one April day long ago when, standing under cover by the farmer's market, we waited for the shower to stop, but it didn't stop so we all got soaked running to the car – Nell, Jake, Tory, Ri, and I. A loaf of sourdough, a bundle of garlic, dripping wet skin. For a long while I watch the sound of our feet splashing in puddles. It's the last of my pictures, out in the weather. Things erode in weather, but not what's essential. Then my heart dissolves this last picture so I may see what's really here.

Yes, says Ri. It's good, my love.

Ours, I say. Not my. Our love.   ...   And I stretch the love as far as I can. Extending our time together. I don't want these words to end. I draw them out like taffy in my mind, like long cello notes. I want our love to continue on the earth – on the back of the wind, in the light of the stars, in a spiraling sound aspiring to –

It makes me wonder, though, says Ri.

What makes you wonder?

Love, and she says the word real casual, as if she's gently digging at the ground with her toe. Does no good just to proclaim things, does it?

I don't know, I say.

Best to be clear, says Ri. How you express love, I mean. Is it the face of the sun? Is it the birth of a child? Is love the spin of the earth? Is it the shapes that the constellations make? Is it every exchange of words, no matter how sweet or how harsh?

All good questions, I say.

And then what happens? asks Ri. That's what I wonder.

What do you mean, what happens?

Say in the future, the earth perfects love, she begins. Say that all human beings become beings of love, what then? What's next?

Why does it worry you? I ask.

Because it's not clear to me, says Rianna. What happens when I am really done because at long last I embody love? What happens when I breathe in moral laws and breathe out love?

I don't know what that means, I say. But Rianna doesn't bother to explain. Either she's ignoring my confusion or she's lost in the thought.

When all human beings breathe as one, and the earth becomes the planet of love – what next? Will we be sad when our world is finished and our love complete? We'll say a lasting goodbye to the world, I suppose. We'll pat each other on the back. Good job, we'll all say. And fade away, placing our story in some memory bank.

You're jumping to conclusions, I tell her. It's much too far in the future.

A girl can still wonder, can't she?

Let everything have its time, I say. Things become however they become. Then they drop a seed. You know about seeds. A seed is planted, something new grows.

That's a very unsatisfactory answer, says Ri.

And maybe she's right, I think. But my mind is a blur with this talk. You've got to keep the story current, I say. Can't jump to conclusions.

Oh. Is that what I must do?

Not you, I say. You're your own captain. I have no authority over you.

I've heard that before, says Ri. Then, is it what you must do? she asks. You, Games, sailing out under the stars. Plugging away. And you, Games, deciding in here. She taps my chest, and I sigh as if the universe has fallen upon me.

I want to do well by life, I say.   And I wait for a response.   I wait for

thoughts
to take shape
out under the stars.

I wait for Rianna to say what she thinks. I wait for her voice to come again and help me to see, to comfort me when the counsel I keep for myself isn't enough. I wait for her hair to fall over the night sky – in whispers of light. I wait for my hand to feel the flesh of her face and for my arms to hold her body as if I could ever, as if I did ever, keep it in place. Yet all of her is without weight and without space, and time is a question and now she is gone. I know this, though I don't know for how long I stand here knowing. I am almost ready to make my way home.

~

Human beings carry love. That love, however, is written on water. They carry it in buckets, in their bodies, in cupped hands from the stream. The words disappear in the liquid. They're difficult to retrieve. Still, humans carry love no matter the troubles, conveying it until eventually they will become what they are trying to say.

It is mankind alone who works with words and with every act to bring love to light. Humans work to bring love like a flower to light in the eye, to bring it as ripe fruit to the tongue, and then as a seed pressed gently into the ground. After which, everything everything again and again until until.

And I see the relentless beauty of the world. I stir up that beauty in my soul by waking to it here where all things, even cold things like the air, even frozen things like the winter ground, even faraway things like stars, are alive and get my blood moving.

> A bird alights upon its branch
> There comes a song
> A boat arrives at the blink of shore
> Something new is born

~

Stars float like seeds, millions of them. It's a perfect night for birth. Though it probably won't be tonight when my granddaughter shows. Not tomorrow, either. Before the end of next week, maybe, twelve days from now. Who knows?

When I was born, there were eyes on me. Hands carried me through the room and placed me where the light though diffuse offered hundreds more welcoming thoughts. *This blanket's for you*, said the light. *This shadow, this window – it's all here for you.* The language of light was strange at first. It would take some time to figure the world. Hours years decades lifetimes. At first, however, I lay beside my mother, quiet in the enchanted world, present in small yet growing touches. And that world persisted in its demand that I someday wake even more, make my way into living, that I might touch and be touched beyond only enchantment but never without it, into the incredible beauty of life that remains my inheritance.

And I didn't have to hold onto life, it held me then in its large and certain hands, as it held me through the years, as it continues to hold today. Nor does it matter so much what's happened to me. It doesn't matter so much what's come and gone in my own specific time. What matters is the consistency of life, like Jell-O like water like rock like fire. The constancy, I mean. Life is bound to the world at the same time as it streams through, encouraging me though not me alone, as if saying:

Games.

What?

It's me again.

Me?

Rianna, she says. Not life.

I know, I say. Sometimes everything blends together. I'd rather we were side by side, though.

We're not that different, you and I, says Ri.

Oh, we're different, I say. And I'm thinking of her body. I reach out to touch it.

Stop it, she says. It's not the time or place. I've got other things to do now.

Sorry, I say.

It's okay, Games. Carry me along like a free gift or a bit of wind you can't contain. That sort of thing. And stop trying to figure everything. I'll do the same. Be ready, though, when answers come.

So, this really is you talking to me, isn't it?

What did I just say to you?

I haven't forgotten. You've got things to do. I know. Well, I've got things to do, too.

So, Games?

Yes.

You going to say hello to your granddaughter for me?

Our granddaughter, you mean.

Ours, okay.

Why don't you say hello yourself? I say.

I will, says Rianna. In time or sunlight or something. But you've got a way about you that conveys things better. I remember when sweet Robin Annelli was born. Our first little bird. You stood in the bedroom. What were you doing?

Listening, I say.

You always listen, and you hear what's best in everyone. That's why I can say anything to you and feel confident. I know you'll hear me right, even if I'm wrong.

You're never wrong, I say.

Of course I'm sometimes wrong, says Ri. But you see it right. You see where life is going and know it is good. That gives me confidence that I'm heading okay. Like a wish coming true inside. And Games.

Yes?

I also listen. I hear what you say.

What am I saying?

You're telling our granddaughter of the incredible beauty of life that is her inheritance. I heard you say that. You're telling her to take up the world with interest and joy. You're saying it doesn't matter so much what words are said but what spirit they are spoken with. You're saying, Be courageous. Permeate yourself with the life around you. Move worlds, move with, move on.

How am I saying all that? I ask. How? I repeat. How?

But not a word comes through, nothing from the farthest stars, nothing up close, either. It sure is difficult to figure things sometimes. So, I gather myself and prepare to leave, my face stung by a wintery cool that tangles my mind even as it refreshes me. And I know it's late. I know it's time. And I'm tired of my questions. Ready for sleep. There's a bed in my house. There are winter mice in the walls, knots on the wooden floor. There are windows in my room to welcome the morning. There are mornings to come, each with a telling light. And this is what I love about days. And this is what I love about stories, too – that I read them according to how I've grown in my soul. I hear them according to what I know in my heart. And I change them according to what I do this moment. And this moment I wonder I walk I return up the road, on the current the river the ocean of

BIRTH

Here's to new beginnings. Here's to what I see taking shape: my little bird and her mama. Rianna holds our child, Annelli Robin Shepard, at her breast. Thick dark hair, pink lips, fresh skin, wings of otherworlds now folded within.

The room is warm and dim, though the morning is cold and bright. Songs of the kittiwakes make a deafening if only imaginary sound in this small space. I like those birds, too, but I shoo them away to keep the peace. There are often birds, and I don't always know where they come from. Or why. From out of the blue they come, or from cliffs that rise above faraway seas, I suppose.

The birds, however, who sleep now in the bed come from whatever means the most to me. And they come to be known for their individualities and for their willingness to be part of our earth. Not to mention – they are easy to love, because they are very becoming. And, as their eyes are still closed, I'm free to look at them without intruding. Mother and child. Girls in the bedroom. Gulls, gulls in this strange light. I stand here, watching. There are shells on the window ledge. The curtains are closed, though not completely. There is a narrow slit for the sun. And the sun slides through, gentle as can be. Rio, too, sleeps gently under tiny Nell. The bed's asleep under both of them. Earth under bed. Turtle under earth, or so I've heard. How far will it go? There's no end in sight.

And I begin now to see, as if for the first time. The twelfth day of Christmas. Epiphany. All's alive and well, nothing to fear. A high near 30 today. A cloudless sky. I see the room open before me – a door. Beyond the first room, another, and beyond that room, a third. Stars have fallen throughout the night to the earth as seeds. This I notice on the floor, where it looks like flowers, bluebells for sure. They've sprouted, even though it is winter. And I watch them sleeping, not the winter flowers, but my girls.

I watch Rianna. She and our little bird, the first of our three children. What would the world be like without them all, without any of my family, any of my flowers, any of my birds, any of these seeds that will one day grow into their most amazing architectures? I don't even want to think about it. Why would I entertain such a dispiriting thought, when right before me on a Friday morning – shells on the window ledge, sun through the slit in the curtain, toying with my mind – lie my wife and our first born? And breathing makes the blanket rise and fall, and turning makes the sun rise more, so that its light strikes the floor where it sticks like honey. And how will they feel to my hands when I touch them? What will they stir in my heart when I, to their waking faces, whisper their names? And who will they be in the world when from out of their dreams they fly?

Ri and our Robin, my sleeping birds. They carry on with light, even in the dimness of the room. So much light, I need my mind to adjust for a moment. Both of them are colors I've got no description for just yet, which I suppose isn't very helpful, though it does give my words something to look forward to saying. It's too early for words, anyway. So, I remain quiet in my watching, and in my anticipation.

We are all I's of life. We are I's of love. We start at birth, and we don't ever stop. Does anyone know what time it is that keeps us going? You need a special internal clock for such measurements. More like an eternal clock.

I haven't been paying much attention to time. It really doesn't matter right now the exact minute. Though as I said, it's early. Half past seven, I'd guess. Here come the hours of waking. Yes. Here comes the middle of winter. Whoosh. Here come the January snows, the woodstove fires. Cold air passes through the jamb of the window into an ever-increasing capacity for warmth. I hear the soft sounds Ri and Nell make in their sleep. Here comes a creak on the wood floor. I keep moving. Inching closer to the bed. Closer still.

And I've got a first story to tell our little bird. Rianna doesn't have to listen if she doesn't want. Though it's going to be something good, so she might give in. I'll keep it gentle and clear – the twelfth type of quiet that expresses itself deep in the heart. I know they both hear me somewhere inside. It's going to be something current, like a river or an ocean or a talking gold dog. A robin and a golden retriever walk into a bar. If Nell doesn't get it this moment, she will in time. When she stretches her wings. When she increases her hold. When the fire in her being burns to know, then she'll understand what the story is saying. She'll recognize its spirit when she's good and ready. So, without further delay, this is the start of it. And here is the rest:

About the Author

Leif Garbisch studied literature at Columbia and Brown, which led to a life of house construction and to a world of inspired writing and photography. He has published four books: *The Shore, Found Light, Transformation,* and *Shared Sky.* His appreciation of birds and stars is exceeded only by his appreciation of his grandchildren. And he enjoys clouds as much as the sun. All of which then gave rise to this book.

Made in the USA
Middletown, DE
23 September 2017